Stellar Endorsements for "Burnt Offering"

"Mary Mueller's *Burnt Offering* is her exclamation point at the end of her epic Ryersen Trilogy. Mueller's prose is, as always, flawless, her dialog relevant and poetic. With a message bigger than these pages yet simple enough to exist in the Northwest Ohio farmlands, Mueller defies the stereotype that says sequels can't be better than book one. *Burnt Offering* stands on its own as a profound statement of faith, family and the concept of home."

– Josh Clark, author of "The McGurney Chronicles" series, the "Dakota Lester" books and the forthcoming novel, "The Streak". –

"This is exactly what Christian fiction should be – real characters living and struggling in our non-Christian world, flourishing despite, or even because of, those struggles by God's grace. Any Christian ever harmed by sin within their family, or who has hurt those they love through their own sin, yet has seen those irreparably damaged relationships reborn through God's love can't help but recognize themselves and their family here. For those still walking that difficult path this story is a beacon of hope; for those who have completed that walk it is a treasured reminder of how faithful, good and loving the God who carried us through truly is."

– Brian Schilton, Author of "Issachar's Heirs" –

Stellar Endorsements for "Mirror Images"

This book should be carried by every Christian book store. In *Mirror Images* the continuing adventures of Matthew Ryersen flow like a cool mountain stream.

– J. Keith Jones
Author of "In Due Time" –

In *The Redemption of Matthew Ryersen"* Mary Mueller crafted a wonderfully realistic story about a man and his need for love and faith. It was a story that begged to be told and its message lingered long after the final paragraph was read. It left a yearning for more about this family and their struggles. We have to wait and anticipate no longer. *Mirror Images* has arrived! In this sequel, Mueller takes us on a journey with Matthew, Will and the others that leads to some perplexing and difficult questions. With her eye on the Lord and her feet grounded in the sometimes painful world in which we live, Mueller has crafted a fast-paced, relevant and engrossing sequel that meets some of the most challenging issues of our time head-on. You will want to read *Mirror Images*, and when you do, it will make you think long after you've closed the book.

– Bill Thomas, Author of
"From the Ashes" –

Mirror Images, the sequel to *The Redemption of Matthew Ryersen* flings you right back into the home of John and Carolyn Abbott, a place where four lonely souls have come to live, heal and find God. *Mirror Images*, by Mary Mueller is beautifully written and witty. It deals with addiction, suicide and bullying in an honest, yet surprisingly quiet voice... so well done, a welcome authenticity in the brassy, superficial culture of today."

– Kathy Frias, Author of
"Rumors of Eden" –

Burnt Offering

Book 3 of the
Ryersen Trilogy

Mary

Mueller

Published by White Feather Press.
(www.whitefeatherpress.com)

ISBN 978-1-61808-093-6

Printed in the United States of America

Cover design created by Ron Bell of AdVision Design Group (www.advisiondesigngroup.com)

Interior wheat stalk photo ©iStockphoto.com/Matt Jeacock

White Feather Press

Reaffirming Faith in God, Family, and Country!

Dedication

To Almighty God,
Who always provides the Lamb for the offering.

To Josh,
who owns this one as much as I do,
with much gratitude.

Acknowledgements

Although writers are somewhat (or more) solitary creatures, we never really write and publish a work in solitude. Everyone has an army, large or small, of people helping to make it happen. And so I offer my thanks and praise:

To the God of the Universe, for the ability to write, for the long life I prayed for to finish this book, for the grace and mercy I had to understand before I could put words to it, for being the One in Whom all things hold together.

To Skip Coryell and White Feather Press for continuing to believe in my work.

To my fellow members of the Writers' Forum for their encouragement, suggestions and critiques.

To Josh Clark, without whose enthusiasm and plotting skills and friendship *Burnt Offerings* would never have made it past the first chapter.

Introduction

Some time later God tested Abraham... God said, "Take your son, your only son, Isaac, whom you love, and go to the region of Moriah. Sacrifice him there as a burnt offering on one of the mountains I will tell you about."

... Abraham took the wood for the burnt offering and placed it on his son Isaac, and he himself carried the fire and the knife. As the two of them went up together, Isaac spoke up and said to his father Abraham, "Father?"

"Yes, my son?" Abraham replied.

"The fire and the wood are here," Isaac said, "but where is the lamb for the offering?"

Abraham answered, "God himself will provide the lamb for the burnt offering, my son." And the two of them went on together.

When they reached the place God had told him about, Abraham built an altar there and arranged the wood on it. He bound his son Isaac and laid him on the altar, on top of the wood. Then he reached out his hand and took the knife to slay his son. But the angel of the LORD called out to him from heaven, "Abraham! Abraham!"

"Here I am," he replied.

> *"Do not lay a hand on the boy," he said. "Do not do anything to him. Now I know that you fear God, because you have not withheld from me your son, your only son."*

(Isaiah 22:passim1-12)

BURNT

OFFERING

Prologue

"REMEMBER THAT YOU ARE DUST, AND TO DUST YOU SHALL return," the pastor's voice intoned, carried through the crowded cemetery on the light early May breeze. Over a hundred people crowded around the raw grave, many standing on grass so green it couldn't be distinguished from the artificial turf attempting to hide the edges of the hole. Overhead, the sky was lightly covered by a scrim of wispy gray clouds, leftovers from the early morning rain, and all the trees around the edges of the cemetery were dressed in fresh greens for the occasion.

"I didn't think he'd come," one elderly woman said to another sotto voce, clasping her black pocketbook against her black spring coat.

"Who is it?" the other woman asked, straining to see where the first one pointed. She wore black, also, but her pocketbook was a patchwork of colors and her sensible shoes were red, the only color competing with the beauty of May except for one bright blue coat in the front row with the family.

"It's that boy – you know. The one who used to live with the Abbotts."

"Oh. Him." The second woman considered for a moment. "I thought he died."

Chapter 1

ALLISON RYERSEN TURNED HER TEAR-STAINED EYES AWAY from the grave to gaze up the sloping road, past all the serious gray funeral home vehicles, past the dozens of cars with little white-and-purple flags fluttering from their hoods, to the gray sky and the grassy hill beneath it. Everything was blurry, because she couldn't seem to stop the tears from falling slowly, no matter how many times she wiped her eyes on Matthew's blue bandana. Blinking to clear her vision a little, she stared at the figure standing just below the crest of the hill, in the middle of the road. As she looked, the clouds parted for a moment and wide beams of watery sunlight fell on the figure, gilding his hair and face and clothing like a Renaissance painting.

Allison gasped, and the sound was not lost on her husband, who put his arm around her and whispered, "What's the matter?"

"Look!" she said, pointing. "It's Will!"

Matthew's arm was suddenly gripping her so hard it hurt. "Will," he whispered.

"Go get him," Allison whispered back. "Bring him down."

Matthew seemed to hesitate, so she shoved him just a little, the way one might shove a recalcitrant horse or an encroaching Great Dane. At that nudging, he took off with a ground-covering stride toward the tall figure still standing unmoving in the road. Allison watched them meet, not touching, standing there like statues, until she thought she couldn't stand it. Why didn't one of them give in and hug the other! Why didn't one of them say something?

"Let us pray," Pastor Corrigan said, drawing Allison's attention back to the burial service.

WILL. HE'S NOT A BOY ANY MORE. OH, LORD, LET ME KNOW WHAT TO SAY to him. Help me to build a bridge.

Matthew stopped about ten feet from his son, unsure how close he was allowed to go.

"Hello, Son."

Slate-blue eyes met slate-blue eyes. "Hey, Dad."

"I'm glad you could make it. Come on down and join us, won't you? Allison would like to see you, and I know everyone else will, too."

"Thanks. I wasn't sure I'd be welcome after all this time."

Matthew's eyes filled with tears he didn't try to hide. "You've been welcome back since the day you left, Will. I've missed you so much – "

"Dad, you have to know it wasn't – I didn't stay away just because of you. There was just so much – my fault – " Now Will's eyes were tearing also, but he seemed to feel more shame, because he turned away, as if to go again.

Oh, no, not this time! I can't take ten more years of this!

Matthew closed the space between them and took Will's arm, turning him around so they were face to face, eye to eye, in fact, as there was not a hairsbreadth of difference in height between them.

"Will, it doesn't matter to me why you left, why you stayed away, even why you came back. You're here, and even today – maybe especially today – nothing matters more to me. I need you, Will, right here with me. Please."

"Dad! Come on – you can't – "

Matthew saw the embarrassment and consternation riding across Will's face on the Ryersen flush that rose up his neck and across his ears and cheekbones. It was like looking in a mirror, and he knew Will must know it, too. They were so alike, although Matthew's wheat-blond hair now had silver frosting, and wrinkles from constant exposure to sun and weather permanently wreathed his eyes. He understood, too, the feelings coursing through his son, because

3

they were alike in that, also, quick to feel and quick to take on a burden of guilt. He liked to think time and experience and the loving corrections of his wife and family had tempered some of that...

Will was shaking his head. "Dad, I – I'm sorry. I should have come sooner. Maybe if I'd been here – " He began to cry in earnest, fumbling in his pocket for a handkerchief.

For a moment Matthew expected him to pull out a crumpled blue bandana, the standard handkerchief for an Abbott family male, and was surprised by the ironed, neatly folded, bright white square. Then he shook off that line of thought and did what he had been wanting to do from the beginning.

This is right. This is where you belong, Will.

Holding Will close in his arms was different now, Matthew realized. The frame was heavier, filled out with muscle, a man's body, not a boy's. The weeping was a man's weeping, too, painful and reluctant, soon to be over as a man's mind told him not to be unmanly. The hands which clutched at him were a man's hands, strong and broad. Even so, his mind recalled the small-for-his-age ten-year-old who had stifled his tears in a couch cushion rather than ask for comfort.

"I've got you, Son," he murmured and held on.

"Amen," Pastor Corrigan said. "Please join us back at the church for a fellowship meal and some time to talk with the family."

People began to mill around immediately, some leaving, some moving forward to speak to the bereaved. Several were staring at the reunion taking place near the hill, but most were still unaware of Will's return. Allison couldn't take her eyes off the two, even as she responded to words of condolence here and there and tried to keep an eye on the rest of the family. At least they were finally in each other's arms where they belonged.

I feel like the watchdog nanny in Peter Pan, Allison teased herself, *herding the people I love together. I wish I could just run up there and – and what? Looks like they have it under control. Oh, God, thank You for bringing Will back! Would it be too much to ask that he would stay? We need him now.*

"Will you come to the church, then, and talk to folks?" Matthew asked as Will pulled away gently and blew his nose.

"I'd rather not. Those people coming up the hill are staring at me, and I'd just as soon not be the topic du jour in front of myself."

"Topic dew what?"

"Sorry, Dad. Today's gossip. Maybe I could just meet you at the house afterwards." He paused, a sudden look of confusion on his face. "I mean – which house?"

Matthew laughed. "It's okay. Come to John and Carolyn's, like always. The door's not locked; you can find yourself some lunch while you wait, because all the dear church ladies have been bringing casseroles and trays of stuff until the refrigerator's full."

"All right. I'll see you when you get back." Will turned away again and made his way to a sleek black car of some breed Matthew couldn't identify but would bet wasn't made in America.

"Will – "

"Yes, Dad?"

"You really will be there, won't you?"

Will looked straight at his father. "Yes, sir, I really will. No running, I promise."

THE FELLOWSHIP HALL WAS FULL OF TABLES AND CHAIRS, WITH HARDLY any room for the well-padded to move between them. A huge buffet of what ten-year-old Gracie Abbott referred to as "funeral food" invited partakers with tantalizing aromas and colors. Several of the older church women presided over drinks and desserts tables, and some kids from the youth group were ferrying plates and drinks to those who were not quite up to braving the lines at the buffet. The air was humid and warm with the steamy scents of food and the breath of over a hundred people.

"Let's sit down," Allison said to Matthew and the others. "I know they have that table over there reserved for us."

"You make a great sheepdog," Matthew muttered into his wife's ear, affection and humor in his voice. "Guess we need one today."

ERIC SHOWALTER, THE MAYOR OF LEWISTON, AND HIS WIFE ANITA SAT with Dr. Nate Hanna, the Abbott family's physician for as long as anyone could remember, and the Harrises, a farm family active on the Lewiston school board and athletic boosters' committee. Al Harris had also been a Future Farmers of America advisor for many years, until long after his own sons had graduated.

"Been quite a time for the Abbotts," Al said. "Couldn't believe it."

"Really," Lynn Harris agreed. "What a shame!"

"Death comes to all of us," Eric intoned, only to grimace as his wife's bony elbow connected unerringly with his ribs. "What? It's true, isn't it?"

"Yes, but maybe you don't want to say it quite so loudly during a funeral meal!"

"Oh. Sorry, folks." Eric gave himself to his ham loaf and roast beef, lest he find himself eating shoe-leather again.

"Always have good food here at funerals," Al Harris said, changing the subject. "Eat up, Doc! You haven't touched a thing."

"Not hungry, I guess," Nate responded, his gruff voice even more gravelly than usual.

The Showalters and Harrises exchanged knowing looks. Everyone in and around Fulton County, Ohio, over the age of forty knew Nate Hanna had been hopelessly in love with Carolyn Seibenek Abbott since they were kids.

"Did you see who showed up?" Anita asked the table at large.

"Who? Where?" Eric asked, echoed by the Harrises.

"That boy. You know, Matthew Ryersen's son, the one who disappeared after those rumors went around – off to college, they said, but he never came back. Until today."

"Which rumors?" Lynn asked. "You mean about how he beat up his father? I heard Matthew almost died! And then I heard the boy committed suicide, but that couldn't be right if he went away to college."

"Well," Anita said, leaning in to speak in hushed tones, "the truth is, nobody knows what happened to Matthew. I don't believe for a minute that Will did it – "

"Oh, that's right," Lynn said. "Your daughter was dating him, wasn't she? So I'm sure you'd know everything!"

"No, no, they were just – ah – school friends," Anita said, obviously trying to distance her child from the unpleasant rumors. "But I do know he attempted suicide, didn't he, Nate?"

"Anita, for heaven's sake, you know if he had I couldn't discuss it! What's the matter with all of you – no hot topics already up for discussion, you have to dredge up stuff that happened ten years ago?"

"Don't be a crusty old thing," Anita teased. "I guess you can't say anything. I'm sorry for asking. Well, Tracy did tell me he tried to kill himself, but I never did learn why. Anyway, he did go away and never came back – until today."

"How'd you even know it's him?" Al asked.

"Oh, you can't miss it! He looks just like his father, only twenty years younger. Same eyes, same face, same hair, same body, even same gestures. It's remarkable, even after all that time apart. Did you see them hugging in the road?"

"I thought we wouldn't ever have to talk about that boy again," Eric complained. "He's gone and ought to stay gone."

"Can't deny the boy a chance to come home for the funeral," Al said. "He is family, sort of. Even if he's a bad guy, he probably has feelings."

"Excuse me," Nate said, gathering his untouched plate and cup and rising, "gotta get back to the office. Nice to see you all."

"Well, he was testy!" Anita said, watching the doctor's back as he hurried through the crowd.

WILL PARKED THE TOYOTA NEAR THE PORCH AND CLIMBED OUT TO STAND under a maple tree, surveying the landscape. It was remarkable how little had changed. The shutters on the house were dark green now instead of black, but the porch swing was the same, and so were the flower beds, spring bulbs rioting already in the mild air. The maples and oaks were all still standing, though he could see where a large limb had been removed from the maple nearest the house. If he let himself, he could readily imagine it was May of 1999 instead of 2009, and Carolyn would call him any minute to come in for lunch.

Although tempted to walk around to the back door, he took himself in through the front, passing into the living room, where he paused again to look around.

John's and Carolyn's chairs still flanked the fireplace, with its figured tiles and carved mantel. The couch had a new slipcover, something with dark green stripes, but the plush green carpet looked as new and fresh as it had ten years before, and the bookshelves were still stuffed with volumes and the occasional treasure. The bust of Christ his father had carved for John long before Will had come to the Abbotts still sat on the bookshelf, surveying the room. Will had never liked that statue; it was creepy, the way it looked like the man was being tortured. Who wanted to watch someone suffer? Shaking off the eerie feeling, Will went through the dining room into the kitchen.

Now, here was change! The room had been repainted some kind of peachy color, and the curtains, which had been white with big red apples, were now a different kind of white material with ruffles top and bottom. The old appliances were all gone, replaced by sleek stainless steel things; even the old porcelain sink had been swapped for a double sink in stainless. The cupboards were all new, some pale wood like birch, with glass fronts. Even the old setting hen and big apple cookie jars were gone. In their place sat a big clear glass jar like the old candy jars in general stores. And it was empty. That had never happened before.

Will put his hand on the cookie jar and tried to imagine – but he couldn't. In that one artifact, the truth had come home. Carolyn Abbott was dead.

Chapter 2

CARS IN THE DRIVEWAY, DOORS SLAMMING, VOICES COMING HIS way, drew Will's attention away from the empty place in the middle of his chest. *Suck it up*, he told himself, denying the tears which had begun to threaten. *You're twenty-eight years old now and you've been on your own for ten years. You can handle this without bawling like a baby.*

Or at least he could have if anyone but Pearl had come bustling into the kitchen.

"Oh, Will," she said, her old, old voice so reedy he could hardly hear her over the pounding of his heart. "Welcome home!" She tottered across the room to him and threw her arms around him, arms now so skinny they looked like parchment-covered sticks.

"Grandma," he whispered, embracing her carefully, noting almost subconsciously that her little body was no longer round and solid, but thin and bony. He laid his cheek on top of her head and saw how thin and sparse her white hair was.

"I've missed you," she said, and at least the tone of her voice hadn't changed. "You might have written more often, or come home sooner. I don't like having to find out what you're doing on those computer things."

"Yes, ma'am," he choked out, but she caught the break in his voice.

"Oh, dear boy, Carolyn would have been so glad to see you."

He caught the break in her voice, too, and it destroyed him, drawing forth the sobs he had been fighting. The old woman held on and patted him as he cried, until he gained control of himself and found his handkerchief again. They parted and looked at each other sheepishly; he wasn't given to public display of emotion, and neither was she. In fact, as far as he knew, Will was the only person Pearl ever hugged, a fact which had given him a smug pride back in his teen years and threatened to do so again now.

"Sorry," he muttered, blowing his nose. "It's just so good to see you, Grandma. I didn't realize – "

"Never mind," she said briskly. "You're here. Can you stay a while? I think it would be good for all of us, including you."

"Yes, I can stay a week if I – if people want me to. If there are things to be done, I can help. You know – around here, or whatever."

"Excellent. Help me get some coffee around now, and we'll take it in to the living room. John's sister and her family are here, and Matthew and Allison, of course."

Will took Pearl's direction to fill a tray with coffee mugs, cream and sugar while she started the pre-prepared coffee-maker and watched it sharply for misbehavior.

"How are you, Grandma?" Will asked. "Looking skinny! You go on some supermodel diet or something?"

Pearl gave a mock sigh of exasperation. "Did we teach you no manners when you were here? A gentleman never remarks a lady's age or her weight."

"Yes, ma'am. Then I guess I won't be asking how old you are, either." He gave her a dimpled grin calculated to melt hearts of stone, even though he knew nothing like that worked with Pearl. It was just habit.

"Sit down with me, Will," she said, no responding smile evident. He joined her at the old kitchen table, somehow comforted to see that, at least, was still the same.

"When you were a boy, you thought I was ancient, didn't you?"

Uh-oh! Warning, Will Robinson, danger! "No, ma'am, not – "

"Of course you did! And I nearly was. Well, ten years have gone by, and now I really am ancient. I'm eighty-six, boy, and not quite the woman I used to be. I'm telling you this, Will, because everyone dies, not just the ones who seem to die by mistake, like David and Johnny and Carolyn. My time is definitely limited, and when I go it will leave another tear in the fabric of this family. You need to start thinking about your responsibility as a member of this family. Helping out for a week is nice, but you need to get over the past and start thinking about the long haul. I'm not going to be here much longer to ride herd on all this, you know."

Oh, man. "Don't you think maybe you could live forever?" Will asked, sounding even to himself like a six-year-old.

"Don't fret about it," Pearl said, reaching across the table to pat his hand. "I'm not dying today. Just think about what I've said. And don't let me catch you telling my age to anyone else, or I'll be after you with a willow switch."

He had to laugh at that image. "Yes, ma'am, I can believe that! Here, let me get the coffee and we'll go hype up the rest of the crew."

WILL AND THE COFFEE WERE WELCOMED INTO THE LIVING ROOM WITH equal enthusiasm, which felt so familiar to him he could once again almost forget ten years had passed. Everyone but Allison had been part of his life from the time he came to the farm to stay with his father.

John Abbott's sister Olivia had married Carolyn Seibenek Abbott's brother Ted, and they had sired four sons, Teddy, Steven, (formerly Stevie), Andrew and Greg, all now adults, Teddy about the same age as Will. Teddy was married to Lisa, and they had three boys of their own; Steven was married to Sherri, and they had two little girls and a boy on the way; Andrew was engaged to Darla Summerville, with a wedding planned for September; and Greg was happily dating his way through the entire freshman and sophomore classes of Ohio State University, majoring in cheerleaders.

They all crowded into the living room with Matthew and Allison and Ed Yoder, the farmhand who had been John's right-hand man since before Will was born. John himself sat in his chair by the fireplace, Gracie on his lap. The Seibenek grandchildren were playing with Legos and dolls on the floor, making navigation of the room tricky, but Will managed to set the tray on the coffee table without a mishap and to hand out mugs to everyone who wanted one. Of all the coffee-drinkers, only Allison used cream and sugar, which were given to her with much teasing.

"I'm used to it," she said to Will in an aside. "Just makes me feel like one of the family."

"So, Will," Ted began, never one to shy away from things, "where you been the last ten years? What's so important off in the big city you couldn't come see us once in a while?"

"Shut up, Ted!" Livvie said, smacking his arm.

"What? All I said was – "

"Shut *up*, Ted!"

Will had to laugh. "It's a long story," he said, "and not all that interesting. I live in Iowa City, Iowa, and teach composition to freshmen at the university there."

"Well, Perfesser," Ed cracked, "git you some overalls and jine me in the barn fer some stall-muckin'. I 'member how much you-all enjoy that."

"Cut the phony accent," Will answered, smiling. "I'll help if you need it, but all I have is jeans and cross-trainers."

"Cross trainer a mean coach?" Ed asked, and he looked serious this time.

"I'll show you in a minute," Will said, rising easily from his cross-legged position on the floor. "Let me grab my bag from the car and change." He paused and looked around, puzzled. "Where shall I – I mean, which room – "

"Matthew's old room," Pearl said. "It's a guest room now. You can leave your things there."

"Oh, but he needs to stay with us!" Allison blurted.

"We'll talk about it, honey," Matthew said quietly. "Just let him go for now."

ON THE SECOND FLOOR, WILL LOOKED AROUND AGAIN. HIS OLD ROOM had been turned into a fairytale princess room for Gracie, he saw, a grin crossing his lips at the change in his former stomping-grounds. Not only was the room an explosion of pink and ruffles and tulle, but also it was an explosion of messy little girl stuff all over the floor and desk and chair.

Matthew's old room hardly seemed to have changed. Everything was still white – walls, window shade and curtains, lampshade, bedspread – and the same austere single bed, desk and ladder-back chair still sat in their usual places. He put his guitar case on the desk, hung his suit and dress shirt on hangers in the closet and draped his tie over the same hook on which his father's only tie had always hung.

Jeans and polo shirt in hand, he stepped across the hall to the bathroom and closed the door behind him, not noticing that now he was able to do that in his underwear without panic.

The bathroom had been repainted at some point, a gray so pale it almost disappeared, and trimmed in warm blue which matched the towels and bathmat. The fixtures here had not been replaced, though, and the shower still dripped.

Home, Will thought, looking at the dripping shower, and a lump rose in his throat. He hadn't expected to feel anything after such a long time. Home now was a high-rent apartment in Iowa, miles and years and feelings away from this old farm. Some of the worst times of his life had happened here. His father didn't even live here anymore. Why should he get all misty about a place he hadn't been able to wait to leave?

Washed and dressed, he went to peek into John and Carolyn's room, just to finish his inspection of the place. The old red-and-blue quilt still covered the bed, and John's slippers still sat on his side of the bed. But there at the foot, ready for her to jump up and slide into it, was Carolyn's bathrobe, the same one he had seen so often as a boy, and her little slippers, and her watch on the dresser-top, and her hairbrush on the vanity – all as if she would be in to use them any minute. He inhaled sharply and caught the lingering fragrance of the shampoo and hand lotion she used, a faint scent of roses hanging on the air.

Carolyn, why? How could this have happened? How could you leave us like this?

"I don't know any of these cows!" Will said, glaring at the half-dozen little Jerseys in their milking stanchions. "Who are they, anyway?"

"Ezekiel and Ecclesiastes, Will," Ed answered, "what do you expect? Cows get old and die. They get sold and replaced. You been gone ten years!"

"Yeah, and a lot is different around here," Will replied, "but some things never change." He took the pitchfork and wheelbarrow and began mucking out a stall while Ed oversaw the milking. It was his least-favorite farm chore, followed closely by anything that had to do with the chickens, but he found his rhythm almost immediately.

"Ah, yes," Ed said, "you can take the farm boy out of the country, but you can't take the country – "

"Can it, Ed," Will warned, trying not to laugh. "I am not now and never was a farm boy."

"Live in Iowa, don'tcha? Big farm state."

"I live in the *city* in Iowa," Will insisted. "Lofts. Starbucks. Theater. Ballet."

"You go to the ballet?"

"I have."

"All them sissy-men in long underwear and little slippers flutterin' around on stage? That kind of ballet?"

"Yep. Opera, too." Will hid his smile as he heaved another forkful of filthy straw into the barrow.

"You happy there?" Ed asked.

"Of course I am!"

"Now, don't go off on me, Son. I just wondered. I wouldn't want you to be unhappy no matter where you was."

"Thanks. Yes, I'm happy. I have a great apartment, a nice car, good friends, a great job – or it will be someday, when I've been there long enough to teach upperclassmen. I like to think my life makes a difference there, and – yes, I'm happy."

"Well, then, that's almost all that matters."

"Almost?"

Ed took out a crumpled blue bandana and blew his nose. Stuffing the bandana back into his pocket, he stared again at the little cows. "If it was up to me, I'd say it's hard to be happy when a man has unfinished business or when he knows he's letting down his family. See, where I'm coming from is, family matters a whole lot. And I think your family needs you, boy. And that matters."

"I'll be right back." Will wheeled the barrow out to the manure pile and dumped his load, face twisted in disgust. *He sounds like Pearl. Of course, why wouldn't he? They've shared Ed's house for twelve or fifteen years, been part of the Abbott family even longer. I know family matters, Ed. I get that. Why do you think I left in the first place?*

WILL ELECTED TO STAY IN MATTHEW'S OLD ROOM FOR THE NIGHT, AND no one contradicted him, although he could see the hurt and disappointment in Allison's face. They had pieced together, at Pearl's insistence, a sort of supper from leftover this and that, and Will had done the dishes while Pearl and John talked Gracie through a heartbreaking meltdown and saw her off to bed. Ted and Livvie had taken their brood home before supper, ready to take the grandkids off their "good behavior" and let them wear themselves out for bedtime. Matthew and Allison had left before supper, too, at Matthew's urging, and Will was particularly grateful not to have to deal with his father just yet, although he knew it was inevitable.

Now he lay quietly in his father's bed, covered with his father's bedspread, listening to the sounds the old house made as it cooled down for the night. He could smell the faint tang of manure from his shoes across the room and knew they were ruined. Oh, well. Tomorrow he would go to the feed store and find a pair of heavy work shoes. It would be just like old times. He would help with chores and talk with people and maybe even call Kevin and Travis. He hadn't contacted his two best friends from high school since the day he left.

The creaky house and the confused call of a late-roosting bird outside didn't mask the sound of John Abbott weeping across the hall. *Oh, crap. What could I do – what could anybody do to make it better? Nothing. There isn't any "better" when the person you love best in the world dies. Poor John! Poor Gracie! I know how it is to lose the woman you love, and I know how it is to lose your mother when you're young. No, nothing is going to help. Not even time.*

"I just don't understand why you didn't ask him to stay with us," Allison said, glaring her most dragon-princess glare at Matthew.

"Honey, I don't want to push him. He's here, and he said he'll stay a week. There's time for him to come to me – to us. This is a big loss for Will, too, you know that. He needs a little time in that house to let it sink in that she isn't going to come around the corner with a plate of cookies."

"What are they going to do?" Allison asked, sitting down across the table from Matthew. She looked around her sunny yellow kitchen, admiring the sunflowers on the curtains and the border at the top of the room. It was a cheery room even on rainy days, and she liked it better than any other room in the house. "I mean – well, Pearl is getting so old and feeble, there's no way she can run that house for John any more. I can't do it, either; I have to work."

Matthew sighed. "I wish you didn't have to work if you didn't want to. You sure didn't marry a man with money!"

"I love my job and we have plenty of money between us. I could have married a doctor, remember, but I didn't want one. You were it for me just about from the day I met you. But what about John's problem? I know nobody's thinking about it yet..."

"Honey, I don't know. This day was hard enough, just laying Carolyn Abbott in the ground. We'll have to worry about it tomorrow. For today, we'll just thank God for His provision and care for us and hope for a good night's sleep. I still have to get up at three to go milk cows."

Chapter 3

WILL DIDN'T WAKE UP FOR THE MORNING MILKING, AND nobody came in to roust him, so that when he stumbled into the kitchen at nine o'clock, freshly showered and shaved but still heavy-eyed and badly in need of coffee, the room was empty, breakfast dishes draining by the sink. The coffee carafe was empty, too, so he opened cupboards until he found what he needed to make some and hovered over it until he could slide a mug in to catch the elixir before it even hit the pot. Eyes closed, he inhaled the steam and voluntarily scalded his tongue to get the magic going.

"Idolatry is a sin, too," Pearl said behind him, causing Will to startle so much that the hot coffee sloshed over his hand.

"Ow!" He set the mug on the countertop and shook the coffee from his hand.

"Put it under cold water," Pearl said, turning on the tap. "I'm so sorry. Had no idea you wouldn't hear me coming."

Sighing with relief as the icy water took the sting out of his hand, Will turned to smile at her. "It's okay. I'm not much good until I've had my coffee, kinda fuzzy-headed. I must have been spacing out."

"You slept late."

"Not really. I mean, it's not like I had to get up. At home I get up around eight every day."

Pearl did that thing she had always done, primming her mouth so the little wrinkles stood out all around it. "You know what they say about the early bird."

"Yes, ma'am, I do. But I'm not big on worms." He dried his hand on the dishtowel and picked up his coffee again. "Join me?"

"I will," Pearl said, filling a small mug for herself and sitting down at the table. "Many a day I've sat at this table drinking coffee with one of you or helping Carolyn with the beans and such." She shook her head slightly. "It isn't going to be the same… but we'll go on and find a new rhythm to the day. Now, tell me all about yourself, Will."

As the caffeine began to awaken his brain cells, Will contemplated the order. "It's really pretty straightforward. I live in Iowa City, Iowa, and teach composition to freshmen at the university there. I have an apartment, a really nice one, and a bunch of friends from the university. And, no, there's no woman in my life right now, at least nobody serious."

"Is this the official biography you hand out?" she asked.

"Pardon?"

"I hear what you're saying, but it doesn't really tell me much about Will Ryersen, the boy I used to know, all grown up now."

"Grandma, there really isn't much else to tell." He met her eyes over his mug and then looked down to sip from it.

Pearl was shaking her head again, more forcefully than before, as she told him, "You know better than to lie to me, boy. We've been over this before."

"Yes, ma'am. So let me just say there's nothing more I want to talk about. Unless you want to ask me how I like teaching composition to five sections of unwilling freshmen."

"Well, heavens, I already know the answer to that! I assume this is an entry level into what you really want to teach."

"Yes! What I really want to teach is modern poetry, mostly American. But it's going to be a few years before I get to do that unless somebody drops dead." He grinned at Pearl. "I don't suppose I could ask you to pray for that, could I?"

"Perhaps not," she said, smiling back at him. "In the meantime, however, you might find Ed and see what needs doing around here."

"May I have something to eat first?" he asked meekly.

"What would you like? Bacon and eggs? I don't have time to make biscuits for you, but there's plenty of coffeecake and muffins and – "

"Just a muffin will be fine. I don't eat much breakfast, just a little something."

Pearl frowned and made tsking noises as she selected the largest blueberry muffin from a plate on the counter. "At least let me get some butter for that."

"No, thanks, really. This is fine." He peeled back the paper and took a bite. "Good. Not as good as – as yours."

"Not as good as Carolyn's. We have to get over being afraid to mention her, you know. It honors the dead to remember them."

Will nodded, his mouth full, but his heart didn't follow. He left the rest of the muffin, chugged the cooled coffee and went out the back door without another word to Pearl.

THAT NIGHT AT DINNER, WILL WENT OVER HIS BIOGRAPHY FOR THE whole family and then managed to turn the conversation to what was going on with the crops and the livestock. He was feeling relatively safe as he took out the garbage after dinner, until he looked over to find Gracie at his side.

"Can I walk with you?" she asked.

"Sure. I'm just taking this stuff to the compost heap."

"That's okay. It's too sad in the house."

"Yeah." Will looked down at the little girl, whose blond head was bent so he couldn't see her sky-blue eyes. Her hair looked like it could use a good brushing, and he noticed her socks didn't match.

"Did you know my mom?"

"I did. She kind of mothered me when I was a teenager. She was a wonderful woman, Gracie, and I remember when she was expecting you, how much she wanted you, then how happy she and your daddy were when you were born. That's about the time I – uh – went away to school, so I didn't get to see her being your mom very much, but I know she was a great mom, wasn't she?"

Gracie looked up at Will with Carolyn's eyes and nodded, "She was. I can't understand why God would take her away from me and Daddy when I'm not even grown up yet. I'm mad at God for that."

Oh, boy, now what? How am I supposed to respond to that!

"Let me dump this bucket," he said, suiting actions to words. The compost heap lay fermenting in the twilight, a faint, earthy odor rising from it. Will took the shovel left there for the purpose and turned under the fresh material.

"Are you mad at God?" Gracie asked. "Your mom died and left you, too, didn't she. I remember Uncle Matthew saying that."

"She did – die – when I was fifteen." He picked up the bucket and headed back toward the house.

Gracie grabbed Will's free hand and dragged against his forward motion. "But are you mad at God? Daddy says we can't be mad at Him, it's bad. But I am. Will I go to hell and never get to see Mom?" Her lip began to tremble.

"Gracie, honey – " Will dropped the bucket and squatted to look the child in the face, taking her other hand in his, too. "God is big enough to understand how you feel, and why you feel that way. He isn't going to send you to hell, Gracie, I promise. He wants to love you and help you through this."

"Nobody can help," the little girl wailed, tears beginning to fall, "because my mom's dead and she isn't coming back and my daddy won't talk about her and nobody understands and who's going to help me wash my hair?"

If You exist up there, You'd better help me now!

Will gathered Gracie against his chest and let her cry on his shirt, fishing a handkerchief out of his pocket to deal with the mess, running his hand over her hair again and again, making some sort of humming noises he didn't know he knew how to do until she quieted and drew back from him, handkerchief mopping at her nose.

"I'm sorry," she said in a tiny, embarrassed voice.

"Nothing to be sorry for," Will said. "I remember how much it hurts. I cried a lot when my mom died, and I did it for a long time, too. Only I didn't have anyone to help me at first the way you do. I know your daddy is having a hard time, but he loves you, Gracie, and I promise he's going to talk to you in a little while. They'll figure out about washing your hair and picking out clothes for school and stuff like that."

"Will?"

"Yes?"

"You didn't answer my question. Are you mad at God?"

She must have learned it from Pearl; she's relentless. "Gracie, I – uh – God isn't really a part of my life, so, no, I'm not mad at Him."

In the faint light of the waning evening, Will could see the shock on Gracie's face as she stared up at him, wide-eyed, her mouth forming an O of surprise. "Are you one of those?"

He stifled a laugh by heroic effort. "One of those what?"

"One of those unsaved people who's going to hell! Oh, Will, I don't want you to go to hell! That wouldn't be good at all!"

Now he did laugh, though not meanly. "I am one of those unsaved people, honey, but I don't think I'm going to hell. Don't worry about it. If God is everything you think He is, then He has better things to do than pick on folks like me."

"Oh, you don't understand," Gracie insisted. She began to drag him toward the house. "You need to talk to Daddy right away!"

ON SUNDAY WILL CONSENTED TO GO TO CHURCH WITH THE FAMILY, BE-cause it didn't seem worth the hassle to refuse. He was there to help, not to upset anyone, he reminded himself, and he only needed to stay until his flight out on Tuesday night.

It had been a long time since he had gone to church here – or anywhere else, for that matter, except for a couple of weddings and funerals in Ames. Nothing had really changed, he saw, as he followed Matthew and Allison down the aisle to the third pew, where the family always sat.

I wonder if the Abbott ancestors paid pew-rent for this pew way back when. Oh, here comes Pastor Miles – look at him, he never changes. Well, hair going gray. And cheaters for reading. Penny sure hasn't changed; not even any gray! Duh; she could be dyeing it. But would a pastor's wife do that?

Somebody managed to brush Gracie's hair and give her matching socks. That's good. And John looks a little better this morning.

How many songs are they going to sing? Let's get this show on the road.

"Pay attention," Gracie whispered from the other side of Matthew. "He's going to do the getting saved part now."

"Thanks," Will whispered back, trying not to laugh again.

"ON SUNDAYS WE ALWAYS HAVE DINNER AFTER CHURCH WITH JOHN'S family," Allison said, "but we thought maybe today you'd come to our house, if you don't mind."

"I guess that's okay," Will answered. "If you don't think we need to be there for them."

"I told Pearl last night we'd be inviting you," Matthew said. "They don't mind; after all, we haven't had a chance to talk yet."

Oh, crap.

"I've had ten years to hone my cooking skills," Allison teased, "so I think you'll be impressed."

"I've had ten years to hone my ordering-in skills," Will said, "so I know I'll be impressed!"

"You haven't seen our house yet, either," Allison said. "It's not as big as the Abbotts', but it's nice. We're happy there."

Matthew turned onto a long, curving driveway and followed it beneath an arch of maples to a red brick ranch-house with crisp white trim. Spring tulips and narcissi were dancing hello in the light breeze, and a huge black dog lazily unwound himself and sauntered over from the front porch.

"You have a dog!"

"Yeah," Matthew said, "I didn't like leaving Allison out here on her own when I have to work nights. So we got ourselves a mighty watchdog." He parked and got out, spreading his legs wide apart. Will's unspoken question was answered without words as the dog charged around the car to jump up and put his paws on Matthew's shoulders. Laughing, Matthew avoided most of the swipes of the huge, wet tongue and shoved the dog down.

"I can get out now," Allison said. "He never, ever jumps on me. But you'd better brace yourself."

The dog went rapidly from Matthew to Allison, but he sat at her feet and lifted his right paw to shake. "Such a good boy," Allison cooed, shaking his paw and petting him. The dog grinned at her and ambled a few steps to meet Will, who was standing very close to the open door so that he could dive back into the car if necessary.

"Give him the back of your hand to sniff," Allison said. "He won't hurt you."

"He could!" Will rejoined, gingerly extending his hand. The dog sniffed, licked and turned his attentions to the rest of Will.

"Tucker! Stop that!" Allison said sharply, and the dog wilted to the ground immediately, looking guiltier than a dog should be able to.

"Let's go on in," Matthew said, his eyes twinkling with laughter he didn't let his mouth express.

Tucker whined as they walked past him, and Allison said, "Oh, all right." He bounced up and led the way into the house, tail wagging.

Will stopped inside the front door to look around him. The living room, dining area and kitchen were all open to one another, making the space seem bigger, lighter, airier than it had from the outside. "Nice."

"Thanks," Matthew said. "Allison has a way with a place."

She showed him the bedrooms, three of them, and the bathroom, and then excused herself to focus on cooking. Tucker stayed close to Matthew, who was staying close to Will.

"Come sit down," Matthew said. "Allison won't need any help for a little while."

No help for it, is there? Will thought. *Time to man up, bite the bullet, take the plunge, uh – well, whatever the next cliché is.*

He sat on the blue couch, which he thought he might remember from Allison's condo, and tried to appear nonchalant. Tucker sat down on his foot and leaned into him, an almost painful weight, but somehow comforting. Matthew took the adjacent chair, tossing a couple of fancy little pillows onto the floor with a smile.

They tried waiting each other out.

"Don't make me come in there and start the conversation," Allison called from the kitchen. "You can do this, guys!"

They laughed together, and Will decided to be gracious, figuring his big-city skills put him one up on his father. "So what kind of a dog is this thing, anyway? He must weigh a hundred pounds!"

"Hundred and twenty, as a matter of fact," Matthew said. "Near as I can figure, he's mostly a black lab, but that size and feathery tail have to come from a St. Bernard or something like that. He's great as a yard ornament, and when he does bark, it's scary as heck, but the fact is he's a lover, not a fighter. He is protective of Allison, though; notice how he didn't jump on her? He's never even tried."

All right, amenities observed. Get it over with.

"Matt – Dad – I want you to know: when I left for college and didn't come back, it wasn't because I was mad at you. I never blamed you for what happened. It was me. It was too hard to be around you, because I could see your scars – " he gestured to the faint lines above and below Matthew's right eye and lower down on his jaw – "and it reminded me every day of what I did. I just couldn't take it. Even after I tried to – kill myself, even after all that therapy, I couldn't get past it."

Matthew's face clouded. "I thought that doctor helped you. I thought you were getting better. He said you were. That's why it was so hard when you just – started having all those excuses for staying away. But I couldn't blame you for not forgiving me for not taking care of you better. I'm so sorry I failed you, Will."

"No! That wasn't it at all!" Will insisted, shocked. "It was what *I* did – or didn't do." Tucker whined and leaned harder into his leg; unconsciously he began to stroke the massive black head.

"I don't understand," Matthew said slowly.

"Can we just – let it go?" Will asked. "Just let the past be past now? I've missed – everyone, and I'm glad to see people again. I'm only here a little while; can't we enjoy this time?"

Matthew appeared to be thinking that over. Will let the silence grow as he petted the dog and turned his gaze to Allison, shamelessly eavesdropping from the kitchen.

"Come set the table, Will," Allison called, breaking the silent stasis. "I can use some help here. Wash your hands first, though. That dog gets into all kinds of nasty stuff outside."

"Coming!" he answered, shoving Tucker aside, no small task, and making his way to the bathroom.

Matthew continued to sit there, silent.

Please don't let him pick now to become assertive! I don't know how to explain any more.

Your manning up didn't last very long, did it? Still as much of a coward as ever.

THE FLIGHT WOULD BE DELAYED BY HALF AN HOUR, ACCORDING TO THE display. Will had turned in his rental car, said good-bye to Matthew, Allison, John and Gracie, and gone through security, only to sit in the little roped-off waiting area with nothing to do but think, his books packed in the bottom of his bag, too shy to play his guitar in public.

Gracie had insisted upon going with them to the airport, even though the midnight flight would mean she didn't get home until hours past her bedtime. She had clung to Will's hand in the back seat and tried repeatedly to talk to him about his salvation. Finally,

Allison had told her to stop it, for which Will was grateful. He didn't want to be mean to the little kid, especially since she was hurting so much, but it was wearing on his nerves.

Talk about brainwashed! he thought now, staring sightlessly out the huge plate-glass window across from him. *Only ten, and she's completely sold on the party line. Well, at least she cares about people. She won't be a bully. She'll be a beauty when she's a few years older, and John will have his hands full with all those farm-boys beating on his door. Especially since she's the heir to the farm, too.*

Too bad Dad and Allison don't have any kids. I would have thought they'd have started a family right away, crazy as Allison is about babies. Dad, too, really. Not me so much, I guess, but John and Carolyn's little boy, David, before he died, and baby Gracie... Oh, well, none of my business.

And what about you, Will? When do you plan to get married and have children? You've met all kinds of bright, attractive, willing women over the years. Most of them were shopping for a husband. Why haven't you been shopping for a wife? It's true, isn't it, what those football players at the high school said about you. Faggot. Queer.

Will jumped up and began to pace the confines of the waiting area, to the displeasure of the dozen or so other people waiting there. *Being here sure brings back memories! I can't wait to get home, where I don't have to think about this stuff.*

But you surely know it's not so easy to put the genie back in the bottle, don't you?

"Did you and Will manage to talk things out?" John asked Matthew as they walked from the barn to the house for lunch.

"Not really. He started to open up, then he slammed the door right in my face again. I could tell he wasn't going to go any further. He said something about it all being his fault, and then – bam!"

"Gracie seemed to take to him."

"Yeah. Will said Gracie's worried about his salvation. He was laughing about it, I'm sorry to say."

"Oh, he's in big trouble," John said, coming as close to a laugh as he had in a long time. "She's praying out loud for him every single night!"

"Can't hurt, can it?" Matthew sighed and held the porch door for John. "We pray for him, too, Allison and I, every night. I hoped I could talk to him about it, but he just wouldn't."

"Whatever you do, don't give up," John said as he washed his hands. "I believe with all my heart that God wants Will Ryersen saved and has a plan for his life."

"Sit down and eat now," Pearl commanded, bringing bowls of tomato soup and a platter of grilled cheese sandwiches to the table. "Where's Ed?"

"Right here!" the farmhand called from the porch as he hustled inside to complete the foursome. "Looks mighty fine, Pearl. Thank you."

"I guess I have a few more lunches in me," Pearl said, seating herself and taking half a sandwich.

"A lot of lunches!" Matthew exclaimed. "You can't leave us now, Pearl. What would we do without you?"

"Same as we always do when someone passes," Pearl said, only the faintest quiver in her voice. "Pick up the pieces and keep moving forward."

"Amen," Ed agreed. "It ain't easy, but it always works out."

"I'm not deaf," John returned. "I get the idea."

WHEN THE LAST OF THE FUNERAL PIE HAS BEEN FED TO THE CHICKENS, when the last of the funeral flowers have begun to wilt and stink in their vases at the nursing home, when the funeral suit and tie have been relegated to the back of the closet again and the white shirt buried at the bottom of the hamper, when the thank-you notes are all written, stamped and delivered to the post office – when there's nothing else to do and nowhere to go and nobody to intervene – then the pain hits.

John Abbott tucked the soft pink blanket close around his sleeping daughter and kissed her forehead gently. Gracie had always been a good sleeper; his attentions wouldn't wake her. "Good night, sweetheart," he whispered as he slipped out of her room and closed the door. He noted in passing how much the room had changed to reflect its ten-year-old inhabitant. As John's son David's room it had been blue, with dinosaur spread and curtains. As Matthew's teenage son Will's room it had stayed blue, but with red and navy accents. John had always thought it looked a little bit like a good motel room when Will lived there – no personal items, always so tidy... And now it was a pink princess room, lovingly transformed by her mother –

Who would never see what happened to that room when their little princess became a teenager. Who would never help Gracie into her wedding dress there or put a bassinet in there for her first grandchild. Who would never –

"Oh, God," John groaned softly there in the hallway, "how can I bear this?"

Chapter 4

"I HOPE YOU APPRECIATE WHAT A FINE FRIEND I AM, MEETING you at the airport in the middle of the night," Trey Sullivan told Will as he hefted Will's overstuffed carry-on into the back seat of his school-bus yellow Mustang convertible.

"It's six-thirty-five a.m., for cryin' out loud, Trey! Hardly the middle of the night." Will shoehorned himself into the passenger seat and buckled up. Trey did love to go fast.

"It's the middle of the night if you didn't go to bed until four," Trey grumbled, sliding behind the wheel. He turned the key and smiled beatifically at the low growl of the engine.

"I do appreciate the ride," Will said. "At the speeds you drive, we'll be home in about a minute and a half, and you can go back to bed. I'm sure you don't have to work."

"Of course not! What do you think I am?"

"Rich," Will answered, but he softened the jab with a grin. Trey was unashamedly wealthy and only had to work if he felt like it in his father's investment firm, but he was generous with his money and never looked down on those who didn't have any.

The thirty-plus miles to Iowa City from Cedar Rapids whined away quickly under the Mustang's tires and Will began to look forward to getting some sleep himself. Rest hadn't been easy on the farm – too many memories to keep him company.

"So how was the trip?" Trey asked, keeping his eyes on the road, where traffic was just beginning to pick up.

"I went to a funeral, man. It was heavy."

"Yeah, but did you get a chance to talk to your dad? Did you meet any hot women? Oh, hey, did you see that old girlfriend of yours? What was her name, anyway – Toni? Tori?"

"Tracy. And, no, I didn't see her. Saw her parents, but only for one of those ever-so-polite handshakes. I started to talk to my dad, but I just couldn't quite – he didn't get what I was trying to say."

"So what else is new?" Trey grinned and shook his head. "Shoot, when I talk to my old man it's like he's speaking Mandarin and I'm speaking Swahili."

Trey expertly maneuvered the little convertible through city traffic and wheeled smoothly into a parallel parking spot in front of Will's apartment building.

"Thanks a lot," Will said, unfolding himself onto the sidewalk and manhandling his bag and guitar case out of the back seat. "I appreciate it."

"No problem! Hey, a bunch of us are going out this evening. Why don't you join us?"

"Wednesday night?"

"Sure. It's hump day for you poor humps. Meet us at McClendon's at five for drinks and then we'll figure out what to do about dinner."

"Sure, why not?"

Will hefted his bags and made his way into the lobby of his building, then took the elevator up to the sixth floor loft which he called home. The building had been a grain mill or something before the city had overtaken it, falling into disrepair and narrowly escaping demolition before the gentrification of the neighborhood. Now it housed upscale apartments and several lofts, not as big as some, but lofts nonetheless. Will had fallen into this apartment by sheer luck, a sublease from an elderly architect who had remodeled it and then fallen ill and ended up in a nursing home but didn't want to let it go. Will got to live there at greatly reduced rent, though still more than he could really afford, in exchange for maintaining the loft and caring for the architect's plants and aging, overweight tabby cat Nero. The cat was currently boarding with Will's downstairs neighbor, Mrs. Gorsuch, who loved the cat almost as much as his owner did and made sure he had treats every day.

Unlocking the modern deadbolt above the beautiful old brass

handle and lock-plate, Will entered and stood by the door surveying his domain. The plants looked fine, which meant Mrs. Gorsuch had come up and watered them at least once, and his mail was on the brushed chrome-and-glass coffee table. Not much of it. No messages on the answering machine.

"I leave a light footprint," Will said, almost expecting his voice to echo in the large, open space.

He unpacked in moments and put everything away or into the laundry hamper. The bag stored neatly in the back of the closet, leaving the room as uncluttered as when he had entered. No mess. No fuss.

As Will hung up his clothes and slipped between chocolate-and-tan striped Egyptian cotton sheets to take a nap before dinner, he thought how different this all was from the Abbotts' farmhouse or his father's tidy little ranch. The architect had kept the exposed heating and water pipes, the I-beams and cross-braces, and double-glazed the huge windows in their original frames. The walls were exposed brick, and no window treatments softened the edges or obstructed the view. It was upscale, uptown, furnished with stark, modern furniture in blacks and tans. It had been dressed for success and always impressed the people he invited in for drinks or to watch a ball game. He knew it impressed the women, and he had also used that in his favor a time or two.

This is the life. This is what I wanted. Nobody here knows who I was, they just know who I am. I'm cool. I'm free. I have it all – or I will have when I get to teach poetry. Nobody can tell me what to do, and nobody can push me around. I'm free. I'm happy.

Oh, really?

"Shut up," Will told the other voice in his head and pulled the expensive feather pillow over his ears.

WILL DIDN'T BOTHER TO SHAVE, BECAUSE THE BLOND STUBBLE WAS AT-tractive to unattached women, but he made sure his hair was artfully tousled and his clothes university chic, in a casual, day-off way. The weather in Iowa City was about the same as the weather in Ohio today, so he didn't need a coat. Locking his door and stuffing the keys into the pocket of his jeans, he celebrated his freedom by running down six flights of stairs, laughing at himself as he found himself puffing a little at the bottom.

It was an easy two-block walk to McClendon's in the mild evening air, and he enjoyed the stroll through the eclectic neighborhood of apartments, dry cleaning shops, cafes and restaurants, bars and boutiques. The neighborhood watchdogs had made sure all the signage was compatible and tastefully understated – no flaming pink neon to announce a bar called "The Pink Flamingo" or anything like that. Will greeted the little Korean grocer on the corner before he crossed the street to enter the gang's favorite bar.

"Here he comes, the world traveler!" Trey announced to the whole place as Will walked in, managing to rouse a cheer from friends and strangers alike. Will rose to the occasion with a very Elizabethan bow, which raised another cheer and not a few cat-calls.

"Whatcha drinking?" the bartender asked.

"Hi, Ned. How about a scotch rocks? Double."

The drink appeared at his hand in seconds, the smoky essence wafting up to entice Will's sensibilities even before he picked up the glass. He took it and joined Trey's table, which was actually two small tables shoved together to accommodate the group.

"Thanks for saving me a chair," he said, sitting and taking a deep first swallow of his drink. They nodded but continued their discussion, which, as far as Will could see, had much to do with the new man under consideration for president of the university. Most of the guys were, like Will, young associate professors from the English and philosophy departments. Only Trey and Josh Baxter were "outsiders," both working for Trey's father's firm.

Liam and Nate, breathing the rarified air of metaphysics and situational ethics, seemed to feel most qualified to pontificate about the poor man's qualifications, but Caleb and Andrew weren't buying any. They were concerned that he might not appreciate the MFA program for which the university was famous, through which Will and Andrew had both received their outstanding higher educations.

"So what do you think, Will?" Liam asked, knocking back his fourth beer and discretely belching into his hand.

"No idea," he breezed. "Haven't met him; haven't heard any hard info; don't really give a care, to tell the truth. Nobody's going to mess with the program; it's too famous. And as a lowly comp teacher, I don't expect to meet the guy until graduation, much less have anyone ask me for my vote."

"Ah, so young, so politically unaware, so innocent," Nate teased. "Come home with me, young Ryersen, and let me teach you the ways of the world." He reached out and patted Will's hand.

"GEEZE, RYERSEN," TREY SAID, SHAKING HIS HEAD AS HE FOLLOWED Will out of the police station onto the sidewalk. "What flipped your switch? I know you hadn't even finished that first drink; were you getting loaded at home before you came? I've never seen anybody go off like that! I thought you were gonna kill Nate – and so did he!"

Will stuffed his wallet and keys back into his pockets and started walking toward Trey's car, parked halfway down the block. "Thanks for bailing me out," he said quietly.

"No prob again, for the second time today," Trey answered, "but what's going on? Did they do something to you in Ohio to make you crazy? You can't just go around punching people and trying to strangle them! What will the dean say?"

"The dean won't know anything about it," Will said, "because your father's big-time attorney got them to let me go without charges. I'm sorry I had to call you; couldn't think of anybody better to waste a phone call on."

"Right. Want to go out for the dinner we didn't get and talk about this?"

"No. Please just drop me off at home."

Trey got behind the wheel, sighing, and piloted the Mustang through the downtown area until he pulled up in front of Will's building. "Déjà vu all over again," he teased. "We're doing this just about every twelve hours now."

"I really am sorry. I'll – I'll see you later."

Trey watched his friend enter the building and sat there a moment, wondering, before driving off.

WILL UNDRESSED TO HIS UNDERWEAR AND WRAPPED HIMSELF IN THE BIG, warm bathrobe his father had bought him years before. It was frayed along the seams and binding and faded to an indeterminate color, and it represented safety to Will. He recognized it as a security blanket, but he didn't care, especially now, after the encounter with Nate. In the bathroom at the back of the loft, he ran the water until steam began to float out of the shower, then stripped and stepped in, standing there in the hot water, washing over and over again until his skin felt tight and raw.

You can't wash it off, you know that. It's not on the outside, it's on the inside. Why are you so upset? It's not as if you didn't know Nate's gay; he hasn't made any secret of it. He's just been waiting for you to give him a signal.

I guess I did that! He won't be quite so pretty for a long time.

Methinks the lady doth protest too much.

Chapter 5

"I NEED TO TALK WITH YOU," JOHN TOLD MATTHEW AND ED that Saturday morning in June as they finished break-fast and prepared to scatter to their day's work. "Let's do it right after lunch, while Pearl's resting and Gracie's still over at Livvie's."

"What's that all about?" Matthew wondered, watching John leave.

"Ain't got the faintest idea," Ed replied.

"Well, I have," Pearl said from her position at the sink, where all three men had forgotten her. "John realizes he has to make some plans and arrangements around here, and he's figured out what he wants to do."

"Plans?" Matthew asked.

"Well, of course. Things can't go on the way they have the last month. It isn't good for Gracie – or for the rest of us. I can't care for this house and that child the way Carolyn did, I'm sorry to say."

"You been doing a fine job," Ed said, "and I thought we was help-ing okay."

"You've both been wonderful," Pearl agreed. "But it isn't enough. Gracie needs more supervision, and as she grows up she's going to need a woman's touch."

"Don't say that!" Matthew returned, moving toward her. "You have to live forever and take care of all of us!"

"Come on, boy," she said, patting his arm but resisting the hug he clearly wanted. "No one lives forever. Even Will understands that."

"You always liked him best," Matthew said, pouting for effect.

"Let's go," Ed laughed, "if you can get past that kindygarden attitude enough to do a man's work. Pearl, you just hold on for now, all right? I'm partial to your company."

AFTER LUNCH, THE THREE MEN REMAINED SEATED AROUND THE KITCHEN table. It was everyone's favorite gathering spot, but for John it was one of the places Carolyn seemed closest, almost as if she might walk in barefoot, carrying a basket of strawberries from the garden, her lips and fingers stained red from the berries, making her blue eyes even bluer, maybe leaving faint muddy footprints on the linoleum. He closed his eyes for a moment and tried to recall the summery smell of Carolyn, that blend of sunshine, berries, Clorox and rosewater.

"I asked you to stay," he finally said, "because it's been a month since Carolyn – died, and we need to make some arrangements here. I've put it off because I can hardly stand to admit to myself she isn't coming back – " He paused to wipe his eyes with his fingers and clear his throat. *God help me, this is so hard.* "Matthew, you may not have known this, but before she – well, before, Ed had been talking to me about retiring."

Matthew was visibly shocked, his eyes wide, face pale. "Are you kidding? Why would you do that? This is your home and you're as much a part of it as anyone!"

"Chronicles and Kings, boy, don't get all upset. Me and John been looking at everything from the long haul, don't you know. I ain't getting any younger, and I been feeling it on cold, wet mornings and evenings. Arthur and me is pretty intimate these days. I'm thinking maybe Pearl and me ought to check out Florida while we still can."

"No! If it's too much for you, I'll just do more and you can take it easier. Pearl can't go to Florida and leave us! You can't just walk out of our lives!"

"Steady," John said quietly. "Nobody's walking out just now. But think, Matthew. I'm fifty-seven and Ed has five or six years on me. Even you're over forty, and you're the spring chicken of the group. We need some younger men in here to keep it going when we can't do it any longer."

"What about Gracie?" Matthew asked. "Isn't it going to be her farm?"

John dropped his head into his hands for a moment. Then he

met Matthew's gaze and said, "Yes, it's going to be hers when I die, if not before. But she's a girly girl, Matthew, and she may not want it. She doesn't show much interest in riding the tractor or doing any of the things boys do around a farm. She's afraid of the chickens and hates to weed the garden – I don't think we're going to see Farmer Grace. That means either she'll sell it outright and use the money to do whatever she really wants to do, or she'll rent it all out and partly live off the profits. But stay here, at least after high school, I doubt it. Either way, my job is to keep the farm a profitable business until Gracie is ready to do whatever she decides to do."

"Makes good sense," Ed agreed. "Me and Matthew and you are going to need help to do that, because I really am getting past it."

"I guess so," Matthew said, rubbing his hands across his face. "So what's your plan?"

"I've been working on it for a couple of weeks, here and there," John answered, "and here's what I have so far: I've hired Cassie Anderson from town to be a housekeeper and minder for Gracie. She'll come in at seven in the morning to make sure Gracie's ready for school, then she'll clean and fix lunch and see Gracie off the bus and into her afterschool routine. If Pearl allows, she'll help with dinner before she goes home. She'll maybe come Monday through Friday, and not on days when there's no school."

"What about now, in the summer?" Matthew asked. "And doesn't she have kids of her own?"

"She has a little boy, Micah. He can stay here every day until they're ready to go home. He's younger than Gracie, and it shouldn't be a problem. Cassie needs the job and we need the help. Pearl can't handle it; haven't you seen how tired she is?"

"Yeah," Ed agreed, "she's been beat ever since the funeral. I been worried about her."

"Okay," Matthew agreed, "so Cassie's a good idea. I know she's a nice woman, because I see her in church with the Sunday School kids. What does her husband say?"

"She's divorced," John answered. "I gather her husband was a mean son-of-a-gun, and he's not great about paying his child support. Cassie's been working at the market, but it isn't really enough. This job will be a big help to her as well as to us."

"Right!" Ed said. "We'll feed her up and make sure she's happy here."

"You're as bad as John for taking in strays," Matthew teased.

"Yeah, and ain't you grateful!"

"The other part is harder to work out," John continued. "I'd like to offer a job to Will's friend Travis. He's kind of marking time until a full-time job opens up with his father, but in the meantime he's been working at that little plant, Lewiston Automotive Supply. He's a farm-boy; we know he had good training. I figure he can work with you on the big jobs, Matthew, and Ed and I will do the easy stuff. You can break him in."

"Oh! Well, I don't think I – "

"That brings me to the third part of this," John said, overriding Matthew's protests. "Matthew, I want to officially make you the manager of the farm. When I'm not around to do it all anymore, you'll still be young enough and capable enough to supervise everything and keep it in trust for Gracie."

"But what about Ed? He's been here so much longer than I have, and he knows everything, and – "

"Me and John have talked about this," Ed said, smiling at Matthew, "and we agree this is the best way. You're a good farmer, Matthew, and you love this place – and this family. You ain't going to up and run off somewhere and leave it in the lurch. You can't afford to buy any sizable place of your own, and why should you? Maybe by the time Gracie might want to sell, maybe you might be able to buy it off her and have it in your name, but, shoot, Son, it's yours in your heart same as it's mine and John's."

Suddenly John was so tired he wanted to lay his head on the table and sleep. "This is what I want, what I believe is best, and I want to do it in writing. Are you with me on this, Matthew?"

Matthew stared at his hands for a long time, while John struggled to stay upright. At last he looked at John and nodded. "If that's what you want, that's what we'll do. I'll try really hard not to disappoint you."

Too tired for further speech, John nodded and left the room, the two farmhands staring after him.

"Tough calls," Ed said. "Grieving and planning plumb wears a man out."

WILL STOPPED IN THE LOBBY TO RETRIEVE HIS MAIL FROM THE ORNATE bronze letterbox sandwiched in among a whole covey of them on the near wall. He skimmed the envelopes as he rode up in the service elevator, telling himself he should really begin to take the stairs regularly to stay in shape, half-laughing at himself, because he remained as thin as his father and got plenty of exercise walking all over campus and biking and playing racquetball with Trey. One envelope caught his eye, and then another.

Inside the apartment, Will tossed the envelopes onto the coffee table while he fed Nero the disgusting stuff that fell into the dish with a wet plop and endured a growl as he tried to pet the cat while he was eating. Leaving the beast to his banquet, he changed into jeans and a plain white tee-shirt and padded barefoot over to the couch to read his mail. The bills were usual and unremarkable, and he put them in a tidy pile for payment. Circulars and catalogues went directly into the brushed chrome wastebasket beside the couch, as did a parking ticket – which he fished back out with a sigh and consigned to the bill pile. Then he used his pocket-knife to slice open the letter from his father:

> Dear Will, it was so good to see you, even if what brought you home was so bad. I love you, Son, and I miss you every single day. Allison misses you, too, and our prayer is that now that you've made it back once, you won't hesitate to come back again. We'd love to have you come for Thanksgiving! Please try. This one will be hard on everyone, especially John and Gracie, and I know it would mean a lot to them, too, if you could be here.
>
> Now here's a piece of news! Yesterday John and I went into Lewiston and met with Mr. Showalter, Tracy's father, who is a lawyer, I imagine you remember. They made out this contract and we all signed it, and what it means – I'm officially the Manager of Abbott Farms! It means I get to boss the new man around and when John retires (or dies, but I'm not going there!), I'm going to be in charge of everything about the farm until Gracie is old enough to decide what she wants to do with it. It's a mighty big job for a boy from Rough River, Kentucky, but I am asking God to guide me and help me do my best for John. I owe him so much more than that!

Ed's talking about retiring – has some notion about running off to Florida with Pearl like a couple of kids eloping. John has hired your friend Travis to work with us so Ed can do less. He seems like a good worker, and of course he's a real nice boy. He asks about you. I bet he'd like to spend some time with you at Thanksgiving, too.

I better get to bed before Allison comes and drags me in by the ear. I love you, Son, and I pray for you all the time. God bless you and keep you safe.

Your Dad

Will carefully folded the letter and put it back into the envelope, to be kept with the rest of the letters Matthew had written over the years. There weren't vast numbers, and this might be the longest ever, but they were precious to Will and he read them over sometimes when the pain and guilt of the past was too much to bear.

Next he slit open the other letter. Even if the return address hadn't just said "Gracie," he would have guessed the author by the loopy, round, uneven letters scrawled on the envelope in blue ballpoint ink:

Dear Will,

Hi. How are you? I am fine now, but I had the flu and threw up all over the living room. Daddy said a bad word and Pearl asked if he wanted to bite the soap. I was so sick, but I had to laugh anyway.

I miss you. Daddy says maybe you will come home for Thanksgiving and I would like that a lot. I think you should quit your job in IowaCity and come home to stay. You could teach at my school, we could use a man teacher in the fifth grade.

When you come home I will show you all my art stuff, we do projects every week, Daddy tries to remember to put them on the refrijurader like Mommy always did.

Now before I run out of paper I will tell you the most important part – I pray for you every morning and every nigt, Will, so you will get saved and be friends woth Jesus. He misses you.

39

Please listen to me and don't go to hell. Matthew cries when I talk about that, you don't want to make your Daddy cry do you of course not.

I love you to! When you come home we will have fun.

Love form your cusun – no, cosin – well, from me, Gracie

Will was laughing and shaking his head as he put this letter back into its envelope and put it on top of Matthew's letter. Nero came over to investigate the unseemly behavior in his living room and sneezed in disgust before curling up on the sisal rug to wash his unmentionables.

You do contempt better than anyone else I know, Will thought at the cat, laughing some more. *And Gracie does unconditional love. What a sweetheart! She's so much like her mother it must kill John to be around her sometimes. Thanksgiving...*

He picked up the guitar and automatically checked to see whether it was in tune, adjusting the strings until he was satisfied. Using the finger-picking technique he was still perfecting, he played the Beatles' "Yesterday" and a Segovia classic something or other whose name he couldn't remember before segueing into "Amazing Grace" without realizing what he was doing.

THE LUMP OVER TREY'S RIGHT EYE WAS TAKING ON A LIFE OF ITS OWN, and the purple color did nothing for his complexion, but he insisted he felt fine and wouldn't miss the chance to have dinner at the loser's expense, even though Will wouldn't spring for the most expensive place in town. They took a booth away from the kitchens and spread the huge bile green cloth napkins over their laps as the server, her black silk Thai skirt and embroidered black silk blouse rustling, set water, menus and a plate of appetizers before them.

"You drink?" she asked.

"Of course!" Trey said. "We drink lots. Scotch, right, Will?"

"Sure."

"Two scotch – soda?" she asked in her broken English.

"No," Trey said slowly, "only ice. Plenty ice."

The girl bowed slightly, but Will caught the vague look of contempt on her face.

"You know, Trey, she probably speaks English as well as you do and maintains a four-point average in astrophysics at the university."

"Or she just got off the boat. Anyway, The Thai Pad has good food, and plenty of it, so just settle back and I'll enjoy – on your dime."

Will did agree it was probably the best Thai food in town, and he was glad to be there. Trey showed no signs of concussion, so Will tried to let it go that he had inadvertently smacked his friend right in the forehead with the ball. He knew he was sensitive about concussions because of the bad one he had received in high school at the hands of Pete Coombs, the football bully, and the beating his – *No! Not going there!*

"You're frowning again," Trey said around a mouthful of noodles. "What's up?"

"Oh! Uh – nothing. Just thinking. My dad and my little cousin want me to go home for Thanksgiving."

"Going to do it?"

"I don't know. It would be a quick visit; we only have Thursday-Friday off. I'd have to leave Wednesday after work, and I have a three o'clock class. Hardly seems worth it."

"Well, you can always come home with me – as usual. I don't know what Mom will do if her 'second son Will' isn't there for the holidays. Heck, I think she likes to see you more than she likes to see me."

"That's understandable. Do *not* throw food at me like a baby! Seriously, though – I think I might go. They're all still hurting a lot from Carolyn's death, and I had a special hand-written invitation from my cousin."

"The little girl?"

"Yeah."

"The one who wants to convert you?"

"Yeah."

"You're smiling, man! What's with that? I thought we had this all talked out years ago, buddy. The God-thing is fine for people with limited intelligence or limited lives, people who need The Big Guy to blame for things or hang onto when times are tough. We don't need all that hocus-pocus, though, because we have scientific truth to back us up. Man is the apex of evolution, and we have everything within us to live happy lives. Look at you, man! You have everything but the girl – and I have a plan to fix that."

Will drained his third drink and stared at Trey across the booth. "What kind of 'plan' are you talking about?"

"My dad's company uses a law firm downtown, Higbea, Higbea, Gutenberg, Leipman and Shaw. I have to go over there sometimes to meet with one of the attorneys, and I've met a couple of paralegals – hot stuff, man! A natural redhead and a probably not-so-natural blonde, and they're looking for companionship. I told them I have a handsome friend with killer manners, and they just about were fighting right in front of me about who gets you and who's stuck with me."

Trey's easy laughter assured Will there would be no hard feelings about which woman went with which guy, and Trey did have a point about the absence of a woman in Will's life. It had been some months since he had broken up with the last girl from sheer boredom.

"Why not? Tonight?"

"Mr. Eager! No, they're classy broads, and classy broads don't go out at the last minute. I'll call them tomorrow and set up for Friday night, okay?"

"Sure. Not like I have anything else to do but grade papers. What's the plan?"

"I think we'll meet at McClendon's for drinks before dinner and see how it goes. If we like them, and I really think we will, we can go to dinner and then back to your place or my place for some action."

"Sounds like a plan."

AND AS PLANS WENT, IT WAS PRETTY GOOD. WILL FOUND THE REDHEAD bright and funny and, as Trey had promised, 'hot.' She was a good conversationalist, seemed genuinely interested in his work, stated clearly that she was not interested in marriage but did like to have a good time. Perfect. He found that three or four drinks into the evening, he liked her even better, although he had a hard time remembering her name from moment to moment. Angie? Alice? Amy? He solved that by calling her 'pretty lady,' which seemed to turn her on and kept him in the running.

When dinner was over, Trey took the blond to his Mustang and bade good-night to Will and Ashley (or Annie?). "Would you like to go to my place?" he asked, holding her arm lightly.

"Sure," she said, and even agreed to walk the few short blocks to Will's building.

In the morning, she washed up and left with a kiss and a wink, thanking him for the whole evening, indicating she would be delighted to do it again soon.

WILL LAY THERE ON THE EXPENSIVE SHEETS, HIS BODY PLEASANTLY tired but his mind twitching. He figured he would probably call her, now that he had her name (Angie) and her number safely entered in his cell phone. It was nice. It was fun. It didn't mean anything. He could do it again and again without guilt. And he probably would.

So why wasn't he sleeping the sleep of the just instead of twitching?

At least he was awake to answer the phone when Trey called, full of congratulations and I-told-you-sos. "Just what you needed, right, buddy? You think too much!"

"Right."

"So you going to see her again?"

"I think so. She was smart and nice..."

"And willing. Don't discount willing."

"I'm not discounting anything, believe me. You score?"

"You gotta be kidding! I didn't even have to tell her who I am." Trey paused. "Nah, that's stupid. She already knew... But so what? We had a good time, and I'm going to see her again tonight. Why don't you call Angie and we'll double again, just like high school."

Not like my high school, Will thought. "No, not tonight. I really do have to grade papers. Not all of us have cushy work-if-you-feel-like-it jobs."

"I'd take offense at that if it wasn't true," Trey laughed. "Okay. Give me a call tomorrow or the next day and we'll go to McClendon's."

THE THIRD LETTER DID IT. AFTER STRUGGLING TO DECIPHER THE ORNATE but wobbly Palmer Method handwriting, Will flopped backward on the couch with the letter clutched in the hand of the arm he threw over his eyes. Nero, sensing an interruption in the force, stalked over, meowling loudly, to jump up on Will's stomach with all four feet. Since Nero weighed twenty pounds on a light day, and since Will didn't see him coming, it was a painful shock.

"Yeeeeeaahhhh!" Will hollered, startling both himself and the cat, who leaped over to the coffee table, laid back his ears and hissed.

"Dumb cat, what's the matter with you?" Will asked, rubbing his bruised abdomen and glaring right back at the cat. "Just because you have more money and prestige than I have, that doesn't mean you get to attack me. Get out of here!" He made shooing motions with the hand that held the letter, as the other hand was busy checking for blood.

As Nero flounced out to investigate the rest of his domain, Will continued to sit there staring at the letter. Pearl had never written to him before beyond birthday, Christmas and graduation cards – with tidy checks in them.

Young Will, she wrote, *I would take it as a personal favor if you were able to come home for Thanksgiving. Christmas seems far off. It would please me greatly to see you, and also to know that you and your father had finally worked through all the pain and misunderstanding of the past. When one reaches my age, one finally realizes how much time one has wasted wondering instead of asking, resenting instead of loving, waiting instead of seizing life with both hands. Don't wait, Will. It is foolish.*

She had signed it, *With love, Grandma.*

"Okay," Will said to Nero, who had returned to fix him with an inscrutable stare, "I'll do it. I'll figure it out and buy a ticket now – or maybe I'll drive home. You prepare your shriveled, stony heart to spend Thanksgiving in the kennel, buster, because Mrs. Gorsuch will be going to her son's house."

McCLENDON's WAS PACKED, FRIDAY NIGHT REVELERS CELEBRATING THE end of the work week and hoping to stir up some action. Trey and Cindy, the blond he was seeing, and Will and Angie were crammed into a mini-booth in one of the corners, the table jammed with beer bottles and hot wings and used paper napkins, sitting closer than they strictly had to and perhaps playing a little footsie under the table.

"I thought you'd come to my house," Trey reiterated. "I told you Mom's counting on it. The girls could come, too; you know it's not only family on holidays. How about it, girls? Want to party with the Sullivans for Thanksgiving?"

Cindy giggled as vapidly as if she had trained to be a stereotype, and Angie leaned into Will as close as she could. "That sounds like fun," she said, stroking his arm. "They have such a nice house, and I'll bet their cook makes a wonderful Thanksgiving dinner."

"She does," Will said. "But I need to go home to my family. My – grandmother is really old, and she asked me to come. She may not have another holiday in her."

"Ooooh," Angie said, "I didn't know. I'm so sorry! I'd hate to lose my grandma."

Will realized he had never asked her about her family and hadn't even known she had a grandmother. They didn't spend a lot of time talking. "So you can see why I have to go."

"Well, sure," she said, "but if she's been good all this time, one more holiday can't hurt, can it?"

"Do you want another beer?" he asked, signaling the waitress, who gave him a look of exasperation which suggested he should get up and go to the bar like a big boy. *Crud. She's running her feet off and I'm sitting here on my butt like a spoiled little rich kid. Trey's rubbing off on me.* Flushed with guilt and alcohol, he took orders around the table and made his way to the bar, where Ned was managing to look cool and under control despite the crush.

"Same?" Ned asked.

"Yeah, all around. No, wait a minute. Give me a scotch, double."

"Gonna be sorry if you mix 'em like that," Ned warned, setting up the beer bottles.

"I don't need a mother, Ned," Will said. "Just a drink. If I can't get it here, I'll go someplace else, where opinions don't come with the booze."

Ned eyed him for a long moment before pouring the drink, which he set on the little bar tray with the three beers as gently as if it were made of eggshell. "I know you don't want to hear it, Will, but this is your last drink. Last time you were schnockered in here you sent a guy to the hospital. You're a mean drunk."

Will considered telling Ned where to put the drink, but he wanted it. "I hear you," he said under the noise of the crowd and carried the tray to his table, where it was well-received.

"Back to your place?" Angie asked, watching Will knocking back the scotch as if it were water. "I know how to improve your mood, guaranteed."

"That's my girl," he said, putting his free arm around her.

"We'll come, too," Trey said. "No reason to break up the party. Plenty of room in your loft for whatever we want to do."

"Sure," he said, determined not to be a mean drunk, "the more the merrier, as they say. Let's go!"

Chapter 6

SUMMER SCHOOL WAS OVER AND THE FALL SEMESTER HAD begun, bringing hundreds of ignorant freshmen onto the Iowa campus, most of them in desperate need of Comp 1 and Comp 2, filling Will's days and nights with frustration, leavened by occasional glimpses of hope as a student actually seemed to comprehend the structure of a sentence, the main idea in a paragraph, the value of an outline. In the spare time he didn't have, he still managed to play racquetball with Trey at least once a week and to do some cross-country jogging as the leaves changed. And more nights than he should have he spent with Angie, who remained ever so willing to be with him on casual terms. If she had ever once hinted at anything beyond what they had, he would have backed off immediately, because he knew he didn't love her, but she even went out with another man several times, making clear her non-exclusivity beliefs.

Will began to think he was developing an ulcer, so he finally made an appointment one October day to see the campus doctor. Fortunately he was able to get in between classes, and the doctor promised to have him out in time to make his next class.

"What makes you think you have an ulcer?" the doctor asked. He was a short, bald man with thick glasses, behind which his watery blue eyes seemed mild and unfocused, an impression Will almost immediately understood to be false.

"Dr. Brown, I have epigastric pain before and after eating, acid reflux, nausea – I feel like crap."

"Mm-hm. Lie back and let me poke around." Dr. Brown's short, fat fingers dug into Will's belly in various places, causing him to wince and grunt with pain.

"Sit up," Dr. Brown said. "All right. You haven't been passing blood at either end, right?" Will nodded. "So I don't think you have an ulcer just yet. I think you have gastritis and nasty acid reflux, which should respond pretty well to a proton inhibitor. I'll give you a prescription, and we'll see how it goes for a few weeks. I hate to put you through an endoscopy if I don't have to."

Will nodded.

"How much you drink?" Dr. Brown asked.

Embarrassed color climbed up Will's neck and across the tips of his ears as he answered, "Not all that much. I don't drink every day or anything. I'm not an alcoholic."

"I wasn't suggesting you are," Dr. Brown replied, his gaze sharpening. "Why would that be the first thing you think if it isn't a problem?"

"My grandfather was an alcoholic; I heard my dad talk about him a lot when I was growing up. I'm never going to be like him!"

"Well, that's good. I suggest while you're having this problem you cut out all alcohol and caffeine. Both irritate the esophagus and stomach." Dr. Brown didn't look up from writing something on the little white pad, tearing off the top page and handing it to Will. "Make an appointment to see me in three weeks unless you get worse. Then come right back, okay?"

"Sure, thanks," Will agreed, shoving the paper into his pocket. *Maybe.*

⸱⸱⸱

"At least tell me you're going to fly," Trey begged, "and not drive the whole way to Ohio."

"Yeah, yeah. I decided to fly, and my plane leaves at 5:07 p.m. from Cedar Rapids."

"Want a ride?"

"No, thanks. I'll drive to the airport and leave my car in the long-term lot. I'll rent a car at the other end."

"Last chance to change your mind and stay home," Trey said. "I know Angie would rearrange her plans to be with you, and Mom said to tell you you're still welcome at the last minute. Why go to all this hassle, bro? Just come with me."

"Trey, I love you like the brother I never had, but this is the right thing to do. I'll come back on Monday and we'll get together Tuesday, I promise."

"How'd you manage Monday?"

"Found a guy who needs the money – teaches the same thing I do, for the same pay, but he has a wife and a couple of rug-rats – and he'll cover Monday for me."

"Okay, then," Trey allowed, "but do me a favor and don't come back from the hinterlands talking like one of those televangelists and spouting the beauties of being saved."

Will shook his head, half-laughing, half-peeved at his best friend. "My dad and all the Abbotts are born-again Christians," he said, wondering why he bothered. "I know you'd laugh at my dad because he's such a hillbilly, but they're all good, kind people. Nobody hits anybody over the head with a Bible or froths at the mouth or anything. They just have a really deep faith."

"Just keep remembering your basic Marx mantra: 'Religion is the opiate of the people.' If it makes them happy, fine. You're too smart and too well-educated to fall for it, right?" He hesitated. "Right, Will?"

"Oh. Yeah. Right."

Tuesday before Thanksgiving, Will went into overdrive to make sure everything was ready for his Monday classes, delivering the material in person to his colleague, Ed Simmons, posting a notice on his office door, delivering Nero in his reinforced cat-carrier to the vet's office, which also boarded pets for short stays.

"Good-bye, you old reprobate," he told the yowling cat, keeping his hands far from the front of the carrier. "I'll be back for him on Tuesday evening," he promised the wary technician, who was now holding the carrier at arms' length. "I promise."

"I'm sure he'll be here," the young woman said, muttering to herself, "Not so sure I will."

It was nearly midnight by the time Will had finished his papers, recorded the grades, eaten a cold hot dog and something in a paper take-out carton which might have been Chinese vegetables, and packed his carry-on bag. He brushed his teeth, took his evening pill and climbed wearily into bed. His stomach burned and threatened to return what had passed as dinner.

You would have had a much better time at Trey's house. You don't owe these people anything. And you know they're going to nag you to talk about the past. A lot of good that will do, right? You are who you are, and you did what you did.

Will turned on the radio to the university's classical station, trying to drown the voice in his head with the mellow strains of Miles Davis.

You think you're sophisticated because you like classical jazz and go to the symphony and read modern poetry and discuss existentialism and relativism like a pro. You know what an imposter you are. You're just one generation from hillbillies who couldn't read more than a feed sack, whose only idea of poetry was a good old gospel hymn. You didn't even know how to tie a necktie properly until you met Trey.

Who knows why he wastes his time on you; maybe because Nate asks him to. Nate likes you. Nate wants you. And you know you want –

"No!" Will cried, sitting up in bed. "It's all lies! It's not true!" He got up and went into the bathroom for a drink of water, turning on the lights as he went until the whole loft blazed with color. He stared at himself in the mirror as if he had never seen that man before, and he couldn't find any evidence of – anything. "I'm just tired, and I'm nervy about going home." He splashed his face with cold water and dried it on the thick bath towel. "Sleep, that's all I need."

Chapter 7

WAKING IN A STRANGE ROOM WITH WALLS PAINTED FIRE engine red, Will was inclined to think he had died in the night and gone to hell. Then he remembered: Allison's folly, his father called it. The amazing guest room. Gold drapes, red walls, black-and-gold bed linens. Supposed to be warm and elegant, Matthew said.

"Well, it's warm, all right," Will murmured from his nest of blankets and comforters. He seemed to be trapped inside them, and he was becoming decidedly sweaty.

Struggling to rise up on his elbows, Will looked down the length of himself to the end of the bed, where he found the source of his discomfort. Tucker had encamped across his feet and lower legs and was sleeping blissfully despite Will's struggles. Apparently dogs were color-blind or had no shame about sleeping in a room resembling a brothel.

"Get up, dog," Will said, not really holding out any hope. Then genius struck. "Want to go out, Tucker?"

The dog was at the door in a second, tail wagging madly and doggy grin all over his muzzle. Will threw on some jeans and a sweatshirt and followed his companion to the front door, listening for sounds of life from other parts of the house but hearing nothing.

"Okay, Tucker, here you go!" Will threw open the door and laughed as the dog cleared the porch in one huge jump and began to run up and down the drive watering the maples.

"I wondered when he'd get you up to go out," Allison said behind him.

"Oh, hi. It was the other way around, frankly. I had to wake him up to get him off me so I could get out of bed."

"I'm so glad he doesn't do that to me," she said, smiling. "I'd be suffocated. But Matthew doesn't let him come into the bedroom, and he does listen to that. Guess he forgot to tell him that means all bedrooms. I'm sorry. He can sleep outside tonight."

"Hey, no problem. I like him. He's a whole lot better than the cat from hell who owns my apartment!"

Allison turned away from the door and looked at Will. "You ready for some breakfast? Coffee?"

"I don't eat much for breakfast, not like Dad and Ed and John. And I'm off coffee these days. But I could handle a glass of milk and a piece of toast. I'll get it." He headed for the kitchen, Allison trailing along.

"Have a seat and let me do it," she told him, gesturing. "I don't get to fuss over you much, and I'd like to."

"Yes, ma'am," Will drawled, imitating his father, and sat at the kitchen table. *Is it an Ohio thing,* he wondered, *or a Midwest thing, or a farm thing? In the city we don't gather in the kitchen like this, but I can't count how many dramas played out in Carolyn's kitchen.*

"Here you go," Allison said, placing a big glass of milk and two pieces of whole wheat toast with butter in front of him. "Want jam? I don't make my own, but I still have some strawberry Carolyn made summer before last."

I remember. It tasted like spring all year round.

"Will?"

"Oh. I'm sorry. I was daydreaming. No, thanks, no jam." He began to eat the toast, washing small bites down with the rich milk, recognizing the flavor of Abbott Jerseys in every swallow.

"Your dad said to tell you to come on over to the farm whenever you're ready. I guess the rest of the family will come around two. I have to get my contribution to the meal ready, but that won't take long. They don't let me cook anything."

"Oh, come on! You're a good cook."

"Thank you! I think so, too, and your father never complains. Not that I've managed to put any weight on him, but he's healthy. No, they just think I'm too busy to cook up a storm like Pearl and Livvie do, so I get to bring veggies and dip and olives and pickles – out of jars. I don't mind." Allison smiled at Will and gestured to his plate. "You can do better than that. Eat both pieces. Drink your milk."

"You're starting to sound like Pearl," Will groused, but he obeyed, hoping the small meal would stay put. He sneaked his pill out of his pocket and swallowed it with the last of the milk.

Nurse Allison didn't miss a thing. "Stomach trouble?"

"Yes, sort of. Doctor says it's stress. Hard life, being a professor *and* a playboy," he said, trying to lighten the mood fast.

"Must be. Can I get you anything else?"

"No, thank you. I guess I'll shower and dress up and go over to the farm. You going to come with me?"

"No, I think you should go early and spend some time with your dad. He misses you, and even more since you've been home the one time."

I MISS YOU, TOO, WILL TOLD HIS FATHER AS HE DROVE THE FEW MILES TO the farm. *I miss all the times we had, and all the times I wished we had. I miss when you'd hug me or smooth the hair out of my eyes or hold my hand for a minute and tell me everything was going to be all right. You'll never know how much I wish every day that I could see you and talk to you without getting sick to my stomach because I remember what I did to you.*

Oh, crud.

Will pulled over on the side of the road and vomited up his breakfast.

"I THOUGHT MAYBE HE'D BE HERE BY NOW," MATTHEW SAID TO ED AS they crossed from the equipment barn to the house.

"Maybe he slept in," Ed said in his usual calm voice. "Boy looked last night like he'd been drug through a knot-hole."

"Yeah, maybe. I guess he doesn't like to fly or something. I wonder what it's like..."

"That's right – you ain't never been on a plane, have you?"

"No. And neither have you."

"Right. Difference is, I don't go wondering what it would be like."

Wiping their feet several times on the mat at the back door, they entered the kitchen, where Pearl was directing traffic as John and Cassie did her bidding. The fragrances of Thanksgiving wove themselves around Matthew, bringing old, familiar memories of holidays past, most of them happy ones, he rejoiced to realize. Sage and cinnamon and the sharp overlay of orange and cranberry were all good reminders this time.

"Where's Will?" John asked, breaking Matthew's reverie.

"Must have slept in, or else he's having a heart-to-heart with Allison. Or Tucker him trapped in the bedroom. Dog's taken to Will the same way he did to Allison."

"Well, I hope he gets here soon," Pearl said, stirring something more vigorously.

"I think your hope is answered," Cassie said, smiling at Pearl and taking the spoon from her hand. "Let me finish this, because I hear a car in the driveway."

In moments they heard the front door opening and Will's voice calling out.

Oh, Lord, let this be the day, Matthew prayed. *Give me the opportunity and the words to make it up to Will and ask him to forgive me. I love him, Lord, and I will do anything You want to help him find his way to You.*

FROM THE FRONT DOOR WILL COULD HEAR THE FAMILIAR VOICES COMing from – *where else?* – the kitchen, including a woman's voice he didn't recognize. *That must be Cassie. Guess she doesn't have a family to go to, so of course they'd have her here.*

Before Matthew could reach him, Will was staggered back a few steps by a flying hug from Gracie, who came barreling down the stairs and leaped at him.

"Hey, short stuff, take it easy," he said, hugging her back.

"I'm just so glad to see you!" Her eyes were dancing with delight and her smile made her little face glow.

"Good to see you, too," Will said, thinking, *How can you be so glad? You hardly know me. All you know is I stayed away on purpose for ten years. You should be mad about that.*

Satisfied for the moment, Gracie stepped aside to let Matthew approach his son. His approach was more measured, as if he were unsure of his welcome instead of the other way around, but Will was so glad to see his father he forgot to be careful and stepped right into a hug.

Oh, Daddy. Please don't let go!

Don't be a simpering fool. He's just being polite. Step away so he doesn't have to feel guilty.

"Good to see you, Dad," Will said, backing out of the embrace.

"You, too," Matthew said, backing up a bit to give Will more room. "I'm glad you could make it."

"Right. Guess I'll go say hello to everybody..."

"WHY DO YOU LOOK SO SAD, UNCLE MATTHEW?" GRACIE ASKED, taking his hand and patting it.

Nailed me, Matthew thought, *just like her mother. Ah, Carolyn, you'd be so proud of her!* "I just – " *Be honest with her.* "I wish I could really talk to Will, Gracie, but there's this big wall between us."

"Why?"

"Before you were born, honey, something happened. I let Will down, and he just can't forgive me. Not that I blame him, because he really needed me and I – I failed him."

"Why?"

"What?"

"Why did you fail him?"

Matthew looked down at the little hand still holding his, the little face so open and full of trust. "I don't know. He needed me to stand up for him, and I backed down instead. I thought I was doing the right thing, what Jesus would have done, but it crushed Will. I should have fought for him, and I didn't."

"Oh. But you didn't know it was wrong?"

"No. But I should have known. I'm his daddy. I should have known."

Gracie's eyes swam with tears, but she didn't turn away from Matthew. "I shut the car door on Greg's finger last summer, remember?"

Hard to forget – all that blood and screaming. "I remember. But that was an accident, honey."

"Well, Mommy said that, too, it was an accident because I didn't know his finger was in the door and I wouldn't have done it if I had known. Right?"

"Of course that's right. You never meant to hurt Greg."

"So isn't that the same with Will? You didn't mean to hurt him. If you had known, you wouldn't have done it. Right?"

Out of the mouths of babes... Lord, You never cease to amaze me with all the different ways you teach us lessons! Thank you for Gracie, her faith and her simple way of looking at the world. Please let her keep that innocent wisdom as she grows up.

"You're right, honey. If I had realized, I never would have done it."

"So you can forgive yourself and not be sad anymore, right?" Gracie tugged at Matthew's hand to bring him down to her level and wrapped her arms around his neck. "I love you, Uncle Matthew, and I don't want you to be sad about Will. There's too many things to be sad about in this family now, and Mommy wouldn't like it."

"Your mommy would be so proud of you," Matthew told the little girl as he hugged her. "You are so smart and so loving – just like her." He set her on her feet again and said, "Let's go see what's happening in the kitchen. Smells too good to stay away any longer."

"So are you going to talk to Will, then?" Gracie asked.

THE ONLY THINGS DIFFERENT ABOUT THIS YEAR'S THANKSGIVING TABLE were the presence of Pearl in the seat at the foot of the table and the absence of pecan pie on the sideboard with the other desserts. Cassie and her little son Micah were squeezed in next to Gracie, and Will was tucked in next to Allison, all of them surrounded by Ted and Livvie and their brood. John managed to say grace without breaking down, although his voice cracked once, and any other tears which flowed while heads were bowed were wiped away surreptitiously on the heavy linen napkins.

Over apple and pumpkin pies with whipped cream, the family chatted casually and ate more than was good for them until Teddy suddenly said, "I miss Aunt Carolyn's pecan pie. Remember when David used to call it 'poison pie?'"

"Who's David?" Micah asked, his mouth full of apple pie.

"Don't talk with your mouth full," Cassie said automatically, wiping his chin with her napkin.

"David is my brother who died when he was seven," Gracie explained. "He and my other brother, Baby Johnny, are in heaven with Mommy now."

"Can we go see them?" Micah asked.

"Shut up, dummy!" Andrew Seibeneck said from across the table, drawing a light swat across the back of the head from his father. "Ow! What did I do? Micah's gonna make people cry again!"

"That's enough," Pearl informed the table at large. "Micah, when people die and go to heaven, we don't get to see them again until we go there, too. That's why it's so important to learn to love Jesus and follow him, so you can go to heaven."

"Do I have to?" Micah asked in a squeaky voice, tears forming in his eyes. "I want to stay with Mommy!"

"You're going to stay with me for a long, long time," Cassie soothed. "Now how about another bite of pie? Want some more whipped cream?"

"Gentlemen," John announced, "we are going to do the dishes after the women put away the leftovers, which I am assured we are too stupid to do. Teddy and Steven, this means you, too."

Twenty minutes later, Will found himself in the kitchen with a towel around his waist and another in his hand, drying silverware. *Been here, done this,* he groused to himself, *and don't enjoy it any more this time than I ever did before. Why can't we just use the dishwasher?*

"Because the silver and good china can get ruined in there," Matthew said, as if he had been reading Will's mind. "Just grin and bear it." He handed Will another bunch of forks and knives.

Will had help from the Seibenek men, and they finished all the sterling and fitted it back into its velvet-lined cases before the rest of the work was done.

"Here," Matthew said, handing Will a dishrag, "go gather up all the linens and wipe off the table. Better check the chairs, too. The younger kids can get messy."

"Great. And what do I do with the linens?"

"Put 'em on top of the washer," John said. "I'm afraid to wash 'em without Pearl's say-so. There's probably some magic formula for pre-treating stains or something."

Will went into the dining room and gathered up all the linens as instructed. He set the big bundle on John's chair while he checked all the other chairs and wiped down the table. As he was gathering everything up again, Gracie came in from the living room.

"Whatcha doing?" she asked.

"Cleaning up in here," Will answered, smiling at her. "Gotta take the linens to the washer and give this dirty dishrag back to my dad."

"I'll do that," Gracie offered, snatching it from him and running into the kitchen before he could even make it through the swinging door. She handed the rag to Matthew, then accompanied Will out the back door into the utility room, where he was dumping the table-cloth and napkins on top of the washer.

"Thanks for your help," Will said, turning back toward the kitchen.

"Can I talk to you?" Gracie asked.

"Uh – sure – I guess so. What's up?"

"This is a really serious talk," Gracie said, "so I need you to come upstairs with me."

In the privacy of her room, door closed, Gracie politely offered Will the chair – his old chair, painted white – at her desk. He sat.

"What's up, kiddo?"

Gracie sat on the edge of the bed, surrounded by ruffles and stuffed animals, cocking her head at Will like a curious little bird. "I need to talk to you about your father," she said.

Will felt the blood leave his head and noticed with detached interest that the spots around the edges of his vision were pink. He took a deep breath and told himself it would be humiliating to faint in front of a little girl.

"I had a talk with Uncle Matthew right after you came," Gracie said, "because he looked so sad."

"Gracie, I don't think – "

"Don't tell me you don't think I'm old enough to talk about things, Will. I'm going to be eleven in January and Pearl says I'm very mature for my age."

"Gracie," Will laughed, unable to stop himself, "you're probably the most mature almost-eleven-year-old I'm ever going to meet, but that doesn't mean it's all right for you to – well, to take on adult issues. What's between Matthew and me – "

"Shame on you! It's not polite to call your father by his first name! You should call him Dad or Daddy. He'd really like that."

Matthew shook his head like a horse being deviled by flies. "I *do* call him Dad, most of the time. For a long time he didn't feel like my dad. There's history you don't know, Grace."

"I know why he's sad, because he told me."

Will felt cold clear through, frigid enough to raise gooseflesh on his arms. The pain in his chest that wasn't indigestion settled in like a knife. He turned away from Gracie so she wouldn't see his face, which he knew was hideous in its guilt. He didn't want to scare her.

"I'm going to tell you, so you might as well just listen," Gracie advised. "Uncle Matthew said before I was born he did something to you that was really bad and hurt you so much you can't stand to be around him. He wishes you would forgive him, but he knows he doesn't deserve it. He said he should have – oh, what did he say? – I think it was he should have fought for you or something like that. Anyway, that's why he's so sad, because he failed you."

She can't have heard it right. Oh, Lord, how could she miss the point completely?

The Lord doesn't have anything to do with this. The girl is delusional. Your father hates you and doesn't want you, no matter how he tries to cover it up. Go home to Iowa, fool. Angie will be glad to see you. She will take your mind off of foolish things.

"So why are you so sad?" Gracie was asking. "Is it really that hard to forgive him? When Daddy yells at me and then says 'sorry,' I don't stay mad at him. I know he loves me, just like Jesus loves me. He just makes a mistake sometimes."

Will turned around, hoping he wouldn't frighten her. "You don't understand, Gracie. You have it backwards. Matthew – I mean, my dad – didn't do anything to me. I was the one. I should have helped him and instead I ran away like a coward. He can't ever forgive me for that – it almost killed him."

The child stood up and tilted her head back to look Will in the eye. "Oh, Will." Her eyes filled with tears, and he prepared to run, but she was faster, surging into him with a huge hug. "Oh, Will, I'm so sorry! You think it's all your fault, and he thinks it's all his! No wonder you stayed away so long." Her little hands were patting his back, as high up as she could reach, and she laid her head against his chest, crying.

He was tempted to hang on, to receive the blessing of unconditional love and acceptance, the amazing feeling of things long frozen melting and warming, but he feared he would contaminate the child and gently moved away from her, leaving the room without another word, only to realize as he stood at the top of the stairs that he had no place to go.

Chapter 8

A TANG OF WOOD SMOKE HUNG ON THE STILL, CLEAR NIGHT air, the reminder of fireplaces and woodstoves staving off the chill and welcoming Thanksgiving travelers home. Tucker bounded off the porch as their cars pulled into the driveway, greeting Matthew, then Allison, then Will as if he hadn't seen them for months.

"Help me carry in the leftovers," Allison told her men. "I swear Pearl must really believe down deep that I don't cook for you, Matthew. We never go over there without being loaded down with goodies."

"Here, Little Red Riding Hood," Matthew said in a growly voice, "let me carry your basket. I want to show you something inside the cottage."

"Hey!" Will said, pretending not to laugh, "TMI! I'm young and impressionable."

"Not likely," Allison said. "You never were. Now help!"

Once the food had been put away and the dog fed, Allison opted for a bubble bath.

"Do *not* say one word about that!" Will warned.

"I wasn't going to," Matthew replied, smiling. "I was just going to ask if you'd join me for a w-a-l-k. We can take T-u-c-k-e-r, too."

"For Pete's sake, do you have to spell for him? I know he's like a kid, but surely he doesn't understand everything you say."

"Well, maybe not," Matthew agreed easily, "but he really does know his name and the w-word. Watch. Hey, Tucker! Want to go for a walk?"

The dog was at the door before Will could recant.

Outside, the night was full of stars, slivers of moonlight gilding the trees and grass, making it easy to see where one was going. Will pulled on his lined leather gloves, glad he had remembered to bring them, and tightened the navy cashmere scarf around his neck. He gave a moment's thought to changing from his light Italian leather loafers but decided not to waste his time. Matthew looked cozy in his Carhartt jacket and leather farm gloves as they walked down the driveway side by side, silent but not necessarily easy with one another.

"Tucker likes to go down the road a piece," Matthew said, "and check out the Millers' place. They have a German shepherd who thinks Tucker's a long-lost brother."

"Glad they don't fight. I wouldn't want to be the one to break 'em up."

"For sure," Matthew agreed. He went on in silence for a while, then turned to look at Will in the starlight. "I had a talk with Gracie earlier today," he said.

"Yes, I heard about that. I had a talk with her, too. Or, rather, she had a talk with me. My job seemed to be to shut up and listen. Matthew – Dad – listen, I – "

"Will, we have to talk about this," Matthew said, talking over Will's stammering attempt to say more. "It's been ten years since you left home, and we've never sorted it all out. Carolyn wasn't that old, but she died anyway. Nobody knows the day and the hour, the Bible says. I don't want for one of us to be gone and the other one wishing he'd cleared the air."

"Dad, honest, it's – "

"No. Just let me say this straight out, Son, and then you can say what you want. I might chicken out again if you stop me now, and we'd never get where we need to be."

Will nodded, feeling the futility of arguing and the hopelessness of every terrible thought being out in the open, no way to pretend anything anymore. They were standing on the frost-crunchy grass along one of the Millers' fields, where corn stubble created a miniature magic kingdom under the starlight and a very real raccoon was ambling down the rows looking for leftovers. Will remembered standing on the verge of a field ten years ago, watching –

"Dad, can I go first? I don't think I can stand it much longer."

Matthew fixed his son with a fierce glare, making Will feel ten again, dumped on the Abbotts' doorstep and dragged off to the social services lady by his unwilling father. Then Matthew smiled and nodded, and the flashback stopped. Will took a deep breath.

"I always was afraid you didn't really want me," he began. "I mean, you gave me away when Mom left me with you, and when the probation officer brought me back to the farm after she died, well, it wasn't easy for either one of us. I know now that you tried to be a father, and you really didn't know how. You ended up doing a good job, Dad, in spite of everything. It's not your fault I never learned how to trust anybody. You tried. You tried hard, I know that."

Matthew laid his hand on Will's sleeve, saying, "Will, I'm so sorry I didn't – "

"No, don't stop me now! The thing is, when those guys at school were bullying me, telling lies about me, beating up on me, you were there for me. You stood up for me. Even that – that night at the Harris place when you saw those guys trying to hurt me and Tracy, you jumped right in, even though there were three of them. And – " Will's voice cracked and tears welled in his eyes as he turned away from Matthew, too ashamed to maintain eye contact. "I was so scared. I was afraid of them like I'd never been afraid of anything in my whole life. When they started kicking and punching you, I should have grabbed the tire iron from the truck and whaled on them. Instead I stood there like an idiot, frozen with fear, then I grabbed Tracy and ran like the coward I am and left you there to die. Oh, Dad, I'm – so – "

Matthew grabbed Will's arm and turned him around, gathering him into an embrace. "Don't you dare say you're sorry!" he said fiercely. "Don't you dare, Will! You did exactly the right thing, the thing I wanted you to do, and I have never, ever blamed you for doing it! Never, do you hear me?"

Will buried his face in his father's shoulder and wept. He could hardly concentrate on what his father was saying, but Matthew's tone was so intense he made an effort.

"It was all my fault," Matthew was saying. "I should have gone to the police in the beginning and hired an attorney to put those thugs in jail. I know you didn't want me to, but you were just a kid, and

I was supposed to be the grown-up. It's a father's job to protect his child, and I failed. Will, I'm so sorry, so sorry I didn't take care of you, so sorry I wasn't the kind of father you needed. I've regretted it every day of my life since then, and I always will. I'd ask you to forgive me, but I know you can't, because I can't forgive myself. But at least know I love you, son, and none of it was your fault."

Tucker came loping back from a visit with the shepherd and wound around their legs, whining at the tension and grief in the air.

Will couldn't bring himself to disengage. He was afraid to look at his father, shamed by the man's humility, stunned by his guilt and grief, afraid he might see that Matthew was crying, too.

All an act, the voice said. *A good act, but not real, just the same. You don't owe him anything.*

No, that's not right. I know he isn't lying. He really believes it's all his fault, and he really believes I can't forgive him. Oh, Daddy –

"Oh, Daddy, I'm sorry," Will said, his voice muffled by the canvas of Matthew's coat. "I should have helped you – and I should have talked to you a long time ago. Do you need me to say it? Then I will: I forgive you, Daddy. Can you forgive me?"

Matthew took Will by the shoulders and held him at arms' length, looking into his eyes in the starlight. "I do forgive you, Son. And I accept your forgiveness." He stood there without moving; Will saw that his eyes were silver in the starlight, and so was his hair.

"There's one more thing, though. Are you freezing, or do we have another minute?"

"No, sir, I'm not freezing. What is it?" *Oh. Of course. I know what it is.*

"I need to pray over you, Will. It's been a long time since I did that. I have a lot to give thanks for tonight, and I want to bless you."

I remember when you asked me to bless you, Dad, when you told me you were going to marry Allison. It's a big deal to you, isn't it. He nodded and bowed his head.

Chapter 9

WILL SPENT PART OF SATURDAY RECONNECTING WITH HIS old friends Kevin and Travis, catching up on some news, congratulating Kevin on his marriage to Susan, their two children, Kevin's job with a big accounting firm in Toledo. Travis was married, too, to a pleasant woman named Julie he had met at Ohio State, and they had three little girls and a boy on the way. Travis had been working for Lewiston Automotive Supply, helping on his father's farm, and now was working for John, living the life he had always planned.

"I tell you, man," Travis said over a beer in his farmhouse kitchen, "this is heaven on earth. Oh, I know, we don't make a lot of money, and the crops are never guaranteed, and there's always something broken down and needing fixed, but I love being here, close to my mom and dad, working on the farm, and living with Julie and the kids – you oughta get married, Will. It changes everything for the better."

Will nodded as if he knew what Travis was talking about and sipped on his ice water.

Kevin, across the table, cradled his beer in one hand and Travis's youngest girl in the other, letting her sleep against his chest. "Trav's right about marriage," he said. "I can't believe you haven't found some smart university babe to settle down with. I mean, you're not as good-looking as Trav and I, but you're not exactly an ogre, either. Nobody in sight?"

"Nah," Will said offhandedly, "nobody worth mentioning. Just hasn't happened."

"It's Tracy, isn't it?" Travis asked, looking sharply for any change in Will's expression.

"I haven't been in contact with Tracy since before I left town. Isn't she married by now?" *I kind of thought maybe she'd replace Susan for Kevin. Can't believe she hasn't found some great guy!*

"She dated some guys in college, I guess," Kevin said, "but she never got serious with anybody. She got her degree in nursing – man, I didn't see that one coming! Anyway, after she got the BS she worked at the hospital for a couple of years, then she joined this medical missionary group and went off to do nursing in Africa. She comes home for a couple of months and then goes back again."

"She's home now, until after Christmas," Travis said. "I just saw her in church last Sunday. You ought to call her."

Will silently cursed heredity as the Ryersen flush crept up his neck and over his ears and cheekbones. He also gave thanks to whatever that apparently his two high school friends had grown up a little, since they weren't teasing him about it. "Maybe I'll see her Sunday. I know Dad and Allison will want me to go to church with them."

"IT'S GOOD TO SEE YOU, WILL," PASTOR MILES SAID, SMILING WITH HIS eyes as well as his lips as he shook Will's hand.

"Thanks. It's nice to be here," *even if it feels weird and I wonder whether the roof will cave in on me.*

"You've been away too long," Penny said, trumping her husband's handshake with a full, enthusiastic hug. "Everyone misses you. Isn't that right, Matthew?"

Matthew and Allison, following close behind Will, both voiced their agreement. Released from Penny's arms, Will looked beyond her to the church's foyer, where many people were talking or pressing on to go out through the big double doors, anxious to get home for Sunday dinner.

"I don't want to hold up the line," he told Penny, passing through the sanctuary doors into the more indifferent crowd.

Many of the same people who had greeted him at the funeral once again said hello in passing, but no one stopped him as he moved toward the doors on the opposite side of the foyer. He was almost safe when he spotted her.

Her hair had darkened several shades, and now she wore it cropped close instead of curling on her shoulders, a boyish cut that framed her face and made those pale green eyes seem huge. She was laughing with another young woman, shaking her head as she turned enough to catch sight of Will, stopping her in her tracks, her eyes widening, her mouth opening in surprise.

He was stricken.

"Will!" she cried, pushing her way past a dozen people to get to him, her hands outstretched, her smile like a lighthouse beacon on a stormy shore.

He took her hands, helpless to refuse, remembering everything he had been trying to forget for the past ten years, good and bad. "Tracy."

"I heard you were in town, but I never dreamed I'd get to see you!" she said, smiling up at him, holding onto his hands as if she had never let them go. "It's so good – how are you? You look wonderful!"

"So do you. I'm fine. Just here for the holidays. You?"

"I'm here for the holidays, too, until after New Year's. Then I have to go back to work. How long are you staying?"

"I'm leaving tomorrow night. Have to be back at work Wednesday."

The smile faded a little, but she brought it back. "Well, I'm sure your family is glad to have you home, even for a little while. It's good to see you, Will. I guess I'd better go; Mom and Dad will be waiting in the parking lot."

No! Can't we – ? "Can we get together for coffee or something this evening? I – uh – I'd like to hear about your work. They told me you're a nurse, a missionary nurse, and that– sounds – uh – interesting." *Suave as ever,* he chided himself, but he didn't let go of her hands.

"Well, I suppose we could... Pick me up at seven, and we'll go – someplace."

"Seven it is! Tracy – thank you."

"I think I just saw fireworks in the foyer," Allison told Matthew as they went through the church doors into the parking lot. "I bet we'll find the seats of the car on fire when we get there."

"What are you talking about now, woman?" Matthew asked.

"Didn't you see it?"

"What!"

"Will running into Tracy. I thought the whole place would go up in flames!"

"Honey, don't get all excited about it. Ryersen men do tend to love one woman, whether it's a good idea or not, but she's almost like a nun now, and they don't have anything in common but a pretty painful past."

"Oh, don't be a party pooper," Allison insisted. "Maybe this is another piece of the healing for Will. Maybe they'll be like us, back together again, more in love than ever, getting married and being happy ever after in spite of the rocky start."

"Are you happy ever after?" he asked softly, drawing her close.

"Most days," she teased, reaching up to kiss him, to the scandalized delight of several other families who were walking by.

"He's in the car already," Matthew said when he had recovered, "so don't tease him, okay? I don't have any idea what might set him to losing his temper or running off again."

"I'd never do that!"

Matthew held the door for Allison to climb in and gave her a warning look as he did so. Will seemed oblivious to the exchange, and Matthew gave thanks for that as he ran around to the driver's side.

"Good service," Will said over the rushing air of the heater. "And you'll never guess who I met in the foyer."

"I saw," Allison said, earning a pinch on her hand from her husband but forging forward nonetheless. "Tracy! Were you glad to see her?"

Will laughed, and Matthew relaxed a little.

"Yes, it was nice. I'm going to take her out for coffee this evening and catch up on ten years' worth of adventures." He smiled at Allison. "Please don't make any more of that than what it is, okay? It's just two old friends having coffee."

"I wouldn't dream of suggesting anything else," Allison said, earning another pinch. "Ouch, Matthew, quit it! Your father," she said, turning around to face Will, "seems to think I'm going to say something about Tracy that upsets you. But I'm not. I just think it's nice for you to see her again after all this time."

"Thanks. I guess it is. Truth is, Allison, I don't know how it even happened. I wasn't going to ask her out, but then I just – did. I couldn't quite seem to let her go without spending some time with her. I mean, she'll be going back to Africa or wherever she works now, and I'll be back in Iowa – who knows when we might see each other again?"

"It's a good idea," Allison said. "You need to get some closure you couldn't get back when you were both so young. Then you can put her behind you and find a nice Iowa girl to give me grandchildren."

"Allison!" Matthew yelled, but both she and Will were laughing at him.

AS HE HELD THE DOOR OPEN FOR TRACY, WILL WAS AMUSED TO SEE that Logan's Diner hadn't changed anything, not even its prices, since 1999. The same miasma of burnt coffee and overused grease still hung in the humid air, and the same kinds of incredibly good pies revolved in the glass case by the counter. He ushered her to the back booth they had occupied a few times and observed the same rip in the near seat, held together with the same silver duct tape.

"This is giving me a severe case of déjà vu," he told Tracy.

"Things don't change all that much in Lewiston," she answered, smiling. "It's one of the reasons I love to come home."

"Evening, folks," a cheery waitress on the far side of middle age greeted them, laying down menus and water glasses. "I'm Helen, and I'll be your waitress tonight. Are you here for dinner, or just for dessert?"

Will looked at Tracy, who shook her head. "How about pie and coffee?" she suggested.

"Sounds good," Will said.

"Well, you're in luck," Helen said, "because we have pumpkin, pecan and lemon meringue, dutch apple, blueberry and Logan's Own Chocolate Cake."

"Oh, cake for me," Tracy said immediately. "I had some last week, Will, and it's wonderful!"

"Fine, make it two," he agreed, "but just water for me. Do women all have a thing for chocolate?" he asked Tracy as they waited. "Allison thinks chocolate is its own separate food group."

"I guess so. It's so good! And for me – it's one of the things I don't get very often when I'm working, so it's a special treat when I'm home."

"Tell me about your work," he said. "I – I have no idea what you did after – well, you know, after I left town."

"Oh." Tracy broke eye contact to fiddle with the paper on her straw and to poke the straw down among the ice bits in her water glass. "That's right. Well, I went to college, same as you did, and got a bachelor's degree in nursing from Findlay College. Then I worked at the hospital, where Allison works, you know, for a couple of years. I did med/surg floor and sometimes the ER It was good; I really love nursing."

She paused as Helen brought the cake and coffee.

"Cream or sugar?" Will asked, pushing the little boxes of packets and the tiny pitcher of real cream toward her.

"Oh! No, thank you. Black is the only way it comes most of the places I work now, so I've gotten used to it." She sipped carefully from the steaming cup and then took a forkful of cake. "Oh, this is decadently good!"

Will contemplated his own cake and took a small bite. "You were saying you worked in the ER," he reminded her.

"Yes. I had a good life going, Will, a great job with great people, a wonderful church family, my own apartment in Lewiston, and I was – " She hesitated, looking down again to avoid meeting Will's eyes, then drew a long breath before continuing. "I was dating a doctor who moved here from the Cleveland area, and it started getting serious. But when he asked me to marry him, I just couldn't do it. I loved him, but just not enough, you know? And then the opportunity came up to go on a medical missions trip to Malawi..."

"Malawi, Africa, right?"

"Yes. Oh, Will, I loved it! It's so beautiful there, and there's so much need! I went on another trip, and another, and pretty soon I just quit my job and went full-time. I go on three- or six-month tours and then come home for a month or more – that's what I'm doing now, taking my home leave before I go back out. We're going back to Malawi next, and then to Ethiopia, I think... It's amazing, Will, just amazing, how people live and how joyful they can be with nothing. You can see God at work in their lives and you can see His creation all around – it's different from Ohio – bigger, more elemental, more varied – oh, I don't know how to describe it!"

He watched her face, lit from within and glowing, and he could see how happy she was. She had moved on and left him behind in every way.

Fool. Did you expect to find her waiting and pining for you?

"It sounds wonderful," he made himself say with warmth. "I'm really happy for you." He could feel the single bite of cake eating away at his stomach.

"Thank you! God has been so good to give me the skills and training to serve Him in such a delightful way. Now what about you? Where have you been all these years? I've heard rumors from time to time, but I'd like to know."

Will pushed cake crumbs around his plate for a moment, wondering how to tell such a boring story after all she had said. "I got a pretty good scholarship to the University of Cincinnati, I think you knew, mostly because Pearl turned out to be a big-time distinguished alumna and a master manipulator, and I graduated with a BA in English. Who knew? Then I got a graduate fellowship to the University of Iowa and got my MFA in American lit and creative writing. Now I'm an associate professor there, teaching freshman comp. One of these days I hope to be teaching modern poetry, but somebody'll have to die or retire first."

"Oh, my, a professor! Well," she teased, "nobody ever expected you'd stay on the farm."

"No."

"And you aren't married?"

"Never even came close."

"So what do you do in your spare time?" Tracy asked, and Will couldn't tell whether she was truly interested or just making conversation.

"Uh – I play racquetball and sometimes I run – but not a lot. Play the guitar – learned that in college, kind of. I see my friends. We talk a lot and act smarter than we are. And sometimes I – no, never mind."

"You're blushing," Tracy said. "Sometimes you what?"

"Sometimes I – I write things. Stories. Poetry. Sometimes."

"Really! I've never known an author before! Have you had any of it published?"

"Some. Half a dozen poems. A couple of stories."

Tracy was beaming. "Your folks must be so proud of you!"

Will shook his head, laughing. "They don't know. I've told hardly anyone at work, even, except the department chair and the dean, which I have to do because being published in something is part of the deal to keep the job. But nobody around here would care; people around here aren't into that kind of thing."

"You've turned out to be a snob, haven't you?" Tracy said softly. "I happen to know plenty of people in this area can read and your father reads poetry. You told me that a long time ago. Shame on you, Will."

Shame on you, Will. Even the good little girl recognizes who you are. Satisfied now that this thing is over? Go back to Angie, back to Angie, back to Angie...

"I'm sorry, Tracy. You're right. I guess this wasn't a good idea; there's no going back, is there?" Will laid his fork down and reached for his wallet. "I'll take you home."

"Before you run away again," she countered, "let's finish the cake and the conversation. You don't get to do this to me all over again, Will." She defiantly shoved the last bite of her cake into her mouth and gave him the evil eye.

What am I supposed to say, Tracy? How am I supposed to act? I couldn't believe you even said you'd go for coffee! What do you want from me?

"Try the cake," Tracy said, "instead of making mush of it. You can obviously use the calories, unlike some of us."

"Are you kidding? Look at you – you're perfect." *Oh, that was suave, too, wasn't it?*

"Thank you, even if there is something wrong with your eyesight. Tell me more about your life in Iowa. Do you live on a corn-farm there, or have you found a big city?"

"I live in Iowa City, where the University of Iowa is located," Will said. "It's not the Big Apple or anything, but it's a real city, with ethnic restaurants and theatre and the symphony and opera and museums and – well, you know, city attractions. I live in a big loft apartment in the city, one of the newly gentrified areas, and I share my digs with the landlord's cat and about a dozen houseplants I have to keep going. That's not my thing, but it's worth it for the rent. I hang with people from the English and philosophy departments, mostly, too good for the engineers but not smart enough for the astrophysicists. We all joke about being 'metrosexuals,' like New Yorkers. My best friend Trey works for his dad's investment firm, but most of my friends are university faculty."

"You do breathe rarified air these days," Tracy said. "And are you happy, Will?"

"Of course I am! Who wouldn't be!"

"Oh, I don't know," she answered. "Me, I guess. I spent the last six months in the bush, sleeping in a thatch-roofed mud hut, sharing my room with two other nurses and every bug in Africa. I cleaned up vomit and diarrhea and pus and blood and rocked AIDS babies while they died. I took a bath in a bucket, with cold water and latherless soap, and only washed my hair once a week to save water. I swallowed malaria pills that turned my stomach and ate fried bugs with my fingers." She paused to look at Will, whose face had grown increasingly pale and horror-stricken. "And you know what?"

He shook his head. "What?"

"I loved it! I can't wait to go back. God is so real in Africa, not just some nice white Guy kind of removed from daily life, but right there helping me through the painful times and rejoicing with me in the good times." She reached across the table to take Will's hand. "Did you ever read the scripture where Paul says, 'I have learned in whatever state I am in to be content'?"

Will shook his head again, looking at their clasped hands. "No, I don't remember that."

"It's so true, Will! If you love Jesus and trust Him, then mud huts and bugs and lions roaring in the night don't matter. And if you don't love Him, then I suspect the best job and the best apartment in the world won't make any difference." She withdrew her hand and stood up. "I guess we should go. I can tell we don't have much in common any more, but it has been fun seeing you again. I'm so happy you're doing well."

If I'm doing so well, why do I feel like I've been run over by a bus? She just told me my life doesn't matter at all, to her or to anybody. The burning in his gut increased.

And this surprises you? Stop lying to yourself. You've known it all along. Maybe it's time to revisit your old way of dealing with pain. The world isn't going to miss you.

"Where'd you go?" Tracy asked, tugging on his arm to get his attention.

"Oh! Sorry. Just thinking." He put enough money on the table to cover the bill and a substantial tip for Helen and helped Tracy into her coat.

"Thinking gets you into trouble, doesn't it?" Tracy asked, walking beside him to the car. "I know that look, Will; it hasn't changed in ten years." She climbed into the passenger seat of Will's rented Toyota and buckled the seatbelt as Will got in on the other side.

They were silent for a while as they exited the downtown area, headed for Tracy's house. Then she turned to look at him in the starlight and said, "May I say one more thing?"

"Of course. I'm not trying to shut you up. What is it?"

"Do you remember when we first met, and you were such an angry, cocky boy? Do you remember how you decided to impress me by carrying around your father's Bible, and how you ended up reading it in spite of yourself?"

"I remember."

"Well, do you remember telling me one day that it was starting to make sense to you?"

"I suppose so."

"And do you remember when your dad brought you home from Chicago after you ran away, how you told me you heard God talking to you, keeping you safe, while you were gone?"

"That was a long time ago," Will said, feeling the embarrassed flush across his neck and ears. "I was pretty young then."

"Okay, but here's what I want to say, Will: I know Jesus loves you and wants to have a close personal relationship with you. He's been talking to you since before I met you, and you know it. I don't know why everything that happened turned you off to the Lord, but He hasn't gone anyplace. He'll take you back any time, the very minute you ask Him to. So please think hard about asking Jesus to be your Lord and Savior. That's where the happiness is."

Don't bother to set her straight. She's ignorant, and she won't listen to anything that proves her worldview wrong. Just take her home and forget about her. Think about Angie, and what you'll do with her when you get back to civilization. Angie...

As Will pulled up in front of the Showalter house, Tracy turned to him, smiling, asking, "Are you coming home again for Christmas?

Because, if you are, maybe we could – you know – have coffee again or something. It really is good to see you again."

I can't believe this! Another chance? "I'd like that a lot, but I don't know whether I'll be back. I hadn't planned – "

Tracy's smile disappeared. "Oh. Of course. I'm sorry; I just thought maybe – "

"No! Listen! I'd really like to see you. Really. I'll try to arrange it, and if I can't, please know it wasn't because I didn't want to. Please, Tracy!"

"All right, then. Take care, Will. Have a safe flight back." She slipped out of the car and ran up the porch steps and into the house without looking back.

Will slowly turned the car around and drove back down the driveway, his heart thudding in his chest. Could she really have meant it? Could she really have been upset when she thought he didn't want to see her?

"HAVE A GOOD TIME?" ALLISON ASKED AS WILL CAME THROUGH THE door, looking up from the nursing journal she was reading with the help of a pair of bright-blue-framed cats-eye half-glasses.

"Yes, I did. It was – good to see Tracy again."

"Doesn't she look cute in that new haircut?" Allison asked, closing the journal and tossing it casually onto the coffee table. She patted the couch beside her in invitation. "Come tell me all about it."

Will turned to the coat closet to hang up his coat and scarf and felt the cursed flush coming over him again. He liked Allison, really he did, in spite of their rough beginning, and he thought she was great for Matthew, but he didn't want to have a heart-to-heart talk with her. Especially not about Tracy!

The phone rang, and Allison got up to answer it.

Saved by the bell! He quickly went to his room to avoid having to talk any more, preferring to consider the evening by himself before going into the details she would try to pry out of him. *Allison's a natural gossip. And she's stubborn! No, I don't want to talk about what's up with Tracy and me when I don't even know that myself.*

I could come back for Christmas, just to see...

You could. Or you could be smart for a change and stay away from those people. You don't have any need for a bunch of ignorant farmers

and farmers' daughters. That girl will try to talk you into joining her church – what a joke. Their impotent god never did you any good before; why would he now? Go home where you belong, to the things that let you forget who you really are.

Will chewed a couple of antacid tablets, kicked off his shoes and lay down on the bed, grabbing the second pillow and holding it over his ears and face until he had to breathe. *Shut up. Just shut up!*

A quiet knock at his door signaled the end of the internal harangue for a while and the start of the inquisition, but instead of Allison, he found Matthew on the other side of the door.

"May I come in?" Matthew asked.

"Sure."

Once inside, Matthew made his way to the black occasional chair in the corner, sitting carefully, as if either his bones hurt or his faith in the chair was minimal. "Not my favorite piece of furniture," he laughed, "but Allie thinks it looks good."

"And whatever she likes, you like, right?" Will said, smiling back.

A flush attacked Matthew, who laughed it off, agreeing, "Yeah, pretty much. I can put up with just about anything that makes her happy, and vice-versa. That's the kind of love I'm still praying for you to find, what I thought you were developing with Tracy way back when." After a moment's hesitation, Matthew continued, "I'm not going to give you the third degree about your evening, and I asked Allie to back off, too. Not fair to pry. I do want you to know we'd be real happy if something redeveloped. That's all." He stood and turned toward the door. "Oh, and we'd love to have you come back for Christmas."

"Dad, I – uh – thanks. That all means a lot to me. I can't imagine anything happening with Tracy now, though. She's got a life mostly in Africa, and we're so different..." Will sighed unconsciously. "I don't know about Christmas; can I let you know?"

Matthew smiled again. "Right up to the last minute. In fact, if you should just decide and turn up on the doorstep without calling, I reckon we'd let you in even so."

Chapter 10

THE WHOLE ROOM SMELLED WORSE THAN ROAD KILL, AND
most of it seemed to be coming from him, Will thought,
as he lay helpless as a turtle on his back, chest heaving, legs quivering, wiping stinging sweat from his eyes with
a soaked wristband. A few feet from him, the inert heap of wet
clothes that had once been Trey Sullivan tried to pick up his
racquet and couldn't manage to lift it.

"I'm dead," Trey moaned, "but it was worth it."

"I'm dead," Will panted, "and it wasn't worth it."

"I'd laugh," Trey laughed, "but I'm too weak."

"I'd love to get out of here," Will gasped, "because it stinks, but I
don't think I can crawl to the door, much less open it."

"They're gonna find us in here tomorrow morning, rotting on the
floor, and my dad is gonna kill me all over again for not dying in the
office."

The thought of fathers took all the fun out of their mutual demise,
and Will wrestled himself to a sitting position. "Let's get showered
and go to McClendon's for a cold beer and some hot wings. I can't be
out too late tonight – early class tomorrow."

"I think I can, I think I can, I think I can," Trey chugged, raising
himself to his feet by inches. "I don't know which one of us stinks
more. Probably you. We either gotta play more often or play less hard.
Man, I'm gonna feel it tomorrow!"

Half an hour later, gingerly perched on a barstool in McClendon's downing his second microbrew, Will privately surmised he would be feeling it tomorrow, too. It almost hurt to lift the chilled glass to his mouth, and he barely had energy to chew the hot wings, much less enjoy them, which was good, because one bite reminded him he was on a bland diet. He was getting ready to suggest they pack it in when Nate and another young man came up to them.

"Hey, Nate!" Trey said. "'S up?"

"I want to introduce you to my new friend Steve," Nate said. "Steve, this is Trey Sullivan, the richest son of a gun in our circle – maybe in the world – and the ever-in-denial Will Ryersen from the university."

"Hello," Steve said in a soft, dreamy voice, his long eyelashes fluttering at them in a girlish way Will found unsettling. "I'm pleased to meet you." He held out his hand to Will.

"No, no, no," Nate chanted, slapping Steve's hand away. "Will doesn't like to shake hands with our kind. Might catch something, if he doesn't already have it."

Thank God I haven't been drinking all evening and I'm too beat up from racquetball to throw a punch, or I'd flatten Nate so bad they'd have to scrape him off the floor with a putty knife!

"Well, we're on our way to a party with some friends," Nate said, "so we'll see you later." He put his hand on the small of Steve's back to steer him toward the door, smiling over his shoulder at Trey and Will.

Out of the ensuing silence, Trey finally said quietly, "You might want to put that down before you break it, okay?" He removed the beer glass from Will's frozen grasp and set it gently on the bar. "Listen, Will, Nate loves to provoke you, because you fall for it every time. He knows you're not gay, same as we all do. If you'd just throw him a kiss or something, he'd give it up. Bullies can't handle it when somebody turns the tables."

Aw, Trey, what do you know about bullies? Or why Nate gets to me so badly? "You're right. He just stirs up some past stuff I'd rather not deal with."

"Oh. Well... if you ever wanted to talk about it..."

Trey was unusually serious, for Trey, and Will acknowledged his friend's effort with a smile. "Thanks. Maybe some time."

"So you want to order a burger and tell me all about your

Thanksgiving?"

Over burgers and steak-fries, which he also couldn't eat, Will tried to explain his trip to Ohio, thinking as he talked how stupid he sounded trying to describe the reconciliation with his father without giving any of the background. He even told about his time with Tracy, figuring it must be the third beer talking but really wanting to say it all out loud.

"Wow! That's the most I've ever heard you talk at one time in the whole – what? – seven years I've known you! So – you going home for Christmas to see her again?"

"I don't know," Will said, "I could, I guess. I mean, I'll have time off from then 'til mid-January. But what's the use? There can't be anything between us anymore."

"You gotta be kidding! There's already something between you! She was practically begging you to give it a chance."

"Nah. She was just wanting to take another crack at converting me, really."

Trey guffawed, causing the people around them to turn to see what the joke was. Red-faced and merry, he told Will, "I'll give you she's a Bible-thumper. I mean, a missionary! That's practically a nun! But I'm telling you, Ryersen, Sister Tracy wants to take off her habit for you."

"I love you like a brother," Will said, "but you don't get to talk about Tracy like that. She's a good woman, not some floozy."

"Floozy!" Trey was choking with beer and laughter now. "Floozy! Nobody in the whole world outside northwest Ohio calls a girl a floozy anymore! Come on, Will, admit it: you got the hots for this chick and all you need is a good shove to go get her."

Will counted the beers Trey had guzzled, coming up with six to his three, which allowed him to refrain from verbal or physical abuse of his friend. "It's time for us to go home, buddy. I'll drop you off, okay?"

"You saying I can't drive?"

"Nope. Just saying you shouldn't, just in case. Come on."

"Let me settle up the bar tab, and we'll be on our way."

In the car, Trey dozed a little while Will enjoyed maneuvering the Mustang through traffic, but he perked up again as they pulled into his parking space. "Hey, how you gonna get home?" he asked.

"I'll catch the bus. There must be a stop around here somewhere."

"Nah. Come on in and I'll call a cab. Or you can sleep in one of the guest-rooms."

"I have to work tomorrow, remember?"

"I know! Take my car. I have another one someplace. Go on! You know you love to drive it."

"That I do," Will agreed. "Okay, I'll drive the Mustang home and I'll leave it at my place with the keys under the mat tomorrow."

Trey nodded in satisfaction and stepped out onto the sidewalk. "Hey, one more thing, buddy."

"Yes?"

"I really don't think you should go back to Ohio for Christmas. Angie's a party-girl to fool around with, but Tracy sounds like she's looking for all the stereotypical stuff – wedding ring, babies, church, minivan..." He turned and made his way inside, listing slightly but managing not to bump into the door frame.

Listen to Trey; he's your friend and he has your best interests at heart.

I wonder...

"WELL, OF COURSE HE SHOULD COME HOME," PEARL SAID AS SHE LA-dled homemade chicken noodle soup into big bowls for Allison to carry to the dinner table. "Don't let that slosh over and burn you."

"Nope, I got it!" Allison took a bowl in either hand and backed her way through the swinging door, repeating the process twice more to set all six bowls at their places. "I know it would mean so much to Matthew, so that's where I'm coming from," she said, slicing a loaf of homemade whole wheat bread into thick slices with a wicked-looking serrated knife so old its blade had turned almost black.

"We all want him here," Pearl agreed, "and not just for a visit. But I have prayed about it, and I think he needs to be here for his own sake. I don't know who his friends and associates are at the university, but they aren't leading him in the paths of righteousness, that's for sure. If Will is ever to find the Lord, he won't do it there."

"Do what?" Matthew asked, coming through the back door with Ed and John just in time to hear the last few words of Pearl's comment.

"Smells mighty good in here," Ed said, sniffing mightily. "Five'll get you ten she's talking about Will."

"Taking odds?" John asked. "I can't endorse that, especially against Pearl! Where's Gracie?"

"She's playing in her room," Allison said. "If all you men are washed up, I'll go call her."

The three held out their hands like kindergarteners, grinning at Allison as they did, and she nodded her approval. Within minutes, everyone was seated around the dining room table preparing to say grace before supper.

"Can I do it?" Gracie asked.

"'May I,'" John said automatically. "Yes, you may."

Gracie waited until she was satisfied that everyone else was in an appropriate state of reverence, heads bowed, hands folded, no peeking, before launching into her prayer: "Dear Jesus, thank You for all this good food. Thank You for the people who made it. Thank You that we are well enough to eat it. Help us to remember the people who don't have good food or nice places to live or good clothes to wear, and help us to share what we have with them."

Gracie paused for a moment, and several people prepared to say "amen," but she started in again with an ostentatious clearing of her throat. "Dear Jesus, we thank You for dying on the cross for us so that all our sins can be forgiven and we can live with You now and after we die. We ask You please to talk to Will so he understands he needs You, too, so we can always have Will as part of our family, now and in heaven. We love Will, Jesus, and we know You love him, too. Please save him! Amen."

Nobody moved. Allison was mopping tears from her cheeks with her napkin, and Matthew was clenching his hands together so tightly the tendons and the bones showed white under the skin.

"Did I do it wrong?" Gracie asked in a tiny voice.

"No, sweetheart," John said, clearing his throat, "you did it just right."

THE WEEKS BETWEEN THANKSGIVING AND CHRISTMAS FLEW BY FOR Will as he administered final exams and began to grade them for five sections. He slept less than usual and dreamed of Lewiston and the farm, and no decision came to him.

"Look, man," Trey said on their way to racquetball, "you need to chill out and let this stuff go. Why don't you call Angie and go out with her Friday night? That'll smooth off the rough edges."

"I went out with Angie last Friday. And we had dinner at McClendon's yesterday."

"Did you go back to her place with her?"

Will felt the sting of heat rising to his ears as he nodded without looking at Trey, remembering all that had transpired in Angie's apartment. "Yes."

"Prime stuff, Miss Angie," Trey approved. "More of that, less of Ohio, that's what you need. That girl back home got you all wound up again about the church stuff. You don't need it, Will. Live in the now and have a good time. Life's sweet!"

"Sweet," Will repeated. *Sweet. Do what feels good and don't worry about the poor souls who get so hung up on morality. That's what I've been doing the last ten years, and I'm pretty good at it. So why doesn't it ever feel like second nature to me?*

"I'm gonna beat your socks off if you don't stop zoning out," Trey threatened. "Here we are, so get ready to go down again!"

SICK OF HIS OWN COMPANY AFTER SEVERAL POST-GAME HOURS OF GRADing papers, Will called Angie after all. *Why not? Trey's right; she's prime stuff.* She was also willing stuff and invited him to come for dinner Friday night.

Enjoy her as much as you want; just don't let her try to hogtie you. You're not going to put a ring on her finger, are you?

Will nearly jumped as that thought came to him. A ring? No way!

Right. She's not the kind of girl you marry. And you're not going to marry anyone anyway, are you, sissy-boy? If you get tired of Angie, just call Nate.

Do not be conformed to the things of this world, said the other voice, the one he seldom heard any more. *Behold, I make all things new!*

"I HOPE YOU LIKE CHINESE," ANGIE SAID. "I DON'T COOK, BUT I'M REally good at ordering in."

"Chinese is great. The Golden Dragon? One of my favorites." He took the seat Angie indicated on the poofy leather couch, sinking in uncomfortably, as if he were being swallowed, and leaned forward to pick up a plate and chopsticks from the coffee table.

As they ate, Angie remarked, "You're really good with chopsticks!"

"Funny the skills you pick up along the way," Will said, shoveling noodles into his mouth without spilling any. "I never even saw chopsticks before I moved here. Never ate Chinese. I don't think my dad likes it; he's kind of picky."

"Do you miss your family?" she asked, dunking an egg roll in plum sauce over and over, taking nibbles.

"No, not much," Will said, but then he thought about it. "No – I do. I didn't deal with it for a long time, just shoved in back into my subconscious, but I think I miss them all the time. When I was home for Thanksgiving, I realized how much those people love me."

"That's not limited to people in Ohio," Angie answered, putting down her plate and scooting closer to Will on the couch.

Oh, no, not the declaration of love, please!

"I care for you a lot, Will. You know I do. You know I'll do anything you want. You don't have to go to Ohio to find someone to – well, to whatever." She draped her arm around his neck, and the powerful musky smell of her perfume rose in his nostrils, overcoming the scents of Chinese food. "Finish your dinner, and I'll show you how much I care, how much I like to please you." She began to caress his neck and ear, which turned scarlet in response.

Exactly what you need tonight, isn't it. Pleasure with no strings. You can use her without making any kind of commitment, and there's no need to feel guilty. She knows the score.

Will felt noodles rising in the back of his throat and stood up quickly, dropping his plate onto the coffee table in case he needed to rush to the bathroom.

"What's the matter?"

He swallowed hard. "Uh – must have been bad shrimp, Angie. I'm feeling kind of sick. I'd better go home."

"Oh, no! I'm so sorry! Let me get you something – Alka-Seltzer or something."

"No, thanks. I'll call you tomorrow."

Will grabbed his coat from the closet by the front door and was away before Angie could make another move. In the car he opened the windows and drew in deep gulps of frigid air until his stomach settled, then drove home with the cold air still pouring over him.

Wimp! Chickening out on a sure thing, where's the smarts in that?

Despite the deprecating remarks, Will couldn't help feeling he had escaped from something. In the loft, alone at last, he fed Nero and flopped down on the couch. After his feast and post-feast ablutions, Nero wandered over and jumped up beside his personal chef, perhaps to critique the meal.

"You have anything to say, do it now," Will told the cat, petting his wide back with the heavy hand which usually elicited a loud purr. This time was no exception. Nero curled up against Will like an old friend and rumbled louder than Will's Toyota.

This is better, just being here with Nero and not trying to be anything but me. It just didn't feel good to be there anymore. Angie acts like a hooker sometimes, but she wants more than that, I know it. And I just don't want to give her any real part of me. If only I had been different, so Tracy and I –

The phone rang.

"Yeah?"

"Hello to you, too," came the sweet voice of his dreams. "I know it's not good manners for the girl to call the guy, but I just wanted to encourage you to come home next week, even for a few days."

"Tracy, I – "

"I've been thinking about you a lot, Will. There are so many things we didn't get to talk about. Is there any chance...?"

"I was just thinking about you when the phone rang. I was wishing we – All right. I'll do it. I'll book a flight somehow and get home as soon as I can."

HE PUT THE TICKET ON HIS VISA CARD. RENTAL CAR, TOO. AN ARMLOAD of Christmas presents. Nero's kennel reservation. *John always taught me you pay off the credit card bill every month to avoid paying interest,* he remembered, *but desperate times... I'll bet I could find a cheaper gym than Trey's and spend a lot less at McClendon's, buy fewer books – drive a cheaper car, for sure – live in a cheap apartment – I make enough money I shouldn't have to be worrying about how to pay off my credit card!*

Then he wondered why he was suddenly wondering about the money and the lifestyle it supported.

Sitting on the plane, ignoring the engines by immersing himself in a current best-seller, suddenly he found himself thinking about it again.

When Tracy leaves Lewiston, she'll be going back to what feels like home to her. A mud hut or a tent, no air-conditioning, no refrigerator full of imported beer, no flat-screen TV. No phone. No bathroom with unlimited hot water. No daily mail service. No computer, no stereo system, no movies, no bookstores, no opera, no ballet, no jazz festival, no haute couture clothing shops, no restaurants with long wine-lists. And she's happy. She doesn't care. She doesn't worry. I wish I could even understand that kind of happiness...

Simple enough. It's delusional. Or it's an act. Or both. Those people think if they act blissful, they are. They think if they waste their time and money on the suffering masses, somehow when they die they'll be rewarded. You know better than that. When you die – nothing. No bliss, no suffering – nothing. You understood that ten years ago, didn't you?

Will determinedly turned the page and focused on his book again. The therapist had told him to redirect himself whenever the old ideas came back. *I'm not eighteen. I'm not in high school. Nobody is out to get me – or my dad. I have a real life, a good life, now, and I'm happy. I'm happy. I'm ... happy...*

BECAUSE OF THE SNOW AND SLEET MIX GLAZING THE ROADS AND COAGU-lating on the windshield of his rental car, the drive to Lewiston took twice as long as it would have in good weather, but Will didn't care. He was glad to be on the ground after a rough landing, glad to be headed for his father's home, glad to be that much closer to seeing Tracy, glad – oh, yeah! – that he had found his luggage without any hassles.

When he pulled into the Ryersen driveway and saw the lights on all over the house, he felt a lift in his heart, almost as if he were coming home. And there was the welcoming committee: Allison in the doorway, Matthew coming down the porch steps and Tucker, shaking snow from his black coat, running to leap up and put his paws on Will's shoulders just as he did Matthew's.

"Get down, you overgrown puppy!" he teased, rubbing the dog's ears and back and finally escaping the welcoming kisses from that huge, wet tongue. "Hey, Dad!"

"Welcome home," Matthew said, embracing his son. "Glad you

could make it. Glad you made it safely! We were a little worried, watching the weather report."

"Kind of a rough landing, but no trouble," Will said, grabbing his suitcase and guitar case and following Matthew into the house. "Allison! Hi!"

"Give me a hug, too," she said, standing on tiptoe to reach him. "I deserve at least as good a welcome as the dog!"

"Fine," Will said, dropping his suitcase to embrace his stepmother, "as long as you don't lick my face."

"No danger of that, I think!" she replied, hugging him with amazing strength for such a little person. "Oh, it's so good to see you!"

Will returned the hug, laughing with embarrassment. "I've only been gone a month."

"I know," Allison said, stepping back to look him over, "but it felt like forever. It feels right when you're here with us and wrong and empty when you're gone."

This is a trap, the voice warned him. *It's the beginning of the campaign to guilt you into leaving your good life to come back to this prison. Don't be fooled.*

"Well," Will said, stepping back himself, "it's nice to be here for now."

When Will woke up the next morning, Matthew had already gone to work at the farm and Allison at the hospital. Coffee was waiting to be brewed, and various breakfast options were outlined in a note from Allison. After a long, hot shower and skipping the coffee for a glass of milk, Will felt ready to consider his day – maybe all his days until his flight home. His primary objective was Tracy, of course, and he wanted to see the rest of his family.

Taking advantage of the empty house, he dialed Tracy's number from deep memory, wondering whether he should be surprised he remembered it.

"I'm so glad you called," she said. "I was worried you might not be able to make it in. Have you been out yet? The roads are terrible!"

"I confess," Will laughed. "I just got up half an hour ago; and, no, I haven't looked outside. I'm afraid the dog will get me." He settled in at the kitchen table.

"It's still snowing, and there's probably half an inch of ice underneath. You shouldn't go anywhere, probably. Did your stepmom go to work?"

"My what?"

"Your stepmom. I'm sorry; don't you think of her that way? If my snowboot's in my mouth, I apologize."

"No, that's okay. I guess I don't *think* of Allison as anything but Allison. I mean, she didn't marry my dad until right before I left, and I never saw them again until the funeral. But she is my stepmother, you're right, and I don't think it bothers me anymore. I was getting used to it before I left home.

"Anyhow, yes, she did go to work, and darned early, too. I think what I'll do is go out to the – I don't know what Dad calls it; it's bigger than a shed and smaller than a barn – the building – and see if there's a tractor with a blade in there. I can plow the driveway for them before they get home."

"That's good of you. It's supposed to stop any minute, so by the time you get going you should only have to do it once."

"Unless it drifts. I seem to remember northwest Ohio country roads drift like crazy. Tracy, I – uh- didn't call to talk about the weather, really. I called to see whether you still want to get together while I'm home. I'm going to be here until New Year's Day, and I'd like to take you out to dinner or a movie or something."

A long pause on the other end set Will to wrapping and unwrapping the cord from his index finger, jigging his leg at the same time.

"If you don't want to, it's okay," he finally said.

"No, that's not it! I just don't know what we're doing. I mean, movies and things are – well – dates. Coffee at Logan's is just catching up on old times. There's a difference, and I want to be sure I understand."

"Oh." He dropped the cord and stood up, pacing in front of the table as he said, "I guess it depends on what you want, Tracy, because I don't really know, either. When I was home in Iowa, I missed you. I thought about you. I really wanted to come back to see you again. But I didn't let myself go as far as putting a label on that."

"Oh." Her voice sounded small and thin to him. "Do you want to put a label on it?"

Yes, I do! I want to call it picking up from where we were before those three football heroes ruined everyone's life. I want to call it dating and falling in love –

No, you don't. Stop being sentimental. Why would she want you, spoiled goods that you are?

"Will?" Her voice wisped over the line, almost not there at all.

"I'm sorry. I really want to spend time with you, Tracy, and I'd like to have more time than a cup of coffee. How can we really figure anything out if we aren't together for more than an hour, and in a public place, at that?"

"All right. Here's an idea: Susan and Kevin are having their annual Christmas Eve open house after church tomorrow night. I could meet you at church, and we could go from there together. It's not a fancy party, just a drop-in thing they do every year. Travis and his wife will be there, too, and everyone brings their kids and their grandmas and – it's just fun. Would you like to try that?"

Church and all the local hicks? Borrow some of Ed's overalls to fit in?

Shut up. "That sounds like a good idea. I'll see you after church."

WILL DID FIND A TRACTOR WITH ITS SNOW-BLADE AT THE READY AND blessed Ed for all those years of instruction about farm machinery. It had been ten years, but he readily remembered how to do it; in less than an hour the drive was plowed and he had shoveled and salted the walks and the porch steps, noting with amusement that Tucker was disinclined to help with any of this and stayed wrapped up in a ball against the house wall on the covered porch.

When his fingers had thawed enough, he spent an hour playing his guitar, pretending he was Django Reinhart for a while, drowning out any nasty voices that might be trying to make him question his decision to see Tracy.

Allison came home, careening down the driveway faster than Will thought she should, around four that afternoon and blessed him with hugs and chocolate chip cookies for his endeavors. Matthew arrived late, but he had called, and the truck was made for hard driving.

"Are you folks going to church tomorrow night?" Will asked as they consumed every bite of the ham and scalloped potato casserole Allison had thrown together.

Matthew and Allison looked at each other.

"Aw, cut it out!" Will implored. "It's not a strange question, is it?"

"No, of course not," Matthew said quickly. "Honestly, though, it is kind of strange for you to be asking about church. Not that it's bad..."

"So...?"

"Yes, we will be going," Allison said. "Do you want to go with us?"

"No. I mean, yes, I want to sit with you, but I need to take my own car, because Tracy and I are going to some shindig at Kevin's after church."

"Oh, the open house!" Allison exclaimed. "That's wonderful! You'll see all kinds of old friends there if you stay long enough. We usually drop in for just a minute on the way home. John and Carolyn used to stop in, too, but I doubt he will this year."

"If you want to ride with us," Matthew said carefully, "then you can take the truck after church and John can drop us off. With the roads so slick, the truck's better than your fancy import."

"Matthew!"

"Honey, I'm just – "

"It's okay, Allison, I know what he means. Thanks, Dad, I think it's a good idea."

"It was good to see you again, Will," Pastor Corrigan said, embracing him. "Merry Christmas! Come around any time."

"Thank you, Pastor Miles. I enjoyed your sermon." *And what a liar I am! All I could think about was Tracy.*

"Here are the keys to the truck," Matthew said, handing them over with a smile. "Have a good time. We'll leave the front door unlocked."

"Aren't you coming back to our house for hot chocolate and cookies?" Gracie asked, rushing up to Will, followed more slowly by her father. "You have to do that!"

"Gracie," John warned, "Will doesn't have to do anything. He has other plans."

"But – but that's not fair! It's a family night, and Will's family, and Mommy won't be there – "

Will's heart nearly broke at the pain in John's eyes as he tried to prevent the meltdown everyone saw coming.

Too late. Gracie began to wail at the top of her lungs, swatting at Allison when she tried to hug her and clinging to Will's arm as if she were grafted in. John, usually so calm and decisive in crisis, stood there frozen as people from around the lobby began to drift toward the drama to see what was going on.

"Hey, Gracie," Will said, squatting down to her level, "let's go over there by the big Christmas tree and talk it over, okay? It makes me really self-conscious, all these people staring at us."

"I don't care!" she screamed, "I want my mommy!"

Will picked her up and shoved her messy little face into his chest, rocking back and forth as if he held a much smaller child. "You have to stop this, Grace. You're hurting your daddy. I know you want your mommy, but so does he, and he can't bring her back. Shhh, shhhh. Just calm down now, okay? He loves you so much, and you're scaring him, too."

Whether she was exhausted or felt she had won the round, Gracie quieted in Will's arms and hung there like dead-weight.

"So will you come back to the house with us?" she whimpered.

"No," Will said, hoping he wouldn't provoke another outburst. "I have a date with Tracy – the missionary lady, remember? But I'll be at your house tomorrow to open our presents – and I have at least one for you."

Gracie wiped her nose on Will's shirt and looked up at him through swollen eyelids. "You aren't supposed to bribe little kids," she said in her best Pearl imitation.

"You are *not* a little kid," Will told her. "You are an alien in a kid's body, and I am sending you back to the mothership. Will you walk or be dragged?"

"THAT WAS PRETTY AMAZING!" TRACY SAID, CLIMBING INTO MATTHEW'S truck. "I can't believe you don't have children of your own. She quieted right down for you."

Will laughed easily. "That's because I'm her special project," he said, "and she doesn't want to tick me off. Hang on – heat's coming!"

"No problem. We know how to dress for the weather here," she teased, "unlike the big city boys. Your feet are probably soaked in those loafers."

"True."

"So what is Gracie's project?"

"Oh. Nothing."

"Will, come on! It's not fair to bring things up and tease me like that."

"I suppose. She's praying every night for my salvation, bound and determined I'm going to 'come to Jesus' and avoid hellfire. Hey, will you tell me where I'm going?"

Directing him to Kevin's home was simple enough, because Kevin and Susan had bought a house on the main road west of Lewiston, not too many miles from the Abbotts. It was bigger than Matthew and Allison's house, with a large yard and a big attached garage, everything hung with Christmas lights or boasting groupings of reindeer or nativity figures.

"Wow. He's bought the whole suburban package," Will said, parking in the wide driveway.

"If you park on the circle in front, it will be easier to get out when you're ready to leave," Tracy said, ignoring the disparaging remark.

"Yes, ma'am."

Inside, the house was just as over-decorated as outside, featuring a gaudy tree of one size or another in every room Will saw. It was also filled with the wonderful smells of Christmas food and the soft background music of Christmas carols and the pleasant din of too many people enjoying one another's company. Will tried to figure out what seemed strange to him and finally realized the voices were all soft and gentle, none of the overloud, abrasive tones of McClendon's. No booze here. Somehow, even though there were far more bodies in one space and far more noise than he liked, it was peaceful.

"Last year I was in Malawi for Christmas," Tracy said, "and I really missed this."

"This? All these people?"

She smiled up at him, nodding. "Most of these people are old friends, and all of them are – well – they're part of home to me. I love what I do, I've told you that, but sometimes I miss all this – the people, the holidays, the rituals, the church – I have a feeling I won't be able to keep going away forever. I'd like to – never mind. Let's find Travis and Julie." She turned away and began to glide through the crowd toward another room. Since she was holding his hand, Will found himself being towed along in her wake.

After an hour of answering the same questions over and over, smiling until his cheeks hurt, Will was past ready to leave. He hated the speculative looks everyone gave as they realized he was alive, here, and with Tracy. But she seemed to be having such a good time he couldn't quite bring himself to spoil it.

"Oh, listen!" she said, and he heard singing from another room. "They're singing Christmas carols! Let's join in!"

Not bothering to see how this suggestion had gone over, Tracy took Will in tow again, leading him into the family room, a large room which easily accommodated an old upright piano and the twenty or so people who were clustered around it. Will had a moment of culture shock as he saw a young woman at the keyboard, reminding him of Pearl playing the spinet in the Abbott living room.

Nestled close to him by the press of people, Tracy began to sing in a lovely, clear soprano, "Joy to the world! The Lord is come!"

Have You? Will wondered. He noted how much more tuneful the carol singing was than drunken karaoke at McClendon's, and how joyful most of the singers looked as they made intricate harmonies without benefit of sheet music. He wondered what it must feel like to be joyful, but he couldn't remember ever having felt that way.

"You're not singing," Tracy said under the music.

"I don't know all the words," he admitted. "This kind of thing wasn't part of growing up for me. Mama and I never went to church that I remember. When I started going to church with the Abbotts, I guess I never tried to learn the songs."

"We can leave if you want to," Tracy said, and he nodded. "Or," she said, "we could go upstairs to the little parlor and talk. Nobody will be there, I'm sure."

"Then let's do that."

At the top of the big old staircase, the hall widened out into a sort of landing, and Susan had created a little sitting area around a bay window that overlooked the side yard, which was currently host to Frosty the Snowman and several plastic penguins with light-up red bow ties. Tracy curled up on the window-seat, and Will sat in the small armchair nearest to her. The sounds of the party floated up the stairs, but they were only background noise.

"This is nice, isn't it?" Tracy asked. "Susan calls it 'the little parlor' for some reason, and we sit up here sometimes with tea and read our Bibles and pray."

"You see a lot of Susan and the others?"

"I do when I'm home. I know it's kind of hokey to keep your high school friends, but they're such good ones. Not everyone from

Lewiston has turned out well, but these guys – you can't ask for better friends. I wish you would reconnect with Kevin and Travis more; I think you'd like them all grown up." She paused and wrinkled her nose, smiling at Will, "Well, okay, Travis will probably never grow up, but he's as good a man as God ever made, and he'd do anything for a friend." She paused again before saying, "Do you have friends like that in Iowa, Will?"

"Of course." Will thought about the men he hung out with. Was any of them the kind of man Kevin was? Even Trey, who really seemed to have his back – could he depend on Trey to be there for him no matter what? Would Trey back him if he decided to do something Trey didn't approve of or believe in? And besides Trey, who?

"I'm glad," Tracy said. "Friends who love us no matter what and help to hold us accountable for our behavior are more important than almost anything except God and family."

"Right. You're right."

They talked for a long time, interrupted occasionally by someone who came upstairs for the bathroom, filling in the gaps of ten years apart. Will found himself describing the plot of a story he was percolating in his mind, something he hadn't talked about with anyone before, and he was gratified by Tracy's interest and intelligent suggestions. A piece he had been wrestling with suddenly fell into place when she made an offhand comment about it, and he could have shouted out loud with delight and relief.

I wonder what it would be like to be able to talk my stories over with her all the time, to have her read and critique them so I could get a fresh view, to watch her face light up when she likes something...

"It's really late!" Tracy suddenly said, staring at her watch. "Oh, Will, we've talked so long almost everybody downstairs has gone home!"

"Guess we'd better go, too, so Kevin and Susan can get some sleep before the kids get up to see what Santa left."

They wandered down the stairs and ran into their hosts at the bottom.

"Gonna spend the night?" Kevin asked.

"Of course not!" Tracy laughed. "Sorry we're so late; we got to talking – "

"It really would be a good idea to stay," Susan said. "While you've been talking, it's been snowing like crazy. Trav went out and plowed the driveway over an hour ago so people could get out, but it seems to be filling in again. I was just coming to tell you Allison called to find out whether you were still here or in a ditch somewhere."

"Ah, nuts!" Will said, shaking his head. "I didn't think – not used to having to account to anybody for where I am." Another thought struck him: "Tracy, what about your folks? It's one a.m.; they're going to think I kidnapped you!"

"They called, too," Susan said. "I told them you were safe inside and might spend the night. They're fine."

"Well... I guess we should stay," Tracy said. "We'll get to see the kids open their presents."

Will shook his head. "I can't. I promised Gracie I'd be there tomorrow – I mean, this morning – when she opens her presents. I need to go home."

"Aw, come on, man," Kevin said. "You can go before noon. Maybe by nine. I'll plow again and get you out."

"No, honest, I can't. Tracy, you should stay, and I'll talk to you tomorrow some time. Thanks, you guys, for your hospitality. It was fun. Merry Christmas!"

They shook their heads as Will bundled himself into his coat and slogged through the mounded snow of the porch and steps to the truck, where it sat by itself on the circle near the front door. Most of its red was covered by snow, and Kevin went out to help Will clear it off.

"You sure your wipers work, and the heat?" Kevin asked.

"Yes. They were working on the way over, so I know they're okay. I'll put it in four-wheel drive and go slow and be fine. Thanks again for the evening. It was good to see you again."

"You, too! Hey, if you're going to be around, how about bringing Tracy over for New Year's Eve?"

Will laughed as he climbed into the truck's cab. "You're going to do this all over again in a week?"

"No, there's a thing at church we all go to together."

"I'll let you know, okay? My family may want to do something."

"Go with God," Kevin said. "We'll be praying for you to make it home safely."

ALTHOUGH TEN YEARS HAD PASSED SINCE HE HAD BEEN A FREQUENT traveler of Fulton County roads, Will's body and hands seemed to remember where the curves were and how fast it was safe to drive under terrible conditions. Unfortunately, the safe speed rapidly became zero. The truck didn't seem to have aged much, bearing up under hard use as the F-150s were famous for doing, and one of the things still working well was its heater, for which Will was utterly grateful. The defroster puffed hot air like a steam-engine against the icy windshield, keeping the inside clear, which would have been a big help if there had been anything but white to see outside. Will hugged what he could see of the yellow line, ever mindful of the huge ditches off to his right and left.

Why didn't I stay at Kevin and Susan's? Ed and John would have milked the stupid cows and let Dad stay home. Whoa! Slicker and slicker! He eased his foot back on the accelerator and slowed even more. *Down to tractor speed. Good news is, I have plenty of gas. Other good news is, at this rate it'll be light before I'm half-way home.*

Lord, please get me out of this!

Oh, great. Now I'm praying. Do I get hit upside the head by a big Hand from the sky for only praying in crisis? Probably. Well, here's more good news: I'm clearly not suicidal anymore, because I really don't want to die in a ditch!

THE LIGHTS WERE ON IN THE LIVING ROOM, ALTHOUGH WILL COULDN'T see them until he was practically in front of the house. He parked the truck close to the walk and sat there for a minute shaking, more frightened than he had realized and not wanting to advertise it. He saw the front door open and his father step out onto the porch, followed by the dog, who leaped off the porch and ran in crazy circles in the yard before watering a tree.

"Glad to see you made it!" Matthew said, welcoming prodigal son and prodigal dog back into the warmth of home. "Tucker, sit down!"

Whining, the dog complied, and Allison was all over him with a bath towel, babbling baby-talk which appeared to take the sting out of the rubdown. Will stepped out of his shoes on the little rug by the door and looked around for a place to hang his snowy coat. The short walk to the house had turned him into a snowman.

"I'll take it," Allison said, adding the coat to the soaking towel and moving as quickly to the kitchen as her huge bunny slippers would allow.

"How was it?" Matthew asked.

"Pretty awful. Can't see a thing." Will shook his head, showering drops of water from the snow melting in his hair.

"How about something warm to drink?" Matthew suggested. "You look kinda cold and miserable."

"Sold!" Will agreed, heading for the kitchen, where Allison already had milk heating in a pan on the stove.

"Did you have a good time until the coming-home part?" she asked, stirring sugar and cocoa powder and vanilla into the milk.

"Yes, I did." Will sat opposite his father at the table, shivering. "I didn't think I would, but I did. It was kind of weird, all those people, and God knows what they were thinking, but everybody was nice enough – and it was good to see Tracy having so much fun talking to people. Thanks!" He took the steaming mug and wrapped his hands around it, almost groaning with pleasure as the warmth seeped into his fingers.

"She's still a nice girl," Matthew said, mirroring Will's action with his own mug. "I always kind of hoped you and she would get together."

"Stop it!" Allison teased, sitting close to Matthew. "You don't get to say things like that if I don't."

"Well, I just meant – "

"I know what you meant," Will said, smiling. "I always kind of hoped that, too. I didn't expect to get a do-over at my age, but, hey – she's willing to talk about it. That's what we did – talked a lot. She's had a really interesting life, working in Africa. But she says she's getting ready to stay home." He sipped the chocolate and closed his eyes in pleasure for a moment. "Oh, man, Allison, this is good. They don't make it this way in Iowa. Of course," he admitted, "I don't usually order it in Iowa..."

"I'll bet you don't!" she said, refilling his mug with what was left in the pan. "So what are you going to do about Tracy?"

"Allie, honey, you can't – "

"Of course I can! Will's full-grown, Matthew, and he knows how to turn off a conversation better than anyone else I know except his father."

"Ouch!" the two men said in unison, laughing together at their matched responses.

"I don't know," Will finally said. "She'll be here the rest of the week, and so will I, so I guess we'll see each other when we can and see where it takes us. She's going back to Malawi January second, for six months, and I have a contract for second semester. Not much either one of us can do before summer."

"You're always welcome here," Matthew said, "and at John's place, for a visit or if you decide you want to come back to Ohio. There are enough colleges around here to find a job – if you ever wanted to, I mean." He ducked his head to avoid eye-contact, but Will could hear the hope in his voice.

Teach in Ohio? I could...

AFTER GETTING TO BED AT TWO IN THE MORNING, MATTHEW WAS GLAD, when the phone rang at seven, that John had told him to skip the morning milking. Even after five hours of heavy sleep, he still felt tired and logy. In fact, he probably would have slept much longer if the phone hadn't been ringing in his ear. It was on his side of the bed because Allison didn't wake up enough to answer it in the middle of the night.

"Hello? Merry Christmas to you, too, Gracie. What's up, honey? It's kinda early."

She wanted Will. Matthew crawled reluctantly out of bed and shivered his way through the early morning chill to wake his son. "Phone, Will. It's Gracie."

"You have got to be kidding! No, of course you aren't. Okay," he yawned, "I'll take it in the kitchen so you can go back to sleep."

"That's not going to happen," Matthew lamented. "The minute that thing rang, Tucker was up and waiting to go out. He's sitting at the front door even as we speak."

Matthew let the dog out as he heard Will pick up the phone in the kitchen and begin to speak. Tucker was out and back in less time than it took Will to reassure Gracie that, yes, he would be there for Christmas dinner and presents.

"She's something else!" Will told Matthew as he helped to dry off Tucker's paws.

"For sure," Matthew agreed. "And she really does have her sights set on you. Has she told you yet that she's going to marry you when she grows up?"

"What! No!"

"Well, she probably will. First, when she was three, she was going to marry her daddy. I guess all little girls go through that. Then when she was seven, she was going to marry me. Allison set her straight on that pretty quick! Now you're on her list."

"No, you have it wrong," Will said, laughing. "I'm on her list, but it's her salvation list. She's bound and determined I'm not going to hell." He took the wet towel back to the utility room off the kitchen and hung it on a little rack above the laundry sink.

"How're you doing with that?" Matthew asked casually, preparing the coffeemaker as he spoke and flipping the switch to get it started.

"Uh – I don't mind too much. She's such a cute kid, and if it takes her mind off losing her mother, what do I care?"

Careful now, Matthew warned himself. *Tread easy here.* "What I meant was how are you doing in your relationship with the Lord?"

"Oh." Will sat down and kept his eyes carefully fixed on the table-top. "Dad, I don't really – I don't really have that kind of relationship. I don't know that I believe any of the Christian religion propaganda. I mean, I'm sorry, I know you and Allison and everybody in the family are believers, but it just hasn't meant anything to me."

Matthew nodded, setting his lips firmly against any errant word that might try to escape imprudently. "Coffee?"

"No, thanks. I'm drinking milk these days. Ulcer."

Lord, help me! How can I get past this polite Will to the hurting kid inside?

He handed a glass of milk to Will and poured a mug of coffee for himself. "Allison will probably sleep until nine if I don't wake her," he said. "Would you like me to fix you some breakfast?"

Will laughed, a simple, easy laugh without undertones. "Have your culinary skills improved any since the last time you tried to cook for me?"

Matthew laughed back. "Not so's you'd notice."

"Then I think I'll stick with milk. You do pour a mean glass of milk!"

"Thank you. There are Christmas cookies from Pearl and Cassie, and probably some donuts in the breadbox if you want."

"No, thanks. I'm not much of a breakfast eater. I'm a lot more like you than I realized for a long time."

Here's an opening! "Yeah, I remember the first time I realized looking at you was like looking in a mirror. Then Pearl and Carolyn were always teasing about how we look alike and act alike, even the same gestures. I've always been kind of proud of that."

"Really?"

"Of course. I'm proud of you, Will, and I want people to know you're my son."

Will ducked his head, but color spread up his neck and delicately colored the tops of his ears.

"I guess that's another reason I was asking about your relationship with the Lord," Matthew continued. "I'm proud of you, and I love you, and I want you to have everything I have and more. God has done miracles in my life, Son, and I want you to have that, too. Don't you ever – I don't know – feel the need for Him?"

Will was staring at his milk as if expecting the Loch Ness monster to swim up from its creamy depths. "Dad, I don't want to get into an argument. I respect that you believe it all and it works for you. I'll even admit I did a little praying myself last night on the way home. But that's just a coward's response to a scary situation. No, I don't need God, whatever that is. I have everything I need, and I can take care of myself now."

Oh, Lord, please help him to see that isn't true without having to go through something terrible! Please forgive him for being – I don't know – ignorant? Help him!

"No arguments, I promise," Matthew said, rising and putting his half-full mug in the sink. "But it's not okay with me for you to keep calling yourself a coward. I need you to stop that. It's a lie, and lies come from the enemy. Let it go."

Will nodded without breaking his monster-watch. "Sure, Dad."

Sighing, Matthew patted Will on the shoulder in passing. "I'm going to hit the shower and get dressed. We'll go over to John's around noon. You better plan to ride in the truck with us; your car still won't be good on the roads."

"Want me to plow out?" Will asked. "Snow seems to have stopped, but the driveway was drifted pretty deep last night."

"Thanks, I'd appreciate it. You can let Tucker out, too. He'll want to roll around in it for a while pretending he's a polar bear."

WHEN THE PACKAGES ARE ALL UNWRAPPED AND THE SCRAPS OF THE meal are all in the garbage, when the parade on television is over and the kids are all engrossed in their new toys or gadgets, when the conversation has died down in postprandial stupor and the weak sunlight outside has been replaced by dreary gray twilight, then Christmas is over and the faint letdown begins.

Carolyn, you would have loved this day, John told her. *I found the book and the art supplies you bought for her last year at the after-Christmas sales and she loved having those last few presents from Mommy. I wish you could have seen her face. She looked just like you. She's almost eleven now, and she's going to be as beautiful as you.*

And Will. You would have been so glad to see Will here, smiling sometimes, talking to people and playing Monopoly with the younger kids. He almost acted like he felt at home here, Caro, maybe more than he ever did before.

And Matthew. So happy to have his son with him, even for a little while, smiling the same smile Will has – except when he'd look at your chair or your place at the table. He misses you, sweetheart, and he sees how much I miss you.

If only you could –

Lord, I know people say they would never wish anyone back because they're happy with You in heaven, so forgive me – but I would give anything, almost anything, to have Carolyn back, even for one day. I miss her so much... Help me not to be bitter, not to lose faith. Help me to believe the pain will get better someday.

"WHERE'S DADDY?" GRACIE ASKED WILL.

"I think he went upstairs," Will said, carefully considering the thousand pieces of puzzle Gracie had dumped out onto the cleared dining room table after her aunt and uncle and their brood had gone home. "I think it was mean of Aunt Allison to pick a puzzle with a picture of a polar bear in a blizzard."

"That makes it harder," Gracie explained.

"My point." He picked up one piece with a black circle in the middle and compared it to the cover of the box. "I think this is the polar bear's nose. It's in the middle, and we can work out from there."

"No, that's not how to do it! You have to make the corners and the borders first, and then you work in. Daddy and Mommy taught me that. Didn't your mommy teach you?"

Will put down the puzzle-piece and took a deep breath. "No, Gracie, my mom didn't teach me much of anything. She wasn't really a very good mom, not like yours."

"Oh. But your daddy, then. Uncle Matthew's a good daddy."

"Yeah, he is. But he and my mom didn't live together, and I didn't come to live here until I was fifteen. I don't think we ever did puzzles and things like that together. I wasn't a very nice kid."

"Really?" She stared at him with huge blue eyes.

"Yes, really. I'm not proud of that, but it's true."

"Oh. Well, that's because you didn't know Jesus, Will. See, when you love Him and have Him in your heart, then you just want to be good and make other people happy – well, most of the time," she owned with a child's candor.

"I want to make you happy," Will said, ruffling her hair, "so let's work on this amazing puzzle and see if we can surprise Aunt Allison by getting it done."

"I THINK AUNT ALLISON'S AMAZING PUZZLE PUT GRACIE DOWN FOR THE count," Allison teased as she and Will carried leftovers into the kitchen.

"You were eavesdropping?"

"Guilty as charged," she laughed, stuffing plastic containers into the refrigerator as fast as Will handed them to her. "I love Gracie and her take on the world."

"May I ask you something, Allison?"

"Sure. Just hand me that big square thing full of turkey."

Complying, he paused a moment to consider his words, then plunged ahead. "I know you love kids. It's obvious watching you with Grace and Livvie's boys and the babies at church and all. So how come you and my dad never had any?"

Allison froze, and that sudden feral stillness wasn't lost on Will.

"Hey, I'm sorry! It's none of my business. Please forgive me."

"Oh, that's all right," she said, straightening and closing the refrigerator door. "You couldn't have known about it. Have a seat, and I'll tell you." She gestured to the kitchen table and sat herself down.

"What's going on?" Matthew said from the doorway, looking at the two of them. "You all right, Allie?"

"I'm fine. Will and I are just going to have a little chat. Why don't you take Tucker for a walk – it's not too cold, is it?"

"Subtle as a meat cleaver," Matthew said to Will in a theatrical aside. "I'll see you later."

"You don't have to go," Will protested.

"Oh, yes, I do. I have received The Message and The Voice and The Look from the little lady, and it's worth my hide to disobey. Mind you, that doesn't mean I'm not the head of this home; I just know when to retreat." Chuckling, Matthew left the room, and in a minute they heard the front door open and close.

"Now, then," Allison said, straightening her shoulders. "Here's my story. Before I met your father, back before I became a Christian, I was kind of a – well, a party girl. I – knew a lot of men, and I got pregnant twice." She hung her head, seeming to force herself to go on, "And I had two abortions. After I met Matthew and fell so hard for him I bounced, I couldn't get past all the God-stuff and we – broke up. While I wasn't with him, I got pregnant a third time and had a third abortion."

Will saw with horror that tears were running down Allison's cheeks. "Hey, it's okay! You don't have to go on!" He handed her a paper napkin, which she used to blot the tears and wipe her nose, crumpling it in her little hand.

"No, I want to tell you." She took another napkin and blew her nose before rising to toss the used napkins into the trashcan. "Do you want some coffee? It could be a long story."

"No, thank you."

"All right, then." She seated herself again and continued, "When I had the third abortion, the doctor told me I was so scarred up from abortions and from an STD that my chances of ever having a baby were less than one in a million. When we started seeing each other again, that's what I told your dad, but he wouldn't listen to me. Told me he already had a son and didn't need any babies to make him happy.

"But all I ever wanted was to be a wife and mother, to have lots of babies. It was always just a huge, gaping hole in my heart. My job, you know, I deal with lots of babies, and some of them I can't help falling in love with. There was one little guy, Benjie, who really got to me – and he died."

"Oh, man!"

"Yeah." She wiped away more tears but continued to speak. "In my family, if you shake the family tree a lot of drunks fall out. I liked to drink and party and have a good time, and I figured out that alcohol could anesthetize that hole in my heart if I drank enough. That first time I called Matthew, when he left the house in such a hurry to come to me – I was drunk as a skunk. And after Benjie died, I started drinking more and more, and more and more often – until the hospital almost fired me. I had to go to inpatient treatment and to be on work probation for a couple of years. But I'm sober today, by the grace of God, and living such a blessed life!

"But I couldn't have any children, and we never really felt called to adopt."

"Wow. I'm – I'm sorry, Allison. I don't quite know what to say."

"Good," she said, smiling through the last of her tears, "because I'm not really finished yet, I don't think. Sure you don't want coffee? I need some."

"What the heck – why not?"

Allison kept talking as she prepped the coffee-maker, flipped the switch and found the mugs. "One of the conditions of my work probation was to go to three or four AA meetings a week and get a sponsor. That's a recovering person of the same sex with more sobriety than you have to guide you over the rough spots and teach you how to work the program. Carol's been with me just about from the beginning. When I get into a patch of 'stinking thinking' and imagine a drink would help, she talks sense into me again. I still go to a couple of meetings most weeks, because I'm a quick forgetter." She laughed as she poured the coffee and set a mug in front of Will.

"Just give me a minute to doctor this," she said, adding four teaspoonfuls of sugar and a generous glug of Abbott milk to her mug. "Want cookies?"

"No thanks. So you're a recovering alcoholic? Nobody ever said…"

"Yep, I am. And nobody ever said because you were never around to say it to."

"Ouch. Okay, I deserve that."

"Yes, you do. You've caused a lot of pain to a lot of really good people over the last ten years. And I know you know that, because I see it. Here's the deal, though, Will, like the rest of the story."

"Go ahead."

Allison took a sip of her coffee and looked Will in the eye. "I found the Lord through Alcoholics Anonymous. He started speaking to me through the program and through people in the program. We'd say the Lord's Prayer at the end of meetings, and the hair would stand up on my arms and the back of my neck because I knew there was something bigger than a bunch of drunks in that room. I know your dad and the family were praying for me for a long time, and that didn't hurt, either. One day I was reading that stupid Gideon Bible they gave me in treatment, and I – "

"You what?"

"I heard this voice say, 'All you have to do is let me love you. All you have to do is ask me.' And I knew Who it was, all of a sudden. I had a bulletin from church in my purse, and it had 'How to Become a Christian' on the back page. I pulled it out and read what it said and then prayed that prayer right there in my bedroom. And so much pain and guilt just – it just went away! I asked God to forgive me and I knew He had."

They sat in silence for a minute or two.

"I'm back!" Matthew called from the living room, "I could use coffee. Is it safe to come in?"

They looked at each other like conspirators.

"Sure," Allison called. "Coffee's made."

"I'm going to a meeting tomorrow night," Allison said. "Want to come?"

"Hey, it's a great story, but I'm not an alcoholic!"

"Didn't say you are. You are related to one, though, so it's legit for you to be there. You might hear something that helps what hurts you." She rose to fill a mug for Matthew, who was coming into the kitchen. "Just let me know; I leave at seven-fifteen."

"I'll get her." There was a decided chill to Anita Showalter's voice as she spoke to Will, and he wondered what had happened since their brief, unremarkable encounter at Kevin and Susan's party.

"Hi, Will!" Tracy's voice seemed as warm and comforting as ever, giving him hope they were all right.

"Happy day after Christmas," Will said. "Did you have a good day?"

"Yes, it was nice, especially after not being sure I'd get home! I'm relieved to know you made it all right; I was worried."

Oh. I get it. Idiot! "I'm sorry, Tracy; I should have called. It just – honestly, it didn't cross my mind anyone would be worried. I'm not used to that."

"Do you think you could get used to it? If we – well – I mean – oh, why is it so hard to talk to you now? It never was before!"

He could hear her embarrassment and frustration through the lines and wished they were face to face so he could put his arms around her and reassure her somehow – honestly? – reassure himself somehow that they could get beyond this.

"Tracy? Listen to me. We're just not used to each other anymore, that's all. And the cure for that is spending as much time together as we can this week. I don't care how we do that – your house, my dad's house, out somewhere – just so we can get past the seventh grade awkwardness and be easy with each other again."

"I think you're probably right," she finally answered, just as he was beginning to sweat. "Why don't we start with you coming here for dinner so my parents can see you're not some big-city player with evil designs on their daughter."

"And what if I am?"

"Then you come here for dinner and fake them out."

Laughing again, he suddenly remembered a previous offer. *No. I don't want to do that. But you know she'd like you to go, and she hasn't ever, ever asked for anything before. It would make Dad happy, let him know I don't hate her anymore...*

"Hey, Tracy, I forgot – I sort of promised Allison I'd go to a – uh – go someplace with her tonight. Can we have lunch instead, or dinner tomorrow night?"

"My mom will probably like the advance notice better anyway, so why not dinner tomorrow night? And maybe – maybe you and I could have lunch somewhere."

"I'LL DRIVE," ALLISON SAID, TAKING THE TRUCK KEYS FROM MATTHEW and giving him a brief, smacky kiss. "You won't know where you're going."

Will gave his father a frantic look. "How can she drive the truck? She can't see over the steering wheel!"

Matthew just laughed and said, "You could meet the dragon, saying things like that. She's driven it plenty over the years, and nary a scratch. Relax, Will, and she'll get you where you're going."

"*She*," said Allison pointedly, "does not like to be talked about as if she were not in the room. Come on, Will, or we'll be late. I don't know how the roads will be."

AFTER A TOTALLY UNEVENTFUL RIDE, WILL PEELED HIS FINGERS FROM the grab-handle and followed Allison down a flight of well-salted outside stairs into the basement of the looming old Presbyterian church in Lewiston, where they entered into a dingy, low-ceilinged room full of long tables, shabby folding chairs and a milling crowd of people.

"I know you don't like this kind of crowd," Allison said over the din of conversation, "but I promise nobody will mess with you. Let's get some coffee, and we'll find a seat."

Will followed her across the room, a progression which seemed to take forever, as nearly every person greeted Allison, many with hugs, some with handshakes, and waited expectantly to be introduced to Will. He was on the edge of panic from all the overfriendly bodies so close to him until one older gentleman in a worn black suit, quite different from the casual or grubby attire of the rest of them, said,

"Is this your first meeting, son?" and immediately went on, "Well, don't worry. It keeps getting better one day at a time, and it works if you work it."

Allison burst out laughing, and it came to Will the old man thought he was an alcoholic. Instead of being insulted, somehow he found it as amusing as Allison did; and with his laughter, the panic went away. "Thanks," he told the old man gravely.

Allison was not so polite. "Doug, you're barking up the wrong tree," she laughed. "This is my stepson Will, and he's *not* one of us. He's just along for the ride."

"Sorry," Doug said, not particularly embarrassed – or sorry, Will thought with further amusement. "Natural mistake."

"No problem," Will said, taking a styrofoam cup from Allison and looking suspiciously at the contents. "What's this?"

"Better not drink it if you're not one of us," Doug said. "That's AA coffee – strongest in the world."

Will put the cup back on the coffee bar.

Sitting beside Allison at one of the long tables, Will listened curiously as the man in the red tee-shirt told his story. It sounded like something out of a bad novel until he began to talk about his recovery process.

"I knew the only way to stay sober was to turn my life and my will over to God, but I just couldn't believe there was anything out there to trust, you know? I figured I could do it on willpower, and I did really well for a year or so. Then I thought I'd reward myself for not drinking, for getting my wife back and keeping my job and coaching my son's little league team..." He hesitated and took a huge glug of coffee, breaking eye contact with his intensely listening audience.

"And that went well, too. It seemed like I could stop after work and have a drink or two with my friends – no problem. If I didn't feel like drinking, I didn't have to. I got promoted, and we had a baby – "

This time the pause was long and teary. No one moved or spoke, just letting the man bring himself under control. Will squirmed in his chair, wishing he were anywhere but there.

"But you know how it goes. One day I was handling the drink, and the next day it was handling me. I lost my job first, then my house, then my wife and my kids – until all I had left was my car and my life, what was left of it. You probably remember me. I came to meetings drunk half the time, and all I really wanted was the coffee and donuts. I'd put together a week or two – six weeks one time – and then I'd be back at it, begging, borrowing, stealing money for a bottle. Living in a flophouse on the wrong side of the tracks. Working a day or two in Toledo if I could get there, or mowing some old lady's yard for a couple of bucks or a meal.

"I ended up in jail, finally, for shoplifting wine from Kroger's. I'd managed to drink half of it before they could stop me, so I was too drunk to worry about being in a cell. Then I went into withdrawal and came to in the emergency room with some doctor yelling in my ear."

"I know that doctor," Allison whispered in Will's ear. "He did the same thing to me."

"I was court-ordered into treatment," the man continued, "and had to go to meetings five days a week – and get slips signed to prove I did it. You may remember how I felt about that, too!"

Laughter bounced around the room; Will gathered they did remember, and it had not been pretty.

"One night Doug over there took me out for coffee after the meeting and gave me The Talk."

More laughter, louder and longer this time. *Have they all had The Talk*, Will wondered. *Is it bad?*

"He told me to get off the pity-pot and take responsibility for my own life, to quit blaming everybody else, including God, to quit whining about what I lost and start being grateful for what I have – you know, The Talk. He gave me a Big Book and told me to read it. He gave me his phone number and told me to call it – but before I took a drink, not after.

"Well, I figured, guy who always wears a suit to a meeting – and a tie – he must be doing all right. And everybody said he'd been sober longer than all the rest of them put together. So I figured – why not give it a try? Now, by the grace of God, I've been sober seven years, six months and five days – but who's counting? And I try to live my life one day at a time, do service to others, ask God in the morning to keep me sober and thank Him at night that He did. If you're new tonight, and you wonder why the heck you're here – keep coming back. If you wonder whether you can do it, or you think you can't – keep coming back. If you think we're all full of it and you can handle it on your own – you'll be back, if you're lucky."

Red-Shirt sat down to boisterous applause and Will let out the breath he didn't know he had been holding.

What Allison called "the meeting after the meeting" began around the coffee-pot after the group had said the Lord's Prayer and disbanded. Will tightened his gut and approached the man in the red shirt.

"Hi," the man said, smiling and extending his hand. "I saw you sitting there next to Allison. You're new, right? I'm Ben."

"I'm Will," Will said, shaking the proffered hand. "May I ask you something?"

"Sure. Want coffee? There's probably still enough in there to crawl into your cup."

"No, thanks. I couldn't drink what I had."

"Okay, then, let's go over there by the inside stairs – less traffic." Ben led the way across the room, brushing off compliments as he moved steadily forward. "What can I do ya for?"

"You said in the beginning of your talk that you didn't believe in God, you thought you could do everything yourself, you thought you were happy."

"That's right."

"And you could handle your drinking. It wasn't a problem for you."

"That's right, too. It wasn't until it was."

"I see how you figured out it was a problem..." Ben laughed and Will forged ahead. "But how did you get to the God part? And do you really need 'God,' whatever that is?"

"Well, I finally got it that I'm powerless – not just over alcohol, but over just about everything except my attitude and my behavior. I'm powerless over my wife and my kids and my boss and the guys I work with and the government – well, you get the idea. That's AA's Step One, by the way. Step Two's the killer for a lot of guys. It says we 'came to believe a Power greater than ourselves could restore us to sanity.' I worked on that for a long time, until one day I just found myself praying to God instead of to myself. And then things started to get easier. The Third Step says we 'made a decision to turn our lives and our will over to the care of God as we understood him.' If you get Two, then Three just makes sense."

"So you just – did those steps and found God."

"Pretty much. I don't go to church or anything, but I talk to Him all the time and try always to ask myself if what I'm doing would be what He wants me to do."

"Thanks. I appreciate your time," Will said. "Congratulations on your sobriety."

"Glad to meet you," Ben said. "Keep coming back!"

Embarrassment scalded Will and turned him brilliantly red. "Oh, no, listen – I'm not an alcoholic. I just came with Allison. Honestly!"

"That's okay, too," Ben said, although his face suggested he didn't believe Will. "Anybody's welcome at an open meeting like this. And, Will? The steps of AA work for anybody who wants to work 'em, alcoholic or not. It's just a good way to live."

Chapter 11

"YOU HAD A LONG CHAT WITH BEN," ALLISON SAID, EYES on the road, expertly downshifting for the curve on County Road F.

"He's a nice guy. They all seem to be pretty nice."

"Oh, mostly we are. Once in a while there's a seriously jerky jerk, but most of those don't seem to last. So what did you think?"

"It was interesting."

"Ah, Will, how polite you are!" she teased. "Well, I won't press you. I just wanted you to see one of the places I draw my strength and hope."

"What are the others?"

"Well, first from my Savior, of course. And from my family. You'd be surprised at what a man of faith your father is, what a prayer warrior. He doesn't think so, of course, but I know so. And John – and Ed – now there's the steadiest man I've ever met, in AA or out of it. And Pearl... I'm going to miss her."

"Wait a minute! What do you mean, miss Pearl?"

"Well, honey, she's older than dirt and getting frailer by the minute. Haven't you noticed a change in her after all this time?"

"Sure. But I didn't think – I mean, are you saying she's dying?"

"We're all dying, Will, from the day we're born. It's just what we do with the time we have that matters. I mean, look at Carolyn. She was too young to die, people say, but God's timetable is so different from ours. And look at her life! She made a huge difference in other people's lives while she was living it. Pearl has been so important to our family, and to a lot of other people. When she goes home to Jesus, she'll leave a legacy of faith here on earth even though she doesn't have any living children or grandchildren. But she is going to die."

Will shook his head, staring out at the snowy landscape gleaming in moonlight. "I'm not going to think about that."

"Here we are," Allison said, not apparently disturbed by Will's refusal to confront reality. "And here's the welcoming committee. You can tell him 'down,' you know. You don't have to let him get slush all over you."

Will tried, but Tucker apparently only listened to Allison, because he was all over Will, jumping and licking until Will had to cling to the truck to keep from slipping on the slush. Inside, the dog escaped having his paws wiped and jumped all over Matthew, too.

At last, dog on the porch again, Matthew in a dry shirt, they settled in the kitchen for some catching up, eating leftover Christmas cookies and drinking coffee that didn't crawl into the cup by itself.

Matthew turned to Will, saying nothing.

"What is it, Dad?"

"I – uh – "

"What?"

"When we go to bed at night, Allison and I pray together. Since we're all three here, would you mind joining us tonight?"

Oh, for – well, what the heck? How can it hurt? "I guess so. But I don't want to – you know."

"Ed used to tell me to just hum along when I didn't know the words," Matthew said, a smile lighting his face as he remembered. "That'll work here, too."

HE SPENT HIS MORNINGS HELPING OUT ON THE FARM, HIS AFTERNOONS playing the guitar or visiting with whoever was free to visit, usually Pearl or Allison, on her days off, and his evenings with Tracy. He wandered out into the living room one night when he couldn't sleep and found Allison's AA Big Book lying on the couch. Having nothing better to do, he sat down and began to read it, never imagining it would be anything but amusing, filled with clichés like the conversations of the people at the meeting.

Tucker, who had been let in for the night because of below-zero temperatures and Allison's soft heart, woke up enough to climb up on the couch and snuggle up to Will. He rested his head on Will's lap and sighed deeply.

"You old reprobate," Will whispered, "you get away with murder, don't you?"

The dog gave a half-whine in reply, and Will used one hand to pet the huge head. He was warm and comfortable and loved unconditionally, and before long his eyes closed and the book slipped from his hand. When he woke up, the dog was gone, the book was on the coffee table, and he was lying on the couch covered by a huge afghan, dreaming of coffee.

"Want some?" Allison asked, waving the mug under his nose.

"Yeah... Bathroom first, maybe..." He wandered away, trying to remember how he had come to be on the couch instead of in his bed.

"Morning's not your time, is it?" Allison asked, handing the mug to him as he sat down again on the couch.

"No, not really. Shoot, I can't drink this. What time is it?"

"If the watch you're not looking at matches mine, it's eleven-fifteen. AM."

"Oh. I forgot I was wearing one... Where's Dad?"

Allison laughed. "Where is he always at eleven-fifteen? He's over at the farm doing something farmish."

"Oh, man. I was supposed to help Ed with an oil change or something. I hope Dad didn't have to do that. He hates the machinery." Will stood, placing his mug on the table. "I'd better change and get over there."

"You don't have to," Allison said. "He called and said to tell you they can spare you this morning and you should rest. Do you need to rest?"

"No, I'm fine. Just need to wake up. Where's Tucker?"

"Outside where he belongs, guarding the property – mostly from rabbits." Allison picked up the mug to take it to the kitchen. "Why don't you shower and dress, and then we'll have lunch. You've pretty much missed the breakfast you don't eat. And you can tell me what you think of my book."

Will presented himself, clean, shaved, dressed in jeans and a plain white tee-shirt swiped from his father, to Allison and a stand-by lunch of grilled cheese sandwiches and tomato soup.

"Nobody opens a can of Campbell's better than I do," Allison declared, setting a plate and bowl before him.

For whatever reason, the meal went down easily, and Will felt amazingly sleepy all over again. He tried to hide a yawn behind his hand, apologizing, "I don't know what's the matter with me. I never get this tired at home."

"If you're not sick, and you don't look like you are, I'd guess you've been wearing yourself out wrestling alligators in your sleep. I have to say you looked pretty relaxed when we found you this morning all snugged up to Tucker, but how many nights have you laid awake or had crazy dreams?"

"All of them," Will owned. "When I'm at home it isn't as bad – but you know what?"

"What?"

"I probably have a drink or two before bed most nights at home. Not a lot of alcohol, not out of control – but I've been thinking about my drinking, and I do drink a lot more than I realized."

Allison nodded. "Do you think it's a problem?"

Will wiped his mouth and pushed back a little from the table. "No, not really. But I think it could *become* a problem, because all the stories I'm reading in your book seem to say it wasn't a problem for them until all of a sudden – it was. And how would I know until after I was in trouble?"

"Are you asking me what I think?"

Will hesitated, having no doubt she would tell him, and in plain language. Finally he nodded, bracing himself.

"Okay. I don't think you're an alcoholic – yet. But I agree with you it could become a problem if you keep going like you have been. 'Normal' drinkers, whatever that means, seem to drink for fun, to complement a meal, that sort of thing. But the people who have problems are the ones who drink to medicate themselves."

"Medicate?"

"You know – like have a drink to kill the anxiety before a party; have a drink to kill the anxiety at the party. Have a drink to tamp down the rage or to kill the pain of a loss or to stifle inhibitions so you can be sexually active or whatever. Basically, alcoholics usually start by drinking to kill feelings. Then they end up drinking because that's what drunks do – keep drinking. So if you're using booze as a sleeping pill, that's self-medicating."

Twisting the paper napkin as if he were making an origami figure with it, Will swallowed a couple of times before looking at Allison again to say, "So I should quit, right?"

"How do you feel about that?"

"I don't know." He scrubbed his fingers through his hair, disordering the damp strands. "It's probably the smart thing to do, isn't it? And it would probably make Tracy happy."

Allison swiped his plate and bowl and dumped them into the sink. Her clear, deep blue eyes were clouded with something and her mouth pursed.

"What's the matter? What did I say?"

"Oh, Will." She looked on the verge of tears, and Will felt the sandwich balling up in his stomach. "Will, honey, the thing is – you can't get sober and you can't stay sober for somebody else. You have to do it for yourself. If, God forbid, your father dropped dead tomorrow, I'd still stay sober for myself. It's not for him, even though being sober is what lets me be with him. Tracy can't be your reason for changing anything, honey. You have to do it for yourself." She began to rinse the dishes, not looking at him any longer.

"I think I'm going to go for a walk," Will said, leaving the table. "I'll be back in a while. Tucker will guard me."

"I'M NOT A DRUNK," WILL TOLD THE DOG AS THEY WALKED DOWN THE plowed road to visit Tucker's friend the German shepherd. "I'm not. But I have been drinking more and hanging out at McClendon's a lot more than I used to. Everybody I know goes there and does that. It's not bad to drink with friends, is it?"

The dog ignored Will and ran ahead, investigating scents along the way, but clearly headed for a destination.

Why am I trying to convince myself it's okay to do something stupid? If it isn't a problem, I can just switch to Seven-Up. If I have trouble sleeping, I guess I need to find some other way to deal with it. Like exercise, or reading the phone book.

Why do you listen to someone who obviously has a drum to beat? She can't drink because she's a weak-willed woman. You're a strong man, and you can do as you please.

Will shuddered, although in his father's spare Carhartt coat and heavy gloves and hat he wasn't really cold. It wasn't about drinking anyway, he knew deep down. It was about – well, about the other part of the program, the spirituality part.

"I wish I could believe that a power greater than myself could restore me to sanity," Will told Tucker. And then there it was again: *All you have to do is ask Me.*

"DO YOU WANT TO GO WITH ME TO A NEW YEAR'S EVE PARTY?" TRACY asked as she and Will demolished hamburgers and fries in their favorite booth in Logan's Diner. "I was invited weeks ago, and I'd love to have you come with me."

"You kinda waited until the last minute to invite me," Will teased, dunking a fry into a pool of ketchup, hoping he wasn't going to pay for this meal in pain later.

"Yes, I did," Tracy said, and she wasn't smiling back. "I wasn't sure how you'd feel about it."

"Why? Is it somebody from the bad old days? Tell me you're not hanging with those football goons!"

"Of course not! It's just that the party's at the church, and Pastor Miles and Penny are hosting it. We'll have a pot-luck supper and play board games and have basketball in the gym and then there'll be a movie after midnight. Will you come?"

The church. Pastor Miles and Penny, fine, but all the church-ladies?

"If you're thinking it'll all be Pearl's generation, you're wrong. It's for the younger generation, from just out of high school to our age. Can you imagine Mrs. Gunderman playing basketball?"

Will had to laugh, imagining Pearl going in for a layup. "I'd like to go with you," he said. "What shall I bring?"

"Gym shoes," she said promptly. "I think I can take you at basketball. We play a lot at the compound in Malawi."

"You're just a girl," Will taunted. "I'll bet I beat you two out of three games of Horse and any team I'm on will trounce your team."

"We'll see, won't we?"

HAVING PREVAILED UPON CASSIE FOR A POT-LUCK DISH, HAVING PURchased a brand new pair of Nikes, Will felt ready to tackle the New Year's Eve party, even if it was in church. *The ceiling never fell in before, so I guess it'll be fine this time, too.*

The foyer had been transformed into party central, he saw, round tables and chairs set up and an incredible array of casseroles and plates of food crowding the long serving counter at the side of the room. Children from toddlers to middle-schoolers were running around, making ear-shivering noises, while their parents held the babies and chatted in small clumps around the room. A couple of teenage girls were pursuing the smaller children who ran off down the long halls. Will took his casserole of chicken-something and Tracy's huge bowl of some kind of pasta salad to the serving area, where he was divested of them by Penny Corrigan and a woman he didn't know.

"Thanks, Will," Penny chirped, giving him a huge smile.

Weaving his way back to Tracy, Will saw her in conversation with Susan and several other young women, most of whom seemed to be holding children under a year old. Tracy had commandeered one and stood swaying from side to side with the baby held low on her hip. She looked so natural – no one would ever have guessed the baby wasn't hers.

As Will was gorging on the sight of Tracy with a baby, feeling a hot longing grow in his chest, Kevin and Travis came up and bore him away in another direction. "Heard you want to kick some butt in basketball," Trav said, "so let's warm up!"

The hoops were down in the auditorium and a number of young boys, teens and a few of the men over twenty, were warming up already. "It's not really my game," Will protested, but they shouted him down and dragged him toward the court. "At least let me hang up my coat!" he said.

"Ah, just drop it over there with those other ones," Travis said, gesturing to the sidelines. "We're ready to rock and roll!"

"Trav, you don't even know what rock and roll means," Kevin laughed, scooping up a ball as it rolled by.

After ten minutes of "warming up," Will was ready to concede that basketball *really* wasn't his game, and he was ready to pay a forfeit to Tracy to avoid making a fool of himself in front of a hundred people, but the guys would have none of it.

"You're saved by the bell for an hour or so," Kevin said as a library bell sounded from the lobby. "Because dinner is served. After that, though – game on!"

And a game it was! Will disgraced himself by not scoring even once and by fouling out fairly early on, while Tracy managed to score three or four times, yelling in a most unseemly manner, "Nothing but net!"

I guess racquetball really is my game. Sure isn't basketball!

"Did we ever settle on a prize for winning the bet?" Tracy asked, wiping sweat from her face with a paper towel. "Because I do believe my team won."

"Miz Tracy," Will drawled, "your team creamed my team. I declare, you are a champion! What would you like for your prize?"

"Let me think about it," she said, smiling up at him. "I'm going to go change back into my party clothes and I'll meet you in the lobby for some games."

"That girl throws a mean elbow," Kevin laughed, coming up beside Will. "I'm gonna have a bruise on my ribs where she checked me. I thought a sweet little missionary girl would play nice."

"Remember how she always wanted to get the highest score on the calculus quiz? She's competitive."

"Pretty, too, maybe even more than she was ten years ago. How's it going with her?"

Will examined his new Nikes for scuff-marks. "Fine."

"Man, you can tell me! Not Trav, because he can't keep a secret to save himself, but me, for sure." Kevin nudged Will. "Give!"

"Honestly? I don't know. I've seen her every day or night this week, and we've talked for hours. I keep wishing things were different... Shoot, Kevin, she's off to Africa day after tomorrow, and I'm headed back to Iowa. Who knows when we'll see each other again?"

"Ever hear of Skype? Telephone? Airplanes? Distance isn't the only thing, is it?"

"Mind your own business," Will said, but there was no rancor in it.

"Let me just say this," Kevin insisted. "Susan and I are praying for you, Will."

"Thanks. I guess. No, really, I appreciate it. I do."

"Come on," Tracy said, running up and grabbing both men by their elbows. "It's time to play games!"

"Could I just go home now?" Kevin groaned, but he followed, as Will did, and they found seats at a table with Pastor Miles and his wife. The game was Scrabble, and Will settled in with a smile. At last an arena where he knew what he was doing.

⚡

"I CAN *NOT* BELIEVE YOU BEAT ME AGAIN!" WILL MOANED, LOOKING AT the scoresheet, where all the numbers damned him in Penny's neat hand. "By a hundred points!"

"Let's gather in the sanctuary," Pastor Miles said, shoving back his chair. "I think the crew has everything set up in there."

"Now what?" Will muttered to Tracy. "Something else you can beat me at?"

"Shut up," she whispered.

Will noted the time: 11:37 p.m. Almost midnight. A new year coming. *I wonder how this one will be different, what new problems will come along... No. Think positively. What new opportunities will come along.*

About three-quarters of the original crowd were left, and they settled into the pews to hear what Pastor Miles would say. Will looked at Tracy, who seemed familiar with the drill, and asked, "Now what? Come on!"

"Shhh! Pastor Miles will say a little something and lead us in a prayer, and then we'll have communion right before midnight."

Communion! Oh, I don't think so.

"Don't you even think about skipping out on this!" Tracy hissed, reminding him of Allison in dragon-mode.

"Wouldn't dream of it," he lied. "But maybe you ought to hold my hand just in case."

Will managed to ignore the pastor by concentrating on the warmth and tingle of Tracy's hand in his, and when the communion trays came around he just didn't take the cube of Wonder Bread or the tiny plastic cup of Welsh's grape juice. But when the count-down started and all the husbands and wives stood up and put their arms around each other, he knew exactly what was happening – and exactly what he wanted. He pulled Tracy to her feet and into his arms.

"Happy New Year!" he whispered and bent to give her a long, gentle kiss.

Chapter 12

JANUARY IN IOWA WAS A LOT LIKE JANUARY IN OHIO, DRY AND bone-break cold. Will took up running on the indoor track at the university rather than his usual runs on the streets of Iowa City and was surprised to find Nate and Steve joining him from time to time. That made him uncomfortable, particularly in the locker room, but running was the best way he had found to let his mind float free. He would feel the heat and the sweat of his exertion and imagine Tracy on the heat-shimmering plains of Africa, holding a little black baby, swaying back and forth to some internal rhythm as she had with the baby at church.

On February second, his birthday, Will received a card mailed from Malawi, wishing him a blessed birthday and reminding him he was destined to be one of God's beloved sons. Tracy had written a brief message in scratchy ball-point scribbles, saying little; but she had signed it "Love," and that was all he needed.

"Here comes the Birthday Boy!" Nate shouted over the crowd as Will and Trey came through the door of McClendon's. Quite a few of the usual gang were crowded around their usual tables in the back, already a couple of drinks to the good. "We saved you the best seat," Nate said, shoving out a chair with his foot. "Hey, Ned, bring this guy a drink!"

The bartender came over to the table, a complete concession, and plunked down a double scotch on the rocks. "Happy Birthday, Will.

This one's on the house."

"Thanks." Will took the glass and raised it to his friends. "Thank you all." He downed it in one long swallow.

Within an hour, everyone at the table was drunk except Will. He had managed to switch to seltzer after the second drink, and he was bemused by the loud, careless young men and women around him. Angie had squeezed in next to him and was practically sitting in his lap, stroking his chest and arm, breathing in his ear, suggesting he go home with her for a really good birthday present. The only one close to sober was Trey, who had also cut himself off after three or four. And Trey was staring at him across the table as if he were a new exhibit at the zoo.

Will excused himself to the men's room, gesturing for Trey to follow.

"Don't be dumb, man," Trey said, "men don't go to the john in pairs like women!"

"Get up and follow me," Will muttered between clenched teeth, his tone so nasty Trey stood up and complied.

In the hallway outside the restrooms, Will said to Trey, "I appreciate the party, and I appreciate that you drove, but I've had enough and I want to go home. If you're not ready, I'm going to call a cab."

"Go home? It's still early! Oh, I get it! You want to take Angie home. I can lend you my car, buddy, and catch a ride with somebody. I know she's eager, so – "

Will shook his head hard. "No, that's not it. I want to go home alone. I don't want to be with Angie at all. I didn't invite her – haven't called her since I got back."

"Wha- I've seen you in here with her – "

"She turns up. I haven't – you know, been with her – since before I went to Ohio."

"You're finished with her, huh? Ohio chick got to you more than you told me."

Will resisted the impulse to break Trey Sullivan's perfect, preppy nose and confined himself to a nod.

"Okay," Trey agreed. "You go out to the parking lot and I'll make our farewells."

"Thanks. I owe you one."

"You have no idea," Trey said, turning back to the bar.

"SO TELL," TREY ORDERED, SLOUCHING DOWN ON WILL'S BLACK LEATH-er couch and propping his stocking feet on the glass and chrome coffee table. "I don't think you've said sixty words about Ohio since you got back, but obviously something pretty big happened there. I'm tired of waiting for you to spill your guts, so this is the 'one' you owe me."

"You want coffee or soda or anything?" Will asked. "A sandwich?"

"Quit stalling – spill!"

"I have pizza in the freezer – no problem to heat it up."

"Will! Stop being somebody's mother and sit down."

Will gave in, if not gracefully, and plopped down in the matching recliner. Nero immediately came out of hiding and lumbered into Will's lap, causing Will to grunt from the pressure.

"That cat's a monster," Trey said idly. "Big as a mountain lion."

"You ever actually see a mountain lion?" Will asked. "Nero's just an overweight, cantankerous, spoiled brat." He idly ran his fingers over and over down the cat's spine, receiving a rusty purr in return. "So. Ohio. It was – odd."

Trey sat quiet through the recitation of events, drumming his fingers lightly on the cushion next to him until Will finally stopped.

"So you made it up with your father, began a pretty good relation-ship with your stepmother, hung out with your high school buddies and fell in love all over again with the girl."

Will laughed a little. "I guess that about sums it up. Not as excit-ing as flying to Rome to spend the holidays like you did, but it was – it was good."

"I've noticed some changes," Trey said. "Like you're not drinking as much."

"Hang out with Allison very long, and you won't, either. She knows how to put a damper on somebody's drinking."

"She tell you you're an alcoholic or something?"

"No. I just got to thinking – well, she talked about how it's a prob-lem if you use alcohol to medicate your feelings." Will concentrated his vision on the cat, avoiding Trey's eyes.

"Uh-huh. I also notice you're not with Angie anymore. Allison give you a safe-sex lecture, too?"

"No. Cut it out! I can't fool around with Angie when I want to rebuild a relationship with Tracy. That's not right."

"Oh, come on. Tracy's in Africa, man. What she doesn't know won't hurt her."

Will's eyes turned stormy gray, snapped back to Trey's. "That's not the way I want to live my life, Trey. I don't cheat on one woman with another, and I don't see myself going into a relationship lying about who I am and what I'm doing."

"The missionary chick gave you a dose of that old-time religion, didn't she?"

Will stood up, dumping Nero and gaining a snarl for his discourtesy. "I think you'd better go home now, before one of us says something we can't take back. It's late, and we've both had a couple of drinks, so let's just chalk it up to that. I'll call you later in the week."

Trey stood also, sliding his feet into his loafers. "Will, don't forget who your real friends are. I'll see you." He left, shrugging into his coat as he went, leaving Will standing there in the living room.

Who are my real friends? Trey doesn't understand. He thinks women are interchangeable. He wouldn't hit on my woman, but he doesn't see anything wrong with having two women on the string at once and lying to both of them! In fact, he doesn't see anything wrong with lying, period, if it gets you what you need...

Look at you, all alone in this big, empty room. Your 'friends' are all having fun while you stand here pretending to be holier than thou, wishing for things you don't deserve, turning down a chance to have some fun with Angie – what a loser. You might as well have a drink so you can sleep.

WILL WOKE WITH HIS HEAD THROBBING AND THE SENSATION OF POND scum on his teeth. *Note to self: don't drink red wine before bedtime.* He managed to brush his teeth and swallow several ibuprofen without getting sick, and he decided a shower would take care of the rest of his hangover so he would be sharp for his ten o'clock class. He started with cold water, which made every muscle ache and twitch but cleared his head, and then eased his way into warm, which relaxed everything.

Standing in the strong flow from the extremely expensive rainforest shower-head, Will was drifting when he heard the Voice.

You have choices, Will. You can live your life with joy. I love you; I want to be the One in Whom you trust.

"Who – never mind; I know Who." *Or I'm losing my mind. I've never had hallucinations from drinking before, and I didn't drink that much...*

He turned off the water and stepped out of the shower, drying himself on a huge towel as soft as a cloud. "I'm not crazy. I didn't hear anything," he told Nero, being careful in his unclad state to stay back from the cat's claws.

Nero seemed to be laughing as he took a swipe at Will's foot and then sauntered out of the bathroom.

Will, wine is not the answer to your restlessness. Your heart will be restless until it rests in Me.

"Just stop it, okay! I don't need to complicate my life with religion!" He dressed quickly, knotting one of his five classroom ties casually and rolling back the sleeves of his dress shirt. As he looked in the mirror to comb his hair, Will realized the plaid of his shirt echoed the plaids of all the flannel shirts his father and Ed had worn over the years. He had to laugh a little, looking at his father's face as he straightened his tie. *No escaping who we are, is there?*

That's what I've been telling you. You are who you have always been, and you will never change. Don't listen to that voice telling you things can be different. It's a lie.

No, Will. Choose this day Whom you will serve. I love you. It isn't about religion, it's about having a real relationship with Me. I will never, ever leave you or forsake you.

"Enough!" Will almost put his hands over his ears, until he remembered that had never worked before. "Leave me alone, all of you!"

He fled the bedroom to feed the cat and grab a bottle of energy-something-or-other he kept in the refrigerator for need-caffeine emergencies. "See you tonight, cat," he told Nero and kept on fleeing, into the elevator, down to ground, out to his car, away to the university.

AFTER HIS TEN O'CLOCK CLASS, WILL DIDN'T HAVE ANOTHER UNTIL ONE, so he went to the cubbyhole they called his office to get a start on grading the stack of papers his first class had turned in. To his surprise, he found Dean Wilson sitting at his desk.

"Good morning, sir," Will said, hanging up his coat and dropping his computer bag on the floor under it.

"Hello, Will," the dean said. "Sorry to surprise you like this, but something has come up and we need to talk."

Uh-oh. This can't be good. "Certainly, sir." Will sat in the straight chair allocated to his students.

"Will, you're a good teacher, and Iowa's been fortunate to have you on our faculty. You've done a pretty fair job of publishing, too, although we might prefer that some of it had been scholarly research. But we understand the budding author," he chuckled.

"Thank you, Dean Wilson." *Please get to the point!*

"Will, we've been given the word from the state that our budget is going to be cut by a significant number of millions of dollars this year. That means we are going to have to make cuts here at home. The English department is not one of University of Iowa's strongest in terms of numbers, despite the writers' programs, and – well – I'm afraid we're not going to be able to renew your contract in the fall."

Will struggled to stay upright on the chair and to keep his face impassive. "I see."

"Well, no, you probably don't," Dean Wilson said, "but I don't have a lot of options. You don't have seniority, Will, and it's always 'last hired, first fired.' I wish I could keep you, because the students like you and your work is good. But we're laying off a number of good teachers because of these cuts."

"I didn't see it coming," Will said, "but I appreciate your telling me in person."

"I want you to know I'll be glad to give you an excellent letter of recommendation when you apply for another job," the dean said. "As will some of your fellow department members. You shouldn't have any trouble finding work."

"Thank you." *Will you please get out of my office now?*

Alone again, Will hung the 'in conference' sign on the outside of his door and closed the solid wood barrier to ensure his privacy. Sinking into his desk chair, he propped his elbows on the desk and put his head in his hands.

What am I going to do?

"THEY DUMPED YOU?" TREY ASKED, HIS VOICE RISING IN DISBELIEF. HE raised his beer and took a swig. "Just like that?"

Will nodded, toying with his glass. "Just like that. I mean, Dean

Wilson was really nice about it, all compliments about my work and my writing, just one dig about no scholarly publications, but the bottom line is: budget cuts equal layoffs, starting with the most junior faculty."

"Man! What are you going to do?"

"I don't know. Look for another job, obviously. But I – I hadn't imagined I needed to, so I haven't been paying any attention to where they're hiring. I've been at Iowa long enough to get a couple of raises, and chances are nobody will start me at that level. I'll have to move, too."

"This stinks!" Trey said. "Drink up. We'll pretend for tonight that nothing is wrong, and tomorrow you'll figure it all out."

Will pushed the bottom of his glass around the table in squares, dragging it through its own condensation. He had taken the first swallow, but it hadn't tasted good. While he had heard the voice urging him to get blotto and forget everything, it just didn't seem a good idea. He looked up at a commotion near the door to see Nate and Liam and several other faculty members coming in, sounding as if they had already begun the drinking process somewhere else.

Caleb and Andrew were with Nate and Liam, both looking as shell-shocked as Will felt. They fell into chairs and shook their heads. "You, too, Ryersen?" Caleb asked.

"Yeah. Both of you?"

"Us and Liam. Good old Nate, he's still in. I guess the philosophy department needs a gay ethician."

"Come on, Caleb," Andrew said. "He's been here longer than we have."

"Whatever. Where's my beer?" Caleb snarled, just as the harried little waitress came over with a tray full of beers.

They drank for a couple of hours, the newly unemployed growing more and more morose and combative, until even Trey's determined good humor couldn't draw anyone out of it. Will had let his beer get warm and switched quietly to seltzer, not telling anyone there was no vodka in it, and the whole feeling of the place, the people, was beginning to drive him crazy.

We're all supposed to be friends, but look at how we turn on one another. No one is even trying to cheer up anyone else or to talk about where they might find another job. Caleb even said he wouldn't tell if he knew, because he has to look out for number one!

"Hey, Will," Trey said softly, "what-say we get out of here? I didn't lose my job, and even I'm getting depressed."

"Works for me," Will agreed, standing and nodding to the others. "Gotta go, guys. I have early class tomorrow."

"So what?" Andrew asked. "Cut it. What are they going to do – fire you?"

"They're paying me to teach it," Will said, realizing he shouldn't bother trying to reason with a drunk even as the words came out of his mouth. "See you, guys."

Will and Trey left to the jeers of the rest of the group, shrugging on their coats and walking the two blocks to Will's apartment.

"Coming up?" Will asked.

"No, I don't think so," Trey said. "I thought I might just go in to my office tomorrow, maybe even before noon. All these lay-offs are making me nervous. What if dear old Dad should decide to follow suit?"

"You'd just charm him out of it," Will said, smiling at Trey fondly. "Thanks for being a good friend. I appreciate it."

"Aw, shucks," Trey joked, waving his hand over his shoulder as he walked over to the Mustang. "Give me a call – we'll go at it on the court."

Inside the building, the chill of February didn't penetrate. Will hung his coat over his arm and walked up the stairs to his floor, feeling virtuous. Inside, Nero was waiting, making surreal noises to express his displeasure at having been left alone again. The light on the answering machine was blinking, informing him he had three messages.

"Shut up, Nero, so I can listen to these," Will said, punching the button.

All three messages were from Pearl, the first just a "call me" message, the second an expression of concern before the "call me," the third clearly a command. "I'm worried about you and I need for you to call me no matter what time you come in."

"How am I supposed to deal with Psychic Pearl?" he asked Nero. "And don't bother telling me to ignore her call. You want to be woken up at three a.m.? Huh? No, I didn't think so." He put some treats in Nero's bowl and lay down on the couch with the phone.

"Ed, it's Will. No, everything's fine. I'm returning Pearl's call – her three calls, really. I'm sorry it's late; I was out. Yes, I'll wait."

Several moments passed, making Will hope he hadn't wakened Pearl. It was ten-thirty their time; ordinarily she would have been asleep.

"Will?"

"Hi, Grandma. I just got in and found your messages."

"You shouldn't be out so late on a work-night," she scolded and Will grinned in the cozy, street-lit darkness of his apartment.

"Yes, ma'am. You're probably right. I was with some friends. What's got you so concerned?"

The old voice quavered as she said, "I was praying for you, as I always do, and it just – seemed to me you're in some kind of serious trouble. I couldn't get past that, no matter how hard I prayed. What's going on, Will? And don't you dare say 'nothing,' because I know better." The usual starch was back in her tone at the last few words.

"Well," he began, trying but failing to figure a good spin for it, "I had a visit from the dean this morning. It seems my services aren't going to be needed come fall. He fired me." *Man, that sounds awful out loud!*

"I'm so sorry to hear that! Obviously not a man of discernment or good sense."

"Thank you," Will laughed. "No, he's a pretty good guy. There are budget cuts at the state level – that kind of thing. I don't have seniority over anybody – last hired, y'know, so I have to go. A bunch of my friends got the ax, too. 'Nothing personal, we'll give you a great letter of reference,' like that."

"Mm-hmm. And what do you want to do now?"

"Well, I have to finish out my contract, this semester and a couple of courses this summer. Then I'll go to some university that's hiring."

"You think you'll find a job easily? Especially if you wait until August?"

"Oh, no, I didn't mean I wouldn't start looking. I'll begin updating my resume this weekend and looking around for what's open. Maybe I'll apply in Maine or California; I've never been either of those places..."

"You might consider applying closer to home," Pearl said.

"Iowa is my home now, remember?" Will asked, trying to be gentle.

"Will, we are still your home on this earth, right here in northwest Ohio. And you will always have a place here, no matter how much time passes, as long as even one of us is left. This is where your roots are; it does no good to turn your back on that, especially when times are difficult. Don't let anything make you forget who you are and where you come from – promise me!"

"Come on, Grandma, lighten up! I'm okay and everything's going to be all right. I'm sorry you were upset, but I don't think God was telling you I'm in any danger."

"Oh, you don't? And how close are you with God these days, boy? Close enough to read His mind?"

Ouch! Pepper, vinegar, hydrochloric acid! "Come on, I didn't mean any disrespect. I just meant I'm fine."

"I know what you meant," Pearl snapped. "I wish you could understand what I meant. You are – you *are* – in danger, boy. The enemy almost got you once, and he's back for another try. Turn to Jesus, Will. He will defend you and deliver you."

Oh, Grandma, don't go there. I can't bear to think of you dying in a religious dementia.

Long after he had said goodnight to Pearl and hung up the phone, Will continued to lie there on the couch in the half-dark, watching passing headlights make patterns on the brick walls, trying to put her remarks out of his mind. Nero came close to consider jumping up for a warm, soft spot to nap but picked up on Will's discomfort and went away again. The hands of Will's watch relentlessly trekked from hour to hour, bringing morning and reality ever closer, but he wasn't the least bit sleepy.

Jesus, if You are trying to get in touch with me, You need a bigger voice or a sign or something. It just doesn't make sense that You care one way or another. If You did – if You ever had – wouldn't my life have been a lot easier?

"Will, you are a jerk," he said aloud and got up to get ready for bed, even though he knew he wouldn't sleep. No matter. He had a good book...

Chapter 13

"Want to meet me at McClendon's?" Trey asked, his voice fading in and out as he apparently moved from one place to another.

"I don't think so," Will said, holding his phone to his ear as he race-walked across campus to his next class, overcoat flapping in the icy wind. "I have to start saving my pennies. And, no, I'm not going to let you buy every time we go out, even though I know you can afford it. I'm trying to cut back on the booze anyway."

"Okay, then I'll pick up a couple of pizzas and come to your place for dinner."

Will laughed, causing several pretty young coeds to stop and stare at him, dreamy-eyed, though he didn't notice them. "Sure, why not? Thanks!"

As he laid out his notes for class, several of the students came together to his desk, shifting from foot to foot with nervousness, looking at one another to determine the spokesperson for the group. Will looked up at them, surprised.

"What's up?" he asked.

"Mr. Ryersen," the pretty brunette with tortoise-shell glasses frames said, "we heard a – a rumor that you've been – well, I mean – that you won't be back next year. Is that true?"

Wow! How embarrassing is this! And how did the word get out so fast? "Miss Evans, it is true. My contract won't be renewed for next year."

"But why?" a reedy boy with bad acne asked in a nasal whine.

"You're one of the most popular teachers in the department. Everybody says so!"

"Thank you, Mr. Burns. I appreciate that. I'm not the only one being let go, and it's not just the English department. State-level budget cuts. It's happening all over the country, I imagine, because of problems with the economy. I'll be sorry to go; I'll miss it. I'll miss my students." He smiled at the contingent fondly; he really would miss them.

"I was going to sign up for Comp 2 with you!" Miss Evans said, looking as if she might be on the verge of some histrionic tears.

"Fear not!" Will joked, trying to lighten the mood. "Associate professors come and go, but Comp 1 and Comp 2 go on forever."

"We don't have to take this," another boy growled. He was tall and heavily built, but not fat, and his dark hair and unibrow reminded Will uncomfortably of Pete Coombs, the football player who had beaten his father to a pulp. For a moment, he felt the old panic and couldn't remember the youth's name.

Anderson, that's it! "It's time to get started, Mr. Anderson. Comp 1 is still part of the schedule, and we have work to do."

"Yes, sir," Anderson agreed without smoothing out his frown. "But it's true," he told his classmates, including those who had come in and were milling in the background wondering what was going on, "we don't have to take this. We can get up a petition and take it to the dean – even to the president of the university. They can't just fire the best teachers!"

"Please take your seats," Will said, raising his voice to be heard and injecting some of Pearl's starch into it. He had begun to do that when he first started teaching, and it had never failed him. It didn't fail him now.

TREY WAS LYING BACK ON THE COUCH, STOCKING FEET ON THE COFFEE table, a half-finished slice of monster meats pizza on the paper plate balanced on his now slightly rounded belly, a bottle of Sam Adams in his hand. Will had assumed a similar posture in the recliner, but his hand held a glass of milk.

"It just never tastes right," he complained, "no matter what brand I buy. Not even the organic stuff. If there's one thing I miss about the farm, it's real Jersey milk."

"You're disgusting," Trey said idly, following his comment with a small, satisfied belch. "I don't know why that raw milk hasn't killed you."

"Never mind. I'm not going to explain dairy-farming to you again, city-boy." Will took another swallow, shook his head in disgust and put the glass on a coaster on the glass end table next to his chair. "You know, I'm going to hate moving. This has been the greatest apartment."

"Maybe you won't have to. Didn't you say some of your students want to start a campaign to get you rehired?"

"Yes," Will nodded, "but it won't work. It's not me, it's a budget thing."

"They couldn't find enough money by cutting something else to fund your measly little salary?"

"Oh, they probably could, but they won't. There are more than just me, and they can't rehire all of us. No, Trey, it's over. This weekend I spruce up my resume and start applying to other universities."

"Start with Iowa State," Trey advised, half-heartedly taking another mouthful of pizza. "Then you won't be far away."

"Pearl wants me to apply closer to home."

"You are home!" Trey protested. "This has been home for you for years! Don't give up before you've even started, Will. They always want to suck you back into that dead-end, small-town mentality, all church on Sunday and pot-luck suppers at the Grange and marry the farmer's daughter and raise up more little hicks who think dinner at Applebee's and taking the kids to an animated flick is culture."

Will put the pizza plate on the coffee table and stood up. "I'm going to clear this stuff away and make sure Nero can't get at it. Back in a minute."

"Oh, hey, Will, come on," Trey called after him. "I didn't mean any disrespect to your folks."

"It's all right," Will said from the kitchen area. "I know we don't see eye-to-eye about life in Ohio. I'm not planning to go there if I don't have to, except to visit. I'm going to apply to schools in California. Maybe I'll learn to surf."

"Right," Trey laughed, settling down again. "I can see it now!"

I wish I could see it now. I can see the ocean and the mountains and the waves – but darned if I can see myself there. I can't see myself any-

131

where but here.

AS JANUARY TURNED INTO FEBRUARY AND FEBRUARY INTO MARCH AND March into April, Will continued to try to come to grips with reality. He got a haircut and had head-shots taken to accompany his resume where requested. He went over and over that resume to make it as clean and professional and laudatory as possible and had it printed on good-quality (but not extravagant) paper with matching envelopes, even though he found most applications were being done by e-mail. He carefully vetted and then obtained permission from the most impressive list of references he could muster and invested in stamps and an expensive pen. He did his homework via Internet, library reference books and word-of-mouth and sent out numerous applications.

Not many schools were hiring; the falling economy had frozen expansion and fueled downsizing everywhere. Those who were hiring tended to promote from within. One or two who did respond positively turned out to be unacceptable to Will for one reason or another.

He dropped his gym membership, although he was still willing to go once a week as Trey's guest to play racquetball. He informed his landlord he would be unemployed at the end of July; the landlord informed Will he would be looking for Will's replacement.

"Have you thought about a non-teaching job?" Trey asked one fine April evening as they left the gym together.

"No. What would I do? I've never had any other kind of job – not counting the work on the farm, which I don't want to do again ever."

"Well, I talked to my dad," Trey said, "and I think he'd consider finding something for you. I mean, you have a degree and you're good with words and all – I don't know what, but there must be something..."

Will was suddenly grateful for the encroaching dark, which hid the tears welling in his eyes. "Thanks. You're a real friend. But, no, I still have time."

"Whatever. The offer's there any time if you need it."

Dear Will, Happy Easter! We are praising the Lord that Christ has died, Christ is risen and Christ will come again! My coworker Sally (actually Sister Sally, a nursing nun whose order runs this hospital) put on a puppet show about the crucifixion and resurrection which was fascinating to children and adults, too. I don't know how much they really understood, though…

We are overwhelmed with HIV patients and tuberculosis patients in addition to our usual load of parasites and malaria and things like that. Babies die of diarrhea here unless their mothers can get them to us in time to give them fluids i.v. Sometimes the mothers and all their children have to walk for days to get here.

Forgive me for sounding gloomy! I really am praising the Lord for His goodness. I'm just so tired…

Well, anyway, I hope things are going really well for you. We'll have to catch up this summer.

God bless you and keep you, Will.

Love – Tracy

Dear Will,

You havn 't called for a long time. I hope you are ok, are you? We are fine. Your dad is fine. Ant Allsion is fine. Daddy gave me a puppy for my birthday, it is a boy named Flash all mixed up colors but not a beegl he has long legs. He learned not to pee in the house, mostly so he gets to sleep in my room sometimes. I let him on the bed if Daddy dosent catch me. I am still praying for you every night so Jesus will save you. But you have to let him do it. I hope you will come visit again soon and I will pray for you like pastor Miles does, with his hands.

Love, Grace

Dear Will,

As you can see, Gracie has sent you a letter to encourage you toward salvation. The child is wise, if not yet well-versed in spelling and sentence-structure. I am praying for you also, that the enemy will not snatch you out of the Lord's hand because of your willfulness.

We are getting along well enough here. The new arrangements seem to work. Cassie Anderson is a competent, quiet young woman and little Micah is a delight. He reminds us all of David, and thus of Carolyn, but day by day the pain is lessening. John is beginning to be himself again, and Gracie's occasional tantrums have passed.

Your father is still not entirely comfortable with his increased responsibilities on the farm. He has no problem with the work, of course; his difficulty seems to be with the title. John thinks this, too, shall pass. Allison is well, working quite a few hours, taking time to do girl-things with Grace. Ed and I are sitting and rocking more, but not necessarily enjoying it more. It is hard to accept the diminishing of one's usefulness.

Do you think you will be able to visit during the summer? I am ashamed to nag, but I feel "time's winged chariot drawing near." I would not want to go without seeing you again.

God bless you, dear Will, and keep you safe.

With love – Grandma

"THEY'RE REALLY LAYING IT ON THICK!" TREY SAID FROM HIS USUAL position on Will's couch. Will fancied the cushion had begun to conform to the shape of Trey's backside.

"Yes, they are. Thing is, I know they haven't conspired. It's like Grandma has this vision of the future or something. And Tracy's half a world away, not talking with my family."

"So what are you going to do?"

"I don't know," Will admitted. "It's not like I have any job prospects, even though I've sent out dozens of applications, on line and by snail-mail. Nobody wants me in academia, but they seem to want me in farm country. I could probably get a factory job; there's a General Motors plant near there."

"You have got to be kidding! Factory work?!"

Will shook his head. "I know – not my kind of thing. But neither is the farm. I can't just go back to Ohio and live off my dad like a leech."

"How long before you have to be out of here?"

"End of August. I can cover the rent until then, and surely something will turn up. I had a couple of really sincere 'if anything opens up, we'll call you' interviews."

"Listen, if for some reason nothing opens up by then, two things: you can move in with me and stay as long as you want. I don't pay rent anyway; Dad owns the building. And I'll talk to him any time you want about a job with us."

"What's today – the fifteenth of June? Summer school is over for me mid-July. If nothing turns up by then, I'll think about asking your father for something."

Trey sat up and looked straight at Will, the lazy comfort gone from his eyes and posture. "There's one more thing..."

"What?"

"You talk sometimes about wanting to be a writer. I mean, you write poems and stories and you took the MFA in fiction, right? What if you just ditched the teaching idea and wrote the Great American Novel instead?"

Will burst out laughing, snorting soda up his nose and driving Nero under the couch, where he bit the back of Will's heel right at the Achilles tendon and peevishly meowed his displeasure with startles and soda-showers.

"Ouch, cat! Oh, man, that hurts!" Will blew his nose into Trey's proffered wad of tissues and raised his feet to the coffee table to avoid a repeat attack. "Sullivan, you are officially crazy. I'm not a novelist, and even if I were, something has to pay the rent and put beer on the table while I'm writing."

"That could be arranged," Trey said, and he wasn't laughing.

"Thank you," Will replied, "but I don't see that as a viable alternative right now. I know you could afford it, and I might be able to get used to being a kept man, but there's no book in me screaming to get out – not yet, anyway. I haven't written anything since last spring. No, it'll have to be something less glamorous. But I do thank you."

"I know when I'm licked," Trey conceded. "But I still believe someday I'm going to be standing in your autograph line in Barnes&Noble."

Dear Will,

I am coming home! By the time you get this letter I will probably be on my way! I told our team leaders this was my last trip, that I am not going to continue on the mission field. When my plane touches down at Detroit airport, that's my last international flight for a long, long time.

I will miss Malawi, especially the dear people here, but I have real peace of soul about my decision. Whatever the Lord has next for me, it won't be overseas. (I know – never say never, never say something couldn't happen! But He told me Himself I'm to go home and work there.)

Please, if you are praying these days, say a prayer for me as I head home. I had a touch of malaria and don't feel the greatest – and it's a thirty-hour flight!

See you soon – Tracy

EVERYONE CAME TO HELP WILL PACK, EVEN NATE AND STEVE AND Liam. Only Angie was conspicuously absent. The beer flowed freely and boxes of pizza and cartons of Thai take-out littered the kitchen area. Putting everything into the storage pod took only an hour or so after it was all packed into cartons. Will was not surprised to note the majority of the cartons were books. Nor was he surprised to hear the complaints of the men who were hauling them from the freight elevator to the pod. He had ordered the smallest pod, because all his worldly goods made a surprisingly small pile.

"What's the deal?" Nate asked as they stood side by side directing the loading of the pod.

"No deal," Will answered. "Just getting the apartment ready for the next guy."

"But Trey said you didn't have to get out until the end of August. That's six weeks yet!"

"I know." Will sighed. "It just doesn't make any sense to hang on here when nothing is breaking for me. I'm going home."

"This is home!" Nate insisted. "I know Trey would let you stay there; he's said as much. Or you could move in with Liam and his girl, or with Angie – I bet she'd take you back in a heartbeat! You could even have the spare room at my place. Steve and I wouldn't mind... No, I guess you would mind. Homophobe." He said it teasingly, none of the sarcasm which usually marked his speech to Will. "I actually am going to miss you, Ryersen. Who'm I going to tease?"

Will gave a bark of laughter. "I have no doubt you'll find somebody. Thanks for the offer, Nate. I really need to go home. They need me there."

Nate snorted his disapproval. "They want to turn you into a Jesus-freak, you know they do. They want you to give up drinking and women and parties and – " He took a deep breath and finished, " – and gay friends."

"Yeah, and I have to shave my head and get a swastika tattoo, too. I'll trade in the Honda for a pick-up like my dad's and put a shotgun in the gun rack on the back window. If you come to town to visit me, Nate, leave Steve here and put on a macho disguise, okay?"

"Good to see you boys making nice, now that there's no future in it," Steve tossed over his shoulder as he handed a box of books to Liam, who was stacking inside the pod.

"Oh, you know how it is," Nate replied, grinning at Will. "He's had a crush on me forever and just now realized how much he's going to miss me."

"In your dreams!" Will scoffed, then blushed deeply. "No, no, scratch that idea!"

"You just remember when the Christians are trying to brainwash you that you have all kinds of friends back here who don't try to manipulate your mind beyond who's buying the next beer. Don't let them get to you," Nate said.

Chapter 14

"This probably isn't exactly what you had in mind, is it?" John asked as he and Will watched the movers unload the contents of the pod into the equipment barn. "But we're glad to store your boxes as long as you need. I'll have Matthew pick up a couple of boxes of mothballs."

"Mothballs?"

"Put them around the boxes and it keeps away mice," John said. "Since Celeste died, years ago, we've never had as good a barn cat, although I think they're all her descendants."

"Okay, mothballs it is. No, this isn't when I thought was going to be my life at this point, but I'm grateful to have a place to come until something happens. And I promise I'm not going to sit around drinking coffee and sponging off you and Dad."

John laughed gently and said, "Never crossed my mind, certainly never crossed Matthew's. You only have to watch the nightly news to see how tough things are all over the country. The unemployment rate in Fulton County has more than doubled. Quite a few of the little factories are closing, and even the bigger ones have had layoffs. We can keep you busy until you find something, if you want."

I sure hope I find something else to do! Will thought. *I do not want to 'keep busy' with farm chores!*

"Welcome home!" Ed called, walking toward them from the house as Will was signing off on his delivery.

"Thanks. It's good to be here."

"Yep. Where you staying?"

"I think I'm staying with Dad and Allison."

"That makes sense," John said, "but you know you're welcome to stay at the house if you want to. Gracie would love it."

"Yep," Ed said again, "be that much closer to her project."

Will shifted uncomfortably from foot to foot and could feel the heat creeping up his neck. "John, is there any way you can get Gracie to back off a little? I'm really not comfortable with being her 'project.'"

"I can try," John said, "but, frankly – I don't think it's going to work. That one has the gift of evangelism for sure."

"You look kind of proud of that," Will said, and John didn't deny it.

"Since you're here," he said, "why don't you come on up to the house for lunch? Cassie always makes more than enough. And Pearl's here. You haven't seen her yet."

"I just got here two hours ago!" Will said, following Ed and John to the house. "But lunch seems like a good idea."

Cassie quickly added another place at the table and filled a plate with some kind of hamburger/macaroni casserole and three bean salad.

"Where's Grandma?" Will asked, sitting down to his full plate and accepting a large glass of milk from Cassie.

"She's lying down in the living room," Cassie said. "She was really tired. I looked in on her, but she was sleeping. I thought I'd just let her sleep and give her lunch when she wakes up."

"Is she all right?" Will asked. He had never heard of Pearl's lying down during the day.

"She's fine," John said. "Just wearing down. She naps most afternoons now, sometimes on the couch, sometimes at home. It revs her up to ride herd on us the rest of the time."

"Ain't that the truth!" Ed laughed. "How about blessing this food so we can eat?"

John bowed his head and the others, even Will, followed. "Lord, we give You thanks for this day and all the good things in it. We thank You that Pearl is still with us, and we thank You for Will's safe return to us. Bless him, Father, and help him to find the work You have for him. Thank you for Cassie and her many gifts, which she uses to help us and to glorify You. Bless this food to strengthen us to do Your will, we ask in Jesus' name, Amen."

He's so sincere. I'll bet John's never had a doubt in his life. It must be nice to have that kind of faith...

"IT OCCURRED TO ME," ALLISON BEGAN LATER THAT EVENING, AS WILL was helping her with the dinner dishes, "that you might not be comfortable in the red room for the duration. If you'd prefer the other bedroom, we can move the desk and things out of there and put in a bed. I just use it for a semi-office-slash-storage-room right now."

"Thanks. It's good of you to offer. I'll be fine in the red room for the time being, although I do admit it took some getting used to the first time."

"I also know you can have Matthew's old room at the farmhouse if you prefer." She didn't look at Will as she said it, suggesting to him that she hoped he would not prefer it.

And, in fact, he didn't. "I like being here with you and Dad," he confessed. "But I want you to tell me if it gets too crowded."

"I promise you I would," Allison said, looking at him now, "but I don't imagine that's going to happen, since you aren't messy. It's almost unnatural, how tidy you are."

"I guess when I was a kid my space was the only thing I could control – something like that."

"Well, whatever, it works for me! I'm going to a meeting tonight, and it's open. Want to come?"

"Oh. Um. Maybe. What about Dad?"

"Dad," Matthew said from the living room, "mostly doesn't go to meetings. I'll be fine here if you want to tag along."

"Well... maybe another time, Allison, okay?"

"Absolutely!" She drained the sink and hung up the dishcloth. "Thanks for your help here. I'll go get ready."

Before Will could blink, she had disappeared into the bathroom, emerging only a couple of minutes later with a fresh coat of lipstick and evidence of a brush having been applied to her hair. She bent down to kiss Matthew full on the mouth and said, "I love you! I'll be back by eleven or else I'll call, okay?"

"Sure," Matthew agreed. "Will and I will amuse ourselves for a bit before I turn in."

"She's a real whirlwind, isn't she?" Will remarked as the door slammed behind her.

"Reminds me of a hummingbird when she isn't reminding me of a little dragon," Matthew said. "She has more energy than any three or four other people I know." He paused, eying Will for a moment. "Would you like to sit down and talk, Son? Or would you rather do something else?"

Will perched on the other end of the couch, not settling in. "I do want to call Tracy," he said, "but there's time to talk if you want to."

"No big thing," Matthew said. "I just want you to know how glad I am you're here. I know you don't think of this as home anymore, but maybe it will be again after some time. I'm sorry about your job, but I'm not sorry you came back."

"Thanks. I – I hope I'm not going to be a burden or a bother to you and Allison."

"Not at all! We're not rich folks, like Tracy's, but we have more than enough to take you in and feed you and clothe you. Now hold on, I see that look coming, but what I mean is you're going to need more jeans and tee-shirts and flannel shirts to hang around here. Those professor clothes won't stand up to the summer or the winter or the work around here."

Will looked down at his expensive chinos and dress button-down shirt and laughed. "I guess you're right. But, Dad, I have enough money to buy my own jeans and blue bandanas and help out with the groceries. When I got the news last spring, I started saving instead of spending. You don't have to worry about me financially."

"How do I have to worry about you?"

"No! That's not what I meant!"

"Will. You didn't answer the question." Matthew's quiet voice and direct look were making Will squirm more and more. "I know you're not all right," Matthew said. "I see it in your eyes. If it isn't money, if it isn't about finding a job, then it's still something. I hope you'll come to trust me enough to tell me, so I can help you."

Everybody in this family has developed x-ray vision! What am I supposed to say? 'Hey, Dad, I'm scared about what's going to become of all my dreams. Hey, Dad, I'm scared about the day I run into Pete Coombs or Chance Rupp on the street in Lewiston. Hey, Dad, I keep hearing voices and I think I'm schizophrenic.'

"You worry too much," Will finally said. "I'm fine. I can handle it.

I really am grateful to you for taking me in, and I'll do my best to pull my weight. Now I think I'll go call Tracy."

WILL RETREATED TO HIS ROOM AND USED HIS CELL PHONE TO CALL TRACY, feeling just a little bit sleazy calling her while lying on his black and gold satin bedspread in his red room. Her mother went to call her to the phone, and quite a few minutes passed before she answered, minutes he used to imagine her face, to imagine what she might say, to imagine getting together with her...

"Hi, sorry I took so long to get to the phone," she said, her voice a little breathless.

"No problem. I've just been home since this morning, but I didn't want to go to bed without talking with you. How are you?"

"Oh... fine. You?"

"I'm fine. Tired from the drive and the unloading and unpacking, but – fine."

"That's good..."

Something wasn't right. He could tell by the griping in his stomach and the hair on the back of his neck. "Tracy? What's the matter?"

"Matter? Nothing. I'm glad you're home, Will."

"So can I come over and say hello in person?"

"Now?"

"Well – yes. It's only eight o'clock. I've missed you – it's been a long time since New Year's Eve."

"You're right; it has. I'd love to see you, Will, but I just... can't tonight. I'm sorry. Maybe I can do it tomorrow."

"Are you going to tell me what's wrong? And don't bother saying 'nothing,' because I can feel it and I can hear it in your voice." He was sitting up now, working his feet back into his loafers.

Tracy's sigh broke over him like an errant north wind. "I'm not trying to lie to you," she said. "I'm just a little under the weather, and I'm really tired."

"You don't sound like you have a cold. What is it?"

"Well... honestly... I had malaria shortly before I came home, and it was a pretty severe case. I'm just not completely over it yet."

"That's really serious, isn't it!" He was reaching for his keys from their place on the dresser-top.

"Will, take a deep breath. Yes, it's sometimes very serious, especially for Westerners like me. I took my medicine, but you can get it anyway. And some strains are more dangerous than others. The one I had this time – "

"This time!"

"I've had it before, but it wasn't this strain. Almost everybody who works a lot in Africa gets it at least once. Anyway, this time it affected my liver. Now before you panic, let me tell you everything is clearing up and I'm going to be fine. But I'm kind of yellow and run down and skinny and I need to sleep a lot."

"I'm on my way," Will said, "so don't go back to bed until I get there." He disconnected and stepped into the living room. "Dad, I'm on my way to Tracy's."

"Okay," Matthew said, "we'll leave the front door unlocked."

Tucker didn't put in an appearance as Will hurried to his car and sped out of the driveway, but Will saw the big black dog loping down the road toward home as he drove toward Tracy's house.

"Dumb dog," he muttered. "Go home and stay off the road. Dad and Allison would have a fit if anything happened to you. Not that I care about you."

Within a mile of the Showalters' house Will saw the flashing lights coming up in his rearview mirror and made some remarks his Christian father would not have sanctioned. He pulled over, took his wallet out of his back pocket and put down his window. The sheriff's deputy came warily up to the car, flashlight in hand, other hand on the butt of his weapon.

"You know how fast you were going?" the officer said.

"No, sir, I don't," Will replied truthfully. "I'm in kind of a hurry, and I guess I just didn't pay any attention."

"May I see your license and registration, please?" the officer asked, holding out his hand.

Will carefully removed the information from his wallet in full view of the deputy and handed it over. The man scrutinized everything carefully and did a visual once-over of Will and the car.

"Have you had anything to drink tonight, sir?"

"Only milk," Will replied.

"You're from Iowa? You're a long way from home."

"I've lived in Iowa for a while," Will said, "but this is my home. I just came back today, but I'll be staying with my dad." He gave

Matthew's name and address and added, "Dad works as farm manager for John Abbott."

The officer's face immediately changed from xenophobic suspicion to smiles and welcome. "I know John – went to school with his wife. Sad, sad thing, her dying like that. I need you to stay in the car while I run your plates and things, but it won't take long."

"I really am in a hurry. Can't you just write the ticket and let me go?"

The suspicion returned to the deputy's face. "What's your hurry?"

"I'm on my way to see my – my friend who's sick. I'm really worried about her because she has malaria. She's just home from Africa, and – "

"Oh, you mean the Showalter girl!"

"Yes, sir."

Suddenly busy with his pen, the deputy didn't bother to look at Will as he said, "I'm just going to give you a warning. Take it easy; these country roads fool you city slickers every time, and you can't ever tell what idiot's coming around the next curve." He handed the ticket and Will's papers back to him. "Have a good evening, Mr. Ryersen, and be careful."

Will pulled slowly and carefully back onto the road and drove two miles under the speed limit until the deputy's taillights disappeared from his rearview mirror. He knew there was only one deputy on patrol for this half of the county, and he was headed in the opposite direction. Will made up time until he pulled up in front of the Showalters' house.

Tracy's mother answered the door, immaculately groomed as always, a decided frown on her face. "Well, I guess you might as well come in. I couldn't talk Tracy out of seeing you tonight. But listen to me, Will. She's a sick girl and needs her rest. Say hello and go home."

I am not sixteen. I am not sixteen. "Thank you, Mrs. Showalter." He stepped past her and caught a glimpse of Tracy lying on the living room couch. She sat up slowly as he entered the room, and Will's heart jumped in his throat, both from the joy of seeing her again and from the fear her appearance shot through him.

"I know," Tracy said, smiling. "I told you I looked awful. But you have to trust me – this isn't as bad as it looks. I'm much better now; my liver enzymes are almost back to normal. It just takes time for the jaundice to disappear from the skin, honestly."

Will sat down beside her on the couch and took her gently into his arms. She was skin and bones. "Oh, Tracy, what have they done to you!" He felt like crying but squelched that impulse lest it frighten her.

"In another week – two, tops – I'll be fine, I promise! You know what I want to do then?"

"What?"

"I want to go to the fair. Do you know how long ago we went to the fair the first time? I want to go with Kevin and Susan and Travis and Julie just like old times."

Yes, I remember. I thought my world had ended when I saw Dad and Allison there together, his arm around her, in front of all my friends. That was the same time all the other trouble started. No, Tracy, those aren't good memories for me!

"I know what you're thinking," she said, snuggling up to him, "but for me that day was so much fun. And I think we could have a sort of do-over, so it could be fun for you, too, from now on. Please at least think about it."

"If you want to do that, I promise we will," he said helplessly. "Just do whatever you need to do to get well. Please, Tracy. I don't know what I'd do if anything – "

She drew his head down to her shoulder and stroked his hair for a moment. "It's going to be all right, Will. Just trust the Lord and let Him take care of everything."

If only. Why did You let this happen to her in the first place?

"WHY DID HE LET THIS HAPPEN TO HER IN THE FIRST PLACE!" WILL SAID.

"I think," Matthew answered slowly, studying his fingernails, "I think God was there to save her from dying, to get her the help she needs. My understanding is that way back when Adam and Eve sinned, the perfect world God intended for us was broken, so we have sin and crime and illness and accidents and death as the consequence of that sin. It's the new natural way of things. Sometimes God does intervene, but most of the time He seems to let things unfold naturally. I don't know why. You can check with John or Pastor Miles, but I don't think they know why, either. God's too much for us to understand."

"That's handy, isn't it?"

"Not at all!"

"When I went to treatment," Allison said, "that was my biggest question: if there was a God, how could He allow babies to die and bad things to happen?"

"They have the answer in treatment?"

"No, they don't, not any more than anybody else does. What they did have was the Serenity Prayer. You know: 'God grant me the serenity to accept the things I cannot change, courage to change the things I can, and wisdom to know the difference.' I learned to use it in most situations, and it really does help."

"Works for non-alcoholics, too," Matthew said. "I've learned to use it myself. You could try it."

"Thanks," Will said, his mouth twisted as if he had bitten into a lime. He walked out of the room and they heard his bedroom door close emphatically.

"Oh, I can't wait!" Allison told her husband.

"For what?"

"For the moment when that boy surrenders to the God of his understanding and finds the peace that's in store for him!"

"I love you so much," Matthew said, pulling his little princess onto his lap for a kiss.

Will threw back the spread and lay down on the blanket underneath, leaving his shoes on the floor. He could hear his father and step-mother talking and laughing in the living room and could imagine they had their arms around each other. He was no longer embarrassed or disturbed by the way they were always touching or at least clearly on each other's radar; he was just longing for that kind of closeness for himself.

My father is a lot like John these days, but Allison – she's newer, not as churchy. But she does have faith, that's obvious.

This is how it happens. This is how they suck you in. Remember what Trey and Nate and Liam told you before you left home. Don't fall for this. They are not your friends; they are only trying to enslave you to a false religion which destroys your free will and brainwashes you. Even the woman wants to trap you. Be a man; don't fall for their illogical fallacies.

Will pulled out his phone and pushed Trey's number, which was 1 on his speed-dial. The phone rang several times before Trey answered, and when he did, Will could hear the sounds of laughter and clinking glass in the background.

"Will, my man! How are you?"

"Hey, Trey! Good. Just wanted to hear your voice."

As they talked Will relaxed and let himself be transported back to McClendon's and the carefree times they had all had there. He remembered the laughter and camaraderie, the hot slide of scotch down his throat and the rising foam of beer in his nostrils, the pretty girls looking for a good time, Angie...

Wow! I haven't thought of her since I've been home. "How's Angie?" he asked.

"Didn't expect that from you," Trey said, surprise evident in his voice. "She's great – looking fantastic. Had some highlights put in her hair and got herself a tattoo right where you can't overlook it. Missing her?"

"No, just wondering. I do miss you a little – haven't found anybody to play racquetball with, or any place to play it."

"You need to think about coming home, man. My offer of the apartment still stands, and I know dear old Dad will make a place for you. He told me so."

Will hung up feeling more dissatisfied than he had when he placed the call. He was bored. He was antsy. He wanted to be with Tracy, but she was still recuperating and not doing anything else. Talking with her on the phone for a few minutes didn't satisfy the need for her at all.

That would be so – So what? Good? Fun? It'd be easier than here in a lot of ways. Trey can afford to let me live there for free, and I could do stuff for him in return. I could see old friends and relax at McClendon's instead of sitting around the living room with my old man and his wife talking religion.

Chapter 15

DESPITE WARNINGS ABOUT THE STATE OF THE ECONOMY IN Ohio, Will had gone at the job search with the same methodical drive he had used in Iowa – and with the same results. The colleges and universities in northwest Ohio and southeast Michigan simply were not hiring. Period. Every door he tried to open crashed shut in his face. His meager savings account was growing increasingly sparse, and he dreaded the day he would have to ask his father for gas money. He saw Tracy for a few minutes on Tuesday and Thursday afternoons, his time monitored by her mother, and sat with her in church on Sundays, defiantly holding her hand, escorting her to her parents' car at the end of the service. Only their phone conversations were keeping him sane.

ANOTHER SUNDAY DINNER AT THE ABBOTTS', AND WILL DREADED IT. He walked in behind Matthew and Allison, bracing himself for the attack, which was only seconds in coming. Gracie ran to him, her feet tangling with the big puppy feet of Flash, and threw herself at him, yelling, "Will!"

Experienced by the past few weeks, Will kept his balance and tossed the girl into the air before setting her back on her feet. "Hi, Gracie. Yeah, hi to you, too, Flash," he said, removing the dog's teeth from his pants leg. Flash had a long way to go to the maturity of

Tucker – well, one could only hope, to more maturity than Tucker...

"I'm so glad you came!" Gracie told him, tugging him into the dining room, where the whole family, Seibeneks included, was gathered. "You're going to sit by me again, isn't that great?"

"Yes, ma'am, it is," he told her gravely, not allowing either his amusement or his despair to show. "But what about Flash?"

"Oh, he doesn't get to sit at the table, silly! I have to put him outside while we eat. Come on, Flash!" She led the large dog out through the kitchen door and Will heard the back door open and close. Flash wasn't trained for much yet, and he couldn't be trusted outside without being on a lead or in a pen.

"How goes the job hunt?" Ted asked, settling into his chair and grinning at Will.

"I wish I could report something different from last week and the week before," Will said, sitting opposite him. "Not a nibble."

"So many people laid off all over the place," Livvie said, putting a huge bowl of mashed potatoes on the table. "I hear it's even worse in the surrounding counties."

"You'd think higher education wouldn't ever go under," Cassie said, placing a large platter of pork chops in front of John. "I mean, how do they expect anyone to find a job if they don't have a good education?"

"That's a good point," Livvie agreed. "It used to be you could do most anything if you had a high school diploma, then it was a bachelor's degree. Now it's a master's degree or a Ph.D. Allie, you can put that applesauce right here, and, Matthew, put the salad over there by Will."

"I *have* a good degree," Will said, hoping he didn't sound as peevish as he felt. "It's just that nobody has a place for me to use it."

"I'm hungry," Micah whined, diverting everyone's attention, for which Will was grateful.

"I heard from Mr. Stemwalter," Pearl said, "that Mollie Rupp is having some trouble with her pregnancy and won't be able to start the year as they had planned."

"Oh, that's too bad!" Allison said, her sympathies immediately engaged by the idea of pregnancy and babies.

"What are they going to do instead?" Livvie asked.

"Mr. Stemwalter said they don't know yet," Pearl answered. Her sharp, dark eyes fixed on Will. "Do you know who David Stemwalter is?" she asked him.

"Uh – no."

Pearl said, "He is the principal of Infinity High School, and I had him in class years ago. He goes to our church, too."

"O-kay..."

"And Mollie Rupp teaches English at Infinity," Livvie said, light dawning across her face.

Will's collar suddenly felt tight, even though it was unbuttoned and open across his throat. *Oh, no, no, no. Not high school. I'm a college professor. Well, associate professor, but even so –*

"You teach English," Allison said, her face also lighting up, "so you could apply for Mollie's job! That would be perfect! Infinity isn't that far from Lewiston."

"Thanks for thinking of me," Will said, trying not to choke on his words, "but I'm not a high school teacher. You have to be certified, state-certified, to do that."

"In Ohio, you can teach high school on an emergency license for a year," Pearl said, turning the full force of that dark-eyed stare on Will.

"I think that's probably enough said for now," John said. "Let's change the subject and let everyone enjoy their dinner."

Will gave John a grateful nod, but he could hardly get a bite past the lump in his throat. His hands were so sweaty he had to wipe them on his napkin in order to hang on to the fork.

High school! There's a come-down! And remember how much fun you had in high school; wouldn't it be jolly to go back into that situation!

"JUST SO YOU KNOW," MATTHEW SAID LATER, WHEN THEY WERE HOME again and walking Tucker down the road, "Mollie Rupp is married to Chance Rupp and they live in Infinity. I'm just letting you know in case you might want to consider that job and might go over there. I'd hate for you to run into Chance unprepared."

Despite the mid-August midday heat, which rose in little waves from the blacktop, Will felt a shiver go all the way through him. "Thank you for telling me," he said. "One more reason not to consider that job."

"Oh, I don't know," Matthew said. "It'd probably be a pretty good job."

"I'm sure it would – for the right person. Tucker, get out of that! What's he got?"

"Dead something," Matthew said and whistled a loud blast. The dog dropped the item and raced to Matthew's side. "Heel," Matthew told him.

"I forget sometimes how gross dogs are," Will laughed.

"True," his father agreed. "So, anyway, you might give Mr. Stemwalter a call and just find out about the job."

"Dad, please – don't. I'm not interested in teaching high school."

Matthew gave his son a leveling look. "You know, Will, sometimes beggars can't be choosers. I remember the year before I got here, when I didn't have a dime or anything except the clothes on my back, when I was hungry enough I'd take any dirty job somebody offered, just like the prodigal son in the Bible. I didn't like cleaning up after hogs, but they paid me to do it and I ate."

"I'd maybe rather work with hogs than teenagers," Will said, but without much conviction. "I'll think about it, okay?"

A COUPLE OF DAYS LATER, AS HE WAS RELUCTANTLY HELPING MATTHEW muck out the barn, Will's phone rang. He leaned the pitchfork against the wheelbarrow and looked at the caller i.d. Tracy!

"I couldn't wait to call you!" she said. "I went to the doctor this morning, and guess what!"

"What?"

"All my blood work is perfect! I'm officially healed, even my liver! Oh, I knew all those prayers would do the trick. Will? Are you there?"

"I'm here. That's the best news ever! Does that mean your mother has to let you off the leash and I could maybe take you out to celebrate?"

"That's exactly what it means! I hear there's a new Mexican place over in Infinity that has wonderful food. Could we go there? I've been on low-fat this and bland that for so long I could scream."

"Anywhere you want. Whenever you want," he assured her.

AT THE LAST MINUTE, TRACY HAD TEXTED WILL TO PICK HER UP HALF an hour later, so by the time he reached the Showalters' house he was twitchier than a Taser victim. Before he could even get out of the car, she was running down the steps, full of energy and light.

Oh, Tracy, I love you!

"Let's make a quick getaway," she giggled, climbing into the car. "My mother is sure the doctor was too lenient and she wants to tell you to take me to the Dairy Queen and bring me right back."

"Is she right?" Will asked, looking at her anxiously. "Are you sure you're up for this?"

"Drive," she commanded. "I'm fine. Do I look sick anymore?"

He was prepared to lie, but it wasn't necessary. "You look beautiful," he told her, taking in her shiny hair, clear skin and green, green eyes, made greener by the deep purple tee-shirt she had tucked into white Capri pants.

When they pulled into the parking lot of Los Gallos, Will looked her over again. "You are probably the most beautiful woman in Ohio, if not in the continental U.S. I'm so lucky to be here with you."

"You are slick with words, aren't you, Professor?" she teased. "Now please feed me. My parents have been raving about this place."

They stood on the sidewalk inspecting the façade of the building, and Will wondered that Mr. Showalter would ever set foot in the place. The chipped paint over brick was so neutral it seemed to disappear in the encroaching twilight, and the sign over the door was obviously hand-painted, featuring three black-feathered, red-beaked, spurred roosters and the poorly scripted 'Los Gallos.'

"I know it looks like a hole in the wall," Tracy said, "but I'm sure the food will be wonderful!"

"I think you're an incurable optimist," Will grumbled, following her inside.

Although they had arrived well past the standard northwest Ohio dinner hour, the restaurant was packed. Wait staff dressed in stereotypical black pants and camisas threaded their way among crowded tables bearing huge trays of colorful food redolent of chiles, cinnamon, cumin and cilantro. A pretty girl whose long black hair hung down her back in a thick braid led them to a table in the back and supplied them with menus, fried tortilla chips and salsa.

Will was reaching for a chip when he noticed Tracy had folded her hands and bowed her head. *Nuts. In public.*

"Would you like me to pray?" she asked when he didn't say anything.

"I guess so."

Will bowed his head, hoping not everyone in the place was watching – or listening, as Tracy invoked a blessing on the food and their time together. He managed to give her an 'amen.'

"I have died and gone to heaven," Tracy groaned around a chip loaded with salsa.

"I may die," Will responded, "if I take a second bite of that salsa."

"Don't drink water!" Tracy warned him. "Just eat some of the chips plain. Water spreads the fire. When the waitress comes, order a glass of milk."

Although the waitress couldn't help laughing, Will forgave her when she returned at speed with a tall glass of milk and then pointed out milder options on the menu. They managed to eat without further incident, and they were agreed that Tracy's father and mother hadn't exaggerated.

"Oh, look," Tracy said suddenly, pointing over Will's shoulder. "It's Mr. Stemwalter and his wife."

"Who?"

"Mr. and Mrs. Stemwalter, from church. You've probably never met them."

Will turned in his chair to watch as the couple approached them, trying to place both the faces and the name, which was familiar. The man was tall and solidly built and had the most outrageous comb-over Will had ever seen. When Tracy introduced them, the man shook Will's hand firmly.

"I think I've heard your name," he said, "but I don't think we've met. I'm the principal of Infinity High School."

Will thought he did a really good job of covering his rush of feelings.

"Will's a professor of English," Tracy bragged. "He taught at the University of Iowa, but now he's back home."

"Really. Where are you teaching now?" Mr. Stemwalter asked.

"I – uh – don't have a new position yet," Will said. "Still looking."

"Mm-hmm. Trouble in Iowa?"

"David!" Mrs. Stemwalter said, flushing.

"No, sir," Will said, gritting his teeth. "Budget cuts."

"I heard Mollie Rupp isn't going to be able to take her classes this year," Tracy said. "If you haven't filled her position, you should hire

Will. American Literature is his specialty."

Mr. Stemwalter's eyes widened a fraction as he looked at Will with a new perspective. "That what you were teaching in Iowa?"

"No, I had sections of Comp 1 and Comp 2. I was sort of in line to teach classes in modern American poetry."

"Well," Mr. Stemwalter said, "if you're interested, shoot me a resume. School starts at the end of the month."

Will was about to say loud and clear that he didn't want to teach high school, but he received a sharp kick from Tracy before he could open his mouth.

"Thank you," Tracy said. "See you both on Sunday."

"What do you think you're doing?" Will asked when they were alone again.

"I'm looking out for you," she said. "You know, whenever God closes a door, he opens a window."

"That's *Sound of Music*, not the Bible," Will snarled. "I can find my own job, thank you."

"I'm sorry," she said, bowing her head and looking miserable, "I won't interfere again. I just so want for you to find a way to stay here."

THE ANGER WILL FELT AT TRACY'S INTERFERENCE DIDN'T LAST THROUGH dessert, a creamy flan that struck both of them speechless for a while. Will was glad to focus on the food rather than to try to speak while he was cursing inside, but that ebbed away, cooled by the soft, milky sweetness of flan and the insistent cry of his heart that he loved her.

"I'm sorry," Tracy said again on the way home. "I shouldn't have said anything. Will you forgive me?"

"Of course I forgive you!" he said, surprised and glad at how easy it was. He pulled the car smoothly to a stop at the Showalters' porch and got out to open her door. Looking once more into those pale green eyes, he gave her his hand and led her up the steps. "Thank you for spending the evening with me. I had a good time."

"So did I. Will I see you Sunday in church?"

"Yes. Take care." He let go of her hand and returned to the car without looking back.

"Call me," she said as she opened her front door, but Will didn't answer.

People really are trying to turn me into a northwest Ohio hick. Teach high school? I'd about rather muck out the barn!

As he drove home, Will glared at the landscape, fields of corn ripe for picking and fields of soybeans just beginning to turn from green to gold, becoming almost invisible as the light faded, but there nonetheless. Crops. Harvests. The cycle of farming. *This is what I tried to escape from in the first place!*

No, Will. You were trying to escape from yourself. No one moves to Iowa to avoid cornfields. No one moves to Kansas to avoid wheatfields. It isn't the farm you hate, and it isn't your family – it's yourself.

"Yeah, yeah, yeah, whoever you are, why don't you tell me something new?"

All right. Not new, but still not clear to you: I love you, Will, and I will never leave you or forsake you. The plans I have for you are good, to prosper you and not to harm you, plans to give you hope and a future.

Tell him to shut up! It's all lies. There is no hope, and there is no future. Things are only going to go from bad to worse. Your bank account is almost empty and nobody wants to hire you. Go ahead and apply for that high school job, and they'll reject you, too. Because you're worthless, and everybody knows it.

Will parked the car and sat there with his hands on the wheel until Tucker bounded up and pressed his nose against the window, whining.

"Tucker!" Allison's voice called, loud enough for Will to hear it through the glass.

The dog dropped to his haunches and sat there looking expectantly at Will, tongue lolling. Will slowly climbed out and stood on the driveway, looking at the dog.

"Hi, Will!" Allison chirped, coming up to them. "I was just letting Tucker out, and he spotted your car. I hope he didn't scratch it!"

"Nah, he went straight for the window."

"Did you have a good time? Like the new restaurant?"

"Food's good."

"Um-hmm. Come on, Tucker, go do what you need to do so we can go in and avoid the mosquitoes."

The dog obediently wandered off onto the lawn and the two of them stood silently watching him.

I wonder what Allison would say if I told her about running into Mr. Stemwalter. She'd probably say it's a sign of God's will. Trey would call it small town coincidence. I think it's plain old bad luck!

"I didn't make my meeting tonight," Allison said, catching Tucker by the collar as he returned to keep him from jumping on Will. "Sit, beast."

"Problem?" Will asked.

"No, your dad and I just got to talking with the folks and the time got away from me. Not a problem. There's a noon meeting tomorrow, and since I don't have to work I'm going to go to that one. It's a discussion meeting, but it's open – so you're welcome to come if you like. Let's go in, Tucker."

Allison and the dog turned away from Will without waiting for an answer, leaving him alone listening to crickets in the hot August night.

Chapter 16

WILL DIDN'T MAKE UP HIS MIND UNTIL THE VERY LAST MINute, but as Allison picked up her keys and walked to the door, he said, "Hey, is it still okay if I tag along?"

"Of course! But hustle, because I don't like to be late."

"I'm ready," he said, following her out the door and into her bright blue car. "What is this thing, anyway?" he asked, trying to fold himself into it.

"Oh, don't be smart about it!" Allison said. "You're not that tall. It's a Ford Fiesta, and I love it."

"Dad says you love anything blue, the brighter the better." He managed to crunch his legs enough to sit down and close the door.

"He's right," Allison agreed, smiling cheerfully. "Blue makes me happy. No coincidence that your father has blue eyes. Just like yours. You can push that seat back a little, I think. Mine has to be right up to the wheel, of course, but there's some leeway for you."

Will managed to find the combination to move the seat back a few inches. It did help, marginally. "Which church is this meeting in?" he asked.

"Oh, this one isn't in a church. It's in a bar."

"What!"

"Easy," Allison teased, keeping her eyes on the road. "The bartender is the owner, and he's recovering. So he decided to start a daytime meeting and keep it right there where he works. The bar doesn't open until two in the afternoon, so there's no – uh – conflict of interest.

Come on!" she said, parking in front and jumping out of the car.

Will stood there on the sidewalk for a moment looking at the building. It was just another Lewiston storefront, nothing fancy, with a red and green neon sign proclaiming "Bob's Place" and another advertising a popular brand of beer. He followed Allison into the building, taking in the smaller-than-McClendon's bar and the row of little square tables pushed together in a line down the center of the splintery old hardwood floor. There seemed to be seating for about twenty in that line, but only half a dozen men and one woman occupied the chairs.

"Hi, Allison," said the man behind the bar, handing her a bright blue mug full, Will presumed, of coffee.

"Hi, Bob!" she responded, bellying up to the bar to add her usual obscene amounts of cream and sugar to the mix. "I brought my stepson Will today."

"Hi, Will," Bob said, holding out his hand for Will to shake. "Coffee? Soda?"

"Water's fine," Will said, thinking it was too hot for coffee. "Nice to meet you." He took a glass full of ice water and followed Allison to the tables.

"I'm Carol," the other woman announced, shaking Will's hand and offering him a seat beside her.

"Nice to meet you," he said, letting Allison sit there and sitting beside her instead.

Within a few minutes, all the chairs were filled and two latecomers dragged bar stools over to squeeze in. After the preliminaries, which included a group recitation of the Serenity Prayer, Carol began a discussion of "praying only for knowledge of His will and the power to carry it out."

That's odd. A bunch of recovering alcoholics worrying about how to know God's will and how to have the power to carry it out. I get it when they talk about how to stay sober, but this goes way beyond that.

"I feel like an idiot sometimes," a swarthy little man with a comb-over to rival Mr. Stemwalter's said, "but I go out in the shed and just yell at God sometimes. Neighbors probably think I'm drinking again. But I don't care. When I get His attention, then He seems to talk to me."

"What? Like you hear a voice?" asked a man even younger than

Will, thin and pale, with a wispy goatee and a bad case of acne.

"Not exactly," the first man said, feeling his way. "It's more like – when I get all the yelling out of my system, I calm down and – well, it's like – I just seem to know what to do." Other heads were nodding around the table, but the younger man looked skeptical. "The other trick, though, is to do what you know you're supposed to do."

"I don't need some spirit telling me what to do," the young man proclaimed, sucking nervously on the straw in his cola. "I can take care of myself."

"That been working for you?" Bob asked, gesturing to the young man's ankle, where an electronic device showed below his jeans. "Community control and all, Teddy? That's the kind of thing my own willpower and my own bright ideas got me, too."

"It's not my fault," Teddy whined. "And when my time's up I'm going to leave this one-horse town for a real city, where things are easier and everybody's not in your business all the time."

Wow. He sounds like me, Will thought.

"Old-timers in AA call that the 'geographical cure,'" Bob said, smiling. "You know: There's too many breweries in Cincinnati, so I'll move to Milwaukee or St. Louis. Trouble is, when I move somewhere, I take me with me. It's not the breweries making me drink – it's me. I'm an alcoholic, and drinking is what I do – unless God gives me the grace to stop."

Teddy glared at Bob but said nothing. Having drained his glass, he began to fiddle with the straw.

"I remember when I hadn't been sober but a year or two," Carol said, "my husband took a job in a new town. I was really set up where I was – a job, good friends, a lot of good meetings to help me stay sober – and I didn't want him to take the job. I told him if he loved me, he'd stay. I went crying to my sponsor, asking her how to make him stay, and she asked me if I was sure that was God's will for us.

" 'Well, of course it must be,' I told her, but she seemed to think maybe I was just being willful. Told me to pray about it twice a day for two weeks and get back to her – and to shut up about it to my husband in the meantime. Oh, I was so mad at her!"

"What happened?" Will asked, forgetting it wasn't his place to speak.

"It was strange," Carol said. "I did what Blanche told me to do, and by the end of the second week I was pretty sure God was telling me to go with my husband."

"Did you?" Allison asked.

"I did. And here we still are, twenty years later. And I could never have found a better group of friends anywhere than all of you are."

"You gave up your job," Will said. "Was that fair?"

"Oh, fair doesn't enter into it, really," Carol told him, smiling so no sting would accompany her words. "I hated giving up my job, that's true. But eventually I found one here – nothing like what I had been doing before, but even more satisfying. The main thing, though, was that I knew God's will for me was to go and He gave me the power to do it, even though I didn't want to."

"THOSE PEOPLE REALLY GET DOWN TO IT," WILL SAID TO ALLISON as they drove home. "No pussyfooting around anything. No excuses for anything. In your face about things."

"Yep. As my treatment shrink would say, 'How do you feel about that?'"

Will considered. "I liked it. I admire those people."

"Honey," Allison said, sparing him a quick glance, "I am 'those people.' They're just ordinary people who happen to have the disease of addiction."

"I didn't mean anything by it," Will said, flushing uncomfortably.

"I know, I know. I just get tired of people demonizing us and acting like we could control it if we wanted to – you know, willpower. Don't you think we would if we could? Can you imagine anybody ever volunteers to screw up their whole life, maybe even die, just for fun?"

"No, of course not. I'm sorry, Allison, honestly!"

"No, I'm sorry. No need to get all bent out of shape about it. People are mostly just trying to do the best they can and to understand things as best they can. I'm fine; let's not tell your father I had a little meltdown."

Will grinned at her. "You keep a lot of secrets from Dad?"

Now it was Allison's turn to flush. "No, of course not! Just the things he doesn't need to know if they would upset him."

"I guess there's a lot I don't know about marriage," Will said slowly, unfastening his seat belt as Allison put the car into park by the porch.

"I don't know how anyone does it without God," Allison said, getting out of the car. "Tucker, sit!"

Will hadn't noticed the dog approaching and was grateful for Allison's order. He walked the two steps to the animal and patted him. "Hey, boy, how are you?" Tucker slurped some kisses on Will's hand and offered his paw to shake.

"Let's take the big baby in," Allison said, starting up the steps. "Tucker, come."

"I wish I could have trained my students like that," Will told her, following the two of them onto the porch.

All three of them went into the house, which seemed unnaturally quiet to Will. Then he realized it was mid-afternoon and Matthew was working at the Abbotts'.

"I have to work second today," Allison said, "so I need to hustle to get ready. You and Matthew can eat at the farm tonight, okay?"

"Sure, no problem. Thanks for the meeting."

"Keep coming back!" Allison said, parodying the traditional AA line. "Seriously. Any time. Oh, and if you want it, the Big Book's on the coffee table."

WILL CHANGED INTO WORK CLOTHES AND HEAVIER WORK SHOES BEFORE driving over to the farm. He found John working on the books at the dining room table and learned that Ed and Matthew were in the fields somewhere.

"Have a seat," John offered. "I never mind taking a break from this paperwork. I imagine there's coffee in the kitchen, but Cassie and Pearl have gone to the store, and they took Gracie with them."

"Where's Flash?" Will asked, sitting opposite John.

"Outside where he belongs," John said. "I should never have let Gracie bring that mutt indoors. Now she wants him in her room every night. I want him outside patrolling the property."

"He sure didn't patrol me when I came in," Will said. "Didn't see or hear anything like a dog."

"I hope that doesn't mean he got hit on the road," John said, a worry frown creasing his forehead. "Gracie couldn't handle that." Deliberately he shook it off. "So what are you up to today?"

"Oh. I went to a noon meeting with Allison, and we just got back. Figured I'd come over and see whether there's anything I can do to help."

"Truth to tell, I doubt there is much until milking time. Unless you want to take a crack at the books here."

"You have to be kidding! I'm a poet, not an accountant."

"Poet, is it?" John asked. "I guess I did hear you'd had some poetry published."

Will blushed and looked at his shoes. "I was just making a point about the math stuff, John. I've written a few things, but I'm not really a poet."

"What is a poet, then?" John asked. "Isn't it someone who writes poetry?"

"I suppose..."

"And you went to an AA meeting. Do you have a problem?"

"No! No, really, I don't. I just went a couple of times because Allison invited me to see what it's all about and I found it interesting. Interesting people. What they talk about is – useful, even if one isn't an alcoholic. I've done some reading in her Big Book, too. It's an interesting philosophy."

"We've talked about the program some," John said. "It's so practical, and it's so spiritual at the same time. It's based on the Bible, you know."

"Uh – no, I didn't know that."

"Wait here a minute," John said, getting up and going into the living room. He came back with a large book in hand. "This is the original Big Book – the Bible. If you like to read interesting philosophy with practical applications, read this." He handed the book to Will, who took it reflexively.

"I have read it," Will replied. "I read it while I was in high school. Great poetry here and there, lots of action/adventure stories." He placed the book on the table. "I think I'll go find Ed; we haven't talked in a long time. Thanks for your time, John."

When Will came back to the house to help the ladies unload the car, he noticed the Bible John had offered lying on the front seat of his own car and laughed to himself. *Gotta love these people for their persistence!*

"Hurry up!" Gracie urged, pulling at Will's arm. "Bring in all the bags so we can finish this job!"

"I'm coming," he told her. "Please hold the door."

Twelve bags of groceries later, Cassie and Pearl were satisfied with the contents of the pantry and refrigerator. Starvation had been fended off for another week. Micah was sitting under the kitchen table with a plate of apple slices and a new book, and Cassie was preparing the vegetables for dinner.

"Let's go outside and sit on the swing," Gracie said to Will. "We need to talk."

They sat side by side, and Will set the swing moving gently with his foot. "What's on your mind, kiddo?"

"Well, you know what it is," she said severely. "I keep telling you what it is. Why are you being so stubborn about accepting Jesus, Will? You know better now; you've been to church enough times, and you're not stupid."

Although he loved Gracie deeply and usually found her amusing in her preacher mode, today it was getting under his skin. "Johanna Grace Abbott," he began and hid a grin as she flinched at the use of her full name. Obviously that name only came up when she was in trouble. "Johanna Grace Abbott, it's rude to keep badgering someone about their faith – or lack of it. It makes a person want to walk away from you and not come back."

Grace's blue, blue eyes filled with tears. *Crud. I didn't want to make her cry!*

"Come on, Gracie. Don't do that! I love you, and I love to spend time with you. But I can't fake a religious experience for you or for anybody else. You wouldn't want me to lie, would you?"

"No..." Her lip wobbled. "I'm sorry, Will. It's just so important! The most important thing in the whole world. Could you at least read some things in the Bible and – and see if they help?"

Oh, brother. How can I say no? "All right, I'll read whatever you want me to read. Your dad gave me a Bible to use just a little while ago."

"Really! That's great! I'll make a list for you and give it to you at dinner!" Heart restored, the little girl jumped off the swing and ran into the house.

Will sat there, swinging idly, and watched Gracie's dog come loping up the driveway. "Where've you been?" he asked as Flash came up the steps to drop at his feet, panting. "You have a pretty good life, you know," Will told him, rubbing his back with a heavy shoe. "Come and go as you please, plenty to eat, the vet if you're sick, no particular job or money worries. No wonder you look so happy."

Flash wagged his tail against the porch floor and nudged Will's foot to keep up the petting.

"I'll bet you don't ever worry about the existence of God or where your next meal is coming from – or about lady dogs, for that matter. They neutered you, right? So all you have to do is chase rabbits and play with Gracie and get tummy-rubs. I envy you, Flash, I do."

The dog looked up at the mention of his name and stood to lay his head on Will's knee. *Dogs love me*, Will thought. *It's the rest of the world I have trouble with.*

Dogs are stupid and nondiscriminating. You are no more lovable today than you ever were.

I have loved you with an everlasting love. You are my beloved child, fearfully and wonderfully made.

All lies. Ignore the lies; embrace the truth. You are worthless and nothing you do matters. So you might as well please yourself. Call Tracy. Take her out. Take what you can get from her.

"No! That's a lie! God, what is this duet in my head? Make it stop!"

"Are you talking to yourself?" Pearl asked, coming out onto the porch. "I heard your voice."

"No! Well, sort of." Blood tinged Will's ears and neck, headed for his face. "I'm trying to turn off this dialogue that keeps playing inside my head. It's too weird – like the voices of good and evil in a cartoon or something. Maybe I need to see a psychiatrist, Grandma. This is crazy."

"May I sit down?"

"Oh, sure! I'm sorry! Here, let me help you get settled." Will handed the old woman onto the swing and held it still for her to settle back.

"Thank you. Now join me and tell me about this dialogue."

Will remained standing, facing away from Pearl and shuffling his feet, wanting to tell her everything and receive her assurance he was all right, fearing to tell her anything lest she think him as crazy as he thought himself.

"Will. Tell me what's bothering you."

Sliding down to sit on the porch floor opposite her, leaning against a pillar, Will took a breath – another – and went for it. The whole dialogue, all the way back to high school.

"After I tried to kill myself, you remember they made me go to a psychologist in Lewiston. I don't think he was as bright as he thought he was, but I know I wasn't easy to work with, either. I finally told him how I heard these opposing thoughts – not really voices, not out loud or anything – and how the one set told me I was all those things I just told you. He said when those ideas came to me I needed to distract myself with something positive, like music or a good book or talking with a friend. Which would have been great, but I didn't think I had any friends any more.

"I managed to ignore them most of the time, though, and that whole thing went away for a long time. While I was in undergrad school I don't remember ever hearing either one of those things, good or bad. I met Trey in Cincy and we got to be good friends, so when it came time for grad school it was easy to apply to Iowa. And what a kick that I got in!

"Trey was getting his masters in business while I was in the MFA program, and we hung out together a lot. I made other friends there, too, and I didn't tell any of them anything about my life before I met Trey. After grad school, I got hired to teach – a really big deal, and I loved it! I found this great apartment through a friend of a friend, and I had a lot of guys to do things with, and I dated some...

"But somewhere in there those voices in my head started coming back. Just a little at first, once in a while, you know? And I'd watch a game on TV or put on some music or play my guitar and it would all go away. But ever since Carolyn died, since I came back to Ohio the first time, it's gotten worse and worse. I think maybe I really am schizophrenic and need anti-psychotic meds." He hung his head, panting a little, as if the telling had been physical as well as mental stress to him.

Pearl closed her eyes for a moment, content to let the silence deepen, then looked at Will as she said, "I suppose you could be schizophrenic. I'm not competent to judge that."

Will looked at her, alarm in his expression. He had not expected her to agree with him!

"But," Pearl continued, "it seems to me there may be another explanation. Would you like to hear it?"

"Yes, ma'am."

"It seems to me you may be hearing real voices, the voices of Good and Evil, God and Satan."

"Oh, come on, Grandma – "

"No, hear me out. That's only polite, you know." Will nodded. "If you are honest with yourself, boy, you have to admit there is good in the world; and if there is good, there is also evil. The Bible is very clear that God is good and equally clear that the devil is evil. The devil is 'a roaring lion,' as Peter says, always prowling around trying to kill our spirits. He is the father of lies, and that's how he gets to us – lying. He tells us things which hurt, frighten, discourage, condemn us so that we give up and let him snatch our souls away from the Lord.

"All these things you've heard over the years – that you are bad, that you are unlovable, that you are a homosexual, that you always hurt those you love, that nobody can ever love you – lies, Will. Every one of them, lies!

"And that other voice you hear – the Voice you first heard in Chicago – that's the Abba God Who loves you and created you for Himself, begging you to let Him love you, begging you to come to Him."

Pearl stood up and forced Will to look her in the eye. "You asked what I think, and that's what I think: you aren't insane, Will. You're the center of an intense tug of war for possession of your immortal soul."

"How can that be?" he asked her, his voice cracking.

She put her arms as far around him as they would reach and hugged him fiercely. "I know it doesn't make any sense," she said, holding on as if she would never let go, "but I know it's true. God made you for Himself. On purpose, knowing everything you are and everything you would do and every time you would reject Him. He won't force you. He will bear the pain of your rejection over and over and still love you, not because you deserve that, but just because He is Who He is. It's for this very thing that Jesus Christ died for you, Will. You don't have to like it. You don't even have to believe it. It just is what it is, and in this life you will never get away from Him.

"I told that to your father once," she suddenly remembered, "that he should read Psalm 139 and understand that God would never leave him or forsake him. He had the same problem you have, you know, thinking he wasn't good enough to be saved, to be loved. He was wrong, of course." She patted Will's back and stepped away.

Will sank down onto the swing as if his legs wouldn't hold him any longer. "I know what everyone wants me to do," he said, rubbing his face with both hands and scrubbing through his carefully combed hair. "You, Dad, Allison, John, Ed, Tracy – even Gracie. Heck, especially Gracie! But I just can't believe it." He buried his face in his hands. "I'm so tired."

"You're tired from fighting," Pearl said, giving no quarter. "Let go and let God take over, and you'll be amazed at how much better you feel."

Will looked up. "'Let go and let God – ' that's an AA saying. I've heard it in meetings. This is too strange, hearing things the same way – even the same words! It's weird."

"No, it's the Lord's way of getting your attention. Now, why don't you just go for a long walk and think things over again. Ask the God you don't think you believe in to reveal Himself to you in specific ways. After all," she smiled at him, "what do you have to lose?"

Chapter 17

"**H**EY, FLASH!" WILL CALLED, BRINGING THE DOG ON the run from the back yard. "You want to go for a walk?"

Flash was apparently as literate as Tucker, because he barked sharply once and took off running down the driveway.

Will followed more slowly, hands in his pockets, pretending he was Sheriff Andy walking toward the fishing hole in Mayberry, hot August afternoon, dusty, dark green leaves on the trees barely quivering in the ghost of a breeze, sky hard blue overhead and cloudless. He rolled up his sleeves as he continued walking, catching up to Flash at the road.

"Good boy," he told the excited dog. "You should wait to cross the road every time until your humans are there to watch for idiots in cars. Let's go through that field to the woods, okay?"

Apparently it was okay with Flash, who followed at Will's heels until they were deep into the field before taking off on his own. Will made his way between rows of corn, unable to keep from noting it would be ready to harvest soon, laughing at his own startle when Flash kicked up a pheasant in a loud whirr of feathers. He could hear katydids and larks in the field and saw the shadow of a red-tail hawk overhead. The corn made its own music, moving imperceptibly when the breeze picked up a little. Drawing a deep breath, Will scented the dry, powdery earth around the cornstalks, the green of the corn, the faintest odor of hogs from the next farm over, even the hot, doggy smell of Flash's coat in the sun.

This smells like home, looks like home, he thought in spite of himself. *I didn't think I missed it, but it's – it's good now.*

Don't be stupid. You hate the smell of hogs. You hate cornfields and wheatfields and soybean fields. Bird songs aren't the same as cool jazz, and this dog is not a friend; he's a stupid animal.

"Hey, Flash, you stupid animal, come back here!"

The dog returned and sat at Will's feet, expectant and glad to be there.

"Yes, you are stupid," Will crooned, fondling the dog's ears gently, "but you're faithful and you're a good dog." He petted the dog for a moment and resumed walking, Flash now staying close to him.

The temperature dropped at least fifteen degrees the moment Will stepped into the woods, where the heavy canopy of maple, oak, and other hardwoods cast a deep green shade over everything. Over many years – dozens, hundreds? – deer and then men had created paths through the woods, and Will followed easily, moving slowly and casually, knowing where this path went and where it came out of the woods on the other side. Flash ranged ahead of him a little way, nose to the ground, delighting in the many animal scents Will couldn't appreciate.

Not too far in, there was a small clearing, probably originally a thicket for deer, which had opened up over the years into a fair circle. John and Ed had placed a couple of rough wooden benches there just under the shade of the trees a long time ago, and Will had sometimes escaped there during his teen years when the pressure of people around him was too painful to bear. Now he sat down on one of the benches and tried to relax his muscles.

"Pray about it," he said, talking to himself with confidence no one was there to hear him except the dog, who was much more interested in whatever animals and birds had passed through recently than in the maunderings of this new man in his life.

"Okay, so I can tell Pearl I did it. Lord, if You exist, if You care about me, I need You to tell me so. I need for you to stop messing with my head and – and tell me what to do with my life."

He waited. Everything was still, even the sounds of birds and insects muted by the weight of the trees and underbrush.

"I didn't think You'd bother to talk to me, but I said I'd try. Okay. Still on my own."

Be still, and know that I am God.

"What!" Will leaped to his feet, all senses on high alert, adrenaline coursing through him like fire in his veins. The dog backed away from him, whining a little.

Be still, and know that I am God. Rest, Will, and let me love you.

Will dropped back down onto the bench, quivering harder than the leaves above him, unable to see anything but the clearing and the frightened dog and his own shaking hands.

"You're really talking to me! I'm not crazy – am I?"

Be still and rest and let me love you.

In spite of himself, Will felt all the adrenaline leaving his body, leaving his arms and legs almost limp. He leaned back on the bench and closed his eyes, letting his breathing slow and his heartbeat become unnoticeable to him. The sun filtered in through the leaves and was warm on his eyelids, almost like fingers gently holding them closed. The tension went out of his jaw, and he noticed it as if maybe it hadn't done that in a long time. His fingers lay limp, and neither of his legs did the jigging dance they so often did when he was worrying. Flash had stopped whining, and the only sound in the clearing now was faint bird-calls.

As Will slumped there, he was reminded of the way his father had wrapped him in his jacket and held him on the way home from Chicago, over ten years before, how safe he had felt as long as Matthew was holding him, how he had missed that ever since. But he felt it now. He was safe.

"Supper's ready," Pearl told the men, who were all seated around the living room watching the evening news.

"Where's Will?" Matthew asked as they gathered at the table.

"I thought he was with you," Cassie said.

"I thought he was in the kitchen helping," Matthew replied.

"I haven't seen him for a long time," Gracie said, frowning. "Flash, either."

"His car's here," Matthew said. "Is he upstairs taking a nap?"

"No," Gracie answered. "I was up there, and he isn't."

"I think he went for a walk," Pearl said, "but that was hours ago. The dog went with him."

"That's it, then," John said. "I'll call the dog."

They trooped to the front porch and John put two fingers in his mouth to produce an ear-piercing whistle. "Flash!" he yelled.

"Didn't realize the boss can bellow like that," Ed remarked to Matthew in a low voice.

John repeated the whistle and the call several times, as they all grew more restive. Then Gracie squealed, "Here comes Flash!"

The dog came loping across the road from the cornfield and up the driveway to drop at Gracie's feet. They looked, but no one saw Will coming through the field.

Matthew took off running, and Flash immediately followed.

"Think that dog thinks he's Lassie?" Ed asked. "You know, like 'Timmy's down the well' or something?"

"I don't think he's that smart," John said. "He's just up for a run. I'll go after Matthew in case... well, I'll just head that way."

"The rest of you back inside," Pearl said, taking Gracie's hand to prevent her exodus. "We'll put the meat back in the oven and see what develops."

As he ran, Matthew prayed. He couldn't imagine Will had been upset enough to harm himself, but it had happened before. The fear tried to choke him, to slow him down and strangle him, but he kept going as fast as he could. *Please, please, please, please –*

Flash had shot by Matthew in the corn and was already into the woods. Matthew couldn't see the dog, but he heard him begin to bark and followed the sound, remembering the clearing. *Please, please, please, please.*

As he came within a stride of the clearing, Matthew heard Will's voice, laughing, chiding the dog, and he stopped to catch his breath.

"What are you barking about, Flash?" Will was saying. "See a turkey in the woods, or what? Settle down, boy. No, I don't want my face washed! Down! Hey, Dad!" he said as Matthew stepped into the clearing.

"You all right, Son?" Matthew asked, trying not to show how out of breath he was.

"Sure. Why wouldn't I be?"

"I just – it's suppertime and nobody could find you."

"Really?" Will looked at the angle of the sun through the trees. "I must have fallen asleep. It wasn't near suppertime when Flash and I came out here."

"I'm just glad you're all right!"

Will stood up and faced his father. "I'm sorry if I worried you. I'm fine."

Oh, God, thank You! He's safe; he's all right – he looks – "Will? What happened?"

"What do you mean?"

"There you are!" John said, breaking into the clearing and into the middle of the moment. "Everything all right?"

"Fine," Will said, snapping his fingers to the dog. "Let's go get supper. I think I'm hungry. I just fell asleep, John, no big deal. Sorry you were worried. I'll apologize to Pearl and Cassie for ruining their meal, too." He headed off through the woods, leaving Matthew and John standing there.

"What's going on?" John asked. "I'm sorry I interrupted."

"I don't know," Matthew said. "We might as well head back and have supper."

Lord, what happened? I know there was something, but I don't see what it was. Did You speak to Will? Did he give himself to You? Oh, please, Lord, if that didn't happen, let it happen soon!

Will made his apologies with much grace and true repentance, which earned immediate forgiveness from the women and Ed and bought him some time to enjoy his meal without having to answer questions. He was really hungry for a change and managed pork loin and applesauce and buttered red potatoes with no gastric repercussions. In true Ryersen fashion, he picked the lima beans out of the succotash, but he kept himself from slipping them to Flash under the table, having seen Gracie reprimanded for the same thing, as Flash apparently refused to remove the evidence.

I must have been asleep for a couple of hours, Will mused, chewing slowly. *But I don't remember falling asleep and I don't remember being asleep. But what else could it have been? I remember feeling safe.*

"What?" He realized Pearl was talking to him.

"I asked whether you gave any thought to the things we talked about," she said.

"Oh. Yes, I did. I – it was – never mind. Thanks for your advice."

"Mm-hmm," she answered. "Ice cream pie for dessert. Gracie, help

Cassie clear the table."

"Why do I have to do it every time?" Gracie asked, her lip on the verge of a pout. "Just because we're girls shouldn't mean we always have to do the housework."

"Stop that!" John told her. "You know the men help out around here plenty, especially on Sundays. Now help Cassie."

"I don't mind helping," Will said, forestalling Matthew's rising.

"You sit down, too," John said. "Gracie has to learn she can't get out of things by pouting. I think I've spoiled her since – well, Carolyn wouldn't have let her get away with it."

"Nope," Ed agreed. "But don't be getting down on yourself. You done a good job, all things considered. She's a good kid."

"See, Daddy?" Gracie teased, coming back in for another load of dishes. "I'm a good kid. Will, I have that list for you; don't let me forget it."

"Wouldn't dream of it, kiddo."

"What list?" Matthew asked.

"List of Bible stuff she wants me to read. I told her I would."

"Oh," Matthew said.

Will looked at his father and could see the prayer happening inside his head. He accepted a piece of pie from Gracie and stuck a fork into it without paying much attention, wondering what Matthew was asking for, figuring he probably knew. He put the bite into his mouth and shuddered. It was strawberries and ice cream and whipped cream and red Jell-O, all mixed into a mush and frozen; the sweetness was as annoying to his teeth as the strawberry seeds themselves.

"You don't like it?" Pearl asked.

"Uh – sure. It's fine," he managed, fool that he was.

"*Stop* that!" Pearl snapped. "I told you, Will, lying is a sin."

"Uh-oh," Gracie whispered.

"Sorry," Will said, face redder than the Jell-O. "Okay, no, thank you, I don't like it and I really don't want to eat it."

"That's better," Pearl nodded. "You don't have to eat it."

"He only touched it with a clean fork," Ed said, "so I'd be glad to help out here."

"How come he doesn't have to eat it, but when I don't like something I do have to eat it?" Gracie asked.

"He's twenty-nine and you're eleven," John said. "When you're an adult, you can choose what to eat and what to leave."

"Not when Pearl's around," Gracie said with a grin at the old woman.

"And don't you forget it! I'm not going anywhere for a while yet."

"May I be excused?" Gracie asked. "I need to get my list for Will. You can meet me on the porch," she offered, "unless they make you do the dishes."

"I think we can let both of you off the hook for dishes tonight," John said. "I'll help in the kitchen, and Matthew and Ed can help me."

"See, here's the name of the book of the Bible, and here's the chapter and verses next to it," Gracie explained, leaning over the back of the swing to look over Will's shoulder as he read the list, laboriously copied in pen on a full sheet of notebook paper.

"You have a lot of things on here," he told her.

"Yes. It's a big book, and everything in it is important. Of course, I don't read so awfully much of the Old Testament yet, because it's pretty hard to understand sometimes. But Daddy has me read the psalms and the gospels a lot."

"You recommend I start with the Gospel of John, is that it?"

"Yes. The whole thing. Then if you have any questions, you can come and ask me and we can talk about it."

"Ask you, huh?"

"Yes. If I don't know the answer, Daddy will, or Pearl, or Matthew. If it's really hard, we can call Pastor Miles."

"What am I looking for in all this?" he asked.

"You're looking for Jesus, of course. For Who He is and how much He loves you and what He wants you to do with your life."

"Of course. Okay, Grace, I said I'd read it, and I will."

She threw her arms around his neck from behind and nearly strangled him with her affection. "I'm so glad! Thank you, Will! I promise you'll be glad, I promise!"

Matthew had fallen asleep hours before, but Will lay there wide awake.

Must be that nap I took. Can't believe I slept for a couple of hours!

I'm sure not sleepy now. Maybe the air conditioning is too cold.

He pulled up a blanket and cocooned himself, curling on his side, but within minutes he began to sweat and flung himself onto his back, blanket on the floor, arms akimbo.

I should have called Tracy. We could have gone somewhere, done something... but she'd ask me what happened, and I just don't know.

He turned onto his other side and pulled just the sheet over himself.

Maybe I need some background music. It's too quiet in the country. I'm used to city traffic.

He turned on the light and found NPR on the radio, turning it low enough to be unheard in the other bedroom. Miles Davis serenaded him gently, and he relaxed into the music for a few minutes. But it was no use.

I'm not hungry, not thirsty, don't have to go to the bathroom... I need to sleep! Just do it.

"Oh, all right," Will finally said, whether to himself or to someone else, and turned on the light again. He picked up the Bible he had left on the nightstand and took a look at Gracie's list, tucked inside it. "Gospel of John, all."

Will opened the Bible, remembering where John was from years before, remembering then that he had started in John the first time.

"Here we go: 'In the beginning was the Word...'"

Several chapters in, Will heard the front door open and close quietly and followed the sound of Allison's footsteps across the living room, to the bathroom, then to the other bedroom. The door opened, closed, opened and closed again. Moments later he heard scratching at his own door.

"Shut up, Tucker!" Will hissed, opening the door. Twice as big as Flash, Tucker still considered himself a lap-dog, and he wanted to share Will's bed. "No!" Will whispered. "It's too hot."

Tucker whined loudly. Will considered for a moment and surrendered.

"All right, here's the deal. Let me get my book and we'll go out on the couch, okay?"

Tucker watched carefully as Will pulled on jeans and a tee-shirt and gathered up the Bible. Content that he wouldn't be shut away from human companionship, he followed Will back into the living room. When Will sat down on the couch, Tucker immediately jumped up to take up the rest of the space.

"Happy now?" Will asked.

Twenty or thirty minutes later, Will closed the Bible in disgust. "It's just not working for me," he told the dog, who opened one eye but decided the comment didn't require any further response.

So now what? I still can't sleep, I'm not hungry, there's nothing on TV at this time of the morning, if I go back to bed Tucker will make a fuss – crud.

Will sat there drumming his fingers on his thigh, wishing he had not finished the novel he'd been reading. His eye settled on the thick blue-covered book on the coffee table: Allison's Big Book. Its plain navy blue paper cover proclaimed in white letters, '...the Basic Text for Alcoholics Anonymous.' He picked it up. The stories in the back half of the book were strange and diverting, so many ways to ruin one's life by drinking.

Start at the beginning, the voice said.

"Here we go again," Will whispered. "Well, why not?" He opened the book.

The "Chapter to the Agnostic" was interesting, all that protestation about not having to believe in 'God' as church defines Him but not being able to stay sober until you believe in 'God as you understand Him,' with all the capital letters. Will wished he could say it wasn't making sense, expected the negative voice to start mocking, but nothing happened, and on he read.

Chapter Five was titled "How It Works," the paper Will had heard read at every AA meeting, the one that started, "Rarely have we seen a person fail who has thoroughly followed our path. Those who do not recover are people who cannot or will not completely give themselves to this simple program..."

That's what everyone at the meetings says is true. That guy – Teddy? – with the ankle bracelet, he didn't seem willing to give himself to it. And he looked like a loser to me!

He read on: "...Without help it is too much for us." *I get that!* "But there is One who has all power – that One is God. May you find Him now!"

If only it were that simple...

"Half measures availed us nothing. We stood at the turning point.

We asked His protection and care with complete abandon."

Half measures availed us nothing... but - 'complete abandon?'

Will noticed the book was shaking, which meant his hands were shaking, so he closed the book and put it back on the coffee table.

'Complete abandon!' Jump off the cliff with no water, just the rocks below, and hope there's a net?

"Oh, God," he groaned, covering his face with his hands.

The bedroom door opened, and he heard bare feet padding toward him.

"You all right?" Allison asked, sitting beside him and putting a hand on his shoulder. "I couldn't sleep, so I – and here you are."

"Here I am. I couldn't sleep either, so I was reading your Big Book again. I was reading 'How It Works.'"

"Mm-hm."

"I was reading the Bible before, because I promised Gracie I would, but I just couldn't get into it. This makes more sense to me. Does that mean I'm an alcoholic after all?"

Allison tried but failed to suppress a grin, which Will accepted without offense. He saw why his father thought she was so cute.

"I don't think that's what it means at all," she said. "I think God just uses different things to reach different people. Remember my telling you this book's all based on the Bible?"

"Yes, I do. The part I was just reading – 'We stood at the turning point' – that's where I am. God did something to me this afternoon, and now I – I have to do something. But then the book says, 'We asked His protection and care with complete abandon.' How can I do that? I don't trust God! Why should I?"

"You want me to wake your dad?" Allison asked. "I'm feeling a little bit inadequate here."

"No! I mean, I don't think he can help, either. There's something broken inside of me, Allison. I don't trust anybody that much. How can I trust what I can't even see?"

"You ever watch extreme sports on TV?"

"Huh?"

"You know – crazy things athletes and idiots do?"

"I suppose I have. What's that got to do with it?"

"Did you ever see those divers in Mexico, the Acapulco cliff divers? They dive over three hundred feet down into the ocean from the cliff-top, and they have to trust that they'll miss the rocks and go into the water where it's deep enough to keep them from getting smashed. Ever see that?"

"Yes. And I was just thinking about that before you came out!"

"Wonder why that was?" she teased. "God's definitely trying to get your attention."

"Are you saying trusting God is like jumping off a cliff?"

"Well, sure it is, until you get to know Him better. All you have to go on is His promises in the Bible – and the experience of all the people who have jumped before you and lived to tell the tale. You have two of 'em right here in this house. You saw your father's struggles with faith years ago, and you've heard about mine. There's John, coming to grips with Carolyn's death, Pearl with the death of her child, all kinds of faith stories right around you if you don't want to look at the really big ones in history."

"So what would it look like?"

"Remember I said, 'I can't; God can; I think I'll let him?' That's it."

"It can't be that simple."

"Sure it can. You decide you're ready to let God be in charge of your life, then you ask Him to forgive your sins and take over. Want to do that now?"

Will had hundreds of reasons burbling to his lips to refuse her. It was too soon, he didn't know whether he really meant it, he didn't know what he believed –

All you have to do is ask Me. I want to forgive you. I want to give you peace.

"Do I kneel?"

"Only if you want to."

Will found kneeling undignified, so he was surprised to find himself kneeling, then lying flat on his face on the carpet. He felt tears running, and then huge sobs were pouring out of him, so hard, so loud he would have been embarrassed if he had been paying attention, but by then he was deep in a dialogue inside his head.

Jesus, help me! Forgive me for my pride and for lust and for being so afraid to trust You and for all the things I've done that hurt other people and for all the things I've done that hurt You. I'm sorry. I'm so sorry! I'm sorry I tried to kill myself all those times instead of trusting You to make my life better. I won't ever do that again, I promise. I want to have peace

and faith and to be – to be – Yours is what I want to be. Please help me!
Make my life into something You and I can both be proud of.

Hard arms scooped him up and a callused hand thrust a wrinkled blue bandana into his hand. He leaned into Matthew's arms and wiped his face. He felt Allison's small arm go around him from the back and felt the same covering peace he had felt in the clearing that afternoon. Loved. Safe. *This is home.*

Chapter 18

THEY HAD TENDED HIM LIKE AN EGG, WRAPPED IN THEIR ARMS, wrapped in their love, as if he would crack and break open if they let him go. They had tucked him into bed and pulled up the covers to make a soft, safe nest and sat with him until he finally fell asleep. It was odd, but comforting, that they had been so gentle and so silent, helping him out of his clothes as if he were a toddler at the end of a long day, smoothing back his hair, his father even holding his hand.

Now his watch proclaimed almost noon, and there was still no sound in the house except the soft snoring – snoring? Tucker, of course, hogging the foot of the bed.

Will sat up and stretched as much as the dog's bulk would allow, rubbing his face with both hands and feeling the rasp of beard-stubble under his fingers.

"Time to get up, dog!" he said, suiting his actions to his words. Tucker rose more slowly and lumbered off the bed, lazy, but still game for an adventure.

"I need a shower first," Will told him. "I feel like Rip Van Winkle. No, I feel like – like – I don't know. It wasn't a dream. It really happened. It really happened!"

Tucker responded to the charged tone of Will's voice, if not the words themselves, and began to cavort around his legs, shoving him toward the door. That kind of verbal energy sounded like a walk to Tucker.

Will let the dog out and took his shower, letting the hot water, then the cool, pound him fully awake and aware. By the time he had shaved, carefully watching his face in the mirror for signs of change, he was almost vibrating with excitement. *What did Dad say? 'You're a new creation in Christ. The old has gone; the new is here.' Lord, what does that mean? I meant it – I'll let You run my life from now on; I'll trust You; I'll obey. But what am I supposed to do?*

"I suppose," he said to himself as he ate a bowl of cereal in big spoonfuls, "I suppose I should read the Bible. That would be the textbook. Dad said John had him read the Book of John first, and that's what Gracie said, too. But it was boring, and it was kind of woo-woo."

He put the bowl in the sink, thinking, *Well, everything that happened yesterday and this morning was kind of woo-woo, wasn't it?*

An hour later, still absorbed in the Book of John, Will vaguely heard the phone ringing. He wasn't going to answer it, since it would probably not be for him, but after three rings he felt as if he should answer.

"I know you probably will think this is odd," Tracy said, "but I just had the strongest impression that I should call you. Is everything all right?"

Will collapsed on the couch laughing. "Oh, Trace, you have no idea!"

"So are you going to tell me?" she asked, a shade of irritation coloring her voice.

"Yes, I am going to tell you, and I'm going to knock your socks off. But I want to see your face when I do it. May I come over?"

"Of course. Now?"

"Right now. I'm on my way!"

"Oh, Will!" Tracy said softly, tears beginning to flow down her pink cheeks. "Oh, I'm so happy for you!"

"I – it's – thank you." He was still overcome and unsure of himself, but the strange feeling of peace remained. "It feels so different I don't know how to describe it. Was it like this for you?"

Tracy wiped her eyes with her fingers and shook her head a little. "I don't know. I asked Jesus into my heart when I was four or five, and I honestly don't remember anything except that I wanted to do it. He's been so much a part of my life all my life – I can't remember the 'before' part."

Will's smile faded. "I wish I could say that. My life would have been a whole lot different if I hadn't been the one running it."

"You weren't," Tracy said. "You just thought you were. God was taking care of you even in the very worst times. If He hadn't been on the job, you would have died a couple of different times. You would never have tried to make peace with your father and step-mother, never come back here when you lost your job... No, you've been cared for from the day you were born."

"Now everything is different," Will said, still frowning. "I agreed to let Jesus take over, but I don't know what to do."

"He's going to tell you."

"Yeah? Will He send me a letter or something? Call on the phone? Do I play Bible roulette and see what my finger falls on? I've heard people do that, but it doesn't seem quite kosher to me."

"We'll pray, silly. And you'll pray by yourself, and listen. And you'll read the Word to become more familiar with Who God is, so when you do hear something you'll be able to judge whether it's His will or not. There's plenty of time to figure things out now, Will, because you're saved. Have I mentioned how happy I am?" She threw her arms around him and hugged him until he forced himself to let go.

"Not too much of that, I don't think," he said, moving away. "Not all my thoughts are holy thoughts."

Tracy blushed deeply and moved away herself. "I'm sorry. You're right, we need to be careful."

"Well, not too careful," Will said, grinning at her and taking her hand. "But I need to go now, anyway. I have to see the family."

On the way to the Abbott farm, Will looked at sky and trees and fields and animals, at birds on the wires and swooping through the air, at kids playing in yards and their mothers hanging laundry on clotheslines. It was beautiful, all beautiful!

In the kitchen he found Cassie making supper, Pearl supervising, and Gracie teaching Micah how to play some card game he didn't recognize. They all looked delighted to see him, and he figured Matthew had already spread the word.

"I'm so happy for you!" Pearl exclaimed, standing laboriously and holding out her arms for a hug.

"Thank you." He hugged her gently and helped her back into her chair. Gracie was next, launching herself at him from the floor with Olympic strength and speed, making him stagger back despite her slight weight. "Thank you, too, Miss Grace. I came to report that I'm doing the Bible homework you gave me."

"Great!" the child enthused. "I knew it would be good for you. Oh, Will, this is so good! Now you won't go to hell and we'll all be together in heaven when we die!"

"That is pretty good," he agreed, laughing, as he set Gracie gently back on her feet.

"Congratulations," Cassie said quietly. "I hope you'll stay for supper tonight. Your dad said we need to have cake, and I've baked one."

"Chocolate?" Will asked.

"With Allison coming?" Cassie laughed. "What else?"

"Well, in that case, I guess I'd better stay."

DESPITE THE CELEBRATION, THE NIGHT BEFORE HAD BEEN SHORT ON sleep and the next morning's chores would still come early. The Ryersens left for home not too long after supper. At their house Matthew asked Will,

"Want to walk Tucker with me before bed?"

"Subtle," Allison sniped.

"Sure," Will said, giving Allison one finger-in-air point for her remark.

They called Tucker from the back of the house and he came at a gallop. "Walk?" Matthew asked. Tucker gave his single bark of approval and took off down the driveway.

The evening was still light, and warm enough to raise a light sweat walking. The dog gamboled ahead of them toward the Millers' farm, where his friend waited, running back every little bit to be sure the men were still following. Matthew was quiet, even though Will had been sure he had something to say. At the Millers' farm, Tucker and his buddy greeted one another and began to chase around the farmhouse yard.

"Do the Millers mind all that carrying on?" Will asked.

"Nah. First of all, they're both kinda deaf, so if the dogs make a racket it doesn't bother them. Second, both dogs seem to know to stay out of the flowerbeds, so Beulah doesn't mind 'em."

"Dad – "

"Yeah?"

"Did you want to tell me something?"

"Kinda thought maybe you wanted to tell me something," Matthew answered.

"Oh. No, I – am I supposed to be saying or doing something now, I mean now that I'm – well, you know."

"Saved, I think the word is," Matthew smiled. "It's okay to say you're saved."

"All right. But what am I supposed to do next?"

"Oh, nothing much except change your whole life," Matthew said.

"Funny, Dad. Can you be serious for a minute here?"

"I am. To live for Jesus is a whole new ballgame. It means giving up all the parts of ourselves that don't fit with what He wants us to be. It means looking at the world with His eyes instead of ours, forgiving our enemies, that kind of thing. It means obeying when He tells us to do something, not whining about it or saying 'I don't want to.'"

"Whoa! I won't ask you to get serious again anytime soon!"

"Let's head back down the road," Matthew said. "Sometimes it's easier to talk when you're moving. Tucker'll come along when he's ready."

They fell easily into step together, same in height and length of stride. Will felt that peace return, that sense of the rightness of things, being there with his father in the growing dark.

"Dad – "

"Yes?"

"Do you think it's all right – I mean, if I were to stay here – maybe not forever, but until I know what God wants me to do?"

"I can't think of anything that would make us all happier than to have you stay right here. You can stay with Allison and me as long as you want to. If you'd rather move to the farm, I know they'd be glad to have you, too. Or if you need a place of your own, we'll help with that until you have a job."

"Thank you. I'm – happy where I am for now." *Happy. Yes, I am.*

They walked along for a few moments more, silent again, but comfortable in it. Will thought about staying, finding meaningful work and putting down roots – a place of his own, a dog of his own? Why not? And Tracy. If he stayed, if he worked, if he was obedient to whatever God asked of him, then maybe she would – she might –

"I want to marry Tracy," he told his father.

"Okay," Matthew said, no evidence of surprise in his voice.

"But I can't do that until I can support her."

"True."

"So I think I should apply for that teaching job at Infinity High."

"Okay."

"Dad, you might show a little surprise or enthusiasm or – something!"

Matthew stopped and faced Will, smiling. "I'm not surprised, Son. I had a feeling that's what you're supposed to do. As for marrying Tracy, I used to think about that way back when you were in high school. I think Ryersen men only love once, and you sure loved that girl!"

"So you'd be okay with all this?"

"Absolutely. Look, Allison left the lights on for us. Let's see if she brought home some of that good chocolate cake so we can celebrate."

Chapter 19

A TEXT FROM TREY VIBRATED WILL'S PHONE. "R U OK?"
Wow! How do I answer that in one text message!
Will shook his head, grinning to himself, and texted, "ok! call me!"

Realizing it would be rude to take a call in one of Toledo's finest jewelry stores, and more than sure said call would come any second, Will stepped out onto the sidewalk, not disappointed when the phone rang.

"You did what?!" Trey yelled into the receiver. "You're going to do what?!"

Grinning some more at his friend's consternation, Will repeated, "I gave my life to Jesus Christ, and I'm going to stay here and teach high school English and try to persuade Tracy to marry me."

"That's what I thought you said," Trey answered.

After an incredibly long silence, Will said, "Hey, talk to me! I know this isn't exactly what I had in mind, but it's what God has in mind. I'm happy, Trey. Be happy for me."

"Will... I mean... Listen, buddy, if the small-town, come-to-Jesus life is really what you want, then of course I'm happy for you. But, man, all that Jesus stuff – we said – we agreed – "

"Yes, I know. 'The opiate of the people.' But when it gets up-close and personal, like God's voice in your ear, Trey, then everything is different. I can't deny this; it happened to me."

"Aw, Will... Do you think maybe – well, maybe losing your job and all has kinda sent you over the edge? Could you maybe be hearing voices and all like a – well – "

Will had to laugh. "Like a crazy person? I thought of that myself. But I don't think so. Listen, if Tracy agrees to marry me, will you be my best man?"

"Uh – of course I will. I can survive a weekend in the country for the pleasure of watching you prance around in the monkey-suit."

"You know what you ought to do? You ought to fly out here and meet my family and see for yourself that I'm not crazy. Or at least no crazier than the last time you saw me. The people here would love to meet you."

Another long silence grew between them, but finally Trey responded. "I guess I could do that. Not as if I have to punch a clock here. But just for a couple of days, okay? I don't want to catch whatever you have."

"Bring some old clothes to muck around in," Will advised.

BACK INSIDE THE JEWELRY STORE, WILL INDULGED HIMSELF IN SEVERAL fantasies before forcing himself to accept the reality that he couldn't even afford the box for one of the beautiful rings he was envisioning on Tracy's finger.

"Thanks for your time," he told the clerk, trying not to blush as he said it.

As he was driving home, his phone rang again, a number he didn't recognize.

"This is Wayne Dennis," the voice on the other end told him. "I teach history and government at Infinity High, and Principal Stemwalter asked me to give you a call. It's our policy to have one or more of the teachers meet with an applicant before he meets with the administration and the Board. Do you think we could get together this evening or tomorrow evening?"

"Yes, sir, I can make either one, whichever you prefer."

Mr. Dennis named the time and gave Will his address, saying, "My wife loves to have people over, so we'll just take advantage of her baking skills and meet here."

This is a lot different from applying for a professorship, Will thought. *He sounds like a nice guy. Maybe teaching high school will be fine. Maybe everything really will fall into place this time.*

"ARE YOU SURE I CAN'T FIX YOU SOME TEA OR HOT CHOCOLATE?" ANITA Dennis asked for the third time.

"Honestly, Mrs. Dennis, I'm fine with water. Really."

"All right, then," she said, frowning a little, "and, please, call me Anita."

"Thanks, honey," Wayne Dennis said. "We'll just sit here and talk and enjoy your lemon meringue pie."

"I get the hint," she teased and left the two men at the kitchen table.

Will looked around as subtly as he could. The kitchen featured a big stove and a granite counter-top, signs of a serious cook. The slight bulge under Wayne Dennis's Ohio State polo shirt was probably another sign. Will tasted the pie and could have wept at the perfection of the explosion of lemon and sugar on his tongue.

"She really is that good," Wayne said, smiling at Will's expression. "Every time." He patted his incipient gut and sighed, "I don't think I have a chance of fitting into my high school band uniform ever again."

Will laughed appreciatively and swallowed another mouthful. "This might be the best pie I've ever tasted, and considering the bakers in my family, that's really saying something."

"So, while you enjoy your pie," Wayne said, "let's talk a little bit about you and a little bit about Infinity High."

An hour and a half passed so quickly Will could hardly believe it. He liked Mr. Dennis, with his wry sense of humor and quick intelligence, his ability to see the bigger picture of things and his obvious, deep love for his students.

He was also getting a less than favorable picture of the administration of Infinity High School, and an even worse picture of the school board.

"Wayne, let me just ask you one thing – I know it's not really my place, but – if the people at the top are as tough to work with as you suggest, why do you stay?"

"Fair question," Wayne replied. "Truth is, most of the time they don't bother me. I do my job and don't worry about the politics of things, which isn't saying I'm not aware of them. And the big thing is, I love the students. They're just such a great bunch of fascinating individuals, with so much potential, a lot of them, that I can't imagine leaving them. If you take the job, I'm betting you'll feel the same way before the first semester is over."

"The job hasn't been offered," Will reminded him.

"Oh, it will be. They'd be bigger fools than I think they are to turn you down."

WILL DREW THE COPY OF HIS SIGNED CONTRACT FROM HIS POCKET AND handed it to Tracy. "You're the first person I've told: I got the job. I'm the new junior English teacher for Infinity High School."

"That's wonderful! Congratulations! I'm so happy for you!" she enthused, looking at the contract and then throwing her arms around Will. "Your family will be so proud!"

"More like relieved," he half-joked.

"When do you start?" she asked, leaning back in his arms to see his face.

"Tuesday there's a teacher in-service, and then we start classes Wednesday."

"But, Will, it's Monday afternoon!"

"I know. I spent the morning at the school, getting my schedule and finding my room and the teachers' lounge and the office – and filling out forms for everything under the sun. I got my books and they gave me a laptop to keep my records on and they gave me a set of keys. Of course, I don't know what they all unlock, but at least I look official."

"How are you going to be ready to teach on Wednesday?"

"I have a copy of Mrs. Rupp's syllabus from last year, so I can copy. And I have taught before, so I know how to handle first day stuff."

"I'm sure you'll be brilliant," she said, Will's faithful supporter no matter what.

"I do have to go now, though, much as I'd rather stay with you." He let her go and turned toward the door. "I'll call you Wednesday night and let you know I'm still alive."

BY WEDNESDAY NIGHT, WILL WASN'T SO SURE HE WAS STILL ALIVE. HE couldn't remember having been this tired since the first day he had baled hay at age fifteen. Apparently Mollie Rupp had been a big favorite, both with the students and with the teachers, and everyone was quick to tell him how wonderful she was and how much she would be missed. The juniors who had had her in sophomore English spent their first classes telling Will he wasn't doing things the way Mrs. Rupp did them. The juniors who hadn't had her spent their time telling him they wished they had her now. All of them managed to find little ways to tease and disrupt, although nothing was really bad enough to warrant action.

"Tomorrow," Will promised himself. "Tomorrow I take charge and show 'em who's boss. God, help me!"

He lay down on the bed with his cell phone to call Tracy because he was too whipped to sit up, and he basked in her sympathy and encouragement.

"I love you," she told him, "and I'm proud of you. I'm going to pray tomorrow goes really well for you."

"What – you didn't pray that for today?"

"Of course I did! But God must have been testing you to see whether you could stick it out."

"For you," he said, "I can stick out anything. If you believe in me, then nothing else matters."

By the end of October, Will had managed to replace Mollie Rupp in the students' affections, probably much aided by bringing in his guitar and singing American folk lyrics to them during the poetry section and giving them the chance to share their own songs or poems. It had been an experiment which really paid off, as half a dozen youth showed real potential as song-writers and poets. Now there was an afterschool writers' group meeting once a month under Will's supervision.

The last Saturday in October there was a couples' baby shower for Mollie Rupp, and Wayne and Anita Dennis insisted Will and Tracy should accompany them.

"I don't want to do this," Will told Tracy, practically grinding his teeth as he spoke.

"It would be rude not to go when you've been invited," Tracy told him. "Besides, we like the Dennises; we'll just hang out with them. Nothing bad is going to happen at a baby shower."

"If it's couples, then Chance is going to be there."

Tracy hesitated, looking down at her feet, where they were firmly planted on the oriental rug in her mother's living room. "I know," she finally said. "But high school was a long time ago, Will. None of us is the same any more. Maybe he's grown up and become a better person."

Will firmly closed his mouth on the invective pouring through his mind and settled for shaking his head. He knew Chance would never change. Once a bully, always a bully.

"We have to buy presents," Tracy said. "Do you want to buy one together or just get them separately?"

"Presents?"

"Will, come on! It's a shower. We take presents for the new baby."

"Oh. Okay. Like what?"

"Do men do this on purpose?" Tracy asked, lightly punching his arm. "All right. I'll pick up something from both of us – and I'll wrap it – and I'll get a cute card. But you have to sign the card."

"Tell me what I'm giving them," Will muttered to Tracy as he maneuvered a large box wrapped in bright blue paper and tied with a huge red satin bow through the throng of people.

"It's a swing," she told him, "one of the things on their wish list. Put it over there by that table with all the other presents."

Will set down his burden and straightened up to find himself face to face with his old nemesis.

"Will Ryersen, as I live and breathe," Chance said, showing all his teeth in a toothpaste-ad grin.

Will felt Tracy's hand clenching on his bicep. "Chance."

"And Tracy Showalter," Chance continued. "Now here's a real treat! Glad you could come."

"Thank you," Tracy said, her voice thready and her palm beginning to sweat through Will's shirt.

"How's life treating you?" Chance asked, blocking their retreat from the table and seeming ready to settle in for a long chat.

I am not in high school any more, Will told himself sternly, swallowing down the acid panic rising in his throat. *And this guy isn't the big football hero any more. He sells real estate. Looks like it, too. Mighty high forehead you have these days, buddy, and starting to look a little bit like your daddy around the middle. You can probably still beat the crap out of me, but I bet you aren't going to risk it here in front of all these people.*

191

"Congratulations on your baby," Tracy said into the void. "I hear it's a boy."

Chance seemed to swell up like a toad with pride. "Yep. Chance, Junior. He's gonna be a football player like his daddy, Mollie says, kicking already."

"That's great," Will said. "Please excuse us."

The mask dropped. "Ryersen, I don't know what made you come back to town, but you aren't any more welcome here now than you were ten years ago. Lewiston and Infinity are towns for real men; you should go back to the city, where all the fags hang out."

"Don't do it, Will!" Tracy said. Will noticed that he had clenched his fist and raised it.

"Oh, don't worry," Chance laughed easily. "He always was a coward. He won't do anything. Just like his old man. Well, children, enjoy the party." He walked away.

"I can't do this," Will said, shaking with rage. "I want to kill him."

"We can't just walk out," Tracy said. "All your friends from the school are here, and they'll start asking questions. Let's go over there and get something to drink. I think I saw Wayne and Anita; we'll sit with them."

Will obtained cola for Tracy and a beer for himself from the drinks counter and led her to a round table across the room where the Dennises sat with several other couples. By focusing on conversation with Wayne, he made it through the longest two hours of his life in a long time before Tracy would allow him to leave.

In the car on the way to her house, Will was silent, gripping the wheel as if to strangle it, breathing unevenly, arguing with the beer sloshing in his belly that it should stay where it was. He parked in the driveway, still silent, and took Tracy's hand.

"You didn't let yourself have a very good time, did you?" she asked, covering his hand with her other one. "Shall we pray before you go?"

"Am I going?"

"Yes, I think you are. You need to deal with some of this anger; I feel like I'm getting testosterone poisoning just sitting next to you. Come on, Professor, let's pray."

"Whatever." He bowed his head and waited for Tracy to begin. After a few moments he opened his eyes again and looked at her. "Aren't you going to pray?"

"I think you're the one who needs to do it," she returned. "You're the one who's so upset."

"Oh, you're not upset? You weren't scared enough to pass out when Chance started talking? I saw your face, babe, and I heard that little whispery voice when you talked to him."

"I was scared. But I reminded myself that the Lord hasn't given me a spirit of fear, but of power and love and a sound mind. Then I reminded myself that poor Chance probably doesn't know the Lord, and he's still living on his old glory days, not having a fruitful life right now. When I did that, I felt sorry for him."

"Sorry for him! If his life isn't perfect, that's what he deserves. I've never met a more —"

"Shh! Don't do that, Will. You need to forgive him and pray for the Lord to save him."

Will let go of Tracy's hand and climbed out of the car. He walked around to her side, opened the door and offered her his hand. "I'll see you to the door."

"That's all right," she told him, exiting on her own. "I can make it from here. Thank you for taking me with you. I hope we'll talk soon. Good night, Will." She turned away before he could kiss her and scurried up the steps into the house.

Chapter 20

"I'M LOOKING FORWARD TO SPENDING TIME WITH YOUR friend," Matthew said as he and Will raked leaves in the front yard.

"I appreciate your taking him in."

"No problem. That third bedroom just sits there, and it wasn't too hard to make it a real guest room." A faint frown creased Matthew's brow and he paused to shove Tucker away from the growing pile of leaves. "This is your rich friend, right?"

"Yes, he surely is!" Will agreed. "Richest guy I've ever met. But you won't know it to talk to him. He's just a nice guy, Dad, nothing to be uptight about."

"I never used to think too much about – well, sometimes I felt like Allison was too good for me – "

"Which she is."

"Don't sass your father, Son. Yeah, she is, and not just because she's an educated woman. But I didn't worry about other people so much. The people we hang out with aren't exactly the upper crust of anything, not even Lewiston, you know. Now here's this young man who can probably buy the whole town and move it to Iowa if he wants to..."

"Dad, I promise, you don't need to worry. Trey's going to be as uncomfortable on the farm as you would be in New York City, and he's going to be glad to meet you. Besides, who can resist Allison and Tucker?"

"You have a point there," Matthew agreed. "Tucker! Get out of those leaves!"

TRUE TO WILL'S WORD, TREY SULLIVAN WAS ALL HUMILITY AND CHARM, greeting Matthew and Allison with deference, embracing Will in a bear-hug full of shoulder-pounding, laughing at Tucker, even though the dog's nails snagged the shoulders of Trey's cashmere sweater.

"Don't worry," he told Allison. "Sweater is courtesy of my obscenely wealthy grandmother, who will send another one this Christmas and never know the difference. Tucker may have done me a favor; I'm not sure this caramel color exactly sets off my lovely blue eyes."

"Well, he's everything you said he'd be," Allison remarked, leading Trey into the house. "You can put your indecently expensive luggage in here," she told him, opening the door to the spare room, "and join us in the kitchen for coffee."

Trey seemed to fit right in, joking with Matthew and Allison and riding Will at every opportunity, just like old times. He seemed to enjoy Allison's lasagna, what she called her 'go-to' company dish, and chocolate chip cookies, and lent a hand with the dinner dishes as if he did that every night.

"Let's take the dog for a walk," Will said, snagging the leash and his leather jacket from the front closet.

"Does he let you walk him?" Trey asked, putting on a similar, though much more expensive, jacket.

"Oh, sure," Will said. "He loves company."

"There's no sidewalk," Trey said as they came to the end of the driveway. "Where do you walk?"

"Follow the dog," Will answered. "We walk on the road."

"What about traffic?"

Will had to laugh. "At this time of night, if two cars pass each other on this road, there's a traffic jam. Don't worry. If something comes along, we just step onto the grass and let it go by. Heel, Tucker."

The dog dropped politely into place at Will's left heel, pushing Trey just a little bit out of the way to get there.

"Well-trained brute, isn't he?"

"In most ways. Can't break him of jumping up to say hello, though. A lot nicer and friendlier than Nero. I wonder how that old cat is doing."

"No idea. I do bring greetings from Liam, though, and from what's left of the gang at McClendon's. Do you miss us?"

"What became of Nate and Steve?" Will asked, avoiding Trey's question.

"They took off for Portland. Steve had a yen to see the Pacific, and Nate thought he might have a job at one of the local colleges. You miss them?"

"Not really. Just curious."

"How do you keep from breaking your leg walking on this stuff in the dark?" Trey complained as he stumbled. "Where are all the street lights?"

"In town," Will said, smiling in the dark. "We go by starlight here, or flashlight."

"Amazing. I like your folks, Will. Nice people. Good-hearted."

"Yes, they are. Don't make fun of them, Trey."

"Hey, I wasn't! I mean it." They walked on a bit farther, quiet and comfortable with it, before Trey asked, "So how are you? How's the job?"

"If you'd asked me that in early September, I would have told you I must have been nuts to sign a contract. They gave me a hard time, breaking me in. But now we're used to each other, and I'm really enjoying the kids. Most of them are bright and funny, and some of them are really special."

"Thought you'd never teach high school."

"I'm learning never to say never. I didn't want to. Even when I applied for this job, it was really because I thought I was supposed to, not because I wanted to. But I've made some good friends and found some real satisfaction in the work."

"And then there's Tracy..."

"Well, yes, there is that. You'll meet her tomorrow night, and I think you'll see why I – I love her."

"You still planning to marry her?"

"If she'll have me."

"Come on, Ryersen, you haven't asked her yet?"

"I'm going to let Tucker off the leash now, so brace yourself." Will released the clip and Tucker spun around their legs like a dervish before taking off down the road, barking.

"What the – "

"His buddy the German shepherd lives over there on that farm, and they love to run around and make a ruckus."

"Ruckus. Dang, Will, you sure sound like a country boy now!"

Will smiled at his friend and kept walking, not the least bothered by what would have been an insult a few months before. "I don't think I'm ever going to be a real 'country boy,'" he countered, "but I'm a lot more comfortable here now than I ever was growing up. I miss the city, I won't lie, and – well – I miss you just a little, but if I need a fix I can drive to Toledo or Indianapolis or Chicago in a few hours. This is home, Trey. It took me a while to figure out this is where I belong, but I know it now."

Trey was shaking his head, frowning, his features deeply shadowed in the faint light. "I know you think you're in love, and you think you've got this new thing with Jesus. But what are you going to do when the thrill wears off?"

"Who says it has to?" Will stopped in front of the Millers' place to watch the dogs gamboling in the moonlight. Trey stopped beside him.

"The thrill always wears off. What happens the day you realize there's another woman out there who's younger and prettier and hotter and – and more sophisticated than your little nunlet, the day you realize you hate farmers' kids who don't give a rip about poetry or books and only want to read the ag news and the Farmer's Almanac, the day you realize you've had the same conversation about the weather and the coffee with your folks every day for the last three hundred sixty-four days and tomorrow you're going to do it all again?"

Will stood very still in the moonlight, the leaves remaining on the Millers' ancient oak tree making patterns across his face, camouflaging his expression.

Trey had a last strike. "And what happens when you finally admit to yourself you're a writer and want to spend time researching and writing the great American novel – and you can't take the time because your job fills up most of it and your wife and kids and dog and lawn – and church – fill up the rest of it? What happens when that's your dream, and you want to do it, and you can't because your brain is dead from years of farm reports and prayer meetings? How thrilled are you going to be then?"

Tucker bounded back across the road and stood in front of Trey, growling, ears laid back. Will softly snapped his fingers and called the dog to him, putting a hand through his collar. Tucker stood obediently, but he continued to face Trey and growl softly.

"I think maybe he's taken offense to what you're sayin'," Will said, the faint echo of Kentucky suddenly in his voice. "Let's head back now. Just step easy, Trey. This isn't my dog, and I can't vouch for him all the way." He clipped the lead back onto Tucker's collar and kept him on a short leash.

"Will, listen, I'm sorry. I didn't mean to stir up anything for you *or* the dog. I just care a lot about what happens to you, and it all looks – dangerous – to me."

"I appreciate that. You're still the best friend I've ever had, and I care what you think. But this time, I think you're wrong. Because of Jesus."

"Oh, please!"

"Hey, wait a minute!"

Tucker began to growl again, and Will spoke sternly to him. The two men stood in the middle of the road, washed in moonlight and regret, looking at one another in bafflement.

"Okay," Will said, "you need to listen: I get it that you don't believe any of the Jesus-stuff; we've had that conversation enough over the years, and I agreed with you until pretty recently. And I respect that's your belief. But my beliefs have changed, and I think you owe me respect for mine, too, even if they're different from yours. I'm not trying to sell you anything or asking you to agree with me – just accept where I'm coming from."

Trey gave a huge sigh. "I don't know if I can. Maybe I should go home in the morning instead of meeting the rest of your family. You can tell 'em I got called back to the office for some emergency or something."

Will burst out laughing. "You have to be kidding! I've been telling my family for years that you're so rich and pampered you only work when you feel like it!"

"Well – well – then tell 'em I feel like it!"

"Come on, let's head back to the house. Allison will give you chocolate something that will make all this seem unimportant." He clapped Trey on the shoulder and began to walk again, forcing his friend to fall into step with him.

TREY STEADFASTLY REFUSED TO CONSIDER GOING TO CHURCH, INSISTING he would sleep in and join them for dinner afterward. Will stopped back at the Ryersen house to pick him up and was pleased to find him there, dressed in his own version of casual, a GQ look he supposed was 'country chic.'

"You might want to lose the ascot," Will said, taking in Trey's five hundred dollar Armani trousers and handmade silk shirt. "I could lend you a Wal Mart tee-shirt; you're likely to get something on that silk before the day is over."

"No problem," Trey laughed, waving his hand in the air. "That's what dry cleaners are for."

"Are you doing this on purpose?" Will asked. "Do you want to make my family dislike you?"

"Don't be dumb. I'm doing it to bug you, Professor. I know how thin-skinned you are. You think Nate was the only one who knew how to push your buttons?"

"Sorry. Let's go, then. No, Tucker, you stay and guard the house."

They left the dog on the porch and climbed into Will's Toyota for the short trip to the Abbotts'. Will was aware of an uneasy feeling in the pit of his stomach and found himself praying the encounter between his family and his best friend would go well.

Matthew's truck and Ed's El Camino were already in the drive-way, and Flash was standing at the foot of the porch steps, barking as soon as they began the long way from the road to the yard. October sunlight bathed the white house in gold, filtered only a little by the remaining oak leaves and naked maple branches. Someone was wait-ing behind the front door, which gaped open just a little.

"Gracie," Will muttered.

"Huh?" Trey asked.

"Our official welcoming committee: Flash-the-dog and Gracie-the-little-dynamo. She's John's little girl, turned eleven last January. The dog doesn't bite, by the way, but he does jump. Step on his toes."

"Country life survival 102," Trey grunted. "Step on dog's toes."

"WILL!" GRACIE YELLED, SLAMMING OUT THROUGH THE SCREEN DOOR and jumping off the porch to grab him around the waist. "I'm so glad you're here!"

"Hey, Gracie," Will said a bit breathlessly, disentangling her. "Good to see you, too. It's been at least half an hour since church. Better call off your dog; he's giving my friend Trey there a hard time."

Flash continued his entirely inappropriate investigation of Trey's person while continuing to growl and bark here and there. Trey stood frozen, hoping not to lose any irreplaceable parts, giving Will a be- seeching look.

"Come here, Flash," Gracie commanded, and the black and white terror immediately moved to her side.

"Thank you," Trey said, clearly meaning it.

"Hi," Gracie said, holding out her hand to shake. "I'm Gracie Abbott, and I bet you're Trey Sullivan, Will's friend."

"Guilty as charged!" Trey said, smiling down at Gracie as he shook her hand. "I'm pleased to meet you, Miss Abbott; I've heard many good things about you from young Will here."

"Ooo, he's fancy, Will!" she said, pinking with pleasure.

"That's one way of looking at it," Will said, giving Trey a slanted glance and a smirk. "Can you keep Flash under control so we can go in to eat?"

In the house they found the usual Sunday dinner activity, men in the living room, women in the kitchen. "I know it's sexist," John had said once when Carolyn and Pearl and Allison had been bustling about while the men watched television, "but I like it this way. It feels like home when the women are taking care of us."

Will imagined all the northwest Ohio families were like that – traditional, old-fashioned, sexist, whatever it was called – the way it had been for uncountable generations. Tracy would be that way, too, he knew. He'd never have to wash a dish or change a diaper if he didn't want to. Not, of course, that he would shirk so-called women's work; after all, he was modern, sophisticated, citified, *and you like making points with the women,* he admitted to himself.

Trey, being metrosexualized, immediately offered to help the la- dies, which earned him points with every one of them and a few dark looks from the men. "We get ours after dinner," John explained. "On Sundays, the men do the dishes."

The meal was an Abbott production number, doubtless in Trey's honor, although Will didn't tell him that. Cassie had roasted a spiral- cut ham and glazed it with something tangy and sweet. It was accompanied by sweet potatoes, new red potatoes, home-made yeast rolls with home-made black raspberry jelly and fresh butter, home-frozen corn and green beans and Allison's favorite death-by-chocolate cake for dessert.

"Ladies," Trey said, leaning back and surreptitiously easing his waistband, "that has to be the best meal I've eaten – well, maybe in forever."

"Suck-up," Will whispered, "you still have to do the dishes."

"Maybe Trey could take a walk with Flash and me," Gracie said, overhearing Will's remark. "I'd like to talk to him."

"Gracie," John warned.

"Oh, no, kiddo," Will agreed. "Not this trip. Maybe next time he visits."

"But, Will! You know how important salvation is!"

Will fought desperately not to laugh as he watched the color drain from Trey's face. "All right, men, let's get this clean-up underway," he said, dragging Trey to his feet and loading him down with the ham platter. "Follow me, buddy."

In the kitchen, Trey leaned against the refrigerator and wiped his face with his hand in a gesture so fervent Will wasn't sure whether he was for real or just hamming it up.

"You have no idea," he told Trey. "She grabs on like a gator and doesn't let go."

"I thought you said nobody was going to hit me over the head with a Bible," Trey said.

"And he meant it," John answered, coming through the door with hands full of leftovers. "But Gracie is a law unto herself in that regard. I promise I won't let her corner you."

"Thanks! I mean no disrespect, John, but I'm just not interested."

"No problem. We'll respect your position."

"Yep," Ed agreed, noisily dumping an armload of dirty dishes on the counter by the sink. "Even if you're wrong." He winked at Will and went back for more dishes.

"I think I'll wash," Matthew said, bringing in a tray of glasses. "Any objections?"

"None from me," Ed said. "I like to protect my dainty hands."

Trey looked at Ed's large, darkened hands, thick with callus and nicked here and there, fingers beginning to be gnarled with arthritis, and laughed out loud.

"Son," Ed told him, faking seriousness, "it ain't polite to laugh at an old man."

"No, sir," Tray gave back, "and if I meet one around here, I won't laugh at him."

They settled comfortably into a routine. Matthew scraped and rinsed everything, then put the silverware and glasses into a sink full of suds. He filled the other half of the sink with warm rinse-water, and John stationed himself there, leaving Ed, Trey and Will to dry things and put them away.

"What about the leftovers?" Trey asked.

"Oh, we ain't allowed to do that," Ed said. "Womenfolk don't think we can figure it out."

"So they just sit here?"

"Until Cassie takes a notion to put 'em away."

"Did I hear my name?" she asked, coming through the swinging door.

"Only in a good way," Matthew assured her.

In minutes she had disposed of all the leftovers according to some arcane formula known only to herself and the men had the kitchen to themselves again.

"So, Trey," John said, handing him a platter to dry, "tell us about your work in Iowa."

Trey launched into a more in-depth analysis of high finance than he had given at dinner and the look of mild surprise on his face suggested he had not expected either the interest or the understanding the men were giving.

"Sounds like you really enjoy your work," John said.

"You know... I guess I do. I like putting people together with other people to make deals, and I like seeing people make money, and I like the rush when the market's wonky and you guess right..." A smile came over his face. "I hadn't thought much about it before. I just show up when I feel like it and mess around for a while and see what happens, but I do like it."

"Maybe you oughta try showin' up more often," Ed said, an implied criticism in his tone. "Might could do a lot of good for folks who don't understand highfalutin' finance as good as you do."

Trey had the grace to look abashed. "You may be right," he said, turning his back to stack a plate with the others on the table.

"What do you do with your time when you aren't making deals?" Matthew asked.

"Well, I see my family a couple of times a week, at least, and I go out with friends. When Will was in town we used to play racquetball pretty regularly, but I haven't found a good replacement since he left. I'm afraid I'm getting soft." He patted his middle ruefully. "Meals like this one don't help, either. I don't know how all you guys stay so thin and fit."

"Come down to the barn with me," Will said, "and I'll show you the local replacement for racquetball. Might want to ditch the Armani pants first, though."

"He seems like a nice young man," Cassie said, eyes intent on her embroidery except for occasional glances across the living room to the area where Micah and Gracie were building with Legos.

"He does care for Will," Pearl said, coming immediately to the only point which mattered.

"I hope he isn't trying to talk Will into going back to Iowa with him," Allison said, voicing everyone's fear.

"Will has a contract with the school and a relationship with the Lord," Pearl countered. "He won't go anywhere."

"But what if he thinks he can do better back there?" Cassie asked. "After all, he can have a relationship with Jesus wherever he is."

"He won't go," Allison told them. "He's working up the nerve to ask Tracy to marry him."

"What would keep them both from moving away?" Cassie asked.

"Oh, I don't think she wants to leave her family," Allison said, "and Will wants what she wants. If she wanted to go away, she could have gone back to Africa or some other country. No, I think her rambling days are over and she's just where she wants to be."

"Maybe Trey can move here," Gracie said, "since his work isn't very important. Then he and Will can play ball together and we can teach him about Jesus."

"You only know one song, don't you, sweetheart?" Allison said, smiling at the girl. "You need to pray for Trey, that he'll learn it's safe to consider our point of view."

"It isn't safe not to!" Grace insisted, flinging her hands wide in exasperation and knocking over some Lego concoction Micah had been laboring at. "Oh, shoot! I'm sorry, Micah! Here, let me help you fix it."

"God bless the child," Pearl said softly, "she has a true heart for evangelism. I hope everyone understands what that is going to mean when she grows up."

"What?" Allison asked.

"Well, most likely she'll feel called to serve the Lord on some far-away mission field where millions of people don't know Jesus. Her passion already is to tell everyone and drag them to salvation." Pearl smiled sadly at her knitting. "I wish I could be here to see that."

"Don't say that!" Cassie cried. "You're going to be here for a long time yet!"

"I'm not having premonitions or prophetic anythings," Pearl said, her dark eyes snapping. "I'm just looking at the facts. It will be nothing but a miracle if I'm still here in another ten years."

"Let's pretend it isn't happening," Allison whispered, her eyes swimming with tears. "You're here today, and this is the only day any of us has."

"Excellent wisdom comes from AA," Pearl said, nodding. "We'll pray for Trey, certainly, and see what God has in mind."

"I'D LOVE TO HAVE YOU STAY LONGER," WILL TOLD TREY AS THEY SAT up late Sunday night in the Ryersen living room, Tucker lying on Will's feet, Trey's up on the coffee table.

"I didn't expect it, but I kind of wish I could. But I really did tell Dad I'd be back early this week to cover a meeting for him while he's at some convention in the Bahamas. I hate having him there; it's hurricane season."

"No hurricane would dare hit your father," Will joked. "Anyway, Dad will take you to the airport in the morning. I can't cut school – sorry."

"No problem. We'll say good-bye tonight. I figure the next time I see you is going to be the wedding – right? Even if I didn't get to meet the bride this time."

"For Pete's sake, don't call her 'the bride' yet! I haven't even asked her!"

"Well, are you going to or what?"

"I want to…"

"But?"

"Well…"

"Bwak, bwak, bwak!"

"Shut up! You'll wake the folks! Yes, I am chicken. What if she says no? You have no idea how hard it was to get her to date me, not just the first time, but the second time, too."

"Hey, buddy, you're one of the good guys. Everybody around here loves you. How can she not? And you've taken care of the one big obstacle, right? The Jesus part?"

"I guess so. Want another beer?"

"Sure."

Will went to the refrigerator and claimed two more beers, noticing the shelf he had filled a few days before was now almost empty. He and Matthew rarely even kept beer in the house, in deference to Allison, but she had been fine with having it there for Trey, along with the kind of yogurt he liked. Tucker, who had followed him, made sad eyes in hope of a treat, so Will gave him some leftover ham.

"You are such a sucker," Trey observed from the living room. "You let the kids manipulate you like that?"

"Nope," Will said, handing Trey a beer, "only the quadrupeds."

Trey drained about half the bottle of beer without stopping before he turned to Will and said, "Before I go – "

"Yes?"

"I don't want you to think I'm disrespecting you or anything, because I'm not, but – about this God business – "

"Trey, come on. Let's just agree to disagree, please." Will took a healthy slug of his own beer, and it burned.

"No, please. I just want you to think again about how different your life is now and how much you liked things the way they were before. We had a good time, and we didn't have to ask ourselves all the time, 'Is this okay?' If everybody agreed and nobody got hurt, whatever it was, was fine. Angie still asks about you sometimes. She hasn't hooked up with anybody permanent. I think she got more attached to you than she planned."

"That's the thing," Will said, seizing the moment. "We didn't plan to get involved or attached, we didn't mean to hurt anybody, we thought we were having fun – and then she got hurt anyway.

Behavior does have consequences, whether we want to think it does or not. You know what else about that little fling? I had to get tested for STDs."

"Yike! You all right?"

"Oh, yeah. But I couldn't touch Tracy, even to kiss her – and that's all you do with a good Christian girl, so don't be going there! – without being sure I was clean. Physically clean. And then I had to start thinking about being morally, spiritually clean. And there's a thing called a soul-tie..."

"What the heck does that mean?" Trey frowned.

"It's a – a – an unhealthy attachment, a spiritual attachment, I guess you'd say, that develops between two people when they – get intimate. And breaking up the relationship doesn't necessarily end the soul-tie. So you can go on to the next person still dragging the last person with you, kind of."

"That sounds obscene."

"It is," Will agreed. "And it can ruin a relationship."

"Like always having three in the bed?"

"Sort of. Even if there isn't a bed involved. It means you can't give your whole heart to the one you love because part of it is tied to somebody else."

"You're saying Angie..."

"Yes. Angie. I had to pray a lot about that relationship and ask God to forgive me for using her and for – well, never mind."

"Oh, don't worry; I get it. 'Fornication is a sin,'" he intoned like a TV preacher.

Will sighed. "I do believe that now. That's why I had to get rid of all that, so I could come to Tracy – clean. So I can marry her, if she'll have me, with a pure heart and the will to love only her forever. Sorry if that sounds preachy – I guess it is."

Trey sighed heavily. "Don't suppose I'm going to get anywhere talking about this stuff with you, am I?"

"I don't think so, no." Will clinked his beer bottle against Trey's. "Let's get some sleep, and I'll see you in the morning."

Trey finished his beer and took the bottle to the trash can in the kitchen. Coming back to Will, he said, "Okay, friend. Just one more thing."

"Yes?"

"If you ever decide you can't do this anymore, if you ever just need a break, you can come to me. I'll always be your friend, even if I don't understand you, and I'll always make a place for you."

"Trey, man, I – "

"No, no getting maudlin. See you in the morning."

Chapter 21

"I HAD THE NICEST NOTE FROM TREY," ALLISON SAID, BRANdishing a creamy ivory envelope that looked like an expensive wedding invitation. "He thanks all of us for making him feel so welcome and all that sort of thing. What a nice guy!"

"He is that," Will agreed.

"He's different from Kevin and Travis, or even Wayne Dennis, though," Matthew observed. "Are you really happy here, Son?"

Will considered. "Pretty much," he said. "I'll be really happy when Tracy and I are married and I find a better teaching job."

"Any progress on that front?" Matthew asked.

"Well – no..."

"She'll never marry you if you don't ask her," Allison observed. "What's the hang-up?"

Will took a chocolate cookie from the box on the table and took a big bite. He knew it wouldn't buy much time, but a guy took what he could get sometimes. Allison set glasses of milk in front of him and Matthew and poured herself a cup of coffee.

Matthew watched his wife doctoring the coffee with cream and sugar and said, laughing, "Why don't you just put sugar in a glass of milk and skip the coffee altogether?"

"Smart-alec." She sat down with them and snagged two cookies. "So, Will?"

"Oh. Yeah." He shook his head a little. "I don't know. I guess I'm afraid she'll say no. As long as I don't bring it up, I can still hope."

"When I see the two of you together," Matthew said, "it reminds me of John and Carolyn or Ted and Livvie – or us –" he looked at Allison. "There's just a connection everybody can see, and it's – " He stopped, the flush rising up his neck and ears.

"What?" Allison asked quietly.

"Never mind."

"Dad, you're blushing like a girl! What is it?"

"You're going to laugh."

"I promise I won't laugh," Allison said, laying her hand over Matthew's.

He wouldn't look at either of them. "It's holy," he said.

HOLY, WILL THOUGHT AS HE DROVE TO PICK UP TRACY. HE HAD BEEN avoiding the football games at Infinity, despite the urgings of the other teachers to attend. They almost implied he was subversive, if not un- manly, for refusing to cheer for dear old Infinity High. Tonight was homecoming, though, and he had agreed to chaperone the dance after the game. Tracy had been delighted to go with him, and he didn't know whether that was his company, a dance, or the game itself. Homecom- ing this year was Infinity vs. Lewiston, the worst possible combination Will could imagine.

Nevertheless, his father's description of good marriages kept re- running in his head at odd moments. He had begun to observe cou- ples wherever he went, honing his writer's skills again, trying to gauge both the visible and the subliminal signs. He had found himself pray- ing about marriage, not just the 'Please let me have her' prayer he had been praying for months, but prayers about his own worthiness. Because how could a man like him be holy?

"Right on time!" Tracy said, running down the front steps to greet him. She was dressed in brown and green, the colors of neither school, probably a smart move, Will thought, and her eyes sparkled with excitement. He opened the car door and handed her in as if it were a limousine.

"You look beautiful!" he told her, leaning over to kiss her as soon as he was seated.

"Thank you! You're pretty, too. Oh, this is going to be so much fun!"

"I hope you think so by the end of the game," Will said. "It's getting colder by the minute."

"Well, it is November. Only two weeks to Thanksgiving, can you believe it?"

"No, in fact I can't. Fastest year I can ever remember."

"Did you remember the blanket and cushions?" Tracy asked. "I have the cocoa." She gestured to a huge Thermos sticking out of her oversized bag.

"Back seat," Will told her. He hoped it would be so cold they would have to huddle together in one blanket.

"Lewiston has a really good team this year," Tracy said. "Almost as good as when we – " Remembering, she stopped abruptly.

"It's okay," Will said, squeezing her hand. "That was then, and this is now." *Even if I never forget it. We're not in high school anymore; Lord, help me to remember that.*

THE HIGH SCHOOL GYM WAS DECORATED WITH EVERY CONCEIVABLE OR-nament in the Infinity Hornets' blue and gold colors. A huge, evil-eyed hornet with blue and gold stripes seemed to be buzzing over the crepe-paper-wrapped thrones of the homecoming king and queen, Bill Tilloch, captain of the team, and Paige Wilcox, head cheerleader, both blue-eyed, golden-haired specimens of teenage perfection. A very young man dressed in baggy jeans and a hoodie, whose sign billed him as "Cee-Jay the Dee-Jay," was set up in one corner to play what passed as dance music these days, and bunches of girls in pretty dress-es danced with each other in the middle of the floor under the disco ball. A few of the team members, hyped up by their 21-7 win over Lewiston, prowled the perimeter near the refreshment tables checking out the girls.

"I think we need to cruise over thataway," he told Tracy, nodding toward the drinks table.

"Oh, yeah," she agreed. "I know how it goes."

"Hey, Mr. Ryersen," one of the boys said as they approached. "Bring your guitar?"

"Not tonight, Eddie," Will said. "I'm kind of outclassed by this music. I just thought I'd get us some sodas."

"Yeah, sure, Mr. Ryersen. Have a good time."

"You, too, Eddie."

"You're such a nice guy," Tracy said. "Dance with me?"

"I will if they play something written before 1985. Which they won't, I'm afraid."

"Maybe I can bribe them," Tracy said, laughing up at him.

They patrolled the gym slowly, drinking lukewarm soda, talking with other chaperones as they met. Near midnight the band suddenly switched from the frantic beat which had characterized the evening to slow-dancing oldies.

"Did you bribe them?" Will asked.

"You know I've been with you every minute," Tracy said. "So now will you dance with me?"

"I don't really know how," he said, embarrassed.

"Easy these days," Tracy said, putting her arms around his neck. "Just put your arms around me and shuffle around."

"What song is that?" Will asked a passing girl.

She laughed and said, "Oh, that's 'Iris,' by the Goo Goo Dolls. It's so last year."

"Okay," Will said to Tracy, "I can shuffle to that." He filled his arms with her and drew her as close as he could, resting his cheek on her hair, breathing in the beloved scent of Tracy, closing his eyes and hoping the song would never end. "I love you," he whispered into her hair, confident she couldn't hear him over the music.

"Thanks for helping me out tonight," Will said as they pulled back into Tracy's driveway. "It was fun being with you."

"I had a great time! Do you want to come in for a while?"

"It's pretty late; looks like your folks are in bed already."

"I know."

How am I supposed to deal with this! Lord, this isn't fair!

"Tracy, it isn't a good idea for us to be alone together in the middle of the night. I want to respect you and treat you like the lady you are, but you're asking a lot of me."

Tracy sighed. "I know. I'm sorry. But we need to talk, and I hate to do it freezing in the car or running the motor and waking my parents."

"Talk," Will said bleakly. "All right."

They hung up their coats and sat down on the couch in the living room, a full cushion between them.

"Do you want some cocoa or tea or anything?" Tracy asked.

"No, thank you. I want to know what's on your mind before I lose mine."

Tracy fidgeted, picking at her cuticles, pulling on her skirt, turning away from him and then turning back. Finally she took a deep breath and said, "We've been seeing each other for almost a year now, Will, and we care enough about each other that we have to be careful not to do anything improper. We've shared a lot about the time we were apart – not the whole story, I suppose, but it seems like a lot. I feel like I know you better than I did when we were in high school, and I – I like you even better than I did then, too."

She hesitated. Will kept looking at her, unsure where this was going, terrified she was about to give him the 'you're such a nice guy, but – ' line.

"I'm twenty-eight now, you know, and – well, frankly, Will, there are things I want in my life that have kind of an expiration date on them. I want to get married and have children and grow old with my husband and have grandchildren. If I don't start pretty soon, I'm going to miss out on the children part, at least. So, see, the thing is – oh, Will, I love you; I've always loved you! – and I want to marry you and have your babies. But if you don't feel that way about me, then you need to tell me and stop hanging around so I can get over my broken heart and try to find somebody else who – "

What?

"Will? Did you hear me?"

What?

"Oh, my – I'm sorry, please forgive me for saying anything. I shouldn't have – "

"Tracy? Did you just say you love me and you want to marry me?"

She nodded, tears dripping from her eyelashes onto her cheeks, eyes downcast.

"Look at me."

She raised her eyes to his, to find the same waterfall of tears starting there.

"I've been trying to get up the nerve to tell you how much I love you, how much I want to marry you, for months. But I couldn't imagine you would want me."

"Sometimes you're so dumb I forget what a great score you got on the ACT," she told him, a smile breaking through her tears like a rainbow. "Do you really want to marry me, Will?"

"Yes! Tomorrow!" He closed the distance between them and drew her back into his arms where she belonged, kissing them both silly before he could force himself to back off.

"I think my mother will probably want some time to plan a wedding," Tracy said. "Do you have any other preferences besides tomorrow?"

"Thanksgiving? No? How about Christmas?"

"When's the end of the school year?" she asked.

"Typically, right before Memorial Day," Will said, "unless there's a bad winter with too many snow days. Then it can run over into June."

"I think a typical June wedding would be nice."

"Aw, come on," Will said, noticing but not caring that he was whining, "how about my birthday?"

"I do *not* want to be married on Groundhog Day," she said severely. "Can you imagine what people would do with that?"

Will had to laugh. "Yeah, they already always ask me if I've seen my shadow. Okay, but *early* June, please?"

"If we can get the church."

ALTHOUGH WILL HAD TEASED TRACY THAT SINCE SHE HAD PROPOSED TO him, she should ask his father for his hand in marriage, he really believed, deep in his old Kentucky soul, that he should speak with her father. He decided to take a chance on dropping in on Monday evening, and he was rewarded with the cool welcome and gimlet gaze he had come to expect from both of Tracy's parents.

"How did it go?" Matthew asked when Will came home.

"About as well as I expected. I protested my undying love – that wasn't hard – and tried to prove I'll be a good provider – that was impossible; he knows what I make – and I asked him for permission to marry his daughter."

"And?" Allison asked, bouncing up and down with excitement. "What then?"

"Then he made me sit there like a little kid in the principal's office while he looked me up and down with those cold eyes, the way he must look at the bad guy when he's in court, until I started to feel guilty myself. Finally Mrs. Showalter gave him the elbow in the ribs, and he said Tracy is old enough to make her own choices, even though I'm not the one he would have chosen for her."

"That's terrible!" Allison cried. "I'd like to give that man a piece of my mind!"

"Don't worry about it," Will said, smiling. "He didn't say no, and her mother seemed pretty happy about it. She went and got the calendar right away and started looking at June dates. And when I excused myself and left, Mr. Showalter shook my hand and said, 'I suppose you'd better call me Eric.'"

"Decent outcome," Matthew nodded. "He's kind of a snob, I think, and he knows your father's an uneducated farmer."

"My father," Will said with deliberate emphasis, "is a godly, caring, decent man who never tries to put anybody down. Eric Showalter should be half the man my father is."

"Group hug, I think," Allison said, wiping her eyes on her sleeve and gathering her two men into an embrace. Neither would have said how happy he was to be there, but it lasted a long time.

THE DAY BEFORE THANKSGIVING BREAK, WHEN WILL WALKED INTO HIS first period class, he found his classroom decorated with white balloons and paper bells and a big sign strung across the chalkboard which said, "Congratulations To The Happy Couple!"

"Surprise!" the students yelled.

Not only the first period juniors were there, but also some of the students from Will's other classes, all bouncing around and cheering like toddlers on Lucky Charms.

"Speech!" Eddie called, echoed by a couple of dozen others.

Feeling heat overtake his neck and ears and turn into a full-fledged blush, Will dumped his papers and laptop on the desk and looked back at the kids in amazement.

"Speech!" they yelled again.

How in the world – we're going to get in trouble if we don't settle down! I guess I'd better stop standing here like a zombie and say something.

"Please take your seats," he began, amazed that they did so. The students from other classes stood politely along the wall, expectant. "I'm – you probably get it that I'm totally surprised. How did you find out?"

"Oh, come on, Mr. Ryersen," one of the girls said, laughing at his ignorance. "It was in the paper, with a big picture and everything. The mayor's daughter – it's no secret!"

"Oh. Well. Thank you all. This is – I appreciate it. So will my fiancée, I know; I'm sorry she's not here to see this. Thank you."

"You said that already," Eddie said. "We just wanted you to know – you know."

"Yes, I do. Well, uh – maybe we'd better get down to work, and those of you who aren't in this class had better get back to wherever you're supposed to be."

"We got permission," Lacy Hamilton said. "Mr. Stemwalter said we could. Most of us had study hall anyway."

"Wow!" Will said. "Big deal! Excellent advance planning."

"And we got cupcakes," Eddie said, getting to the important part.

"I WISH I HAD BEEN THERE," TRACY TOLD WILL AS HE DESCRIBED THE first period engagement party. "Cupcakes and everything. They really like you, Will, and Mr. Stemwalter must really like you, too."

"You'd never know that," Will said. "I hardly ever see him unless there's a teachers' meeting, and when I do he always has his face buried in that oversized coffee mug of his. He sort of nods and grunts and slurps all at the same time. I think he just figured it's the last day before break and nobody's going to do any work anyway."

"You are still coming for dinner tomorrow, aren't you?" Tracy asked, a sudden nervous quiver in her voice.

"Of course."

"I know you've always been with your family, but it seemed really important to my mom to have you here."

"No problem, honey. Allison said husbands always go to the wives' families for holidays and I need to get used to it. Only one who's given me any grief is Gracie."

"I'm sorry for that, but I'm glad you're going to meet my grandparents and my aunt and uncle. You already know Baby Sister, but I promise you won't have to spend too much time with her and her husband. If you do get stuck with them, just talk about horses. She's as horse-crazy now as when we were kids."

"You don't really call her Baby Sister all the time, do you?"

"No, of course not. I call her Lisa – unless she's bugging me."

"Trace?"

"Yes?"

"Can we go to the Abbotts' later in the evening for a little while? I'd like for you to meet my family, too, and to spend some time with them. Pearl isn't going to be around forever, and she's pretty special."

"I already told Mom and Dad we'd leave at some point to do that. I want to get to know your family, too. Don't worry, Will, I'm not going to try to separate you from them. Not that I even could. I don't think you realize how much they mean to you, but when you talk about any of them, your face lights up and your voice gets all mushy."

"Does not!"

"Does too. I love it. I love *you*. Thanks for calling; I'll see you to-morrow."

"DON'T YOU CARE FOR THE SQUAB?" ANITA SHOWALTER ASKED WILL.

"Mom, don't pester him," Tracy said. "Will just doesn't eat much." She squeezed his hand under the table and smiled at him.

Will took what comfort he could from Tracy. In fact, between being nervous at meeting most of her family for the first time and being faced with what was essentially a half-raw pigeon on his plate, he was scarcely able to swallow anything.

The long mahogany table was gowned in lace over damask, appointed with silver candelabra and a huge silver epergne full of strange fruits Will knew to be kumquats and pomegranates and star fruits, set with gold-rimmed, fluted china, heavy, patterned silverware and Waterford crystal glassware for water, red wine, white wine and champagne. The main course had been plated in the kitchen, served by the maid, each plate a visual masterpiece of glazed squab with raspberry coulis, a couple of tablespoons of purple potato/parsnip puree, a small bundle of haricots verts, which looked like stringy green beans to Will. Each butter plate bore a small croissant, a pat of butter with a rose embossed on its center and a delicate little knife just to spread the butter. A tiny silver bowl of strawberry jelly was passed around the table so a few people could place a scant teaspoon-ful of the quivering red stuff next to their butter.

Will thought longingly of turkey and dressing, of real mashed potatoes and gravy, of enough jam on the table to load up a roll until it dripped.

"Tell us about yourself," Tracy's grandfather commanded, glaring

216

at Will from eyes the color of good whiskey. He also was an attorney, and cross-examining was apparently his forte.

Will explained his education and work history, including his present job, aware the grandfather was not impressed.

"You expect to support my granddaughter on a high school teacher's salary?" the old man asked.

"Yes, sir," Will said as steadily as he could, aware that Tracy was squeezing his hand hard enough to cut off the circulation. "I know I won't ever earn what you and her father do, but we won't starve and our children will have what they need."

"That, young man, is a matter of opinion."

"Oh, stop it, Carl," Tracy's grandmother said, laying a spidery hand on his sleeve. "They love each other and they know what they're doing. At least she won't be living in some hut in Africa any more – will she? You don't intend to take my granddaughter back to some foreign country, do you?"

"No, ma'am," Will laughed, "I surely don't. I do not have a call to foreign missions."

"Well, that's a relief!" Eric Showalter said, smiling at his daughter, if not at Will.

"I've been gone a long time," Will said to Tracy's sister Lisa. "Tell me about what horses you have now."

WILL SURVIVED SEVERAL HOURS WITH HIS FUTURE FAMILY BY REMINDING himself how much he loved Tracy, but he was glad when she finally said they could leave to visit the Abbotts. Entering the farmhouse was like entering another country, one where everything was bigger and louder and warmer, even the mingled odors of the feast reaching out to welcome them.

This is home, he told himself, sniffing appreciatively while receiving a hug from Allison and another from Pearl.

"Tracy!" Gracie yelled, barreling in from the kitchen, followed by Micah Anderson.

Tracy gave both children big hugs and squatted down to listen to some tale little Micah wanted to tell her about pie and whipped cream.

"Glad you could come," Matthew said, giving Will a hug.

"Me, too. It's good to be home."

"You just live down the road," Ed said. "Ain't like you been gone more'n a day."

"I've been gone to a whole other world," Will said, hugging Ed for good measure. "You have no idea."

Tracy stood up and put her arm through Will's. "I'm afraid my family was pretty rough on Will," she explained. "And I don't think he liked my mother's fancy French Thanksgiving dinner."

"No offense intended, honey," Will said, "but it just wasn't what I'm used to for Thanksgiving. And I don't think I want to eat squab again ever. I'm sorry."

"Oh, don't be sorry!" Tracy said. "I don't care that much for it, either. Mom just likes to show off her Culinary Institute training for Grandma and Grandpa." She turned to address Allison and Matthew, who were still standing there. "My father's father and mother. They're pretty – uh – what would you call it, Will?"

"In words of one syllable? Snobs. Look-down-their-noses snobs. I guess there are certain types who become attorneys and doctors, men with a really strong sense of their superiority to everyone else. And the wives seem to pick it up."

Tracy sighed. "I'm afraid you're right. Grandpa's the worst, but Mom and Dad can be awfully starchy."

"No matter," Pearl said, taking Will's other arm. "They'll learn to love Will as the rest of us do, and he'll learn to handle them. Now come into the kitchen and let me fix you each a plate."

"Oh, don't bother," Will said.

"Nonsense. He didn't eat a thing, did he?" she asked Tracy.

"No, not very much," Tracy agreed.

"A marriage lesson," John said to Will. "Do not argue with a woman when she's on a mission."

In the kitchen, they sat at the table and let Pearl fix plates for them. She was used to Ryersen men and didn't put much of anything on Will's plate, but she made sure he had some of everything. "You can eat all of this," she said sternly, "so don't bother pushing your green beans under the potatoes."

"He doesn't do that!" Tracy exclaimed in disbelief.

"Oh, indeed he does, just like his father."

"Hey, would you mind not talking about me like I'm not here?" Will asked. He bowed his head over the plate for a moment and picked up his fork. Buttery rich mashed potatoes melted across his tongue. *This tastes like home.*

Chapter 22

"SO WHAT DO YOU WANT FOR CHRISTMAS, GRACIE?" WILL asked as she accompanied him and Flash toward the barn through the wet leaves and icy drizzle of the second week of December. He had offered to make sure the cows were watered and had enough hay to keep them happy until morning, to lock up the chicken coop and make sure things in general were buttoned down. *I must want to be on the right side of Santa's naughty or nice list*, he thought, *because none of this is my idea of fun. But Dad and Ed looked so tired...*

"Well, I'm almost twelve now, you know," Gracie told him, "so I'm too big for toys. My friend Alyssa has a really neat jewelry-making kit, and I'd like one of those. I'm going to get my ears pierced – I almost have Daddy talked around to it – and then I could make my own earrings or trade with Alyssa."

"Okay. I'll look for that."

"Thank you, Will. I'm getting you a necktie to wear to school, but I haven't found just the right one yet."

Wonderful. My neckties are going to be like Wayne's sweaters. "That's great, sweetheart. Here, peek in and see if all the hens are in there."

"Why me? You said you'd do it." Gracie was more afraid of and disgusted by the chickens than Will, and that was saying something.

"Never mind," he sighed, peering into the gloomy depths of the chicken coop, holding his breath against the ammoniac smell. As far as he could tell, all of them were there, roosting quietly, as if they never turned into vicious attack-chickens.

"I'll lock the door," Gracie offered, fitting the padlock into the hasp and clicking it shut. With the expertise born of experience, she pulled on the lock to make sure it held and spun the dial for added safety. "No dumb old raccoons or foxes are going to get Mommy's chickens."

"Nope – all secure. Let's check out the barn."

"Will, what are you getting Tracy for Christmas?"

"Oh. Honestly, Gracie, I don't know. She doesn't seem to want much, you know? She doesn't love clothes or shoes the way her mother does, and she doesn't read a lot of books or collect movies or anything... I don't know."

"I know."

"Come inside where it's warm," he said, ushering her into the barn. Some of the cows were still outside in the lot, milling around slowly; most were inside in their stalls, munching hay or lying down ruminating. They gazed at the intruders with calm brown eyes and lowered their long eyelashes coquettishly when the two passed by.

"I know what you should get Tracy," Gracie repeated.

"Okay, kiddo. What?"

"An engagement ring. She needs a ring. You should have given her one when you asked her to marry you. My daddy says your daddy gave Aunt Allison a ring when he proposed to her. He did it on Christmas, too, right in front of everybody. Of course, I wasn't born yet; I was just on the way."

"I was there," Will said, putting extra hay into several depleted mangers. "I remember the whole thing."

"Well, then?"

"First of all, kiddo, I didn't propose to Tracy; she proposed to me."

"No way!"

"Oh, yes, way. Second, I didn't have much money, and I couldn't afford a ring."

"Oh. I didn't mean to embarrass you, Will. But you have your good job now, and you don't have to pay rent or anything, so you must have some money saved up. It wouldn't have to be a big ring."

"Johanna Grace, don't give me puppy-dog eyes, please. I actually think you have a pretty good idea. But don't tell anybody and spoil the surprise, okay?"

"Maybe I should go with you to pick it out," the girl said. "You might not know what a woman likes."

"And you would?"

"Well, I'm almost a woman," she said with great dignity. "And I do like jewelry."

"Gracie sent me," Will told Tracy as he stood on her front step the next evening.

"Oh, well, then. I guess you'd better come in, hadn't you?" She stepped aside to let Will enter and led him into the living room.

Will hated the living room. It was perfect and cold and sterile and held the ghosts of Tracy's parents when they weren't there. He wished he had asked her to come to him. But the roads were a little slick, and he didn't want her to drive if she didn't have to.

"Would you like some tea?" Tracy asked. "We could go into the kitchen. Mom and Dad are watching some improving show on TV in the family room."

"No, thank you. Let's just sit down a minute. I want to – I need to – "

"Is it going to be bad?" Tracy asked. "Because if it's going to be bad, I need to brace myself."

"I don't think it's too bad," Will said, smiling at last and dragging Tracy down onto his lap on the couch. "I just feel kind of stupid. But that's nothing new, either."

"Quit that! Just tell me what Gracie said."

"Well – she asked me what I'm getting you for Christmas, and then she vetoed my ideas. She says what I need to give you for Christmas is an engagement ring."

Tracy froze in Will's arms.

"So I wanted to ask whether you'd like to have an engagement ring, honey, and if you'd like to pick it out."

"Oh, Will!"

"You're not going to cry, are you?"

"Yes!" she sniffled, wiping her eyes as she said it.

"But I thought – I hoped you'd be pleased."

"Oh, I am! I don't need a ring – well, except a wedding ring – but I would like an engagement ring of some kind in the meantime. I know that's worldly and selfish of me, and I'm sorry to be so shallow, but – "

Will kissed her until the heat dried her tears and said, "Let's go to Toledo Saturday and pick out the ring you want."

THEY HAD SEEN THE STORE ADVERTISED ON TELEVISION, BUT THE COM-mercials didn't do it justice. As they entered through the elegant front door, Will felt suddenly very much a farm-boy. The walls were richly papered in soft neutral tones, the carpet was a foot thick, and the lighting was subtle and indirect except for the overheads, which cast beams to splinter into thousands of brilliant rays as they broke against the diamonds in the display cases.

"Wow," Tracy said softly, holding tight to Will's hand. "Nothing like this in Malawi!"

"Nothing like this in Iowa City that I remember," Will said.

"May I help you?" asked a middle-aged woman dressed with careful understatement in a draped black jersey dress with a high neck. Her artfully blonde hair was swept up and back into a simple chignon, leaving her ears and neck bare. Her hands were lovely, pale and slender, with long fingers and perfect oval nails lacquered in a soft beige polish. Will understood immediately that she was the canvas to show off the jewels.

"We're looking for an engagement ring," he said, giving his voice a ring of confidence he didn't feel.

"Do you have something in mind?" the woman asked, "or would you prefer to look around for a while first?"

"Let's look," Tracy said, and the woman nodded, smiled and removed herself behind one of the display counters, in sight but out of the way.

"Oh, everything's so beautiful!" Tracy exclaimed, turning around and around without going anywhere.

"Do you have any idea what you want?" Will asked. "I've never bought jewelry for a woman before."

"Good! That makes me very happy. I don't know... I always thought I'd want a diamond, but my birthstone is an emerald – and I love sapphires – and pearls – and – oh, I don't know!"

"I wish I could give you one of each," Will said, putting his arm around her and drawing her toward the first case, "but I don't know whether I can even afford one, unless it's small."

"Well, small is fine! What do I need with a huge rock weighing down my finger while I'm setting up an i.v. or fixing a pot roast?"

"You cook pot roast?"

"Sure. American pot roast, too, not French."

"Will you marry me?"

"Uh-oh. I thought we had that part settled."

They wandered the store, looking at everything, trying nothing, until finally Tracy said, "I love a lot of these, but honestly – not one of them seemed to speak to me. Thank you so much for your time," she told the elegant saleslady, "but what I want just isn't here."

Will expected the woman to be snippy after following behind them at a discreet distance for an hour, but she gave them a lovely smile and wished them well. As they reached the door, she called them back and handed them the card of another store.

"I think you may find what you're looking for there," she told them.

"Can we go there?" Tracy asked. "I know you aren't big on shopping. We could go to WalMart and get it over with."

"Get in," Will ordered, handing her into the car. "I want to go with you to as many jewelry stores as it takes until we find the ring that will make you happy. Honestly!"

Within fifteen minutes they were in another neighborhood, this one composed of older buildings and smaller storefronts, but all beautifully preserved and equally elegant. The name of the shop on the card was 'Treasures.' The shop itself had one large front window and a narrow door. In the window sat an old three-drawer dresser with a mirror on top, its drawers spilling old lace and linen and long strings of pearls.

"Oh, how pretty!" Tracy said. "It must be an antique shop. I wonder why she sent us here?"

"Want to go in? I think I can survive a few ruffles."

Inside, they looked around at dusty wooden floors and turn-of-the-century oak display cases. One whole wall had built-in open shelves which someone had rigged with lights to bring out the beauty of Victorian china and glassware displayed there. Around the narrow store were tiny islands of interest: an ancient buggy full of old dolls in high-necked, lacy dresses with puffed sleeves and big ribbon sashes; a roll-top oak desk with a pile of old books and several pairs of very old spectacles artfully arranged; and a wash-stand with a beautiful hand-painted ewer and basin, next to them a china shaving mug and straight razor.

"Hello, folks!" came a cheery old voice from the gloom at the back of the store. A little white-haired man who looked like he might be as old as Pearl came hobbling forward as fast as he could go, which wasn't a great speed. He wore an old-fashioned brown suit and olive/orange swirled wide tie, and his glasses perched almost on the end of his nose.

"Is he for real?" Will whispered to Tracy.

"I'm Oliver Edmunds," the old man said, holding out his hand to Will. "Delighted to have you in Treasures! Welcome, welcome!"

"Thank you," Will said, shaking hands and finding Mr. Edmunds's grip surprisingly strong.

"What a lovely store you have," Tracy said.

"Thank you, my dear. Are you young folks looking for anything in particular?"

"The lady at the jewelry store across town sent us here," Tracy said.

"Oh. Andrea. Yes, she does that sometimes, for special people she thinks will prefer what we have here. Were you looking for an engagement ring, then?"

"We were," Will agreed. "But this doesn't seem to be the kind of place – "

"Just follow me to the back," Mr. Edmunds said, moving away as fast as he could. Will and Tracy grinned at each other and followed.

There along the back wall was another display case, higher than some of the others, and all its lighted shelves were filled with jewelry.

"Oh, this is beautiful!" Tracy cried, dropping Will's hand and practically pressing her nose against the glass. "Where do you get all these beautiful things?"

"I buy them at estate sales, for the most part, my dear. Sometimes someone brings a piece in to sell on consignment, too. I'm particularly fond of pieces from the Victorian and Edwardian eras. They're considered hopelessly old-fashioned by young people nowadays, but they always seem to me to have a story behind them."

"You can feel it," Tracy said, "the sense of history."

Will said nothing. Tracy and the shop owner examined various pieces and she tried on several rings; but she didn't ask his opinion, so he didn't give it. In spite of himself he was drawn into the age and ornateness of the pieces, wondering who had worn them in the beginning, and had they been happy...

From his vantage point several feet back from the case, Will spied a satin-lined box on the bottom shelf. The lining was faded, but it must have been almost cobalt blue before time and light had bleached and frayed the satin. The case itself appeared to be leather, worn off at the edges, held together with a delicate brass hinge. Two rings sat in the slots, one a plain gold circle, so thin it seemed almost worn away, but still gleaming brightly, and the other a raised enameled forget-me-not flower with a tiny diamond at its center, green leaves spreading out over its thin gold band.

"May we see the forget-me-not, please?" Will asked.

Mr. Edmunds drew the little box almost reverently from the case and set it on the counter in front of Tracy. "Ah, yes, the forget-me-not. One of my favorite pieces. It has a long history."

"What is it?" Tracy asked, her eyes never leaving the rings.

"In the 1850's a handsome young man who was a member of one of the city's wealthy families fell in love with one of the leading debutantes of the day and asked her to marry him. He designed these rings himself and had them made for her so that she would remember him when he went on his long sea-voyages. He captained a tall ship, you see."

"And he died at sea?" Tracy asked, her eyes filling with tears.

"Oh, no, my dear! He came home an even wealthier man and built his bride a huge home and filled it with children. They both lived to be quite old and died peacefully within a few months of one another. The rings were worn by the eldest daughter, and by her eldest daughter, but then there weren't any more daughters and the daughters-in-law wanted modern jewelry. So eventually the rings came to me as part of the estate sale. The legend in their family, though, which the relatives told to me, is that every woman who wore these rings lived happily ever after."

"Oh, come on," Will sneered. "You don't need to make up a story like that to sell us. If she likes the rings, we'll take them."

"Will, don't be rude!" Tracy said, blushing. "I'm so sorry. He isn't usually disrespectful. It's a lovely story, Mr. Edmunds. And I do like the rings. May I try them on?"

Will couldn't believe they fit so perfectly and looked so pretty on Tracy's hand.

"This is why Andrea sends certain people here," Mr. Edmunds said as he swiped Will's credit card and wrapped the fragile old box in pale blue tissue paper. "She has a sense sometimes that someone will be happier with the old things. I know you are going to live in the joy all the other wearers of these rings did, and I'm so glad to be able to give that to you!"

"Are you sure they're what you want?" Will asked as they drove home. "If you change your mind, we can take them back."

"I'm not going to change my mind at all. I love them! I will have a jeweler check the mounting of the flower and the diamond to be sure I don't lose them. Thank you so much, Will! It's a wonderful Christmas present!"

"THIS IS THE BEST CHRISTMAS EVER!" GRACIE DECLARED, AND WHO would question her?

Allison was slowly wandering around the living room gathering torn, crumpled wrapping paper and discarded bows, stuffing them into a lawn and leaf bag, adding the occasional pretzel or cookie crumble to the mix. Everyone else sat or sprawled on floor or furniture with the faintly glazed eyes of surfeited lions.

Gracie, however, was revving her engines, fueled by candy and excitement. She bounced over to Will, where he lay on his back on the floor at Pearl's feet and dragged him up by the unresisting hand.

"I want you to play your guitar," she instructed. "We learned in Sunday School that 'Silent Night' was written to be played on the organ, but the mice ate the organ – well, some parts of it, anyway – so the guy had to play it on his guitar. I want to hear it the way it's supposed to be."

"I don't play the organ," Will said, trying to remember whether he had brought the guitar with him. He knew her in this mode; she wouldn't give up.

"Your guitar's in the guest room with your coat," Tracy said from Carolyn's chair. "Want me to get it?"

"No, you just relax. You look good there," he smiled. "I'll get it."

Accompanied by Gracie, Will dragged his tryptophan-drugged body up the stairs. "I'll tune it up here," he said, taking the instrument from its case.

"Thank you again for the jewelry-making kit," Gracie said, perching on the guest bed to watch Will work the strings. "I love it!"

I'm glad," he replied, "because I had a hard time finding it. Got the very last one. I think this is still off..."

"You did good with Tracy's ring, too, even if the diamond is kind of small. But I love the flower, and so does she."

"Glad you approve," Will said, grinning at Gracie and nodding to himself in satisfaction at the mellow sounds from the guitar. "You were right – she did want a ring."

"I know," the girl said, no trace of smugness at all in her voice. "I prayed about it and God told me."

Will stood abruptly, suddenly uncomfortable with the turn of the conversation. "Let's go make music, kiddo!"

IN THE LIVING ROOM, PEARL WAS PLAYING CHRISTMAS CAROLS ON THE piano, and everyone was gathered around singing. Will came reluctantly into the room, holding his guitar by the neck, feeling terribly self-conscious as he realized he had never played for any of them before, although Matthew and Allison had probably heard him playing softly to himself at night.

As 'O Come, All Ye Faithful' ended, Gracie said, "Now Will is going to play 'Silent Night' on his guitar!"

There was an immediate exodus from the piano to the rest of the room, to Will's further embarrassment. He sat down on the ottoman and cleared his throat, embarrassment staining his neck and ears as he said, "I hope you won't be disappointed. I just about never play in public – not that good. I'll try..."

He bent his head to the instrument and placed the fingers of his left hand on the frets. After a couple of experimental strums he began to finger-pick the deceptively simple melody, laying down increasingly layered, rich sound as he forgot anyone but God was listening. On the second time through, Gracie began to sing in a clear, childish soprano, joined by Tracy's soprano, Matthew's almost-tenor, John's baritone, Cassie's faint alto, Allison, Ed, Pearl, Olivia, Ted, all the Seibenek family members, until the mellow guitar was supporting a small choir through the last verses.

"Amen," John finally said when the silence had eased.

"You've been holding out on us," Pearl said.

"No, ma'am," he rejoined. "Just never came up. While I was at UC I had to take some electives, and music theory was one they offered. I did it in honor of you, Grandma, but then it led to guitar lessons. I found out I love Segovia, and so I studied picking, too. Not that I think I'm Segovia!" he laughed.

"Of course not," Pearl agreed. "But you are a very much better Ryersen than I had realized."

"Will you sing to me?" Tracy asked.

"Who said anything about singing?" Will asked. "I might play for you sometimes."

"I heard you singing," Gracie said. "Don't lie and say you can't."

"Busted," Allison muttered, laughing.

"I think it would be wonderful for you to play and sing for our children someday," Tracy insisted, her eyes dreamy.

"I DON'T UNDERSTAND WHY I COULDN'T JUST WEAR MY OWN TUX," Trey complained as he and Matthew, John, Ed, Kevin and Travis all paraded around the rental shop in front of Anita Showalter. "It's an Armani, for Pete's sake!"

"That's why," John laughed. "It would ruin the effect of all the others."

"No, no, no," Anita said to the harried salesman, "you can surely see that sleeve is too short! Get a longer length."

"Who *is* this woman?" Trey asked Matthew under his breath.

"Bride's mother. Queen Bee of Lewiston. Her husband's the mayor."

"Got it," Trey nodded. "Like my mother. Where's Will, anyway?"

"In school," Ed grumbled, as if it were a personal affront. "But he didn't escape the dragon-lady, either. Come back looking like he was drug through a steam-pipe. I don't get why we have to do this in March, when the wedding's second week of June. What if we was to gain weight or something?"

"You may *not* gain *or* lose weight before the wedding," Anita said, having caught the last line of the conversation. "My daughter will only marry once, and I intend for it to be perfect."

"I don't see how it could be anything else," Trey said smoothly, raising smothered laughter in the other men.

"YOU SURE YOU WANT TO GO THROUGH WITH THIS?" TREY ASKED WILL, slouching down on Allison's blue couch and swigging his beer from the bottle as if he had been born to it.

"With what?"

"The wedding, stupid! That woman is something else. At least you and Tracy should be thinking of moving about two thousand miles away, or, I'm telling you, Will, she's going to be running your lives every minute of every day."

"I doubt that," Allison said, coming into the living room with her coffee in hand. She perched on the other end of the couch and grinned at Trey. "You underestimate both the groom and the bride. Anita didn't want Tracy nursing poor, sick natives in Africa, either, but Tracy just did it. So, how's life in Iowa?"

"Going okay, I guess. My dad has me working on some interesting financial stuff, and I found a new guy to play racquetball with. Not as good as you, buddy, and not as competitive, but I'm training him."

"Any special girl in your life?" Allison asked.

"Nah. I like variety – and no strings." He finished the beer and put the bottle on the coffee table.

"Put a coaster under that!" Will said, doing so. "I can't believe your mother didn't raise you better than that. Want another one?"

"Sure. And, no, my mother didn't raise me better than that; but Nanny and the housekeeper did. Sorry, Allison."

Will brought two fresh beers back from the kitchen and sat down in the chair across the room, slinging one leg over the arm. "I haven't found anybody around here who plays racquetball," he said. "Mostly it's basketball. At which I am not a star."

"Tomorrow's Sunday," Allison said, "and we'll be leaving for church around nine. We'd be delighted to have you go with us."

Trey flushed a little and took a sip of his beer before saying, "Uh – thanks, but I'll pass."

"I remember you didn't go the first time you were here, either. I wish you'd try it; you might like it."

"Allie, I don't think – " Will began, looking at Trey to gauge the damage.

"Allison, let me explain," Trey said, sitting up and carefully placing the sweating beer bottle on the coaster. "I respect your beliefs, but

I can't buy into them. To me, it's just foolishness – and foolishness that has caused a lot of pain and grief and social oppression over the centuries. So, no, thank you, I don't see any reason to waste my time on church."

The silence seemed to vibrate like a tuning fork until Allison broke it to say, "I'm sorry I pushed about it, then, Trey. I won't do that again, I promise. You just sleep in, and we'll have a good country dinner when we get home. I think I'll go find your father now," she said to Will. "See you in the morning."

Trey stood as Allison left the room, running his hand through his hair, shaking his head. "I'm sorry, Will. I should have kept my mouth shut." He flopped back down on the couch.

"I don't think she was upset," Will said. "When Allison's mad, she breathes fire. Dad always calls her his 'dragon-princess.' I'm sorry I didn't head her off before she got on you."

"You still in love with Jesus?"

"Don't do that, man, okay? Yes, I am, and that's how it is. If I don't push you, you don't push me, either."

"But, Will, it's so different from how you were in Iowa City! Like you're some completely different guy, someone I hardly know."

Trey's hurt and confusion showed in his eyes as well as the tone of his voice, filling Will with sadness. "I'm still your friend," he promised, "still the guy who can beat you at racquetball and stay awake while you sleep through the opera and drive your Mustang better than you can – "

"Now hold on!" Trey said, the light of competition replacing everything else. "No way do you drive the Mustang better than I do!"

"Okay, that was an exaggeration..."

"That was a lie! Doesn't your religion say 'Thou shalt not lie?'"

"You know it does, so quit pushing. All I'm saying is, I'm still your friend. I love you like a brother, Trey, and I never forget all you've done for me over the years. I want to be your friend forever."

"Well – well – nothing's going to change that! We're as much 'until death us do part' as you and Tracy will be."

Will smiled and nodded, but his heart lay heavy in his chest. *Oh, buddy, if you only understood. We're not going to be together forever unless you get it about salvation. I don't know how it is in heaven, but I'm afraid there's going to be a huge, black, empty place beside me where you should have been.*

"I HAVEN'T ASKED," ANITA SHOWALTER SAID CAREFULLY, SIPPING HER Earl Grey tea from a see-through white china teacup bordered with tiny pink rosebuds, "because one doesn't want to seem intrusive, but what are your plans for the rehearsal dinner?"

Allison looked long at Anita over her own delicate teacup, considering all the possible answers running through her mind and discarding them one at a time as too crude, too mean, too flip, too nasty... "We're having it, as you know, in the banquet room of the Infinity Marriott. The hotel is catering, and the meal features roast beef and twice-baked potatoes. There will be flowers on the tables, there will not be alcohol served, the napkins will be linen, the background music will be canned."

"My dear," Anita ventured delicately, "if you wanted to serve a nice wine with dinner and to offer cocktails beforehand – well, I understand Mr. Ryersen – that is, that the expense might be more than you had planned. However, Eric and I would be glad to assist with the bar bills, as our contributions to the festivities."

"How very kind of you," Allison said, channeling Melanie Wilkes, "but that won't be necessary. Will and Tracy are fine with no alcohol being served, as are the rest of our family and friends. I'm sure your side of the family will have no trouble with one completely dry evening, right?"

Anita set down her teacup with just a hint more emphasis than necessary. "Of course we won't! It's not as if we're alcoholics." Realization dawned, along with a rather unbecoming blotchy redness of neck and face. "Oh! I didn't mean – "

"No offense taken," Allison assured her, smiling freely. "I know I'm a recovering alcoholic, and so does just about everyone who knows me. And I'm all right around other people's drinking, so the reception isn't going to be a problem for me. No drunken behavior from the Ryersen side, I promise."

"Oh, no, I would never suggest..."

"Well, you just did," Allison rejoined, "but I don't mind. Look, Anita, we get it that the Ryersens aren't good enough for the Showalters, from your perspective, but this wedding is happening and these two people have gone through hell to get to it. Can you just love them both enough to pray for their happiness and support them with more than your money?"

The Showalter living room rang with silence.

"I have to go now," Allison finally said. "It's almost time to start dinner for my guys. Thank you for the tea and the little chat, Anita. It certainly has been interesting." She picked up her purse and showed herself to the door, Anita a couple of steps behind her, protesting politely. "See you in church, Anita."

"I CAN'T BELIEVE YOU JUST WALKED OUT ON HER!" MATTHEW GASPED, holding his sides, which were beginning to ache from laughter. The remains of their lower-class farm family supper of hot dogs and potato chips and pickle spears still lifted pungent reminders across the dining room table and he shoved his plate away.

"Aw, it wasn't that bad," Will said, his own laughter a shade less wholehearted.

"Are you referring to the meal or the meeting?" Allison asked, pretending to be haughty about it.

"The meal," Will said. "I like hot dogs. As for the conversation with my future mother-in-law, better thee than me! I know you're not afraid of her – or anybody. And she needs to get off Tracy about things. So, thank you."

"My pleasure, so to speak," Allison said. "And I'm not afraid of the Showalters; they're snobs and they try to be bullies sometimes, but they don't have any real power over us, at least not as long as Tracy holds to what she wants. Since she seems to want you."

"She offered to write our vows for us," Will laughed. "So they would be 'classical and memorable.' I thought that was really nice of her, don't you?"

"I figure a writer like you would rather do his own vows," Matthew said. "You don't need anybody interfering in anything unless you ask. Allison managed to do our wedding without any unsolicited advice, and it was perfect."

"See how he knows exactly what to say?" Allison asked Will. "You need to take a note here."

"Yes, ma'am," Will replied, grinning at his stepmother. "I do remember it was a nice wedding, and everyone seemed to have a great time."

"Except you," she said softly, sorrow fleeting across her face as she remembered the time.

"That wasn't because of you!" Will hastened to say. "It was just because of everything else going on with me. I was only out of the hospital a couple of weeks, just had the stitches out of my arm, still had the crazy thoughts in my head... But I was glad for you and Dad, Allie, truly I was. It was so right for you – and look how it's turned out!"

"You're right," Matthew agreed. "We're still living together, still talking to one another, still – "

"Careful, Dad!"

"I was going to say: still in love."

"Right."

"Well, it's true," Allison said. "I love your father more today than I did the day I married him, and I pray that will be true for you and Tracy, too."

"I don't know whether I can love her any more than I do now," Will said. "I don't think there's room inside me for any more love than this."

Chapter 23

"**S**EE YOU IN THE FALL, MR. RYERSEN!" SEVERAL STUDENTS hollered as they charged out of the stuffy classroom into the heady air of a summer full of freedom.

Will grinned and waved a casual good-bye, sharing their excitement.

"Last day feels great for everybody, doesn't it?" Wayne Dennis said, coming into the relative quiet of Will's empty classroom. In honor of the day, he wore an orange-and-green plaid shirt with a wide teal-colored tie striped in two different but equally disgusting shades of brown. Just below the wrinkled knot a large, faintly orange grease stain paid tribute to a fallen slice of pepperoni from a pizza circa 1983.

"Nice tie," Will snickered.

"Thanks!" Wayne said enthusiastically. "My granddad gave it to me when I graduated from Ohio State. It was his favorite tie."

"I can see why," Will said, poker-faced.

"I'm looking forward to sleeping in every day for a month!" Wayne said.

"You and me both," Will agreed, stuffing the last of his papers into his back pack and cradling his laptop in its carrying case. "But it was a good year, for me, anyway."

"Yeah, me, too," Wayne said. "Great kids, great graduating class. I don't like the rumors I hear floating around about the budget, but as far as I know, nobody got laid off."

"I sure hope they get this economy thing under control pretty soon," Will said. "I don't want to worry about another lay-off just when I'm starting married life."

They walked into the hall together, and Will locked his door for the last time that year.

"Only two weeks til the wedding," Wayne said. "Ready?"

Will laughed. "Well, Tracy says she is. I think all I have to do is smile a lot and show up on time for things. Anita has given me list after list, and I check things off and return the lists to her."

"God bless the mayor and his mayoral wife," Wayne intoned. "You got time to get together for lunch one day? Sort of in lieu of a bachelor party."

"I'll make time. The more I hang around the house, the more someone will figure something out for me to do. How about Monday?"

"Deal. Meet you at Logan's at noon, how's that?"

<hr />

"I'VE ARRANGED FOR A TASTING AT NOON ON MONDAY," ANITA SAID.

Will and Tracy were opening presents in the Showalters' living room and Anita was arranging them on a linen-draped table, rearranging as needed for artistic effect. Tracy was writing down descriptions and names in a fancy book, using a faux-quill pen.

"I have a lunch engagement on Monday," Will said, carefully folding a huge sheet of wrapping paper printed with gold bells and ribbons. "I thought we did the tasting thing a couple of months ago."

"We did," Anita agreed, to his surprise. "But I just wasn't happy with several things, and I told the caterers they have to do better. We'll see. You can change your plans, Will, because this is important."

I wonder whether this is the time to start asserting our right to make our own choices. 'Begin as you mean to go on,' right?

"I'm sorry, Anita, but you should have checked with me before planning to have me there. I won't be changing my plans."

An ugly, mottled flush came over the older woman's face as she narrowed her eyes at Will. "Don't be ridiculous. This is more important than anything you could have to do."

"Mom!"

"It's okay, Tracy. Anita, I understand how important this wedding is to you, so I'm going to forgive you for being so rude. But I am not changing my plans at the last minute. And I expect you to not take it out on Tracy. You can handle the tasting all by yourself if you want to, because you're the one who's having issues with the menu. I'll enjoy whatever you choose." He ripped open the big box he had unwrapped and drew out a large... "Look, Trace! A great big silver something-or-other!"

"I HAVE NEVER, EVER SEEN MY MOTHER AT A LOSS FOR WORDS BEFORE," Tracy giggled, snuggling up to Will on the couch and laying her head on his bony shoulder.

Will wrapped his arm around her and leaned back, feeling the tension ease out of him. "I hope I wasn't rude. I didn't mean to be. It just came to me, that old saying, 'Begin as you mean to go on,' and I figured if we don't take a stand now, she'll be telling us what to do about everything. Your mother's a nice woman, honey, but she does love to be in charge."

"I know! And I always want to stand up to her. But it's usually easier just to go along, unless it's something that really, really matters to me – like marrying you."

"I know she didn't want you to." Will sat up and leaned forward, elbows on his knees, hands running through his hair. "Are you having any second thoughts?"

"Me?" Tracy leaned forward, too, and began to rub his back in soothing little circles. "I haven't had second thoughts for a long time, certainly not since you moved back here. What about you?"

"No! Never!"

"Then we're good to go," she said.

Almost good to go. There are still things we've never talked about. Now?

"You're being awfully quiet all of a sudden," Tracy said. "Is something bothering you?"

"No, of course not. Yes." Will shook his head as if to clear his ears. "You know I love you, right?"

"Uh-oh." Tracy moved away a little.

"Tracy?"

"Yes, I know you love me." She was watching him now as if he were coiled to strike, but Will didn't notice because he was looking at his feet.

"You and I – back in high school, we – I mean we didn't – "

"Is this going to be a sex talk?" Tracy asked, torn between laughter and concern at Will's discomfort. "Because my mother and my doctor both gave me that already. They were substantially different talks, too," she laughed.

"I wasn't – you know – a virgin then," Will said. "But I didn't – never after we started dating again. Then in college and after – well, there were a few girls –"

"I understand," Tracy said gently. "You weren't a believer then; you thought it was all right. It's what a lot of people do, isn't it?"

"Yes. It's what a lot of people do. Just before everything fell apart in Iowa, there was one particular girl for a while. We were – intimate. I know now that it's a sin, and I get it that it can be dangerous. I had myself tested in Toledo, and I'm clean. I wanted you to know that. You and I are a whole new thing, and it will be safe for you."

Tracy stood and walked across the room, Will's eyes following her. "Will, I need for you to tell me the truth: the last girl, in Iowa – do you still have feelings for her?"

"Oh, honey, I never did have feelings for her! She's a nice person, but there was never anything between us except – well, you know."

"Are you sure she felt the same way?"

Wow. Am I? She did seem to be getting clingy. "I thought so," he said, "but I can't swear to it. I hope so. I wouldn't have wanted to hurt her."

"Would you say you're over her?"

"Over – Yes, of course I am!"

"Because I would *not* like to find another woman in my bed."

Will stumbled to his feet and moved toward Tracy, but she moved away from him again on an angle, putting the coffee table between them. "And I mean that spiritually as well as physically," Tracy continued. "If you can't come to me whole-hearted, then we need to call it off."

"Tracy!" Will heard the desperation in his voice, but it was an accurate reflection of his feelings.

She sat down in one of the silk-upholstered armchairs, tears gleaming in her eyes, and motioned for him to return to the couch, which he did, sinking down into the cushions as if his legs couldn't hold him any longer.

"Sometimes," Tracy said, "when people get really close, emotionally or physically, they – they leave little bits of themselves attached to the other person spiritually. And so the person carries that around with him – or her – and carries it into the next relationship. In marriage, it's good to be really close – that two becoming one flesh. But those soul-ties with other people can kill a relationship."

"I know about soul-ties. Why didn't you say something before?" Will asked, anger rising up to companion his distress. "It's kind of late to want to see my little black book, isn't it?"

Tracy nodded. "I don't know – I was just praying about us last night and it came to me. I'm sorry it's late, but it's not too late – is it?"

"I guess that depends on what you want to do about it. Shall we rewind, and I'll lie?"

Tracy came to Will and sat beside him again. "I thought maybe you could pray about it and just – you know – deliberately let go of anything that's stuck to you."

"Great! You want to watch? And what about you, Trace? I know you dated some guys. You have any sticky stuff to get rid of?"

"I did date some, and I have prayed that if there was anything that shouldn't be there, God would remove it in Jesus' Name. I would never, ever come to you less than clean, Will, because I love you and want to have the best marriage in the world with you."

Why don't you tell her you've already taken care of it?
We know who's damaged goods here, and it isn't the girl.

Tracy watched Will jolt as if he had stuck his finger in a lightsocket. "Are you all right?" she asked.

"Fine." The reply was automatic. *I didn't think I'd have to hear that voice again! Lord, what is this!*

"I'm going to pray," Tracy said, putting her hand on Will's, "because I don't know what's going on, but it isn't good."

Will bowed his head and let her cover him with her words, but he wasn't paying attention. He had his own prayer going on. *Father God, please deliver me from that voice! I do believe You are Lord and he is already defeated. I know I'm not who he says I am. Help me to believe it! Help me to let go of Angie and anything else that might come between Tracy and me. You've given me the second chance with Tracy, Lord; please protect it.*

"I'm all right," Will said. "It's gone. All of it's gone, Tracy. I promise."

"Nervous?" Trey asked, straightening Will's tie with the expertise of years of tuxedo-wearing.

"Why would you think that? The sweat pouring off me? The shaking hands? I'm scared to death!"

"Never too late to say no," Trey offered, mopping Will's forehead with a starched white handkerchief. "We can be on a plane to Iowa in a heartbeat. Angie'd love it!"

Not now! Not Angie now! Please, God, take her out of my head.

"No, stupid, I'm afraid I'll step out there in front of all those people and she won't show up. She'll figure it out that she's way too good for me and leave me there swinging in the wind."

"The women are in the building," Trey said, patting Will's shoulder. "I saw the bridesmaids – who are fine, by the way – and heard the dulcet tones of the bride from behind closed doors. She didn't sound the least bit hysterical. No, brother, she's going to run down that long aisle to grab hold of you and never let go."

"I hope so! Oh, man, I think I'm going to throw up."

"Take a deep breath," Matthew advised, coming up behind them. "Mind over matter. I did not throw up the day I married Allison."

Will had to laugh in spite of himself. "Probably the only important date on which you didn't!"

"What's with you Ryersen men?" Trey asked, looking from one to the other.

Two nearly identical wheat-blond heads turned toward him; two nearly identical sets of slate-blue eyes took his measure under identically arched golden brows. They were practically mirror-images, and handsome ones in their black tuxes.

"Some people get drunk, some people eat everything in sight, some people – whatever – but Ryersens puke," Matthew said.

"Not my first choice for a hereditary trait," Will muttered, breathing through his mouth.

"No time now," Trey said, taking Will by the elbow and steering him toward the door. "The prelude music is starting. Show-time!"

"You can still say no," Eric Showalter murmured to Tracy as they stood at the head of the aisle, poised to take their first step toward the altar.

"I've waited for him for thirteen years," she whispered, smiling. "I love you, Daddy, and I know you mean well, but be happy for me today. Will is everything I ever dreamed of."

"SHE'S A BEAUTIFUL BRIDE," ALLISON WHISPERED TO MATTHEW, WIPING her eyes again on his handkerchief, an ironed white replacement for his usual blue bandana in honor of the day.

"Not as beautiful as you were," Matthew whispered back.

"Look at him," Allison said. "His face is radiant! He loves her so much. I hope she's as worthy as she seems. I wouldn't want to have to hurt her."

"MAY I BE THE FIRST TO INTRODUCE TO YOU MR. AND MRS. WILL AND Tracy Ryersen!"

Chapter 24

SUMMER LINGERED INTO FALL IN NORTHWEST OHIO, BUT GENtly, allowing the wheat to ripen, the soybeans to turn gold and the corn to fill each ear with plump, juicy kernels. The night skies were full of stars and the mornings offered pearly rose-and-gold sunrises to call sleepers gently into the day.

"I think all this beauty is for us," Tracy told Will as they sat on the tiny terrace of their Lewiston apartment drinking coffee in the October dawn. "God is demonstrating His love through creation."

"Mm-hmm," Will murmured, letting the steam from his mug rise over his face like a kiss. He didn't care about the philosophy of morning; he wanted to get through it and wake up. He was grateful for the coffee, though; he had begun to drink it regularly again not long after the wedding and was overjoyed to find it acceptable to his stomach.

"I have to get ready for work," Tracy said, "and so do you."

"Mm-hmm," he answered, not moving.

"Will, come *on*. Have breakfast with me."

He rose and drew his wife to her feet, leading her inside with an arm around her waist. "No breakfast, thanks, but I'll sit with you."

"You should eat something," she fussed. "Breakfast is the most important meal of the day. How about scrambled eggs? That's quick, lots of protein."

"How many months have we been married?" Will asked. "Four? You try to feed me every day, and every day I tell you no. Honey, I'm fine; I just don't like breakfast. Please, don't – "

"Don't what?" She was glaring at him, hands on her hips, pulling the silky yellow bathrobe close around her.

"You really are beautiful," he said, admiring her, meaning every word. "Let's forget breakfast – "

"You are not going to sweet-talk your way out of this. You were going to say, 'Please don't nag me,' weren't you?"

Will gave up on the idea of making love to his wife and nodded. "But I don't mean it in a bad way."

"Suit yourself," she snapped, taking a small skillet out of the cupboard by the stove and slamming it down on the burner. "I'm having scrambled eggs."

"I'll make your toast," he offered, but she shooed him away. Unwilling to risk an all-out argument, he retired from the field and took a shower instead.

Must be her period, he mused as he dressed. *Tracy isn't snippy or petty about things. Maybe I should ask her – or maybe not.*

They passed each other wordlessly a time or two as Tracy got ready to go to the hospital and Will made sure he had everything he needed for school in his back pack. As the little Westminster wedding-present clock in the living room chimed seven, they met at the door.

"Don't leave me without a kiss," Will begged, dropping his pack to put his arms around his wife. "I love you, and I'm going to miss you all day. I'm sorry for anything I said that hurt you."

Tracy let him hold her for a moment, then hugged him back. "It's all right, Professor. I'm just in a mood, I guess. I love you, too, and I'll see you for dinner." She gave him the kiss he craved, with interest, and Will headed off to school whistling. Life really was good.

"WHAT I THINK," GRACIE TOLD WILL FIRMLY AS SHE WALKED DOWN THE road with him following Tucker, "is that it's time for you and Tracy to have a baby."

Will stopped dead and looked at the girl for a long moment. "Is that so. God tell you this, too, kiddo?"

Gracie grinned back at him, shaking her head. "Nope. I just think so. I'd like to have a baby to play with and take care of – but of course I'm too young to do it myself, and I'm not married. So you and Tracy should give me one."

Will shook his head, laughing, as he said, "You are the most amazing girl, Johanna Grace Abbott! How selfish is that? Tracy goes through all that hassle, we put up with the expense and the sleepless nights and the worries after the baby comes, all so you can play with it for a few minutes and then give it back when it needs something? I don't think so." He resumed walking, whistling Tucker back to keep pace beside him.

"I don't think it's just selfish," Gracie argued, catching up. "I mean, it is, sure, but I know Tracy loves babies. And every couple wants to have children, don't they?"

Will considered. "I don't know. We haven't been married very long, kiddo, and we're still getting used to what being married is all about. It might be a good idea to wait a while longer. When the time comes, I'm sure we'll talk about it."

"You mean you didn't talk about it before you got married?" Her tone suggested something scandalous about that idea.

"Have you talked to Tracy about this?"

"Not yet. I thought I'd tell you first, and you could tell her."

Oh, God, help me. "Some things are private to a husband and wife, Gracie, and I think this is one of them. I do appreciate your – ah – interest, and I promise I'll keep it in mind as we go along, okay?"

"Well, I hope you don't take too long," she huffed. "I'm not getting any younger, you know, and neither is Pearl."

THE IDEA, ONCE PLANTED, TOOK HOLD LIKE BINDWEED. WILL BEGAN TO notice babies in the supermarket and the big-box store and all over the place in church. He also noticed again, as he had some time back, his wife's open-hearted response to those babies.

And he noticed how tired those mothers pushing carts looked, how short-tempered some of them were. He was taken aback to see one weary woman slap her whining little boy across the face when he refused to move out of the cookie aisle without a package of Oreos.

I don't want to see Tracy looking like that, all used up and at the end of her rope. And babies are expensive. If we stay as we are, we'll be able to afford the down payment on a house in a couple of years, a good down payment so the monthly payments don't break us. She hasn't said anything, so maybe she doesn't really care that much anymore. I don't need a kid to be happy, do I? No. I don't want the bother or the expense or the responsibility.

Sunday dinner with the Abbotts remained the focal point of the week; Will and Tracy had been folded into it seamlessly, Tracy quickly finding her place among them and enjoying her time in the kitchen with the women preparing and serving the meal. She also enjoyed the relaxing time after the meal when all the women sat around the living room and left the clean-up to the men.

This Sunday seemed to be needlework day, although Allison never did more than pretend to knit. Even Gracie seemed to be crocheting something out of white string.

"I need to get myself a project for Sundays," Tracy said, examining Allison's bright blue whatever-it-was.

"Do you know how to do needlework of some sort?" Pearl asked.

"As a matter of fact, I do. My Grandma Keppler, Mom's mother, taught me to knit and to embroider when I was little. I used to have fun doing it back then. In Africa, I taught some of the women how to use a treadle sewing machine, too. That was fun!"

"Well, then, I guess you just need to decide what you want to make," Pearl said.

"What are you making?" Tracy asked, looking at the tiny needles and mint green yarn Pearl was manipulating with expert fingers.

"Oh, just booties," Pearl said.

"Really? Who's having a baby?" Tracy asked.

"Nobody that I know of. I'm just planning ahead, you know."

"Planning ahead?" Allison asked.

"Well, yes. I'm sure Will and Tracy will have children one of these days, and if I shouldn't be around to see them, I want to know they have some things I made for them."

Gracie dropped her crocheting and ran to Pearl, squeezing in beside her on the sofa. "Don't say things like that! You can't die and leave us! You can't!"

"Mercy sakes, child, I didn't say I'm dying. I just said I want to be sure there are things here whenever."

"But you meant it, I know you did. Otherwise, you'd just wait until Tracy says she's pregnant. Please, Pearl, please don't leave me!" Like a much younger child, Gracie threw her arms around the frail old lady and buried her face in Pearl's shoulder.

"There, there," Pearl soothed, patting Gracie and enduring the prolonged embrace, her dark eyes dimming with tears. "I'm trying to stay as long as I can. I don't want to leave you, but no one can promise to live forever. You know that, Grace."

Allison and Tracy were watching the scene with tears of their own. Nurses, they knew the clock could only count down from here for Pearl.

"She took her mother's death so hard," Allison said, "but Pearl was here for her, like a rock. Pearl has always been here, all her life. And all my life as a Ryersen, too."

"Tracy," Gracie said suddenly, sitting up and wiping her eyes, "you and Will need to hurry up and have a baby. Then Pearl will feel like she can't go until he's big like me."

The women burst into laughter, which drew the men in from the kitchen, hands wet and faces curious. But no one would tell them what was so funny, or why they were crying at the same time.

"What was that all about?" Will asked Tracy that night as they climbed into bed. The nights were just becoming chilly, and Tracy had taken to wearing a long-sleeved nightgown. Will hated the nightgown.

"What?"

"Come on, honey. That laugh-cry episode in the living room." He moved closer to take her in his arms. "I know something was happening."

"Well... Of course there was. It was silly."

"So tell me," he urged, kissing her neck. "It's making me crazy."

"Not too hard to make you crazy," she teased, turning onto her back and looking over at him. "Okay. Pearl was knitting, and I asked what she was making. She said she was making baby booties, so we all wanted to know who's pregnant." She hesitated.

"So who is?"

"Uh – nobody. She told us she's planning ahead, in case she isn't here when – "

"When what?"

"Well, when you and I decide to have babies. She wants to be sure they'll have things she made for them."

Will felt unmanly tears welling up and tried to turn away before Tracy caught him, but the light shimmered in his eyes and she put her arms around him.

"Oh, Will. I know you love her so much and you're going to miss her terribly. But she's in good shape for as old as she is. I don't think you have to worry right now."

"She could have a heart attack and die in her sleep any night, just like Carolyn. We could wake up tomorrow morning and she'd be gone."

"Or we could wake up tomorrow morning and drive over there and she'd be scrambling eggs and frying sausages and forcing you to eat them like she's done a hundred times."

He sighed. "You're right, I know you are. 'Sufficient unto the day are the evils thereof' and all that."

"Do you want a baby?" Tracy asked. "Because I do."

Will sat up abruptly, all thought of sleep gone. *I knew this would happen sometime, but I thought I had more time. How do I answer that?*

"Will?"

The next thing you say is going to make or break your marriage.

"Will?"

"Wow. Tracy. Uh – honestly – I guess I figured we'd have kids sometime, but maybe not so soon. We haven't even been married a year yet."

"Is a year a magic number?"

What! "No! I mean – I've read that couples should get to know each other as a couple before they have a baby. I don't know how long the article recommended, but a year seems like a reasonable time period."

"I see." Tracy was sitting up by now, too, her arms wrapped around her knees. She didn't look at him, and Will felt the twelve inches between them as if it were a mile.

"Honey, I didn't realize you wanted to do this now."

Not good enough. She was shaking her head, still not looking at him.

"Come on, Trace, I can't do any better and still be honest. I suppose it might be fun to have a little rug-rat running around the house."

"Kindly do not refer to our future children as rug-rats," she said, ice crystals forming along the edges of her words.

"Fine. Children. Little angels, even though I know they're not.

If you want a baby, Tracy, we'll try to make one. Starting now." He reached for her.

She pulled away.

"Or not. Let me know." He lay down and turned his back and prayed for sleep.

Will was grading papers at his desk in the apartment's second bedroom, which served as his office, when his cell phone rang. Shoving his red pen aside, he opened the phone to see Trey's name come up.

"Hey! What's up?" Will asked.

"Just checking up on you," Trey replied. "Haven't heard from you in two weeks and wondered if you drowned in a hog trough or something."

Will laughed, feeling the residual tension in his shoulders melt out. "Just busy, and nothing new to report. How about you?"

"Couldn't be better! Met a cute girl at the office and we're hanging out pretty regularly. She's blond, built – smart, too. Great sense of humor. And my dad has decided I'm responsible enough to send me on – get this! – an 'overseas acquisitions' trip!"

"Wow!" Will leaned back in his ergonomically correct chair and teetered back and forth, smiling to himself at the sound of Trey's voice. "That sounds really impressive. Where are you going?"

"Oh, buddy, you're going to hate me! I'm going to London and Paris and Monte Carlo! Be gone two weeks, unlimited expense account, rent a Ferrari, eat at Maxim's, gamble in the casinos at Monte Carlo – live large and love it!"

"I won't hate you, but I do think I'm going to be sinfully jealous. Congratulations!"

"You know the only thing that would make it better? If you came with me."

Will dropped his feet back to the floor and ran his free hand through his hair, sighing. "I wish. Don't tease about something like that, man. It's too sweet."

"Who says I'm teasing? Meet me at JFK on the appointed day and we'll fly away. Think of it, Will, all that romantic stuff you used to talk about when we were in school – being a starving poet in Montmartre, seeing the chestnuts in bloom – well, of course, they won't be at this time of year, but – walking along the Seine drinking wine from the bottle and eating fresh bread, visiting the Louvre and the cathedrals – sunning ourselves beside the lavender fields in Provence – well, I guess we can't do that either at this time of year, but you get the idea. You could start your novel, just like Hemingway did."

"I have a job here, and a wife," Will said slowly. "I'm not free to pack up and leave when I feel like it."

Long silence. Then Trey said, "Yeah, that's right. I forgot for a minute. Well, I'll bring you souvenirs." He cleared his throat and said, "So how's married life treating you?"

It's pretty shabby at the moment, Will thought, but he didn't want to admit that. "Great!" he enthused, making a face to himself as he said it.

"Yeah? Well, that's good; I'm glad for you. Hey, I have to go, but say hi to Tracy for me, okay?"

"Sure will."

"And – Will – take care of yourself, buddy."

Long after the conversation was over, when he should have been grading papers, Will continued to sit there, thinking of all the things Trey had offered.

We did talk about all those things. I was going to travel and see the world, especially Paris, no matter how corny that is. I'd love to have a cheap hotel room and a laptop and just write and look out over the city…

That's never going to happen now. You're stuck in this boring place with your boring job and your boring, vanilla little wife. You won't ever write that book you thought you could write. This is it.

A knock on the door jolted him out of his reverie.

"Will, your dad's on the phone."

He went out to the kitchen, where the land-line presided, picking up the receiver without saying anything to Tracy.

"I could use a hand over here," Matthew explained. "The water-line to the kitchen sink broke, and we're in a mess."

"Do I need my scuba gear?" Will asked. "If not, I'll be there in a few minutes."

"What do you need scuba gear for?" Tracy asked when he hung up.

"Oh, I don't. Dad needs help with a broken water line in the kitchen. Want to come along?"

"No, thank you. I'm going to do some laundry so I have clean scrubs for the rest of the week."

She turned away; he let her.

"I hope I'll be home before you go to bed," Will said, grabbing his leather jacket and heading out the door without waiting for a reply.

"I TURNED IT OFF AT THE MAIN VALVE," MATTHEW SAID, HANDING WILL a pair of big, ugly black rubber boots. "But there's water all over the kitchen and living room. Those Eye-talian loafers, as Ed says, won't stand up to it."

Will toed off his loafers in the entryway and slipped easily into the boots.

"I have most of it shopvacced up," Allison said, coming into the entryway. Her scrub pants were wet to the knees, as were her bare feet. "It must have let go for some reason while we were at work, because when I came in it was a river in the kitchen!"

"We'll get it taken care of," Matthew promised. "Ed gave me all kinds of tools and pipes and things."

"Do you know how to use them?" Will asked, "Because I sure don't!"

"Why didn't Ed come?" Allison asked.

"Because I don't like to ask him to take on a hard project, especially in the evening. And I need to learn."

"It's a guy-thing, Allie," Will said, grinning at her. "You just go rest your pretty little self on the sofa with some bon-bons and we he-men will figure this out."

Mostly because of Ed's instructions before Matthew had left the farm, and Matthew's own begrudging experience with farm machinery and milking machines, they did manage to finish reconnecting the line with good pipe within a couple of hours. Allison had managed to stay out of their way for the most part, pretending she was taking them seriously, and they hadn't killed each other, so Will figured it was all good.

"It's not too late," Matthew said. "Want to walk Tucker with me?"

"Sure. Let me change my shoes again."

Tucker was waiting on the porch as if he had known what was coming, and he snuggled up to Will in a frenzy of affection.

"Dumb dog! I just saw you two hours ago and petted you enough to last a week."

"No such thing as enough for this dog," Matthew said, patting the huge head himself. "He's such a baby. All Allison's fault."

They strolled down the driveway and made the automatic turn toward the Millers' farm, Tucker loping ahead a little, exploring new smells along the way.

"I thought Tracy might come with you to keep Allison company," Matthew said.

"Nope. She had some things to do."

"Too bad; please give her our love and tell her we missed her."

"Sure."

They walked a little farther in silence before Matthew looked at his son by moonlight and asked, "Is everything okay?"

"Sure. Why wouldn't it be?"

"I don't know. You just seem kind of down. Work going okay?"

"Fine."

Tucker had reached the Millers' property and begun his carouse with the German shepherd, so they stood silently side by side to watch the two dogs romping.

Will was tempted to say something, but the voice reminded him: *It's none of his business. You don't need a lecture from Pseudo-Dad.*

No. I'm not listening. Go away, in Jesus' Name!

"Dad?"

"Yeah?"

"It's not all okay."

Matthew turned to face Will, even though it was hard to see his face in the moonlight filtering through the maple-tree branches at the edge of the Miller property. He smiled a little and said gently, "Tell me."

The floodgates opened and Will poured out all his grievances with Tracy, with work, with life in general, hating the sound of his own voice but unable to stop himself. He told his father about his conversation with Trey and his reawakened yearnings for travel, adventure, writing. He told him about Tracy's wanting a baby. Finally he stopped, hanging his head like a bad dog. Matthew put an arm around his shoulders and squeezed for a moment.

"That's a lot of stuff," Matthew said.

"No kidding!"

"I gather you and Tracy haven't talked about any of this."

Will shook his head, pulling away. "Not since that first 'discussion' about a baby, no. We're barely talking at all."

"I guess that means you're not praying together, either."

"No. I guess we hadn't been doing as much of that as we did at first even before. Now she's all about what do I want for dinner and do I have clean shirts and she'll see me later because she's going to her mother's."

"You haven't been married quite six months yet," Matthew said. "It's bad that things have fallen apart so fast, but it's good that they haven't had time to freeze that way. What do you want to do?"

Will gave a bitter chuff of laughter. "Do? What can I do? I'm stuck."

"Tucker, come on! Time to go home!" Matthew called and stepped back onto the road. The dog ran up and circled him a couple of times but gave up when he saw neither Matthew nor Will was going to play. He began to plod slowly home. Will fell into place beside his father.

"There are some things you can do," Matthew insisted. "You can pack a bag and leave. Go back to Iowa and go with Trey to Paris and write your book. Or you can pack a bag and move out and get a room and file for divorce. Or you can go home and take your fist to Tracy for not being more accommodating to your needs and wants, even if you haven't told her what they are."

"Dad! Are you nuts? I can't do any of those things! Do you think I'm like my grandfather, that I'd beat a woman?"

"No, I don't think you're at all like your grandfather," Matthew said. "I'm just saying things you *could* do, not things you would do. But they are choices; you have to know that so you understand really well that whatever you do, it's because you choose it and reject all the other possibilities.

"So," Matthew continued, "there are the better ways. You could go home and tell Tracy you feel bad about this gap between you and you want to close it. You could beg her pardon for any way you've hurt her. You could be honest with her about any way she's hurt you. See, I think sometimes we hurt the people we love and we don't even realize it. And we can't ever make it up if we don't know we did something wrong. Then you could ask her to pray with you, the real deal, together on your knees, and see if that doesn't make a difference. And you could choose to pray for your wife every day."

"You take lessons with Pastor Miles, don't you?" Will asked, laughing. "All right, I hear you. Thanks for listening."

They were back to the Ryersen house now, and Tucker was scratching at the front door, hoping Allison would let him spend the night indoors.

"I'll say good-night here," Will said. "Tell Allison I love her."

"Of course. I love you, and I'll be praying for you. Let me know if I can help."

Will gave his father a brief but heartfelt hug. "I love you, too. Thank you – I mean it."

Driving the few miles from his father's house to his apartment, Will considered what he had told his father, and what his father had told him. Choice. Free choice.

Right, but it isn't free. Choose one thing, lose another. Choose the old things and break the new vows. No, that's not cool. Lord, why do you make the rules so hard?

He had no idea that his last question was exactly the same one his father had asked more than a decade before, but he might have found it comforting if he had.

Chapter 25

WAYNE DENNIS WAS INFAMOUS FOR HIS SWEATERS, AND Will wasn't sure whether the man realized it and played to the crowd or was blissfully ignorant of the ridicule he received behind his back. Today's version was a bilious yellow-green with a huge turkey appliquéd on the front, the whole thing tufted like a chenille bedspread. Will tried not to look at it too much as they sat opposite one another in the teachers' lounge over lunch, because it really was making him sick.

Wayne, on the other hand, seemed in a fantastic mood; Will feared his perpetual grin would let his lunch dribble out the sides of his mouth as he shoveled in forkfuls of whatever casserole was left over from last night. Will himself was picking around the edges of a piece of take-out pizza, cursing his own stupidity for bringing something spicy.

"I have news!" Wayne finally said.

"Figured it was something," Will said, ribbing him.

"Big news!"

"Well, spill it!" one of the women teachers called across the room from her post by the coffee-maker.

"Anita and I are going to have a baby!"

The room was crowded with teachers, and they all broke out in cheers and congratulations, coming to embrace Wayne or pound him on the back.

"Little surprise package?" someone said.

"Well, I guess you could call her that," Wayne said. "We thought we were pretty much beyond this stage. But durned if I don't feel blessed! Anita, too. It's a girl, and we're spending our spare time googling names on the Internet and buying pink stuff again. Anita's four months along; we didn't get it that she was pregnant until she started to show!"

Will stood and quietly dumped his pizza into the trash. "Congratulations, Wayne," he said as he left the lounge.

His first class after lunch was a study hall, the worst time to have one, and he had worked all year so far to contain the rebellious and wake up the sleepers. He heard rumors from Wayne that some of his techniques didn't sit well with the older teachers, but a prof had to do what a prof had to do. Only today he wished he could just go home and leave them to do whatever.

"Mr. Ryersen!" one of the football players called out even before Will had put his things on the desk. "Hey, Mr. Ryersen, we have an idea!"

Will felt a small thrill of adrenaline. "Who are 'we,' Eddie, and what's the idea?" he asked.

"You know how you were challenging us to act more grown-up and do our homework?"

"Yes, I do seem to recall beating that drum fairly often in here," Will said, smiling.

"Well, me and the guys decided it'd be a real challenge if there was a prize. So here's what we think: if we can behave every study hall until the last one before Christmas, we win and you have to pay a forfeit."

He could see the gleam in twenty-eight pairs of eyes. They had it planned out, the sly devils.

"So who decides whether you've behaved?" he asked.

"You do," Eddie said. "That's only fair."

"Sounds too good to be true," Will returned. "And if you win, what's the forfeit?"

"Oh, it's nothing bad," Eddie's little girlfriend with the strawberry blond ponytail told him. "You just have to wear the same tie every day from the last class before Christmas through Easter Sunday."

That didn't sound too bad, so he nodded. "I think I could do that, gang, but you have to really buckle down. No talking, no notes, no texting, no iPods hidden beneath the textbooks; do your homework and show it to me on your way out of the room. No unnecessary bathroom passes. I have to take your word on that, but if this is an honorable wager, you have to behave honorably."

They all nodded and murmured their agreement in unison. Will had to laugh to himself as he watched every single student in the room take out some kind of work and apply himself or herself to it.

"Y'know," he said, "if you keep this up, your grades are going to improve so much Principal Stemwalter will think I'm teaching you to cheat."

WILL WAS STILL LAUGHING WHEN TRACY CAME HOME FROM WORK, tired, crumpled, not in the least friendly-faced. He saw her, really saw her, for a moment and moved to her with his arms open. "Honey, are you all right? You look worn out."

"Thanks," she said, spurning his embrace. "I know I look awful, but you don't have to rub it in."

Stung, he opened his mouth to retaliate, but something held back his sarcastic comment. "I only meant I love you and I'm concerned – and I wonder whether you'd like me to make dinner."

Tracy dropped her bag and her jaw at the same time. "Are you serious?"

"Sure."

She went into the living room and sank down on the couch. "I'm sorry I snapped. I am tired. We have a lot of sick kids right now, so I've been working peds with Allison. Not my favorite floor – it's too hard to stay objective." She laid her head back and closed her eyes. "I ought to change clothes, but I really am too tired."

Will knelt at her feet and removed her shoes and socks. "Just put your feet up and take a nap," he offered, lifting her legs to the cushions. "I'll figure out something to eat for when you wake up. Does anything sound good?"

"Honestly, no. I'll just have a bowl of cereal or something..."

"Sleep," he whispered, bending over to kiss her forehead. As he did that, she smiled, the first smile for him in days, warming him like a fire in winter.

Will would not call himself a good cook, but he could make do after all those years of living alone. He found leftover broccoli and a wedge of cheddar cheese and a carton of eggs and prepped his ingredients for an omelet. It would go together easily whenever Tracy woke up. He set the table and tore up lettuce for a salad, smiling to himself as he remembered Carolyn making this meal a long time ago. There was bread for toast, or English muffins – plenty of butter – some kind of jam in a jar in the refrigerator – all set.

Lord, help me to love her unconditionally, to treat her like a princess, to forgive the things that hurt and to put a guard on my lips so I don't strike back. I want my wife back. I want to have a good marriage. That's not unreasonable, is it? Amen.

THE OMELET TURNED OUT WELL, IF HE DID SAY SO HIMSELF. WILL FURther distinguished himself in his young wife's eyes by doing the dishes and cleaning up the kitchen. He sent her off to take a long bath while he did his homework, grading essays and beginning to put together an exam, and expected to find her asleep when he came to bed at midnight.

"I thought you'd be asleep," he said as he undressed and hung his pants in the closet.

"I did sleep a little while, but then I woke up again. So I've been reading." Tracy indicated the open Bible on her lap as she sat there in bed.

Will climbed in beside her and propped up his pillows, too. "Is there something you want to talk about?" he asked, expecting the usual negative.

"Yes." Tracy closed the Bible and put it on her nightstand.

Will looked at her expectantly, waiting, but she just looked down at her hands and said nothing. Finally he asked, "Tracy? What is it?"

Tears began to trickle down her pale cheeks, and her eyes remained hidden behind those long, dark lashes. He looked down on the tender skin in the part of her wavy hair and felt his heart breaking for her. But she wouldn't let him put his arms around her.

"Will, I'm sorry," she whispered. "I didn't mean to do it, truly I didn't. I don't know how it happened – it just did."

The hand Will had tried to place on her shoulder dropped to the bed with a lifeless thunk. *She's telling me there's some other man!*

What did you expect? You aren't man enough to hold her. Women

are fickle.

Lord, please, this can't be!

"I think you'd better tell me straight out what you mean," he made himself say.

"Please don't be angry," she begged, finally looking at him through tear-drenched eyes. "I know you didn't want to, but we're going to have a baby."

What?

"Will? Please say something!"

Ask her if it's yours, if you dare.

"Are you sure?"

She nodded. "I took two tests, a couple of days apart. I have some of the early symptoms, and both tests were positive. It threw me off because I had a period, but there's no doubt."

"Oh. I thought the pill..."

"Nothing is foolproof," Nurse Tracy said. "And before you ask, no, I didn't stop taking it. It just fails sometimes."

"Oh. So now what?"

"What do you mean?" she asked, a perplexed frown crinkling her forehead. "Now we get used to the idea and feel happy about it. I know you didn't want a baby yet, but since it's coming anyway, we can have all the fun other new parents have, imagining boy or girl, picking out names, shopping for baby things, daydreaming about what he or she will grow up to be... God has blessed us, Will! We need to thank Him."

He took in the change from penitent tears to blazing excitement, happiness, her cheeks now gone from lily to rose, her smile camera-worthy. "You're really happy about it, aren't you?"

She nodded, the roses deepening in her cheeks. "Oh, yes! I've always wanted babies!"

I'm about to put my foot in my mouth. I should just shut up. But if I wait, it will be too late.

"Trace, you're young enough to have a baby any time for years. We haven't even been married a year yet, and it's too soon. We should have decided this together, and, no, I'm not happy."

The roses bled out of her cheeks and the tears dried in the heat in her eyes. "Get out of this bed," she told him in a low tone that singed his ears. "Get out of this room."

He went.

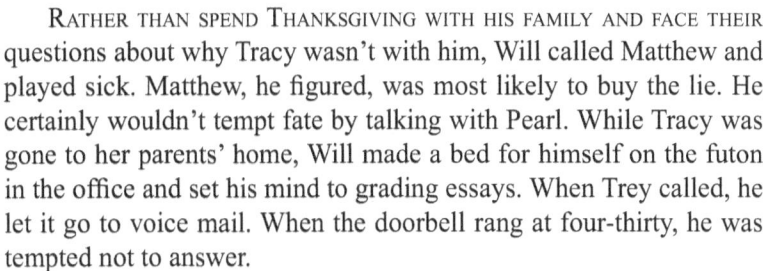

Rather than spend Thanksgiving with his family and face their questions about why Tracy wasn't with him, Will called Matthew and played sick. Matthew, he figured, was most likely to buy the lie. He certainly wouldn't tempt fate by talking with Pearl. While Tracy was gone to her parents' home, Will made a bed for himself on the futon in the office and set his mind to grading essays. When Trey called, he let it go to voice mail. When the doorbell rang at four-thirty, he was tempted not to answer.

However, the ringing bell was followed by some intense pounding, so he went, pulling the door open to find Allison on his porch.

"Let me in!" she said, pushing past him. "It's freezing out there!"

"What are you doing here?" Will asked, not offering to take her coat.

"I'm on my way to a meeting, and something tells me you should come with me."

"Oh. No, thanks. Uh – I'm not feeling well, and I have a lot of work to finish before Monday."

Nurse Allison inspected Will briefly and snorted. There might have been a faint whiff of sulfur about it. "You aren't sick any more than I am, and I'm in top shape. I don't know what's going on, and it's none of my business if you don't want to tell me, but don't try to b-s a b-ser. You need a meeting. Get your coat."

Will had heard Matthew say Allison was dangerous when she was angry, and he thought maybe his father didn't exaggerate. She certainly looked capable of knocking down any wall he might try to erect. *Why not go, if it gets her off my back?*

"All right," he said, putting on his black leather jacket. "Where are we going?"

"First Presbyterian," Allison said. "They always have a special late afternoon meeting on Thanksgiving, Christmas, New Year's Eve and Fourth of July. Days drunks are likely to get thirsty."

"Are you thirsty?" he asked, climbing into her little blue car.

"No, but I don't want to get that way. And I figured you need a meeting. Matthew was fine with it; he never objects if I say I need a meeting."

"Well, he's not stupid!" Will laughed.

"It's not far from here," Allison said, putting the car in gear and backing out like a race driver. "Anything you'd like to tell me before we get there?"

"For Pete's sake, Allie," Will said, clinging to the grab-bar, "if you'd slow down we could be in plenty of time, but safe, too!"

"Chicken!" she teased. "You know you have a love for speed; I saw you driving Trey's rent-a-Porsche. Now, really, what's going on?"

Will debated, but somehow he felt Allison would understand and probably not judge. "Okay," he said, "here goes: Tracy's pregnant and I wish she weren't."

Allison pulled the car so abruptly to the curb that Will's head smacked the window.

"What did you say?"

"I said Tracy's pregnant and I hate the idea."

"That's what I thought you said. Oh, Will."

Will couldn't remember having seen Allison so white since Carolyn's funeral, and he couldn't remember ever having found her at a loss for words. Worse still, big tears were filling up her eyes and running over!

"I'm sorry, Allison! I didn't have any idea I'd upset you so much, or I would have kept my mouth shut. Please don't cry."

Allison wiped her eyes and said some things Will hadn't realized she knew before looking at him again and shaking her head. "I don't think we'll be going to the meeting," she said. "We're going home. Your father won't be home for hours yet; I can feed Tucker."

"All right. But, Allie, I – "

"Just don't talk yet," she said, pulling back into traffic and negotiating the turn which would take them to the Ryersen house.

Will sat in uncomfortable, obedient silence for the short drive, knowing what he had triggered and wondering how to get past it, until they fishtailed into the gravel driveway and exited to receive Tucker's customary greetings.

"Come in," Allison said, opening the front door. "You, too, you big galoot," she told Tucker, who immediately went in and made himself at home, sniffing, rubbing against his humans, making conversation in a whiney tone.

"Sit down," Allison said, plopping down on the blue couch without making the customary offer of coffee. She still had Will's hand-kerchief crumpled in her hand. Will sat, also, in the adjacent arm-chair, jigging his leg nervously.

"Allison, I'm sorry I said anything. I know this is a touchy subject for you, but –"

"Touchy?" she asked. "Yes, I guess you could call it touchy. Will, what possesses you?"

"Look, I know not being able to have kids was a bad thing for you, and I'm sorry about that, but this is different."

Allison glared at Will and gave a decidedly sulfurous snort. "You are an idiot," she said, and he definitely saw fire hanging on her words. "An idiot. Let me tell you something, Professor; Tracy really wants this baby. I was there when she took the test, and I have never, ever seen anyone so full of joy at a positive result. If you give her a hard time about this and steal her joy, she will never forgive you. And nei-ther will I! So man up and support your wife and stop thinking just about yourself."

She stood up, stalked into the bedroom and slammed the door.

Ignore her; she's a hysterical female with problems of her own. She's jealous because she can't have a baby. You know you aren't fit to be a father, any more than your father is.

Lord, what can I do? I don't want this baby! I don't want any more changes in my life! But I don't want to lose Tracy; she's everything to me. I can't live without her.

Will knocked on Allison's bedroom door and asked her to take him home. Allison didn't seem inclined to forgive so easily. Although she gave him a ride back to his apartment, she refused to talk to him.

This is one hard woman! he thought, thanking her for the ride and closing the car door gently. He watched the little blue car drive away fast, no wave from the driver, no glance in the rearview mirror.

As twilight settled in, still no sign of his wife, Will made him-self a peanut butter sandwich and washed it down with a local beer. He spent an hour on his exam questions but couldn't really concentrate on them; nor could he find anything worth watching on television – all football games. Restless, he wandered the apartment, which only took two minutes, and finally pulled out his guitar case.

Being alone was a luxury in some ways; he hadn't played and sung to himself for a long time. Feeling melancholy, he went through his repertoire of Dylan songs before settling in to pick some classical jazz. Gradually all the knots eased out of his neck and back and shoulders and the music took him to that deep place he only reached once in a while, the place where peace abounded and God was real and present.

Why can't it always be like this? he wondered. *Why can everyone but me feel this peace and trust all the time? Lord, what do I have to do?*

His fingers slammed across the strings in a huge discord as the moment was lost forever. As he started to put the guitar back in the case, he heard Tracy coming through the front door.

She saw him sitting there on the living room floor and turned her back.

"Welcome home," Will said, thinking several words he wouldn't say in front of her. "Did you have a good time at your folks' house?"

"Fine."

"Are those leftovers?" Will asked hopefully, indicating the shopping bag she carried.

"Yes. But I'm sure you're too sick to eat any, aren't you."

Will thought several more strong words. "Tracy, let me put that stuff away for you, and then we need to talk."

"I think you've already said everything there is to say on the subject," she replied, slipping past him to the kitchen, where he could hear her banging things into the refrigerator.

Ignore her. She just wants to torment you and make you feel guilty. Stick to your guns.

Will shook his head sharply and followed Tracy into the kitchen. "Honey, I don't blame you for being angry, but I need to tell you something. Please hear me out."

"Fine." She sat down at the kitchen table and glared at her husband, waiting.

Will sat opposite her and drew a deep breath. No time for cowards, no time for spin-doctors, he knew. *Tell it like it is.*

"Allison came by late in the afternoon to take me to a meeting she said I needed. In the car, she asked me what was going on, and – well, I told her." Will shuffled his feet and peered at Tracy from under his eyelashes. "She was furious. She bawled me out up one side and down the other, and she scared me to death! I know why Dad calls her the dragon-princess!"

He waited for a smile but didn't get one.

"Well, anyway, I'm sorry you're upset. I never want to hurt you."

"I know I need to forgive you," Tracy said, still glaring, "but I don't think I'm quite ready to do that yet. I'm going to bed. See you in the morning."

Will didn't miss the sheen of unshed tears in Tracy's eyes as she left the room.

You see? No matter what you do, it isn't good enough. Her mother's daughter.

WILL SLEPT ON THE FUTON IN THE STUDY AND TRIED REALLY HARD NOT to say anything offensive, a good trick when he wasn't sure what might be the wrong thing at any given moment. He spent his time on school work and self-pity, since obviously no one understood him. Friday passed in cold isolation, but on Saturday morning John called and asked whether Will could come by to lend a hand with some glitch in the computer. It was a relief to have somewhere to go where people would talk to him, so Will texted Tracy, who didn't respond, and drove to the farm.

"I appreciate your taking the time to help me," John said, greeting him with a smile and a cup of coffee, "because this thing is driving me nuts. I guess I'm too old to be computer-savvy."

"Aw, come on, John. You were using a computer when I was still in high school." Will shrugged out of his jacket and slung it on the hall-tree, managing not to spill his coffee in the process.

"True," John agreed, "but this is the new and improved model, and I can't even work the mouse right."

The new computer was a pc laptop, and Will found his way around it easily. Then he settled in to be the teacher John needed.

Two hours later, John declared himself brain-dead and suggested they take a break. "I happen to know Cassie baked a coffee-cake and expects us to spoil our lunch with it," he said, leading Will into the kitchen.

Cassie served up large wedges of coffee-cake and topped off their coffees, but she threw them out of the kitchen because she was making turkey-noodle soup with the carcass of the Thanksgiving bird and needed all the table and counter space.

"Might as well get comfortable in the living room," John said, gesturing to the mess of papers around the computer on the dining room table. "We can ignore all this until my brain is resuscitated."

"I'm fine with that," Will agreed, "but you know you're not that bad. All you needed was someone to show you where things are." He sat down on the couch and put his coffee on the end table.

John sat in his usual chair by the fireplace and dedicated a few moments to enjoying the coffee-cake, which, Will agreed, was worthy of homage. When Will's plate was empty, John cleared his throat and said, "I have to confess, Will, I had an ulterior motive for asking you to come over."

Huh?

"You know how family is – we talk. It's hard to keep a secret."

"Yes?"

"Allison told Matthew what happened Christmas day, about the baby and your wanting Tracy to get an abortion."

"Allison told Dad," Will said slowly, heat rising in his face and in his stomach, "and Dad came running to you, and you've been deputized to talk to me."

"No, Will, nothing like that."

Will stood up and gathered his dishes. "By the way, that's not what I said. I'll be going home now. Glad I could help with the computer, John. Call me any time."

WILL TRIED TO STAND AND REALIZED TUCKER HAD COME OVER AND parked on his feet, his head on Will's thigh, troubled eyes fixed on Will's face. He reached out and petted the dog absently, touched to see that somebody cared how he was feeling.

"Let's go for a walk," he said suddenly, and Tucker made it to the door before Will made it out of the chair.

Clipping the leash to Tucker's collar and pulling on his jacket and gloves, Will left the house to step into a cold gray wind. Although Tucker immediately turned toward the Miller farm, this time Will dragged him around to go the other direction, toward a woods he hadn't explored yet about a quarter of a mile from the Ryersen house. He walked as fast as he could, feeling his ears and nose getting colder and colder as he faced into the wind, wiping his nose on the back of his wrist when he realized he had no handkerchief.

"Into the woods!" he said to Tucker, who really needed no encouragement. He seemed to have found a scent to follow and was tugging at the leash.

It was a pine woods, different from the hardwood areas more common in the county, and the even placement of the trees made Will think it had probably been planted on purpose rather than growing up wild. The trees were so tall he could hardly see the tops when he looked up, and the wind was noticeably less as soon as he stepped under their shelter.

"If I let you off this leash, will you stick around?" he asked the dog, who was whining to go on. "I don't want to go much farther, myself."

Freed from constraint, Tucker took off, nose to the ground, to find the critter whose scent he had picked up earlier. Will sat down on a deadfall and leaned his face on his hands, elbows on knees. He didn't have any plan or any prayer to offer; it was just a time to be.

Tucker came loping back to check on Will and to see whether Will wanted to play fetch.

"I can't throw a stick in here, dummy," Will told him, dropping the proffered stick on the ground. "Too many trees. What's the matter? Couldn't you find your rabbit?"

As the dog despaired of play and wandered off again, Will thought about dogs and cats, wondering how Nero was doing, and Flash... Gracie took good care of Flash. Gracie was really a nice kid, and smart and funny...

Suddenly Will flashed back to the last days he had spent on the Abbott farm, just before he had attempted suicide and then left home, when Gracie was just a tiny infant. She had been such a pretty baby, already a mirror image of Carolyn, and she had been such a good baby, rarely crying. Will remembered how she used to smile and flail her chubby little arms and legs whenever she saw him, making tiny cooing noises like a pigeon. He remembered carrying her in his arms for long walks around the farm, pointing out flowers and trees and squirrels and other animals to her as if she could understand him, pouring out his aching heart to her where no one else could hear them.

I loved her, that baby. I wonder if some part of her remembers that now, and that's why she's so attached to me. I felt as if I should keep her safe from all the bullies in the world. When I had to leave, I missed her.

And I love her now, almost grown up as she thinks she is... Tracy's baby might be a little girl like that, all pink and pretty. Or a feisty little boy who looks like Dad and me. A real person.

Could I have killed Baby Grace like some stray cat? Of course not! And Tracy would say this blob she's carrying is just as much a real person as four-month-old Gracie. Not just Tracy's baby, either; I made it, too. Oh, God, what's the matter with me!

"C'mon, Tucker," he called. "Time to go home."

Chapter 26

"Hey, Will, how was your holiday?" Wayne asked as they met at the coffee-machine in the lounge. His sweater du jour was orange and Chinese red checks, with cables knit down the front for good measure. Will turned his head for a moment to quell the vertigo before responding automatically, "Just great. Yours?"

"Great! Anita's folks came to spend the weekend and we had a blast. I have the greatest in-laws!" Wayne stepped aside as Principal Stemwalter came over, brushing down his comb-over, reaching for the coffee pot. "Morning, boss."

"Mmphf," Stemwalter replied, filling his huge travel mug and emptying the pot. "Ryersen."

"Good morning, sir," Will said to the man's departing back. He looked at the empty pot and shook his head. "Nuts. I'm not too good to make coffee, but I don't have time."

"By lunch break one of the women will have done it," Wayne soothed, "and probably washed out the pot, too."

"It's just getting seasoned," Will teased. He felt the acid burn in his stomach and said, "I probably don't need it anyway. See you later."

"Yeah. You guys need to come for dinner this week. We were just saying we haven't seen enough of you lately. We'll pig out on Anita's cooking and play Sequence or something."

"Thanks." Will hurried out, thinking, *Just what I need, to have them see how angry Tracy is with me – and why. Anita will start all that sappy ooo-ing and ahh-ing and it'll make things even worse. Shoot, even Wayne's excited about having a baby. Well, not me.*

Maybe it was normal for the kids to have trouble settling in on the first day back from a four-day weekend, but Will had no patience for it. By the end of the day he had sent three boys and one girl to the office and yelled at his first American Lit class. Only the study hall bunch had been superlatively well-behaved. He had looked spitefully for the least breach of conduct but had been unable to find one.

I know they're up to something. But if this is the result, how bad can it be?

He drove home, tired and hungry, looking forward to dinner. Tracy had had the day off, so he was hoping for a big meal. Instead, he found a dark house, a cold kitchen and a note:

I have gone to Mom's for dinner; don't know when I'll be home. T.

"So what am I supposed to do for dinner?" Will asked the blank walls. He opened the refrigerator door and stood there for a while, but he didn't find any leftovers. He opened the freezer, but nothing beckoned from there, either. "Well – "

He considered ordering pizza, but his stomach had that newly returned burning sensation that told him he would regret it. Finally he settled for a bowl of Cheerios and sat down to more paperwork. By seven o'clock, that had lost its charm, too.

Lord, please, what am I supposed to do? I said I was sorry, and I am. I couldn't lie about being excited, but I'm willing to go along. What more can she expect? It's not fair to be punished for being honest.

Will could almost hear Pearl's voice all of a sudden, saying, "Nobody ever said life would be fair." He started to laugh out loud.

Then he clicked out of his grading program into Word and found his fingers stuttering over the keys almost as if he were not in control of their direction. He hadn't written anything since he had left the university, but within a short time the hesitation was gone and words were flying onto the page. He didn't notice the passage of time and was heart-thumpingly startled when Tracy walked into the study and said, "What are you doing?"

Will gasped for a breath and said, "Oh, nothing much. You startled me."

"I know I did. I called when I came in, and when you didn't answer, I was afraid something had happened to you."

Will hit 'save' and turned to face his wife, curious to see real concern on her face. "I was pretty into it, I guess; I didn't hear you at all. Thanks for being concerned."

"You're welcome. What were you writing?"

Honesty, remember?

"I suppose it's a short story," he said, no longer meeting her eye.

"That's great! But you look – Will, are you embarrassed?"

The Ryersen flush again. "I guess so."

"But why? I know you used to write, before you came here. I – I read some of the things you had published." Now she was turning pink, too. "I thought they were really well-written. They were awfully dark, though. But why be embarrassed?"

He took a deep breath and let it out in a whoosh. "It's expected for English professors to write at the university level – part of keeping the job. I used to get flack for it 'only' being fiction, but it was, well, normal. Out here in farm country, though – a writer? I don't think it's going to be considered very manly by the farm crowd. I had enough of being called a faggot when I was a kid."

Tracy's eyes filled with tears and she crossed the room to put her arms around Will, drawing his head against her chest. "Oh, Will, you're as much a man as any man I know. Those idiots were just – idiots. You can't let them define you or stifle you all these years later. I love you, and I'm proud of your work. I hope this one gets published, too!"

Will took advantage of her grace to put his arms around her and tell her how much he loved her. He was tired of sleeping on the futon, tired of the distance between them, tired of the empty place that ached all the time because her love wasn't filling it. As he ran a hand down her side and over her abdomen he felt a small, hard knot low in her belly. Shocked, he drew back his hand, but she pressed it back.

"That's our baby growing," Tracy said. "Now, when I take my clothes off, you can see it." She paused for a moment and then said, "Would you like to see?"

The month between Thanksgiving and Christmas had passed in a rapid blur. Will had found himself pressed into service decorating trees in three households and was heartily tired of all the bustle Abbott and Ryersen women could create over tinsel and wrapping paper. He did approve of all the baking, of course, and paid himself in cookies whenever he could get away with it.

"Gonna get a paunch if you're not careful," Ed teased as he raided a rack of cooling cinnamon stars in Cassie's kitchen.

"No, he won't," Gracie contradicted. "Will's skinny. Just like Matthew." She took one little star for herself and savored it in tiny nibbles. "Are you going to have a boy baby?" she asked Will. "If you do, I bet he looks just like you and Matthew."

"Too soon to tell, I think," Will replied with his mouth full. "I think we can find out next month, if Tracy wants to."

"Don't you want to?" Gracie asked, licking cinnamon and sugar from her fingers.

"Wash your hands," Will said semi-automatically, and she turned to the sink. "I don't really care that much what it is," he answered her question. "Just as long as it's healthy."

"Kinda fun to think of you with a little perfessor," Ed said. "'Course, a pretty little girl like Tracy – that ain't bad, either."

"You aren't going to live to find out if you don't stop stealing cookies," Pearl said, coming up behind them. She glared at all three, but it was evident from the twinkle in her eye that she was teasing.

"Yes, ma'am," they said in unison. Will spoiled the effect by taking several more of the little cookies, leaving only half a dozen or so on the rack.

"I came in to tell you there's a surprise for you in the living room," Pearl said.

"It isn't Christmas," Will said. "Do I get to open my presents early for some reason?"

"Well, I guess you'll have to find out, won't you?" Pearl said. "Go on. I want to see this."

Will, Gracie and Ed followed Pearl through the swinging door into the dining room, whose table was piled with boxes, bows, wrapping paper and tape, and into the living room, where the rest of the Ryersens and John sat in quiet expectation.

Will looked at them with a question in his eyes and then looked around the room.

"Merry Christmas, buddy!" Trey said from his post by the front door.

Will stood frozen, mouth dropping open, and then closed the distance to his friend in a few steps. They were hugging, pounding one another on the back, and Will felt some very unmanly tears threatening. He stepped back, still holding Trey's forearms, and gave him the onceover.

"What are you doing here! Why didn't you call? I'd have picked you up at the airport."

"He did call," Tracy said, "and we decided it would be fun to surprise you. John picked him up."

"Let the boy get his coat off," Pearl said, "and then we'll have some cookies and coffee. Not cinnamon stars, unfortunately, because they seem to have mostly disappeared. Gracie, come help me get things together."

"Aw, Pearl, I want to watch!"

"No," John said, "go help in the kitchen. You can stay with us then while we talk."

Gracie appeared to be considering a pout, but she gave it up and followed Pearl out of the room. Will hung Trey's cashmere overcoat and scarf on the hall tree and sat beside him on the couch, Tracy snugged up against his other side.

"So what possessed you to come right before Christmas? How long can you stay?"

"I missed you," Trey said. "You hadn't called or even e-mailed in forever, and I was afraid something was wrong. So I called, and Tracy told me about the baby and the writing and it just seemed like a great time to see you all again. Holiday spirit and all that. Besides, my parents have decided to do Christmas in Spain, and I wasn't really into that. So I decided I'd spend it with the Ryersens and the Abbotts if they'd have me."

"And of course we'll have you," Allison said. "It's good to see you again!"

Trey accepted a mug of coffee and a napkin from Gracie and observed that Matthew, Will and Tracy received glasses of milk.

"Stomach acting up again?" he asked Will.

"Some. Besides, milk goes better with cookies than coffee any day. Want some?"

"No, thank you. This is great coffee – and those look like prize-winning cookies," he added, taking several of different kinds from the plate Gracie was passing.

"In fact, some of them are – or were," John said. "Mostly family recipes handed down and tested at county fairs for a hundred years."

Will watched a reverent look come over Trey's face as he bit into an apricot bar, which was one of Pearl's family recipes.

"You could have stayed at the farm," Will said, dumping Trey's matched luggage in the study. "The bed there is a lot more comfortable than this futon."

"Speaking from experience?" Trey teased.

"As a matter of fact, yes," Will said, shaking his head. "Long fight – but it blew over. Otherwise, I'd have to offer you the couch in the living room. Come to think of it, it's probably more comfortable."

"This will be fine. Roughing it builds character." He helped Will to open out the futon and put clean sheets and blankets on it. "It's early – you have to get to bed yet?"

"No, that's my dad who gets up before the chickens. Tracy's probably about ready for bed, though. She gets really sleepy at night right now."

"Oh. Okay."

"Trey?"

"Nothing. Just thought we could talk a while, the two of us. If Tracy wouldn't mind. But it'll keep til tomorrow."

"Let me go say goodnight and tell her what we're doing, then we can talk as late as you want."

Trey wasted no time when they were ensconced on the living room couch with beers and pretzels. "I met a woman. I think I'm in love."

"Congratulations!" Will replied. Then he considered. "You don't look happy about it."

"I'm not. This wasn't in the Sullivan Plan at all!"

Will laughed, just a little, and took a small swallow of his beer before saying, "Man, the Sullivan Plan is fifteen or twenty years old! You have to expect things to change in that much time."

"Why? It's a good plan – love 'em and leave 'em and not get serious about anyone before I'm fifty – and then only a wealthy younger woman who doesn't want more than two kids."

Will shook his head at Trey. "It seems God changes our plans while we're not looking. I didn't imagine I could ever find Tracy again, and I never wanted to end up teaching high school in northwest Ohio. I thought I'd have a novel published by now, or a book of poetry, and be going on book tours and getting tenure at the university. And here I am, married, wife pregnant, teaching American Lit to high school farm kids, no books, no tour..."

"Yeah, exactly. Nothing you wanted except maybe Tracy has happened. And if it hadn't been for her, maybe you would have those other things, or at least be on the way. I want to be free to flit from flower to flower like a bee, to travel, to work as little as possible until I take over the business for the old man – and I can't do that if I let myself be tied to Claire. But I – I think I love her anyway."

Will laughed again at the sight of his best friend tearing at his usually impeccably coiffed hair and looking wildly around the study, as if an answer might be written on the walls. He noted to himself that Trey hadn't even risen to the mention of God, a sure sign he was confounded.

"So tell me about this woman – Claire?"

"Yeah, Claire Kennedy. And, yes, she's some kind of distant relation to *the* Kennedys. I met her at the country club at some black-tie fundraiser my mother dragged me to, and it was all over in about five seconds. I turned on the charm, and – "

"And she was all over you; I know how it goes."

"No! She wouldn't even dance with me. It took me weeks of brutal self-abasement and groveling to get her to go out with me – for lunch, for Pete's sake! Not even for dinner. Then she quizzed me about my goals in life – like I could tell a chick I want to hit on about the Sullivan Plan – and explained she found me quite handsome and charming, but shallow. Shallow! Me!"

"If the shoe fits..." Will murmured, drawing a glare.

"And she told me she's the head of some foundation in Ames, where they do good works – I didn't even understand some of what she was saying. And she doesn't want to waste her time, at her age, which is all of twenty-seven, going out with men who aren't marriage material. She – you're really going to laugh now, buddy, but she's a Christian." Trey hung his head and moaned. "Do you know what that can do to a man's love-life?"

"That I do!" Will responded, managing by intense will-power to keep from rolling on the floor with laughter. "Oh, man, Trey, you're in a mess! Congratulations. You know what? You didn't even talk about how beautiful she is or what she looks like. It's all over."

Trey had managed a smile or two, fairly acknowledging why Will was so transported by his story, but now he sobered. "That's exactly it; it's all over before it can really get going. She likes me, but she isn't going to date a heathen, because for some reason I don't understand she can't marry one."

Will sobered, too. "It's a God-thing," he explained. "The Bible tells us not to be unequally yoked with unbelievers. It doesn't lead to a good marriage when the two people have radically different beliefs about the most important things."

"Oh, come on! You believe that?"

"I wish I could tell you it's nonsense, but I do believe it. God is too important to put aside in a relationship. Tracy always knew that, even though I didn't. If Jesus hadn't gotten ahold of me, we wouldn't ever have gotten married."

Trey drained the last of his beer and went to the refrigerator for another. He held one up to Will, who shook his head no.

"So what am I going to do?" Trey asked.

"You only have two choices, right? Give her up and date some-body else, or start studying religion. You're a smart guy, so you've probably figured out already that those are the choices. And you've probably figured out you need to ask Claire to teach you."

"You know where I stand on all that."

"Sure do. All I can say is, God can change your heart – if you let Him."

"I think I'll check out the futon," Trey said, turning toward the study, beer still in hand. "Thanks for listening. Hey, don't tell Tracy, okay? I don't want her laughing at me – or trying to convert me."

WILL WOKE EARLY THE NEXT MORNING, AS EXCITED AS THE STUDENTS that it was the last day before vacation. He dressed up a little, crisp white shirt and bright red tie, and hustled out the door to wind up the week. He made it through the morning, even though everyone was antsy and distracted, and had a quick lunch with Wayne. Then it was time for his after-lunch study-hall and the judging of the wager.

"So, Mr. Ryersen!" Eddie piped up even before Will could get seated, "what do you think? Did we win?"

"Eddie, we'll have to see how things go until five minutes before the closing bell. I'm not going to announce the winner now and have a whole period of chaos."

"Fair enough." Eddie turned to his classmates. "Settle down, guys! We gotta make it through this class!"

"I don't have any homework," came a grumble from the back of the room. "What'm I supposed to do?" This complaint was echoed by more than a few others.

"Attention, here, please," Will said. "I know many of you don't have homework, but every one of you has at least one textbook. So study for exams. No talking, et cetera, remember?"

Pretending to study things on his laptop, Will was secretly proud of the class as they struggled against nature to remain quiet and in control of themselves. With ten minutes left in the period, he rapped on his desk, the sound loud in the silent room.

"Ladies and Gentlemen, I am proud to announce that every single one of you has fulfilled the terms of the wager. You've been the best-behaved, hardest-working class in the school. Maybe *ever* in the school. Congratulations – you win!"

The quiet was erased by loud cheering and a few ambitious whistles, so that Will had to quiet them to avoid an invasion from the hall Nazis or the principal.

Eddie marched to the front of the room bearing a tie-box with a big red satin ribbon around it. "Mr. Ryersen, you remember the terms, right? If we win, you have to wear the same tie every day until the day after Easter."

"Yes, I remember," Will grinned. "I figure this one will do for most occasions without getting me in trouble with my wife."

The class began to giggle.

"Well, see, we have this tie as a gift for you, and this is the one you get to wear." Eddie proffered the box.

I'm so stupid! Should have foreseen this and set it up differently. Oh, man!

Will took the box with two fingers, as carefully as if it were ticking. "Thank you, guys. Really."

"Open it," came a girl's voice from the back of the room.

"Open it. Right." Will slowly untied the red bow and placed the ribbon on the desk. He slowly opened the box...

Chapter 27

TREY WAS UNQUESTIONABLY THE HERO OF CHRISTMAS. His second suitcase had been full of gifts, and each one had obviously been chosen with knowledge and great care. Gracie became his slave forever when she opened the Tiffany robin's-egg blue jewelry box to find a pair of small cultured pearl stud earrings inside.

"How did you know what I wanted most!" she cried, throwing herself on Trey for a big hug.

"A small bird told me you are going to get your ears pierced for your birthday in January," he said, hugging her back, "and my mother told me a lady always wears pearls."

He had wrapped a picture of an elaborate baby stroller for Will and Tracy, in addition to their individual gifts, and promised it would be delivered if Tracy approved it. "If you don't like this one, pick out the one you want and let me know. The young prince deserves the best possible carriage."

"How do you know it won't be the young princess?" Tracy asked, smiling in spite of herself.

"Just a hunch. And if it is a princess, then so much the better. She'll need all kinds of extra-special, beautiful things. And *I* shall become her favorite uncle by showering her with gifts."

"You can be *my* favorite uncle in the meantime," Gracie said.

"IT'S INTERESTING," ALLISON SAID TO MATTHEW AS THEY GOT READY for bed that night.

"What is?"

"The way Trey can throw his money around and still not seem obnoxious about it. He spends it as if he were printing it himself, but he doesn't make anyone feel small. He never condescends."

"You're right. I guess he makes fun of himself so much it all seems like a game or something. I really like the guy, if he would just let the Lord get ahold of him."

Allison snuggled up to Matthew's back and threw her arm across his chest, where he took her hand and held it close. "We should pray for that more often."

"Or just sic Gracie on him," Matthew teased. "She'll bring him to heel."

"Can't you just see Gracie, in her high-heeled shoes and pearl earrings, bringing the gospel and the fashion word to primitive tribes in the Amazon?"

"Honey," Matthew said, laughing, "you have a way better imagination than I do. I just thought of her bullying Trey into reading the Book of John and then giving him the Four Spiritual Laws as an ultimatum."

"Whatever," Allison yawned. "I like him and I want to know I'll see him in heaven."

Matthew caressed her hand over and over as her breathing slowed and deepened. He would never, ever say Allison snored, but she did make some little dragon-like rumbles. He prayed his way to sleep, thanking God for all their many blessings and seeking protection over his beloved family.

"I BET IF WE GO INTO TOLEDO WE CAN FIND A PLACE TO PLAY RACQUET-ball," Trey challenged.

"Man," Will said, "I haven't played since I left Iowa! It'll kill me!"

"Naw, it's like swimming or riding a bike – you never forget how. And I don't play all that much, either. Come on, Ryersen, give it a try. Humor your guest."

"Well, if you put it that way..." Will logged onto the Internet and googled racquetball courts in Toledo. Sure enough, there were several possibilities, and a couple of phone calls found one with an open court in an hour.

"Get your gear," Trey exalted, "and we're off!"

"Let me at least ask Tracy if it's okay with her," Will said, but Trey had gone before him.

"She said if you could find a court she was all for it. Now stop procrastinating and get your gear."

Will found a gym bag in the back of the closet and put in shorts and shirt and underwear and shower gear, but he had no idea where his racquet had gone.

"Not a problem! They'll rent you one there," Trey said, picking up his own bag and racquet, which showed he had plotted this out before he left Iowa.

"Do I at least get to drive?" Will asked.

"So," Trey said, scrubbing the water out of his hair with a mono-grammed towel, "I guess we aren't as good as we used to be."

"Nope," Will agreed, applying deodorant liberally, his towel cinched around his waist. "Lack of practice on this end, but probably old age on yours."

Trey snapped Will with the end of his wet towel and turned to putting several manly products into his damp hair, inspecting himself in the mirror over the sinks. Will dressed as quickly as he could and ran his fingers through his hair as means of grooming.

"I do miss playing with you," he allowed. "You ought to visit more often."

"Or you should come home and visit us." Trey buttoned his shirt and reexamined his reflection, judging it good. "I'd like you to meet Claire. She'd like you and Tracy – maybe give me some cred, that my best friend's a Christian."

"I can't see how she wouldn't like Tracy," Will agreed, putting everything, including his wet towel, into the gym bag, "but that's not going to make the final difference, I can guarantee it."

As they walked to the car, Trey kept shaking his head, until Will finally asked, "Do you have water in your ears or something? You remind me of Tucker with a flea."

"Ha ha. No, just thinking. I know you're right about Claire. I guess I'll have to study up on stuff. You going to help me?"

"Sure, why not?" They settled in for the ride home. "The first thing is to – uh – "

A silence fell over the car. Trey sat very still, waiting, like a rabbit under the shadow of the hawk. Will felt scalded with embarrassment as he realized he had no idea how to begin to introduce his friend to the Lord.

After nearly ten minutes of increasingly uncomfortable silence, Trey laughed and said, "Maybe I should ask Gracie, huh? She's never at a loss for words."

"Maybe you should," Will agreed. "And I bet we could set you up with Pastor Miles for an hour or two while you're here. How long are you staying, anyway?"

Now it was Trey's turn to be embarrassed. "I – well, I hoped – I mean – "

"As long as you want," Will said, smiling without looking at his friend.

ON SUNDAY MORNING TREY AGREED TO GO TO CHURCH AND DRESSED IN the Armani suit and tie he had brought for any possible formal occasion. Tracy was admiring his polished appearance when Will came out of the bedroom in navy slacks, a white dress shirt and The Tie.

"What is *that!*" Tracy shrieked, pointing, as Trey forgot all good manners and gaped.

"What is what?" he pretended.

"I think she may be referring to your cravat, old man," Trey said in his best British accent. "It is rather – unusual."

"Don't give me a hard time, okay? This is my forfeit."

"What have you forfeited," Trey asked, "good taste?"

"You can't possibly wear that to church," Tracy said severely.

"Sorry, honey, but I have to. My students won the wager, and this is my forfeit. I have to wear it every day from Christmas through Easter."

"Oh, no," Tracy moaned, "no. No. You can't go out of the house like that. No."

"It does have a certain – je ne sais quoi," Trey said, suppressing a chuckle.

Will turned to examine himself in the mirror on the wall. The tie was impossibly wide, teal with two different hideous shades of tan stripes. A large orange circle of embedded grease sat right below the knot. It was, in fact, Wayne Dennis's grandfather's memorial tie.

"Please, Will, not to church," Tracy begged.

"I promised," he told her, the red in his cheeks contrasting badly with the orange grease-spot. "Let's go."

"Nice tie," Ed remarked, turning a laugh into a cough.

"Handsome," John and Matthew agreed, snickering.

"Whatever has gotten into him?" Allison asked.

"He hates me," Tracy moaned. "He's trying to humiliate me. My parents are going to have a heart attack. They've already asked me why I couldn't have married Trey instead of Will."

"I am not hard of hearing," Will intoned solemnly, "and I am not unaware of the particular charms of this tie. But a deal's a deal."

"Maybe next time you'll think it through better," Pearl said, no expression whatsoever on her face. "Now we need to get seated before they begin without us."

"Sit by me," Gracie told Trey, taking his hand. "I can explain things to you as we go along."

Will didn't miss the panicked look Trey threw him, but he didn't try to stop Gracie, either. *She loves this sort of thing; let her do it.*

The worship team stepped onstage to begin the call to worship, picking up their instruments and microphones, fussing with their music. The bass guitarist caught sight of Will and began to smile hello, only to be arrested by the vision of Will's tie. Will gave him a ferocious glare, and the guitarist shook his head, trying to get back into the mood for worship.

"How embarrassing!" Tracy whispered, hiding her face on Will's shoulder.

"Buck up!" Trey whispered from her other side. "In a few weeks nobody will notice anymore."

"Pay attention!" Gracie hissed, pinching Trey's hand. "You need to hear everything."

Sunday dinner at the Abbotts' was always a great meal, and today's roast with potatoes, carrots and parsnips was no exception. The men rose lethargically from plum tart dessert to begin their Sunday kitchen routine, but Gracie clamped onto Trey's wrist.

"I need for you to stay with me," she said firmly. "We have a lot to talk about."

"Gracie..." John warned.

"No, it's okay," Trey said, rising with the girl. "I do need to hear a lot of things. If I may be excused, please."

"Oh, you're so polite!" Gracie enthused. "Come with me."

"HOW'D IT GO?" WILL ASKED, TRYING NOT TO SMILE AT THE SLIGHTLY harried expression on Trey's face. He himself was feeling terrific, replete with dinner and a brief doze after the dishes, neck free of the dreaded tie until tomorrow.

"It was brutal!" Trey moaned, wiping imaginary sweat from his wrinkled brow as he settled on the couch next to Will. "She brought out the thumbscrews. She threatened me with unspeakable horrors. When I didn't capitulate, she brought out the ultimate weapon."

"She cried, right?"

"Great big crocodile tears. About broke my heart." Trey didn't look like he was joking anymore.

"So..." Will managed once again not to smile, but it was harder this time.

"So I told her I'd think about it and read the Bible." He shook his head and ran his hand over his perfectly coiffed hair. "I can't stand to disappoint a pretty little girl like that, but – dang, Will – it just doesn't – "

"Yes, I remember. Just do the reading, because there will be an exam, and she's merciless once she gets started."

"I'll be going home soon."

"Don't think that makes you safe! Remember the letters she wrote me?"

"Aw, man..."

Will watched the exact moment when Trey's designer-tanned complexion drained of color to resemble bad cottage cheese.

"Here she comes!" Trey hissed. "Hide me or something!"

Now Will did laugh. "Not a chance, buddy."

"There you are!" Gracie said, advancing purposefully toward Trey. "I have something for you." She handed him a package clumsily wrapped in Santa paper and tied with a green ribbon which had seen duty before. "I know you're going to like this!"

Trey had automatically taken the parcel and was weighing it in his hand, looking at it with the same enthusiasm he would have awarded a dirty diaper or a pail of fish guts.

"Go on; open it!" Gracie insisted, her eyes dancing.

Trey untied the ribbon and unfolded the paper with the terrified precision of a bomb disposal expert and laid bare the deadly contents. "Uh – thank you, Grace. This is very nice of you. But don't you need your Bible?"

"Oh, it isn't mine," she explained, "it's an emergency copy. We always keep some around so we have them when somebody needs one."

"Well, I wouldn't want to deprive someone who needs it," Trey tried.

"Oh, no," she countered. "Nobody needs it more than you do."

That did it. Will collapsed back on the cushions, roaring with laughter despite the evil glare his friend gave in response. "She's got you, buddy. Just say 'thank you' and ask her for your reading assignment."

Faithful to his word, Trey began reading with the Gospel of John, but he refused to discuss his reading with either Will or Gracie. "I'm doing what you asked," he told Gracie. "Now don't bug me."

Gracie took the rebuff with more grace than her family would have expected, perhaps aided a bit by a private word from Pearl.

Will and Trey played racquetball twice more, splitting the wins, and they spent several evenings enjoying the mellow sounds of Will's guitar, singing along sometimes, accompanied by Tracy.

But Trey decided to go home on New Year's Eve day rather than face spending the evening in church.

"I love you like a brother," he told Will, "but not enough to go through that." He caught a late afternoon flight out of Detroit.

Will stood at the fence for a while watching planes come in and out, shivering in the cold and feeling the chill deep inside himself. *I miss him already. It was like having a brother here, and now the place he's supposed to fill is empty. Lord, how can I stand eternity without my best friend? Please let him find You somehow, in spite of himself, the way I did.*

Chapter 28

W HEN SCHOOL RESUMED, MR. RYERSEN WAS THE HIT OF Infinity High School in his new tie. The teachers all remarked it, including Wayne Dennis, who praised it highly as "a lot like one of my best ones." The students, after their five minutes of hilarity, settled in to work with the usual mix of enthusiasts and slackers to liven his classes.

"I hope we all make it to graduation," Will told Tracy. "At this point I'm not sure I'm going to survive until Friday!"

"I hope you are," she said, "because Friday after school we have the next ultrasound, and we should be able to tell the baby's sex if we want to. Do we want to?"

Will sat down rather heavily on the kitchen chair and made eye-contact with the linoleum. "Uh – whatever you want, I guess." He hesitated, then went on, "Trace, I don't really – I mean, I know the ultrasound is a big deal to you, but – "

"You don't want to go, do you."

"Well..."

"Never mind, then. My mother will take me." Tracy quietly left the room, leaving Will in communion with the linoleum.

Why couldn't I just have said yes and pretended it's great? It means so much to her, and she means so much to me...

Will's cell phone rang, Matthew's ring.

"Hey, Dad."

"Will, are you all right? I was just turning out the cows and I got this – feeling – "

"Funny you should mention it. No, I'm not all right, I'm so screwed up and I don't know what to do about it. May I come over?"

"Sure. Come to the farm, because I still have some things to do here. I'll be in the barn, so wear your boots."

Will found his farm shoes in the utility closet and put them on before grabbing his old parka and hollering to Tracy that he was going to the farm. The drive was uneventful, as the snow and ice from earlier in the week had been driven off by a scouring northwest wind. He parked at the house and hiked back to the barn without meeting anyone but Flash, who greeted him but didn't accompany him on the trek.

Inside the barn, Matthew was shoveling manure, Will's least favorite job in the whole world.

"You don't have to help," Matthew said preemptively, "just sit on the straw over there and tell me what's up."

"Thanks." Will plunked down on the bales and inhaled their still-potent summer smell.

Matthew kept shoveling, although he spared a long look at his son. Finally, as the silence stretched between them, he said, "I'm going to dump this load on the manure pile, then I'll be back to talk." Will nodded.

Several of the Jerseys were in their stalls, rustling the straw and breathing audibly, their warm, sweet aroma as pleasing as their manure was not. Will felt the peace of the old barn surround him like a cocoon.

"Okay, what's up?" Matthew asked, dropping down beside Will with an audible grunt. "And don't say 'nothing,' because you asked to come over, remember?"

"Yes, sir." Will ran his hands through his hair, causing the wheaten strands to stand on end in longish spikes. "I did a really dumb thing, and I don't even know why I did it." He paused; Matthew waited. "Tracy told me she has to have an ultrasound on Friday. She made the appointment for after school so I can go with her." He paused again.

"And..."

"Well, I don't want to go – and I sort of told her that."

Matthew huffed out a huge breath. "Oh, brother. I can imagine how well that went over."

"She said her mother will take her – and then she walked out of the room." Will ruffled his hair again and jiggled his foot. "Dad, I don't know why I said that! Why didn't I just lie and say I'd love to go with her and I'd love to know the sex of the baby?"

"Not your smoothest move ever," Matthew agreed. "I don't usually recommend lying, though, especially not to your wife. The Bible says, 'Be sure your sin will find you out,' and that's been my experience with trying to lie."

"Well, the truth sure didn't go over well!" Will got up and began to pace back and forth in a short line in front of his father.

"The question now would seem to be what can you do to make it right, agreed?"

"Yes, sir."

"So sit down for a minute and we'll figure it out." Matthew patted the straw beside him and Will sat down again.

"First," Matthew said, "I think we need to pray. I don't feel like one of those TV advice-givers, but the Lord always knows what's best."

I wouldn't expect any less of you, Dad. "Sure. Let's pray."

Will sometimes thought his father had a wide Quaker streak, because often Matthew's first response in prayer was a long silence. Will didn't usually fare too well in silence; he didn't know what to do with it. Now he clenched his fists and waited it out, because he had no idea what to say.

"Did you hear anything?" Matthew asked.

"Hear – uh, no, not really."

"I've been reading in Ephesians," Matthew said at last, "and this morning I read the end of chapter four, where it says, 'Be kind and compassionate to one another, forgiving each other, just as in Christ God forgave you.' That's just one place the Word tells us to be loving to others and to put their needs before ours, just the way Jesus did for us. So I think maybe you need to stop thinking about what you want or don't want and start thinking about what's best for your wife and your child. The Lord didn't save you from hell and damnation just so you could have a good time and get whatever you want. You signed on to do His will, whatever it is."

"Wish you'd quit beating around the bush," Will said, sarcasm oozing from his very pores. "Hard to know what you really mean." He stood up again, turning to look down at his father. "I wish you could manage to be wrong just once when we have these little talks."

He extended his hand to Matthew and pulled him up from the straw into a hug. "I love you, Dad, and I'm so grateful to have you in my life. I'll talk to Tracy."

Matthew surreptitiously wiped his eyes on his sleeve and followed Will out of the barn, back to Will's car. "I love you, too," he said, smiling. "Give her my love and tell her Allie and I can't wait to find out what this baby is!"

WILL FOUND TRACY IN THE KITCHEN FIXING DINNER AND SPARED A MO-ment to thank God for a wife who could be crushed and angry and still care for him and his needs. *I know I don't deserve her, but thank You for giving her to me anyway.*

"Dinner will be ready in half an hour," Tracy said, her voice flat and even.

"Thank you. Uh, Trace, is it something that will keep?"

She looked at him now. "Keep?"

"I mean, can you stop for a while and talk with me?"

"I guess so. It's just spaghetti." Tracy turned down one burner and turned off another and wiped her hands on the towel by the sink. "What is it?"

"Can we go into the living room?"

Tracy followed Will and sat on one end of the couch. After a moment of consideration, he sat at the other end, turned toward her, respecting her distance.

"I want to apologize for my behavior a while ago," he began. "I'm really sorry, honey. I'm an idiot. I want to go with you to the appointment Friday."

Tears spilled over as Tracy said, "Don't lie to me, Will. I know you don't want anything to do with this baby."

"Please hear me," he begged. "I'm not excited about having a baby, but I'm happy for you, because I know you want it. I mean that, honey, honestly I do. I want you to be happy and I'm going to try harder to want what you want. I promise you I mean that." He scooted over to put his arm around her, handkerchief in hand, but Tracy wasn't ready to concede.

"How can I believe you? I see your face whenever anybody talks about the baby. I see the phony smile you put on when people congratulate us. You – well, you've been avoiding me – you know – "

"Oh, no! That's not true! I want you as much as I ever did, Trace. You're beautiful to me. I've just felt like – well, maybe you wouldn't want me, because you're mad at me."

Tracy threw her arms around Will and kissed him soundly, clarifying her feelings and soothing his ego. "I haven't put the spaghetti in the water yet," she said, "if you want to have dinner wait a little longer."

"So," THE ULTRASOUND TECH SAID AS SHE SQUIRTED THE SLIMY GEL onto Tracy's rounded belly, "do you want to know the sex of the baby?"

Tracy looked at Will, who sat beside the bed holding her hand, a bit sweaty and green around the gills. "What do you want, Will?"

"Honey, I want whatever you want. It doesn't matter – I mean, it matters, but – "

"Let's do it," Tracy said, laughing.

The procedure didn't take long. Will was amazed at the clarity with which he could see his unborn child, including the obvious.

"Is that what I think it is?" he asked.

"Yes, sir," the tech replied, laughing. "You have a son." She began to remove the wand from Tracy's belly.

"No, please!" Will said urgently. "Just a minute more!" He couldn't take his eyes off the screen.

"Somebody's falling in love," the tech said in a low aside to Tracy. "We see it all the time with fathers, when they first see the baby like this."

"Are you falling in love?" Tracy asked him on the drive home.

Will laughed as the blood crept up his neck and across his ears and cheekbones. "I guess I am. What we saw today isn't just an idea – he's a person. He has a face. He sucked his thumb."

"Now that we know," Tracy said, "we have to decide a couple of things."

"Decide what?"

"Well, first of all – do we tell anyone – or everyone? Then, what are we going to name him?"

"What do you want to do?"

Tracy swiveled her head to look at Will, noting the flush had faded to pale. "Are you going to ask me what I want to do about every single thing?"

He paused. "Well, probably."

"No good, Will. You ask what I want – well, I want you to get involved. Don't dump all the decisions on me."

"Oh. But what if I really don't care, like whether we tell people or not, or just have no idea?"

"Come on, Professor. Make a choice."

"Well, then, uh – I think we should tell at least our families. Because they are going to drive us crazy asking, and because it will help them to pray better."

"I think you nailed it that time," Tracy teased. "Now what about names?"

"Do we have to decide this minute? There must be a million boy's names out there, and that's just in English." Will pulled the car into their parking space and came around to hold Tracy's door.

"I have some ideas," she said once they were seated at the kitchen table.

"Okay..."

"I'd love to name him after his daddy."

Will jumped up, shaking his head. "Oh, no! That's no kind of name for him, Trace. I don't even have a middle name. I don't even have a real first name, just a nickname. No, our son needs a real name."

Tracy came and put her arms around him. "I had no idea you don't like your name. I think it's a good, strong name and it fits you. But if it's no good for you, let's find something else. Think about it, and we'll talk more about it. Now I need to call my mother and tell her it's a boy. She's going to start giving us names right away!"

WILL DECIDED NOT TO TELL HIS FAMILY UNTIL SUNDAY DINNER, WHEN they could all hear at once. Tracy warned her mother and father to say nothing if they ran into any of Will's family at church, and Anita retaliated by beginning a series of e-mails of acceptable boys' names, many of them featuring 'Eric.'

"Maybe I should just change my last name to Showalter," Will grumbled.

"Mother would love that," Tracy laughed, "but I wouldn't. Don't let her get to you; remember how you handled the wedding stuff."

When the remains of dinner littered the table and the German chocolate cake was just settling, Will cleared his throat and called for everyone's attention. He was secretly pleased that even the Seibenek crew was present this week, and the telling would be finished in one take.

"Tracy and I have something to tell you," he began.

"About the baby!" Gracie squealed, drawing excited noises from the Seibenek grandchildren.

"Quiet down," John said, quelling the outbursts with one calm command. "Go ahead, Will."

"Tracy had an ultrasound on Friday, and – you tell them, honey."

Tracy turned rosy and began to smile the kind of smile that melts hearts and makes children laugh. "It's a boy!" she said.

From the general confusion of congratulations, Pearl's voice emerged: "Thank You, Lord, for this blessed son to bring joy to Tracy and Will and to carry on the legacy of redemption."

"Amen," they all murmured.

"So what are you going to call him?" Gracie asked.

"So, Mr. Ryersen," Eddie said before class started. "Heard your baby's gonna be a boy. Whatcha gonna call him?"

Will flushed and sat down, half-laughing. "Eddie, how in the world did you find out about this?"

"Well, my mom knows your stepmom from the hospital, and she said..."

"Never mind. I get it. No privacy at all."

"So what are you going to name him?" Melissa Yoder asked.

The teachers' lounge was no different. The naming of the Ryersen heir was the prime topic of conversation day after day.

"With a last name like Ryersen," Wayne said, "figure he needs a good Viking name, like Erik or Sven or something."

"Don't be silly," the Spanish teacher chimed in. "He should be named after his father. What is your full name, Will?"

"You know my full name," he said, embarrassed. "Will Ryersen. Not William, and no middle name."

"Oh," she said, as if it were, indeed, an inferior name.

Several weeks went by, and the overt interest diminished at school, but it surfaced again in the renegade study hall, where Eddie suggested a lottery. "We all put up names and you draw one out of a hat. That name goes to the kid, and the winner gets some kind of prize."

Will was laughing again in spite of himself. "Eddie, that's a fantastic idea, but I have a feeling you guys will come up with names like Batman or Chili Pepper and my wife will kill me."

"Nah, we wouldn't do that to you," Eddie insisted. "We'll pick good Bible names, like Hezikiah or Shadrach or Malarky."

"That's Malachi," Melissa said in a stage whisper.

"Well, thanks, guys. I'll take the idea to my wife and see what she says."

Settled in to watch the news after dinner, Will drew Tracy down onto his lap and asked, "How would you feel about a son named Shadrach Malarky?"

"What!"

"The kids in study hall want to set up a lottery to name the baby. They'll each put a name in the hat, I'll draw one out, that will be the baby's name, and the winner will get a prize – as yet to be determined."

Tracy doubled up as much as she could with laughter. "Shadrach Malarky, huh? My mom will love that!" Her eyes twinkled green sparks as she said, "Let's tell her that's what we've decided."

"Maybe not..." Will said. "But maybe we do need to get serious about a name, because the rest of the world is set on picking one for us."

"I bought a book," Tracy said. "It has a thousand names for boys."

"Did you read it yet?"

"Well, not the whole thousand, but some of them. I liked Michael and Gregory and Declan – that one's Irish – and Curtis..."

"I... see..."

"Well," she said a touch defensively, "it's better than Shadrach Malarky."

"You better quit saying that name," Will warned, "or we'll end up calling him that for a joke and it'll stick. How about biblical names for real?"

"Seriously? I didn't think you'd want that."

Will was hurt. "Why wouldn't I?"

"Oh, I don't know. Just – sometimes you don't seem too into the Word and things like that. I don't mean to hurt your feelings, Will. I just don't want to name our baby some name you'd – well – dislike."

Will settled Tracy back against his shoulder and began to run his fingers through her curls. "Let's start over, okay? I'm fine with Bible names as long as they're not too dorky, like – uh, like the one the kids suggested."

"Okay. Let's just start naming off some of them and see what we like."

An hour or so later, when Will was about to despair and had a cramp in his leg from holding his wife on his lap, she said, "What about Isaac? I like that name because it means 'laughter.'"

"I think we have a winner, folks," Will announced to his imaginary audience. "Isaac James Ryersen."

Chapter 29

FEBRUARY BROUGHT A LONG, RAINY THAW WHICH BLOSSOMED the forsythia and redbud, turned the wheat emerald green in the fields and caused showers of pink and white petals on each wind as apple and cherry and pear trees bloomed. Farm animals stumbled around in deep mud and farmers stood glumly at the edges of fields too wet to work.

Long gray skies shortened tempers and chilled relationships or heated them to boiling.

English students were bored with everything, including their favorite teacher, who was more disinterested in them each day.

"How long til Easter vacation?" Will asked Wayne over lunch. He was sharing the leftover lasagna and salad Anita had sent for the two of them, thinking if Anita's cooking couldn't sweeten their moods, nothing could.

"It's late this year," Wayne said. "Infinity may be the last system in the state to tie its spring break to the holiday."

"Think we'll make it through March without a riot?" Will asked.

Ever the optimist, Wayne assured him, "Of course we will! It's not that long, and it'll freeze and snow again any time now. Northwest Ohioans are like Yoopers; we thrive on cold weather." He scraped some escaped tomato sauce off the front of his mauve and blue checked sweater. The pale orange residue left behind made an interesting contrast.

"If you say so," Will grumbled.

He was about to continue his litany of complaints when he felt the buzz of his cell phone and yanked it out, fearful it would be Tracy.

To his relief, it was Trey. "Hey, buddy!" Will said joyfully. "Good to hear from you!"

"Time to talk a minute?"

"Yes, a minute or two. I'm on lunch break. You'll hear the warning bell, I guarantee."

"Good. Listen, Will, Claire and I were talking, and I had this idea..."

"Go on."

"Well, we'd – that is, Claire and I, we'd like to invite you and Tracy to spend Easter with us."

Will's mind blanked. "In Iowa?"

"Duh. That's where we are, bro. My folks will love having the two of you at the house. You know there's more than enough room. I want you to meet Claire."

"Uh – thanks, that's really nice of you... Trey, it's kind of a big church holiday, and our families both expect us to go to church and then – "

"I know," Trey said. "I understand. But, see, Claire's family is like that, too, so I figured we could all go to church with them. It's not too bad there..."

Will was beginning to grin. "You've checked it out?"

"Yes... Like, don't laugh, okay, but I'm going almost every week."

Heroically Will bit the inside of his cheek to keep from laughing out loud. "I think that's great, Trey! I'd love to go to church with you sometime. I just don't know about Easter."

"Will, could you maybe not say no until you talk it over with Tracy? And – and maybe pray about it?"

Will stopped laughing. "Okay. I'll talk with both of them tonight and let you know as soon as I can."

"Sounded heavy," Wayne remarked as Will pocketed his phone and began to shovel the last few bites of lasagna into his mouth. "Better eat your salad."

"You sound like my family. Ryersens don't like green vegetables." He put the lid back on the salad container with a decided click.

"So what's up with Trey?" Wayne persisted, not the least bit self-conscious about his curiosity.

"He wants Trace and me to come to Iowa for Easter to meet his girlfriend and go to church with them."

A small glob of Italian dressing dripped from Wayne's fork to add shine to the tomato stain on his sweater. He reminded himself to chew and swallowed the last bite of his salad. "I thought this was your atheist friend. Don't we pray for him to get saved?"

"That's the one! My niece got ahold of him when he came for Christmas and started him on a scripture-reading program, and this girl of his is a Christian who won't even date him if he isn't headed toward salvation. Sounds like maybe she's having a good effect; he's been going to church with her."

"That's fantastic!" Wayne began, but whatever else he was going to say was bisected by the warning bell.

"WELL, I THINK IT'S EARLY ENOUGH THAT I CAN GET THE DAYS OFF FROM work," Tracy said. "I wasn't scheduled for Easter Sunday, anyway. One of the nonbelievers always volunteers to work the Christian holidays for one of us."

"Do you want to go to Iowa? Will you be able to fly? It's a long drive."

Tracy was folding laundry and paused, towel in hand, to consider. "I think it should be all right. The baby isn't due until June, after all. People fly pretty close to their due-dates. I'll ask Dr. Dana if you want to go."

"Let's find out. I hate to leave the family, but it seems like this means a lot to Trey."

Dr. Dana confirmed that the pregnancy was progressing perfectly and saw no reason Tracy couldn't fly to Iowa. She gave the usual caveats about drinking plenty of fluids and getting up to walk around, but otherwise it was fine. Will made the reservations before he told his family, although Tracy had already gone to drop the news on her parents.

"They weren't too happy," Tracy said over dinner. She looked pale and tired, and Will felt a wave of resentment against his in-laws. They had no right to upset her.

"They can just get over it," he snapped. "Did you tell them it's a ministry opportunity?"

"I did," Tracy sighed, pushing broccoli around her plate but not putting any into her mouth. "I'm afraid it didn't go down too well, after Africa. They sort of thought I'd never do anything remotely missionary ever again. I'm too tired to eat. If you'll excuse me, I'm going to go lie down."

Will was on his feet before she was. "Honey, are you all right? Should I call the doctor? Is Isaac okay?"

Tracy gave him a tired smile and patted his cheek in passing. "We're both fine. I'm just tired. Leave the dishes and I'll get to them later. I know you have papers to grade."

"This is all your mother's fault," Will snarled, taking her arm and leading her to the bedroom.

"Please don't blame her," Tracy said, kicking off her shoes and flopping down on top of the spread. "I'm tired because that happens to pregnant ladies. I'm fine, I promise."

"All right," Will agreed with his mouth, covering her with an extra blanket.

Returning to the kitchen, he put away leftovers, did the dishes and wiped down the counters and table, praying for Tracy and Isaac as he went, not even noticing that all his prayers now included the child he had not wanted.

"I HEAR WILL AND TRACY WILL BE GOING TO IOWA FOR EASTER," JOHN remarked to Ed and Pearl as they were watching the evening news.

"Yep," Ed agreed, "Matthew said Trey invited 'em to meet his girlfriend. Seems she's a good Christian girl and he wants to make points."

"It will seem – I don't know – not quite right for them to be away for the holiday," John said. "I've gotten used to having them around. I know Matthew and Allison are kind of sad about it, but they're not saying anything. Matthew figures it's a chance to work on Trey for salvation."

"That's exactly what Gracie said," Pearl smiled. "She said she should go along to be sure Trey is getting the message."

"What did Will say about that?" John asked, an answering smile on his face.

"I believe the phrase went something like, 'Over my dead body,'" Pearl said, almost laughing, "but he was very polite with Gracie. Now, why don't we pray for their trip and for Trey's salvation?"

MARCH FROZE THE BUDS OFF THE FRUIT TREES.

"Pearl is really fussing," Allison told Matthew, Will and Tracy as they walked together into the Chinese restaurant in the Lewiston mall. "She's convinced there won't be any apples for applesauce and nothing to use for jam and jelly."

"Isn't she getting too old to can?" Tracy asked, easing her girth into the booth.

"Don't tell her that!" Matthew laughed. "She hates to give an inch to old age."

"She may be right," Will said. "Ed was telling me the same thing."

"We'll just have to see what God sends," Matthew answered. "He surprises me all the time, with one thing and another."

They ordered large dishes to share and tucked into the meal with enthusiasm. "I'm always surprised," Allison said, "to see a Ryersen man eating Chinese. I don't think Matthew ever even tried it until a couple of years ago."

"I can learn new things," Matthew said, pretending to be affronted. "Nice thing about Chinese is you can get all kinds of things without green vegetables."

"When do you leave for Iowa?" Allison asked, poking her husband in the ribs at the same time.

"We'll leave on Good Friday," Tracy said, "and we'll come back on Tuesday. Will has school on Wednesday."

"Taking your racquetball gear?" Matthew asked.

"Yes, and my guitar, at Trey's request. Feels like I'm going to have to perform all kinds of ways for my room and board."

"Bet it's fancy room and board, too," Allison said. "Great big house, servants, all that?"

"Oh, yeah," Will said, smiling a little. "But his mom and dad are really nice people, and they never made me feel like the peon I am when I was there. They'll love Tracy, and the whole baby thing – honey, I guarantee you are going to be treated like a queen and held up as an example to remind Trey how much his mother wants grandchildren."

THE CADILLAC WAS LONG AND BLACK AND VERY SHINY.

"Will," Tracy whispered, "that's practically a limo!"

Trey, who claimed "twenty-twenty hearing," laughed as he expertly loaded the Ryersen suitcases into the trunk. "It's dear old Dad's Caddy," he said, sliding into the driver's seat. "I thought it would be more comfortable for you, Tracy, than the Mustang. Especially with the luggage."

"I keep expecting to see the chauffeur with the funny hat," she said, only half-joking.

"Oh, Mumsy needed him to drive the Rolls," Trey dead-panned, leaving her horrified for a moment before assuring her it was a joke. "Don't let the Sullivan gelt make you nervous, okay? It's just this thing my father can't help, and my parents are really nice people. They're looking forward to meeting you, Tracy, and Mom can't wait to start spoiling Will again." He gave a mock frown and said to Will, "Mom always liked you best."

The Sullivan house would certainly be called a mansion in Lewiston, Ohio, but Tracy was rapidly overcome not by the wealth but by the warmth of the home and its inhabitants.

"It reminds me of the Abbotts' place," she told Will as they crawled into a bed so huge she wondered whether she would need a GPS to find him in the dark.

"Huh?"

"Don't play stupid, Professor! I mean, the Sullivans are so nice and the whole place just says 'welcome.' Not like Mom's house, where everything feels like it's covered in plastic."

"Just remember you're the one who said that," Will teased, demonstrating that a GPS would not be needed as he drew her into the circle of his arms.

On Friday morning, as Trey's mother served them a farmstyle breakfast, minus bacon or sausage, she said, "Will you two want to go to church with us today?"

Tracy looked up sharply, confused and curious. "Church? I thought – uh – "

"Trey isn't a believer," Mrs. Sullivan sighed, sitting down with them to add cream and sugar to her coffee and stir it with a silver spoon, "but his father and I are. We're Catholics, and on Good Friday we go to a special service from noon to three, the hours Jesus hung on the cross, to pray and to watch with Him."

Trey came straggling in and poured himself some coffee, seeming as comfortable with the paper-thin china cup and saucer as Will was not.

"Some breakfast, darling?" his mother asked.

"No, thanks, Mom. Coffee's fine. I aim to drag the Professor off to the racquetball court this morning and beat the pants off him, so I don't need to weigh myself down with your excellent cooking."

"I was just inviting Will and Tracy to go to church with us," she said, smiling fondly at her boy. "Will you join us?"

"Sure, why not, for part of the time, anyway," Trey said casually, well aware of the effect this was having on his mother.

"I guess we're going to see how the Catholics do it," Will said to Tracy. "If I survive racquetball. What will you do while we're gone?"

"The dishes?"

"Nah," Trey said, "we have an app for that. Take a nap, or wander around and see what amuses you. We have a great film library and a real library – a real one, with the little ladder and everything – and a grand piano and a billiards table – all kinds of toys."

Mrs. Sullivan shook her head at her son. "The 'app' you are referring to is your mother today, young man, and I will be glad to have Tracy's help. Then we'll just see... Maybe I'll give her the keys to the Mustang and let her take a drive." A furtive smile lifted her unpainted lips and she raised her cup to her mouth to hide it.

"I THOUGHT YOU'D HAVE A HEART ATTACK WHEN SHE OFFERED TRACY the Mustang," Will chortled as they drove that vehicle back from the club.

"Yeah, well, I did, too! Man, she knows how to play me!"

"She's your mother, stupid. She's had thirty years to practice. And you know it goes both ways."

"I suppose. So, are you okay with this church thing?"

Will laughed, running a hand through hair still damp from the showers. "Sure, why not? I don't think it's going to hurt us to see how some other faith does it. You're the one I'm surprised at."

"Well – I figured, why not? I know it'll make them happy. But we'll go with Claire on Sunday, okay?"

"Seriously?"

"Yes, loser, seriously."

"If you keep calling me 'loser,' I'm going to have to call for a re-match."

"Any time, buddy. You used to be the man, but you ain't no more. We're having dinner with Claire tonight, by the way, so don't let Mom rope you into any promises. I know she'd like to have you with her every minute, but I want you to meet Claire and get to know her."

"Don't you bring her home to mother and daddy?" Will asked.

Trey hesitated long enough for Will to give him the once-over. "I have, a couple of times. It was – awkward. I think my mom knows I'm serious about this one, and she's funny about it. Keeps pointing out Claire's not Catholic."

TRACY KICKED OFF HER SHOES, PEELED OUT OF HER CLOTHES AND PULLED on her nightgown. "I'm so tired, Will, I really need a nap." She crawled into the big bed and pulled the luxurious down comforter over herself.

"Shall I join you? I think we have a couple of hours before we have to get ready to go out to dinner." He stripped off, folded and hung his clothes, and hers, too, and climbed in next to her. "So what did you think of the service?"

"I've been in Catholic churches before," Tracy said, yawning. "I really like the liturgy, the way they take everything so seriously, all the responsive prayers – some of the music – it's different, but it doesn't feel wrong – mostly..."

"Can you imagine Pastor Miles leading a three-hour service like that?" Will laughed. "And, frankly, I thought the rosary stuff was boring. But there's no denying those people were grieving for Christ's suffering and giving thanks that He paid the price."

Tracy said nothing; her slightly raspy breathing told Will she was fast asleep.

WILL WAS SURPRISED TO LEARN THAT CLAIRE HAD DRIVEN INTO TOWN TO meet them at the country club for dinner and really glad he had brought a back-up tie. He wouldn't tell the students he had forsaken his forfeit for these days among the rich and famous. He knew Tracy was feeling just a bit country mouse in her soft green pleated maternity dress and flat-heeled shoes, especially as Claire floated up to them.

She was taller than Tracy and reed-slender, with long, dark hair pulled back into a soft knot at the nape of her neck and pale blue eyes shaded by long, dark lashes. He couldn't tell whether she had used mascara on them or not. Her little black dress looked like something out of the Vogue magazines Tracy's mother devoured, and her matching pumps had high stiletto heels. A small diamond watch glittered on her thin wrist and matching studs graced her tiny ears.

"Oh," Tracy breathed almost silently.

"You are perfect," Will told her quietly. "Perfect. Look at Trey."

"This is Claire," Trey said.

Tracy looked at him, and then at Will. "Goner," she muttered out of the side of her mouth.

"I'm Claire Kennedy," the beautiful young woman said warmly, holding out her hand, "and you must be Tracy and Will. I've wanted to meet you for such a long time!"

Will pushed three skinny asparagus spears, four tiny purple potato halves and bits of perfectly grilled salmon filet through a gloppy butter sauce and realized how much he had come to prefer home-cooking. Pearl would never have allowed such skimpy portions or such odd seasonings. He could see his father obediently slapping a huge spoonful of butter-and-cream-mashed potatoes onto his plate and ending up eating every bite under Pearl's watchful eye. Tracy seemed to be faring better, but she had learned to eat bugs in Malawi.

Dessert redeemed the meal, as mousse au chocolat melted in their mouths. Will also observed that neither Trey nor Claire was focused on the food.

"All right," Claire said after the waiter had refilled their coffee cups and Tracy's tea cup. "Let's get down to it."

"Pardon?" Will said.

"Just listen," Tracy said. "She has an agenda."

"Yes, I do." Claire had the decency to blush just a little, setting off her pearly skin against the black of her dress and making her even more beautiful. "Trey and I are strongly attracted to each other. He's a wonderful man, what people would certainly call 'a good catch' in every way, but we have a problem. I know you two are strong believers, and I am, too. No matter what I might want, I can't marry a man who doesn't believe as I do." She turned beseeching eyes to Trey. "I just can't."

Will had heard this part before. "And your agenda is…"

"I'm hoping you and Tracy can convince him to become a Christian."

Silence hung over the round table.

Finally, Tracy said, "Oh, Claire, if you're a Christian, then you know we can't do that. Only the Holy Spirit leads people to Christ."

"I know that," she said, "but you can explain things to him. You're his best friend, Will! He loves you. He'll listen to you."

"I can't believe you're sitting here listening to us talking about you," Will said to Trey. "Did you know about this?"

Trey nodded. "I did. Thing is, buddy, if you could do it, I'd love to have you sell me. I want to be with Claire more than anything. But I just can't – "

So what am I supposed to do!

"Where's Gracie when you need her, huh?" Trey asked, sadness in his eyes and in his voice.

"Trey," Tracy began tentatively, "could you – could you maybe pretend there's a God and – well – maybe ask Him to help you?"

"You mean pray?"

She nodded.

"Right here?"

"Well, I guess so. I mean, there isn't anybody seated near us and the waiter will stay away if we don't call him. It's – it's as good a place as any."

"It's not a church," Trey protested.

"Doesn't need to be," Will finally chimed in. "I think I met God in an AA meeting one time."

"Please," Claire begged, "try it for me if you won't do it for yourself."

"Out loud?"

Will had to laugh at the horror in his friend's voice. He knew the feeling. "No, you don't have to pray out loud if you don't want to. Just shut your eyes and go to it. The waiter will think you've passed out."

Trey guffawed in spite of himself, and the exchange seemed to ease something in him. "Whatever. Okay, here goes." He bowed his head a little, closed his eyes and frowned ferociously.

Will did the same and suspected the women were praying, too. *Please, Lord, speak to him, draw him to Yourself!*

When Will came to the end of his prayers, he opened his eyes slowly to find the other three still wrapped in silent concentration. Several more minutes passed before Trey opened his eyes and looked around like a baby waking up from a nap.

"That was weird," Trey said.

Tracy and Claire snapped to awareness and stared at Trey expectantly. The silence stretched out until Will wanted to fill it with – with anything.

"I think it's time to go home," Trey said. "Claire, I'll walk you to your car."

They left Will and Tracy sitting at the table.

"Don't bug him when he comes back," Tracy warned. "Just don't say anything about it unless he brings it up."

Will gave her a carefully manufactured look of affront. "You think I would – "

"Yes. But you better not!"

"HE NEVER SAID A WORD!" WILL COMPLAINED AS THEY SETTLED IN their luxurious guest room for the rest of the evening. "He didn't make a joke or anything!"

"He obviously had some kind of encounter," Tracy said, "and he's not ready to share it yet. You're his best friend, Will. He'll probably tell you even before he tells Claire. For now, just come to bed and we'll watch television for a while."

Tracy's calm eased the tension out of Will and he settled in to watch a silly movie with her. But from that evening until they were saying good-bye at the airport, Trey never said anything about those minutes of prayer.

Chapter 30

WILL WALKED INTO THE FIRST STUDY HALL AFTER EASTER wearing his forfeit tie and set a plain blue on blue striped tie on his desk. When the class had come to order, he thanked them for their cooperation first semester and slowly removed the offensive tie. He noticed as he laid it on the desk that the grease spot below the knot gleamed almost irides-cent in the fluorescent light.

"I want to thank all of you for this amazing experience," he told the class, deadpan. "It has really been – an experience. Now, Eddie, I think you'd better return the tie to Mr. Dennis, don't you?"

"Mr. R," Eddie said, playing to the crowd, "Mr. Dennis told me this morning he wants you to have it as a token of his esteem."

AS WILL WAS DESCRIBING HIS STUDY HALL TO TRACY, HIS CELL PHONE went off.

"It's Wayne," he told her, taking the call. "Hey! What's up?"

"I am!" Wayne hollered through the phone so loudly even Tracy could hear him. "We are, as of twelve minutes ago, the proud parents of Amelia Faith Dennis!"

"Congratulations! I take it everything's all right?"

"Couldn't be better. I sure hope it goes as easily for you and Tracy. We were only here an hour. Baby looks just like her mother, and she has all her fingers and toes. She's beautiful, Will." He paused for some audible snuffling. "Sorry. I'm just so grateful to God – you know."

"Yeah. That's great news, Wayne. Give our love to Anita. We'll try to get over there tomorrow to see them."

"Do that! Hey, Will?"

"Yes?"

"Anita and I would like you and Tracy to be godparents for Amelia."

Will stood there in shock for a moment before gathering himself to say, "Thank you. Of course we will."

"Of course we will what?" Tracy asked when the call was over.

"Be godparents to the new little Dennis, Amelia Faith. Would you like that?"

"Certainly! What an honor. Just think, Will – maybe someday Amelia and Isaac will fall in love and get married..." her voice trailed off and her eyes were miles and years away.

"Honey, that's a great idea – if she turns out to be good enough for him."

"Never let Wayne hear you even hint at that!" Tracy warned, laughing.

"Time for the last ultrasound," Dr. Dana told Tracy and Will. "I'd say this boy is big enough and strong enough to come any time now."

Tracy shifted uncomfortably on the examining table, trying to balance the bulk in front of her and relieve the pressure on her back. "I'm ready any time he is," she said.

"The baby isn't due for a couple of weeks," Will protested. "Isn't it bad if they come early?"

Dr. Dana gave Tracy a steadying hand down from the table and smiled at Will. "You aren't going to be one of those hysterical fathers, are you, Will? At this point the baby can come anytime safely. We'd worry more if he were late. Now go get the ultrasound and enjoy it!"

Will put his arm around Tracy to walk her to the ultrasound lab, letting her lean on him some. "Back hurt a lot?"

"No more than usual these days," she said. "I really will be glad to get this over with. Waiting is hard when you feel like you're going to explode any minute."

She crawled up onto the ultrasound table and the tech handed her a sheet. "Just assume the position," the tech joked.

Will loved the ultrasounds. Isaac became more a person every time they saw him, his face and hands and toes and everything so clear and so developed. He couldn't remember that he had ever not wanted this baby. He loved his son and knew he would die to defend him.

"Here we are," the tech said, turning the screen to show them. "He's pretty big now, not so much room to move around in there anymore. I'd say he weighs about eight pounds and is probably twenty-one inches long."

Will tried to imagine eight pounds. Eight boxes of butter. Less than one of his hand-weights. Bigger than a roasting chicken but smaller than a ham...

WHILE TRACY WAS SHOPPING WITH HER MOTHER, WILL AND MATTHEW rearranged the living room furniture to accommodate the rocking chair Will had found at Treasures, the store where they had found Tracy's rings. It was almost a hundred years old, the oak darkened by time, the rockers and the arms wide and the seat deep. Allison had rocked in it for a while and then found pillows to pad the back and sides, pronouncing it perfect. Will hoped Tracy would like it; she had said they needed a rocker, but she hadn't said what kind.

"It's a big one," Matthew said. "Allie had a hard time reaching the ground to rock it. But Tracy likes old stuff, so it should be just the thing." He looked around the living room, which they had furnished in comfortable cast-offs, many of them antiques by default. "It looks like it belongs here."

"She said she needs it for nursing the baby. I don't know why."

"Neither do I," Matthew said, regret in his voice. "I never was around when you were a baby. I feel bad about that now."

"Ah, it's no big deal, Dad. I didn't know the difference."

"No, but I do," Matthew said. "I hope you and Tracy will let me spend time with Isaac."

"Dad! Don't be dumb! Of course you can spend time with Isaac. We want him to know you and Allie and the rest of the family. Tracy's family, too, I suppose – maybe not as often..."

"Will," Matthew cautioned, "you can't win coming against Tracy's folks. You have to love them and make them as welcome as you can, or it will backfire on you. And there's one more thing about it..."

"What?"

"God says to love them the way He loves you. You don't have to like them, but you do have to honor them and feel compassion for them and such."

Will snorted. "Right."

"I mean it, Son. For Jesus'sake if not for Tracy's."

"Sure, Dad." *As if that were possible!*

"You need to pray for them, both of them, every day. It's a funny thing, but doing that leads to loving them."

TRACY WAS SNUGGLED INTO THE ROCKER, HER FEET ON A HUGE OTTO-man, Will seated on the floor opposite her playing his guitar.

"I know Isaac hears the music and likes it," Tracy said, idly strok-ing her belly, "because he always kind of surges toward it and then gets really quiet for as long as you play. I'll bet you'll be able to play him to sleep after he's born."

"He'll be the only kid on the block who likes jazz guitar," Will said. "Hope the other kids don't make fun of him." He struck a dis-chord and slapped his hand against the face of the guitar.

"Nobody is going to bully our son," Tracy said gently. "He'll be strong and brave and happy and smart and, most of all, godly…"

"Godly." Will put the guitar down and stared at his wife. "I haven't even been thinking about teaching him to know the Lord! I have no idea – "

"Not to worry. We'll work on it bit by bit and take lessons from your family and Kevin's family and Trav's and pray about it – God will show us the way."

"That's easy for you to say!" Will snapped, standing up and begin-ning to pace around the small living room. "You were raised like that. Not me."

"Maybe you need to go to a meeting with Allison," Tracy said, smiling. "Isn't that where they talk about living one day at a time? Or we could recite scripture: 'Sufficient unto the day are the evils thereof' or such." She rose from the rocker in stages and put her hand to her back as she lumbered over to Will. "Now give me a hug and stop worrying."

THE LAST DAY OF SCHOOL WAS THURSDAY, JUNE SECOND, AND WILL felt the usual mix of relief and regret as he said good-bye to the last of his students. He threw his laptop and a few other work-related items into his backpack and turned out the lights.

"End of the year blues?" Wayne asked, coming up behind him.

Will turned around to enjoy for the last time that year the spectacle of Wayne Dennis, this time in a madras print shirt in pinks and oranges and a bow tie in bile green with prison-uniform-orange polka-dots.

"No blues here," he laughed. "Just tired. Tracy isn't sleeping much these nights, so I'm not, either."

"Oh, yeah!" Wayne commiserated, walking beside Will down the long terrazzo hallway. "Better do your best now, though, because once Isaac gets here, it's all over."

"I thought babies sleep a lot."

"Oh, they do. Just not when you want them to. And if Trace is nursing, he could wake her up every two hours around the clock." Wayne shook his head in faux sympathy, but his grin gave him away.

They burst out the double doors into the parking lot with as much enthusiasm as the students had fifteen minutes before. "I'm going to take Anita and the kids to Disney World," Wayne said. "Then we're going to spend the summer sitting around the pool and sipping cold drinks, maybe listening to baseball – maybe not. No school thoughts before August first."

"Hope it all works out that way for you," Will replied. "I expect I'll be changing diapers and pushing strollers and doing housework."

"Reckon so, but you won't mind. There's something so great about holding your child, watching him grow and change – it really is a miracle. Can't wait to meet Isaac!"

They parted at their cars and Will drove home thinking about what a good friend Wayne Dennis had turned out to be.

Lord, bless him and Anita and the kids, please. They're such good people. And please, Lord, bless Trey and call him to Yourself. I'm sorry I haven't been praying much for him; I guess Tracy and the baby are more on my mind these days. Bless them, too, and let everything be all right. Please.

"YOU DON'T HAVE TO GO TO CHURCH IF YOU DON'T FEEL UP TO IT," WILL said for the tenth or eleventh time that morning. "It's okay. I'll stay home with you."

"Don't be silly!" Tracy said, struggling into her maternity pants. "I'm fine – just big as a house – and about as graceful. Besides, it's Pentecost Sunday; that's special."

As they joined the Abbotts in the third pew, Gracie grabbed Will's hand and said, "I have something to tell you!"

"Okay. Let's get Tracy seated first, okay? It's hard for her to stand around."

"Oh, I'm sorry! Here, Tracy, you go on in."

Tracy maneuvered her belly past the back of the pew ahead of her and took a seat in the middle of the row. Allison sat on her far side and Will moved in next to her near side.

"Now, Gracie, what is it?"

"I had a text from Trey!"

"Really? I didn't know you were phone buddies."

"We aren't, but we are Facebook friends. That's fun, only Daddy doesn't let me be on there very much."

"Daddy's a smart man," Will said. "So what's up with Trey?"

"He has this girlfriend, Claire – you met her, right?"

"Yep."

"Well, she believes in Jesus and he wants to marry her, so he's been working on believing in Jesus, too, and he texted me for some more reading assignments, and I sent him some, and I think he's really close, and – "

"Come sit down, Grace," John called from the other end of the pew. "Go around; don't climb over Tracy."

"That's great!" Will said, giving Gracie a gentle shove toward the front so she would go around the first pew and be seated before Pastor Miles and the worship team came in.

The worship leader had selected several songs about the Holy Spirit to go with the theme of Pentecost, and Will thought about the words as he was singing them. He had once heard Pastor Miles say to be careful about singing the lyrics if you didn't mean them. He never thought much about the third Person of the Trinity and didn't understand the people who went on and on about being "filled with the Spirit."

I should ask Dad about this, or maybe John.

He was distracted from the sermon by Tracy, who couldn't seem to sit still. He asked if she needed to leave, but she told him she was fine. He put his hand on the small of her back and rubbed a little; that seemed to help.

As they left the pew and started back up the aisle at the end of the service, Allison came up beside Tracy and said quietly, "Time to go to the hospital."

"What!" Will said much too loudly.

"Shh!" Tracy insisted, jabbing him in the ribs. "Don't make a scene!"

"She's in labor," Allison said softly, "and she has been for an hour or longer. I make her contractions to be eight minutes apart, which means you should get a move on."

How could she do that? Will wondered. "All right, let's go! Stay in the foyer with Allison, honey, while I get the car!" He ran to the parking lot and was back much faster than was safe amidst the people walking to their cars and backing out of parking places.

"Will," Allison said, as she helped Tracy into the front seat, "do not speed. It isn't that far to the hospital, and you have time. Matthew and I will stop at the apartment for her suitcase and meet you there. It's all fine."

Will heard the voice of Nurse Allison and was immediately calmed. If she wasn't calling an ambulance or pulling on a pair of latex gloves, they had time.

Not as much time as he had thought, according to a labor team nurse named Terri.

"You let it go a long time," she remarked to Tracy as she expertly inserted an i.v. line on the first try. "You're almost at nine."

"Nine what?" Will asked.

"Centimeters," Terri said. "Ten is fully dilated and probably ready to push. Didn't you know you were in labor sooner?" She adjusted things Will didn't like to look at and directed him to a place next to Tracy's free hand. "Hold on to her hand," she told him.

"I thought maybe – during the night – but my water didn't break and it sort of stopped, so I decided it was just my back aching. Then in church I was pretty sure – oh!"

"Breathe through it," Terri coached and Will remembered his Childbirth Ed class instructions.

"When does she get the epidural?" he asked.

"I don't want it!"

"But, honey, it hurts."

"Stupid man, don't you think I know that! Oh, here it comes again!"

On the next contraction her water broke and a crew of nurses assembled, along with Allison, who was not in uniform.

"Where's Dad?" Will asked.

"In the waiting room praying," Allison said. "I'll wait with him if you like, Tracy."

"No, stay! I don't want you to go!"

"All right. I called your parents and they should be here soon."

"No, I don't want my mother in here!" Tracy shouted before she fell into the grip of another contraction. Will noticed they were much closer than they had been, and lasting much longer.

Dr. Dana entered the room, gowned and gloved. "Hi!" she said with her usual enthusiasm. "Terri tells me we'll be meeting Isaac in just a little while! Now, Mother, all you have to do is follow my lead and we'll do just fine. Daddy, you all right?"

"Uh – sure." *Are you kidding! No, I'm not all right, and Tracy isn't, either. Why don't you give her something to knock her out and send me to the waiting room!*

Will really didn't have much sense of time after that, or of what was going on around him. He was praying for Tracy and the baby steadily on the inside and doing whatever he was told to do on the outside. Soon Tracy was pushing, making noises he didn't think a human could make, and suddenly a slimy mess squirted out into Dr. Dana's hands. It made a funny, yawping sort of noise, and Dr. Dana said,

"Welcome to the world, Isaac."

Will would have liked to see his son, but his eyes were too full of tears.

Terri wrapped the baby in a blue blanket with white bunnies on it and laid him on Tracy's chest. Her arms automatically cradled her son and her face was radiant.

"Want to cut the cord, Daddy?" Dr. Dana asked, and Allison laughed.

"No, he doesn't," she said, taking Will's arm and leading him a couple of steps to the nearest chair. "Put your head between your legs for a minute, and you'll feel better." She stood with her hand on the back of Will's neck, shoving him down, and told the room at large, "Ryersen men don't do too well with medical messes, and they vomit really easily."

There was general laughter, including Tracy's.

"I saw how white he got," Dr. Dana remarked. "Let's get young Isaac cleaned up so his daddy can hold him without passing out."

"Eight pounds, seven ounces," one of the nurses called out moments later, "and twenty-one inches long." They were wiping the baby down and doing other things Will couldn't see, even though he was now sitting upright, all of them cooing at the baby and chattering away about how cute he was.

"You did a great job, Tracy!" Dr. Dana enthused, "And you don't even need any stitches. I wish all my first-time mothers were as easy!"

"Doctor," Terri said suddenly, "would you come here, please?"

Something in the nurse's tone rang an alarm in Will's head. "What's wrong?"

"Nothing," the doctor said automatically, leaving the bed to go to the baby's side.

Will made to follow her, but she gave him a stern look and said, "Sit with Tracy."

"What's wrong with my baby!" Tracy cried, grabbing Will's arm.

"Shh, honey, I don't know. It can't be anything serious, or they'd be running that funny little basket-thing down the hall somewhere. Just relax; you've done a good day's work."

"Oh, God, please take care of my baby!" Tracy wailed, tears running down her cheeks and puddling at her collarbones.

Will sat on the bed and folded Tracy into his arms, smoothing the tears from her face. "Let's just pray and not expect the worst," he said, folding one of her hands inside his. "Lord, we thank You so much for Isaac, and for all the good women who helped to bring him into the world today. We ask You to protect him and give him perfect health and we trust him to Your care, in Jesus' Name. Amen."

Time passed, what seemed a long time, as the pediatrician joined the phalanx of nurses and Dr. Dana around Isaac. Will could hear their steady murmur and held on tight to the lack of urgency in any of the voices. Finally both doctors came over to the bed, the pediatrician holding Isaac like a football.

"What's wrong with him!" Tracy demanded.

"Well," the pediatrician, Dr. Lokeitz, said, "we hear a little bit of a heart murmur, but nothing serious. Not uncommon for some babies to have a slower closing of that hole between one side of the heart and the other. He's nice and pink and not in any distress, so I think it will close itself over the next day or two. Here, Daddy, they said you haven't had a chance to hold him yet."

Dr. Lokeitz thrust the tidy bundle that was Isaac straight at Will, as if he were handing off a pass, but Will had never played football. He stepped back.

"Here, honey," Allison said, taking the baby and coming up to Will slowly, "just hold out your arm with a crook in the elbow for his neck – that's it – let your hand support his bottom – exactly. Now you can use your other arm for extra support under him if you need it, or you can use that hand to unwrap and examine him." She took Will's arm and guided him to the bed. "Sit here by Tracy so you can both look. There!"

"Let's give them some time before we call in the grandparents and the rest of the family," Allison suggested, and doctors and nurses quickly flowed out of the room ahead of her. In moments the three were alone.

"Thank you," Will said to his wife. "Thank you for marrying me and thank you for our son. I love you so much – "

"He looks just like you," Tracy said, her smile tired but shining.

"He does? I think he looks kind of like Winston Churchill."

"You take that back!" Tracy ordered, poking his ribs. "Isaac is beautiful!"

She leaned over and unwrapped the bunny blanket, exposing arms, legs, diaper and long-sleeved undershirt. The umbilical stump and its plastic clamp stuck out between the top of the diaper and the bottom of the shirt.

Will poked toward it with his finger. "Does that hurt?"

"It doesn't seem to. It'll dry up and fall off in the next week or ten days."

Will pulled the blanket back over the stump. "Gross," he said.

"I'll take him if you don't want to hold him," Tracy replied.

Will was surprised by the wave of feelings that washed over him at her suggestion to give the baby up. He tightened his grip and stood abruptly to make sure she didn't take him. Late afternoon sunlight was streaming in through the window, and Will walked over to stand in its rays, examining the still face of his son in the light.

"I am never going to let you go," he said softly. "No one will ever take you away from me. I'm going to take care of you and love you all your life, and nothing bad is ever going to happen to you. Nothing is ever going to hurt you, I promise."

Chapter 31

AFTER DINNER, WHICH HAD BEEN SERVED FANCY-RESTAU-rant-style with candles, and wine for Will, and a linen tablecloth, Tracy nursed the baby again and fell into a doze. Will sat in the recliner by the bed holding his sleeping son, marveling at the constant parade of expressions across the tiny face and the random starfish movement of the tiny hands.

"Lord," he prayed, "thank you for this child. Thank you for our son. Thank you for Isaac. Thank you for Tracy. Thank you for bringing them both safely through this. Please bless us, Lord, and help us to be worthy parents for Isaac. Help us to do everything right. I know that's not reasonable, Lord, but it's not too much for You to arrange. Help him to grow up strong and healthy and secure in his faith..."

His prayer was interrupted by the entrance of Dr. Lokeitz and another doctor Will didn't know.

"Sorry to disturb you," Dr. Lokeitz said in a tone which suggested he wasn't sorry at all, "but I wanted Dr. Gable, here, to take a look at Isaac."

Tracy had been awakened by the doctor's voice and said, "Why?"

"Well, I just want to make sure everything's all right," Dr. Lokeitz said, not looking Tracy in the eye, Will noticed.

Dr. Gable took the baby from Will and laid him out on the bassinette. Will saw that the doctor's hands were as big and thick as hams. Those huge hands unwrapped the baby and laid a huge stethoscope on his tiny chest. He listened for a long time before moving the bell to another spot and repeating the procedure. Then he seemed to be putting Isaac through a series of exercises.

"What is it?" Will demanded. "Why are you doing all this? Who is this guy, anyway?"

"Dr. Gable is a pediatric cardiologist," Dr. Lokeitz explained. "I want him to listen to the murmur, just to be sure I'm not missing anything."

"Hmpf," Dr. Gable muttered, hanging his stethoscope back around his neck and walking away from the baby.

Isaac apparently didn't like to be left uncovered, because he began to cry. Before the nurse in the background could get there, Will had the baby in his arms again, wrapping the blankets around him and speaking softly to him. "It's all right. Daddy has you now."

"What about his heart?" Tracy asked. "I thought you said it would be all right."

"I did," Dr. Lokeitz said. "Don't get upset, now. It's just wiser to take advantage of an expert when he's in the building."

"So far, so good," Dr. Gable said. "Probably nothing to worry about. I think you ought to keep him on oxygen overnight and keep checking him every hour or so, but he'll probably do fine for now."

"For now?" Will asked, the hairs on the back of his neck prickling.

"For now. If the hole doesn't close in a couple of days – maybe a week – then we have to determine how bad it is, what we might need to do about it. It might need a surgical repair, which I can do easily. I've done thousands of them. Usually no residual problems after that."

"Usually!"

"I'm as good as they come," Dr. Gable said matter-of-factly. "But no one can guarantee anything working with babies. I'm not going to lie to you."

"I wish you had," Tracy muttered, swiping tears from her cheeks with a corner of the sheet.

The nurse stepped forward to take the baby from Will. "We need to get him back to the nursery now," she said gently. "I'll be really careful of him, I promise."

"Go with her," Tracy urged from her bed. "I'll be fine here, Will; you go with Isaac."

"That won't be necessary," Dr. Lokeitz said, but Will interrupted.

"I think it will," he said. "I'll carry him. Lead on!" he told the nurse.

THE NURSE TOOK ISAAC FROM WILL'S ARMS AT THE NURSERY DOOR AND commanded him to stay on the outside. "You can look in through the glass," she said. "We can't have you spreading germs to the other babies."

She took Isaac to a bassinette in the far corner of the room all by itself and laid him on his back on the mattress. She turned on a light over the unit and then stripped the baby to his diaper. She wrapped something around his foot just below the toes and something around his arm. Then he saw her put a tiny two-pronged tube into the baby's nostrils and fiddle with dials where its clear green tube ran into the wall.

Lord, if he's all right, why are they hooking him up to all these machines?

Nurse Terri came up beside Will, the kittens on her scrub top and the long, bouncy pony-tail she had made of her dark hair making her look like a twelve-year-old, saying, "I know how scary this looks, but it's all just precautionary. Isaac is fine; we want to be sure he stays that way. When Eileen is through fussing over him, I'll let you go back there and sit with him for a while. I'm off shift pretty soon, but I'll tell the night nurse you can be with Isaac as much as you want."

"Thank you!"

"The way to thank me is to gown up when they ask you to and stay out of the nurses' way, so I don't get in trouble for bending the rules for you." She smiled to take the sting out of her words, and Will felt impossibly grateful.

"You'll want to go back and forth to your wife," Terri said, "because otherwise she'll be down here, too, and she needs her rest."

"Got it," Will agreed. "Be nice, be inconspicuous, be clean, be attentive to wife. Thanks again for all you've done."

Moments later, Will found himself swaddled in a yellow, paperish robe and matching over-shoe booties, washing his hands like an extra on "General Hospital" and fighting an urge to say, "Clamp!" or "Scalpel!" or "Clear!"

Before he could install himself next to Isaac's bassinette, another pony-tailed brunette, this one as tall as Terri was diminutive, came up to him, all smiles.

"Hi, Mr. Ryersen! I'm Leslie Overmyer, used to be Leslie Brant. I'm a good friend of Allison's and I used to know your father, years ago. I'll be Isaac's nurse tonight, so if you have any questions – just let me know."

"Small world, isn't it?" Will remarked. "Thank you. Can I just go over there and stay with him?"

"Yes, you can. I'm going to put a rocker there so you don't have to stand all the time, and you can be there as much as you want unless something goes wrong with him or with one of the other babies and we have to clear the room of all nonmedical personnel. But I don't anticipate anything like that; all the other babies are fine and rooming-in with their mothers. If you leave to go to see your wife or anything, you need to put your gown and booties in the receptacle outside the door and re-gown before you come back in."

"Got it. Thanks again." Will smiled briefly at Leslie and walked across the room to Isaac's corner, where the machine was beeping softly as it monitored pulse, blood pressure and oxygen levels.

"Hey, baby," he said softly, extending one finger to touch Isaac's cheek. The baby turned toward his hand, eyes wide, as if he were examining his father. "Welcome to the world," Will said. "I hope you like it. I hope you have a wonderful life. But first you have to get over whatever has you stuck in this nursery instead of in your mama's arms, so be a good boy and get well, okay?"

I'm talking to a baby as if he could understand me. They'll think I'm nuts and kick me out of here. Well, I'm not going to leave my son alone. They'll just have to lump it.

Hours passed as Will stood over the bassinette or sat in the rocker beside it, never taking his eyes off Isaac except when he left to check in with Tracy. She was becoming increasingly agitated by the separation, so he sat with her for a while, holding her hand, praying with her, stroking her hair until she began to doze. But every minute his mind and heart were turned toward the nursery, and every prayer was a plea for Isaac to be well, to come home to his parents.

Around three in the morning Tracy woke up again and sent Will back to the baby. He kissed her and promised to report if there were any changes.

Gowned and scrubbed again, Will silently entered the nursery and made his way to the bassinette in the back corner just in time to see Isaac wrestling the tubing off his face, grimacing ferociously with the effort.

"Way to go, Son!" Will whispered. But Leslie arrived almost at once to put the cannula back.

"He needs to have the oxygen for now," she said calmly, tightening the elastic as she spoke. "It's good that he doesn't like it and has the strength to fight, but he has to have it. So don't let him pull it off, okay?"

"Okay. How's he doing? I mean, nobody has really said what's going on."

"Doctor will be in around seven tomorrow morning, maybe a bit earlier, and he'll explain everything to you then, all right?"

"No," Will said, "it's not all right. He looks fine, he's alert and strong enough to go for what he wants, so what's the matter with him?"

Leslie shook her head. "I'm sorry, but I'm not allowed to discuss things with you if the doctor hasn't already explained. Isaac is all right, and he'll be all right, so you can wait to talk with the doctor." She left the room to avoid the confrontation she could see coming.

Will pulled out his cell phone and considered calling Allison, but he realized the time. She was undoubtedly asleep.

Why didn't somebody tell me something sooner? Why didn't I ask? When did I turn into a sheep, just doing as I'm told without question? Lord, what's wrong with our boy? Please help him!

Will sat down beside the bassinette and watched Isaac breathe. He noticed the baby was making a funny little noise with some breaths, and he noticed his skin wasn't quite as pink as it had been. He put his forefinger on the palm of Isaac's hand and reveled in the way the tiny fingers clutched and held.

That's right, Isaac, hold on to me! You hold on and breathe, baby. Don't stop! God, don't let him stop!

Nurse Leslie came back and adjusted the oxygen flow; in a few minutes the funny little noises stopped. "It's called grunting," she told Will. "It's a sign of respiratory distress. That's why he needs the oxygen, to get him over the hump."

"Why does he have respiratory distress, and why didn't somebody tell me earlier?"

"Dr. Lokietz or Dr. Gable will be in later, and he'll explain every-thing," Nurse Leslie said. "Just be patient. Isaac is doing fine, I prom-ise."

The big clock on the nursery wall read 6:37 AM when Dr. Lokietz breezed into the nursery and made a beeline for Isaac's corner.

"Good morning, Mr. Ryersen!" he said in the annoying, brisk tone of the habitual early riser. "Up all night?"

"I was, mostly. What's going on with our son, doctor?"

"Tell you what," Dr. Lokietz said, "why don't you go get some cof-fee and join your wife in her room? I'll examine the baby and look over some of my other ones here and join you in her room in a while."

"You expect me to leave him?"

Dr. Lokietz laughed. "Well, yes, I do, Mr. Ryersen. He's in good hands with me; I'm a pediatrician, you know." He kept smiling, urg-ing Will to relax and go with the flow of things.

"I'll see you in Tracy's room, then," Will said, stroking Isaac's tiny arm for a moment before walking out of the nursery.

Tracy was sitting up in bed with a glass of milk in one hand and the television remote in the other, mindlessly channel-surfing, but keeping her eye on the door.

"Oh, Will! I'm so glad to see you! How's Isaac?"

Will sat on the edge of the bed, taking the remote and turning off the television. "I guess he's all right. Dr. Lokietz just came and said he'd talk with us here in a little while. He basically threw me out of the nursery, but I thought that would be okay. How are you?" He bent over to kiss her and noted she had brushed her teeth.

"I'm fine. Tired, of course, and kind of sore. But fine, really. I'm just worried about the baby. All the other mothers have their babies in the rooms with them, nursing them and holding them and chang-ing diapers – " She teared up and wiped her eyes on the sleeve of the hospital gown. "I'm sorry. I just want my baby!"

"I know, sweetheart. And we'll have him soon. Let's not worry before we need to, okay?"

The nurse came to check Tracy and booted Will out into the hall. Then she mustered towels and washcloths and toiletries and ushered Tracy into the bathroom to take a shower while Will cooled his heels on the small sofa in the room. Tracy returned to her bed, a bit breathless but clearly glad to have shampooed her hair, just in time for breakfast.

"I swiped a tray for you, too," the nurse said, and Will saw with gratitude that Nurse Terri was back for the day-shift.

"Thanks," he said. "Haven't had anything but vending machine coffee since dinner last night."

"Not good for you," Terri teased, setting up Tracy's tray on the bedside table and then putting Will's on the little dresser-top by the bed. "You can pull up that chair and eat over here by your wife," she offered before breezing out of the room.

"She's so nice," Tracy said, pouring milk on her oatmeal and sprinkling sugar on top.

"She is," Will agreed. He gave the oatmeal a jaundiced eye and poked at the scrambled egg mix with his fork. "I know these aren't farm-fresh eggs."

"Oh, don't be picky," Tracy teased. "Eat everything – it's free, and you're going to need your strength."

Will grunted but began obediently to shovel egg stuff and bacon strips and limp white toast into his mouth. He was hungry, and it was manageable if he didn't chew much and washed it down with coffee.

As they were finishing their breakfasts, Dr. Lokietz and Dr. Dana came into the room together.

"Okay, Mother," Dr. Dana said. "I examined you earlier and have the results of your blood work back from the lab already – a small miracle, I might say – and you're good to go home after lunch. I'll want you to keep taking the prenatal vitamins – you'll have a new scrip for those – and to take it easy at home for three weeks. That means no more than one or two trips a day up and down stairs, no laundry, no heavy lifting, no driving. Your job is to make milk, rest and take care of your baby. Daddy and the relatives get to do the housework, the shopping, anything the least bit heavy. After three weeks, you can drive and begin to do things again, but slowly. I'll see you in six weeks for your final checkup. The nurse will have your appointment time with your discharge papers. You bring the baby when you come so I can check him out, too. That's the most fun of all – seeing how much they grow and change in six weeks." She smiled a huge smile and shook hands with Tracy and Will. "Call if you need anything; otherwise – have a great time with your new addition to the family!" She was gone before either young parent could say anything.

"She has a mom in labor down the hall," Terri said.

"Now," said Dr. Lokietz, "let's talk about Isaac."

"HE'S GOING TO DIE, ISN'T HE?" TRACY ASKED, HER VOICE UNNATU-rally calm.

"No, of course not," the doctor replied, a touch of exasperation in his tone. "I told you – it's not a serious problem."

"I don't believe you," Tracy said.

"Trace, come on!" Will interjected. "Don't go jumping to conclu-sions! Dr. Lokietz, tell us again."

"Isaac has a problem called ASD, atrial septal defect. The hole be-tween the two atria, the upper chambers of the heart, didn't close at birth the way it's supposed to. It's not all that uncommon. Sometimes it just takes longer to close, days or weeks instead of hours. I can hear a little murmur, the sound of the blood flowing from one side to the other, that's how we know it's there. We'll ultrasound it to see how big it is, and if it's too big we'll do surgery to close it. But most times we just wait."

"What will happen to Isaac?" Will asked.

"Best scenario, the hole closes on its own soon and nothing hap-pens. No problem ever. Worst scenario, it gets worse over time and surgery is necessary."

Tracy's nails dug into Will's hand painfully. "You mean open heart surgery, right?"

"Yes, but it's routine work."

"There's no such thing as routine open heart surgery on an infant, at least not on our infant!" Will said. "What are the chances you'll have to do that?"

"I can tell more after the ultrasound," Dr. Lokietz said, determined to keep the mood in the room calm. "If the hole is really small, many times we don't do anything but wait and see how it goes as the baby grows. If he gains weight and has normal development and doesn't have breathing problems – well, some people go all their lives with a mild heart murmur and no complications. Let's just wait and see, all right?"

"Go back and stay with him," Tracy said to Will. "Don't leave him alone. Pray over him! I'm calling Pastor Miles and your dad and the Abbotts."

Will hurried through the ritual to get himself ready to enter the nursery, begrudging every moment, and hurried to Isaac's side. He noticed his son was sleeping peacefully and seemed to be breathing easily. He was a lovely soft shade of pink.

He's all right. Thank you, God!

Terri appeared at his side. "I need to take him for the CT scan now," she said, detaching Isaac from his tethers to the machines. "I'm going to wheel him down in his basket; would you like to walk along?"

"Sure. Hey, what about his oxygen?"

"They told me to take him off and see how he does," she said, gently removing the cannula from Isaac's nose and laying the tubing above his head in the bassinette. "It's okay. He's been doing just fine most of the night."

Will followed shot-gun as they took an elevator into the bowels of the hospital and down a long corridor, through a mechanical door marked X-Ray. The hallway on the other side of the door was no wider, but it was much brighter. Isaac screwed up his face and squeaked a protest.

"He knows what he likes and what he doesn't," Terri laughed. "I pity you when he hits the terrible twos."

"Do not put word-curses on me," Will laughed in return. Then, "So you do think he'll live to be two, right?"

After a pause, Terri looked him straight in the eye, no laughter now. "Yes," she said. "I do."

Chapter 32

WITH A MINIMUM OF CURSING UNDER HIS BREATH, WILL detached the car-seat cradle from its base and carried it to the apartment swinging from one hand while he lugged Tracy's suitcase in the other, leaving her to unlock the door. Once inside, he gave a huge sigh of relief and leaned back against the door as if to bar it to all intruders.

"Home," Tracy said softly. "It's only been a day and a half, but it feels like forever."

"Now what?" Will asked, feeling stupid.

"Now... I guess we unpack the baby things and set up shop while Isaac is still sleeping."

"I'll do that," Will said. "You –uh – maybe you go lie down with the baby or something."

"Okay, I will. Give me the baby seat – "

"Oh, no! It's too heavy for you," he said, pulling it out of reach. "I'll carry him into the bedroom for you and put it on the bed beside you. Then if he cries, all you have to do is lift him out."

"I think," Tracy said, following Will into the bedroom, "I could get used to this kind of treatment. You know what? In Malawi, they carry the baby in a sling, the water on their head and the toddler on their hip all at the same time."

"We are not in Malawi," Will told her repressively, carefully positioning the baby seat on his side of the bed, away from the edge. "Get your nightgown on and get into bed."

"You'd better expect my parents at the door any minute," Tracy warned, her voice muffled as she pulled the short cotton summer nightgown over her head. Its mint green complemented her eyes, and the ruffles made her look as young as Gracie. "They didn't get nearly as much time as they wanted at the hospital."

"Yes, I imagine my side will show up, too, although Allison will make them hold off longer. We do have a pretty spectacular baby to show off. But I'm putting up a 'No Visitors' sign for the rest of today. Period."

Cassie and Pearl had left several casseroles and salads and a huge plate of cookies, so it was no problem for Will to provide dinner for the two of them. He watched Tracy nurse Isaac several times, sitting beside her on the bed, his arm around her shoulders, feeling a kind of proprietary delight in their trio. Who could have known it would be even better than the duo?

In the night Will got up to stand over the cradle which had once been David's, and then Gracie's, watching the slight rise and fall of Isaac's chest, the occasional grimaces or stretches or squeaks he made in his sleep. He couldn't see anything wrong with the baby, no strange color, no blue around the lips, no gasping or grunting for air – the things the doctor had said would be signs of trouble.

Father, You know every cell of Isaac's body, every hair on his head, every bit of him. Please heal this one tiny imperfection. Dr. Lokietz says it may heal up on its own – it's not that bad, nothing to worry about. The scan didn't indicate any need for surgery. Please heal the hole in his heart so he can be just as perfect on the inside as he is on the outside. Please don't let anything happen to him!

Pastor Miles called them up onto the platform and asked Will to introduce Isaac to the congregation. "This is Isaac James Ryersen," Will said into the hand-held microphone, holding the baby up just a little to show him off. "He was born on Pentecost Sunday, two weeks ago, and he weighed eight pounds, seven ounces. He was twenty-one inches long."

"Is he a good baby?" Pastor Miles asked, grinning.

"Of course he is!" Tracy said indignantly, not following the 'script' of the introduction ritual. Everyone laughed, but it was the loving laughter of family and friends and people who had been there.

"He doesn't sleep all night," Will said, "but he doesn't cry much."

"Most of you know," Pastor Miles said, "that Isaac has a little problem with his heart. So today we're going to pray for God's healing, and I'd like you all to continue to pray for it."

Will deliberately forced himself not to clutch Isaac too tightly as the prayers washed over them. Tracy stood close, one hand on Isaac's chest, the other on Will's rigid arm, focused on prayer but never forgetting for a moment for whom she was praying.

SUNDAY DINNER WITH THE ABBOTTS WAS EXACTLY AS IT SHOULD BE, wonderful aromas of roast chicken and broccoli and mashed potatoes and blackberry cobbler with vanilla ice cream, lots of laughter, arguing over whether the men really had to do the dishes. Everyone vied to hold the baby, who didn't seem to mind being handed over every few minutes.

"He smiled at me!" Gracie insisted, despite being told two weeks was too young for a deliberate smile. "No, he really did. He likes me best because I'm the youngest."

Ed, reaching to take the baby from Gracie, paused for a moment and said, "I think she's right! He's smiling at her right now!"

"It happens," Pearl said. "Not very often, but every once in a while God makes one who's attuned from the very beginning. He's smiling because he knows he's loved."

"But all babies are loved," John protested.

"Not all," Allison said, anger and sadness mingling on her face. Then she took a deliberate breath and shook it off. "But this one – he's loved so much he'll be the worst spoiled brat in town."

Matthew took the baby from Ed, somewhat gingerly, and sat down beside Will on the couch. "You must have looked just like this," he said to his son, smoothing the light blond hair which grew in funny swirls around the baby's head. "I wish – "

I do, too, Will thought, *but now I believe you. When I see you with Isaac I know you would have loved me just like this. I don't have to be jealous of David anymore; you really do love me now, and you love Isaac. I'll bet you'd give your life for him in a minute, just as I would.*

"I know Isaac's the most important thing right now," Gracie suddenly said, "but I have an important announcement." She waited, still as a statue, for all eyes to be upon her. "I had a text from Trey." She paused dramatically. "He accepted Jesus as his Savior while he was at church with Claire!"

"Today?" Will asked.

"Yes! Just this morning!" Gracie was practically dancing in circles. "Oh, let's pray and thank Jesus for this!"

When they had finished, Will said to Tracy, "I need to give him a call."

"It's time for us to head home anyway," she said. "Isaac will want a meal and a nap pretty soon, and we might as well be settled in. Thank you all so much for another wonderful dinner!"

WILL TIPTOED OUT OF THE BEDROOM, LEAVING THE BABY SLEEPING IN HIS sleeping mother's arms in the middle of the bed. He went to the living room and stretched out on the couch with his phone, punching in Trey's number three on speed dial. The phone rang four times before Trey answered, breathless.

"Congratulations!" Will said. "Gracie told us today is the day!"

"Yeah," Trey said. "I just – it just – He – "

"With you all the way," Will laughed. "Are you with Claire? Is she happy?"

"Yes, and yes. Oh, man, you have no idea! She said she'll marry me, Will!"

"Wow! Double congratulations then! Did she set a date, or is she going to test you first?"

"December twenty-fourth. Says she needs that long to put together a wedding. Didn't like the idea of eloping to Vegas. I suppose, being a Kennedy and all... Hey, you'll be my best man, won't you?"

"Of course I will. So when are you and Claire going to pay us a visit and meet Isaac?"

"Oh. Yeah. Well, when's a good time? I know you have the summer off, but maybe Tracy isn't up to visitors yet."

"Oh, she's fine," Will hastened to assure him. "Since we don't have room for you here, you'd have to stay with Dad and Allison or John or get a hotel. I mean, you'd need two rooms, right?"

"Do not insult my bride-to-be," Trey intoned, pretending to be offended. "We're fine in a hotel – if there is one."

"Do not insult my town," Will gave back. "Lewiston has several fine options, including a Holiday Inn and a Motel Six."

"Well, it will be slumming," Trey mused, "but we'll survive. Let me check with Claire and get back to you." He paused, then said, "Hey, Will? About today..."

"Yes?"

"Well, I need somebody to tell me what to do next. I mean, it's not as if it all gets zapped in there when you say the prayer."

"You're right. Keep reading your Bible and praying, that's most important. Then get with somebody whose faith you admire and ask him to mentor you. Have you been going to church?"

"Yeah, I go with Claire. But her church is kind of a long drive to make every Sunday."

"Oh, really? Then you need to be checking out churches close to home. Find one this week and start going. Join a men's Bible study, too."

"Uh – okay. I don't remember you talking about a men's Bible study."

"Just do it, Trey. You need support you can't get from your family like I can, and it's not fair to Claire to make her your only teacher. Talk with her and call me soon about when you can come; I really want to show off my son to you. And I want to give you a hug, too; I'm so happy for you!"

"Are they coming soon?" Tracy asked sleepily from the doorway.

"Hi! Did I wake you?"

"No, it just happened. Isaac's still asleep, so I put him in the cradle. What about Trey?"

"He and Claire are engaged! Wedding December twenty-fourth. I'm going to be best man. And he sounds really happy about being saved, but really confused. He didn't talk about it until the end, when he asked me what to do. Like I'm ready to mentor anybody! Anyway, he's going to check with Claire and let us know when they can come for a visit. I thought that would be all right with you – isn't it?"

"Of course! He's your best friend, and I like Claire, too. Maybe they can stay at Mom and Dad's – "

"I think a hotel will be better, don't you?"

"I wish," Tracy said, coming over to lie down next to Will on the couch, "that you'd get along better with my parents. I know they're difficult, but they love us, really they do, and they want to spend more time with Isaac."

Will tried not to communicate the shudder that ran up and down his spine. "I know, honey. I just – "

"I know you 'just.' Has Dad had a little talk with you recently?"

"No. Is he going to?"

"I think so. They're so happy about Isaac – only grandchild, a boy – you know – and they want to do things for him."

"Things?"

"Well..." She hesitated, then plunged in. "They think we should have a minivan now that we have a baby and all his gear, and your car is kind of old, in their eyes, so they want to give us a new minivan, one with all the bells and whistles, you know... And the apartment is really too small now; you've lost your office to the nursery – so – "

"So?"

"So they want to buy us a house. Not a big, fancy house," she hastened to add, "just a three-bedroom ranch like your folks' house."

"Does there happen to be a three-bedroom ranch available just down the road from your parents?" Will asked softly.

Tracy leaned up on her elbow to look Will in the eye. "Yes, kind of. Not far from them. And they want to give us a Buick or Honda vehicle, something strong and well-made – and before you have a tantrum, I want you to know I told them no thank-you to both of these things. So there."

Will drew her down onto his chest and ran his fingers through her hair. "I appreciate that your folks want Isaac to have nice things. And I understand why they think what they can provide is so much better than what I can provide – because it is. But the thing is, I can provide for my family, even if it isn't fancy. I won't put my son in a cheap car seat or an unsafe car, and I won't let him sleep in a box on the street, either. The Toyota runs like a top for now, and we can look for a larger apartment any time you're ready. I figure in another year we'll have enough money saved for a down-payment on a house. Do you mind very much not having the fancy stuff?"

"Of course not," Tracy said, patting him. "Every time you worry about that, just think: Malawi – mud hut – no flush toilets. Oops! There's Isaac." She stood and quickly moved toward the bedroom, where the baby was winding up to a scream.

"Lord," Will said, "I thank You for the ways You provide for us, for all our needs. Please help me to be patient with Tracy's parents and to remember their choices come from love – for Tracy and Isaac, anyway."

Chapter 33

"**D**O YOU WANT ME TO GO WITH YOU?" WILL ASKED AS Tracy dressed Isaac in a puppy-printed blue onesie and a sailor-suit with short legs.

"No, of course not. We'll be fine. It's my six-week check-up, and I know you don't want to be any part of that."

"Uh – not really. But I could watch Isaac while you – do whatever you have to do." Will took the baby from her and swaddled him expertly in a light receiving blanket, also printed with puppies. "I could carry the car seat for you. It's heavy."

"It's not too heavy," Tracy said patiently. "I lug it – and him – around all the time now, and it's fine. You just use the time to work on that short story you've been hinting at for months or to work on your syllabus for fall semester." She retrieved the baby and buckled him into the carrier.

Will waved them off and wandered back into the living room, where his laptop sat open on the coffee table. The story had been banging around in his mind for a long time, trying to write itself even as he tried to shut it down.

That's stupid. Why wouldn't I write it? Let's see how it goes; it's been a long time, and maybe I've lost my touch, but...

"You're really into it!" Tracy said, smiling down at Will as she set the baby carrier on the floor beside him. "You didn't hear us come in or anything."

"Oh! Hey. What time is it?"

"It's two-thirty in the afternoon. After my appointment, we went to celebrate my new freedom by having lunch with Mom and then doing a little shopping. Did you have lunch?"

Will considered. "Uh – no. I guess I lost track of time." He saved his document and shut it down before Tracy could get a look at it.

"So it's going well?" she asked, sitting beside him.

"Yes, I guess so. I have a couple of thousand words, and I don't think they're too bad. So what did Dr. Dana say?"

"She said I am free to resume all activities."

"God is good," Will said. "Did she say anything about Isaac?"

"Of course! She said he's handsome and obviously intelligent and wonderful and apparently thriving. Smart woman."

"Did she listen to his heart?"

"Yes." Tracy was quiet for a moment, then added, "It's still there, the murmur. But she said it doesn't seem to be causing any problems. He goes in to Dr. Lokietz in two weeks, and I'm sure he'll say the same thing."

"Of course he will. I just wondered," Will said.

"Let me fix you something to eat while Isaac's still sleeping," Tracy said, heading to the kitchen. "I know you don't care about eating, but you need to keep up your strength."

"So tell me about his feeding patterns," Dr. Lokietz said, handing Isaac back to Tracy, who sat down again next to Will, cradling the whimpering baby in her arms. Isaac did not like to be undressed and subjected to cold stethoscopes and otoscopes.

"Well, he's nursing. I haven't given him any formula or cereal or anything, just the nursing."

"How often does he nurse?"

"Oh, all the time!" Tracy laughed. "At least every two hours, even at night. I'm so grateful I don't have to get up and go to work."

"How long does he nurse?" the doctor persisted.

"At a time? Oh – I don't know – fifteen minutes, maybe? Is that right, Will?"

"I think so. About that. Why?"

"Does he go to sleep after he nurses?"

"Usually," Will said. "He's a good baby."

Dr. Lokietz sat on the little wheeled stool and glided over to Will and Tracy. He pursed his lips for a moment, then said, "Isaac looks fine, but he isn't gaining weight the way he ought to be. He isn't nursing strongly, or long enough. I suspect he lacks the energy and has to work too hard at it, and that's why he doesn't last longer at a time. I want you to make an appointment with Dr. Gable. In fact, I'll have Sharon see whether he can see you today yet."

"But – he's pink and he waves his arms and legs around and – and – " Tracy said, her face white and her arms clasping the baby tighter.

"I know this is hard to hear," Dr. Lokietz said, "but I'm not the expert; Dr. Gable is. Let's just let him figure it out."

Will put his arm around Tracy and held on. "It'll be all right, honey. Just take a deep breath. God will care for Isaac, you know He will."

Ten minutes later Sharon informed them they could go straight to Toledo to meet with Dr. Gable in an hour. "He cleared a couple of things to make room for you," she told them, "so be sure to be on time."

Dr. Gable's office, in an annex of the hospital in Toledo, was not designed to distract and delight healthy children. It was formal and dimly lighted, sort of like a funeral home, Will thought. But – of course. Only very sick children and their desperate parents came here...

And they waited.

After an hour and a half, Will went to the window and asked how much longer it would be. The receptionist gave him a withering look.

"Doctor is a very busy man," she said, her voice scathing. "You will have to wait your turn. You don't even have a real appointment."

"No," Will returned, "but I do have a real baby, and a real wife, who is panicking."

"Please resume your seat," the receptionist said, unmoved. "Doctor will be with you shortly."

Admission to the inner sanctum came after two and half hours of waiting, during which Tracy had retreated to the restroom twice to nurse Isaac. They were placed in a small examining room and instructed to strip the baby to his diaper.

"I'm not going to do that," Tracy said. "He hates being undressed, and there's no need to make him suffer any longer than he has to. We could be waiting in here for another hour or two."

"Okay," Will agreed. "It doesn't take that long to take off his clothes. We'll wait."

As he finished speaking, Dr. Gable knocked once and immediately entered the room. "Sorry to keep you waiting so long," the doctor said. "I know it's hard when you don't know what's happening. But I want you to know that now that I'm with you, I will take as long as I need to." He stepped over to Tracy and extracted Isaac from her arms. "Now, little fella, what's going on with you?" He put the baby on the examining table and deftly stripped off his clothing. Isaac howled.

"He doesn't like to have his clothes off," Tracy said, embarrassed.

"Of course he doesn't," Dr. Gable agreed. "Now let's have a look and a listen." He made no effort to quiet the baby, but watched closely as he cried and waved his arms and legs about. "Does he cry like this often?"

"No," Will said. "He doesn't cry much. If you let me pick him up, he'll stop right away."

"No, no," the doctor demurred. "Let him cry." He continued to watch as Isaac suddenly stopped yelling and lay quite still. "So when he cries you usually pick him up and quiet him right away."

"Well, of course we do!" Tracy said. "It's not nice to let him cry like that! He can't know what's going on in his world or what to do about it."

"Would you say this is the longest he's ever cried?"

"Of course it is!" Tracy snapped.

"Wait a minute," Will said. "He's getting at something. What is it?"

"Look at Isaac's fingertips," Dr. Gable said softly. "See how the nail-beds are kind of dusky? He stopped crying because he ran out of oxygen."

They looked at the tiny hands in horror. "No," Tracy said, "no, that can't be."

"See how still he is now? He's recovering his energy. I'm going to take a listen to that murmur, then we'll ultrasound him. But I think what we're going to find is that the problem isn't resolving – it's getting worse."

ALLISON CALLED TRACY'S PARENTS AND PASTOR MILES AND ASKED them to meet the family at the Abbott house at seven that evening. She did a load of laundry and ate several Snickers bars and talked for a few minutes with her sponsor. She made sure Tucker's food and water dishes were full on the porch and spent several minutes petting him.

Then she went inside and wept until Matthew came home.

"I didn't want to believe it," she told her husband as she blew her nose on his blue bandana. "I kept telling myself I didn't see what I saw. But I knew, Matthew! Oh, how can God let this happen to Isaac!"

"Honey, it'll be all right. God can heal Isaac, or God can use the doctors to heal him. He loves Isaac, too, and He has plans for Isaac's life. It isn't like this appointment was the end of the line, is it?"

"I'm sorry," she said, stepping into his hug and holding on as if she might be swept away by a wave at any moment. "I know you're right. I know. But I'm so scared – and Will sounded so terrified – "

"And that's why we call the troops together," Matthew said, keeping his little wife anchored. "We'll pray together and cry together and make plans together and everything will be all right."

They arrived at the farm to find everyone else already there, including the Seibeneks. Will and Tracy sat on the couch in the living room, leaning on one another and holding hands while Gracie held Isaac close to her chest and seemed to be talking to him under her breath. Pastor Miles and his wife Penny stood behind the couch; John sat in his chair and Pearl in Carolyn's, while Ed and the Seibeneks and the Showalters sat on dining room chairs brought in for the occasion. Matthew and Allison took the last pair of chairs.

John began, "Thank you, everyone, for coming on such short notice. Will and Tracy have something they need to share with us, and then we need to pray. Go ahead, Will."

"Today was Isaac's two-month check-up," he began slowly. "We saw the pediatrician, and he – he didn't like the way Isaac – he – " Tears welled up in Will's eyes and his throat closed. He shook his head.

"He sent us to Dr. Gable in Toledo," Tracy continued, patting Will's hand. "The pediatric cardiologist. He – well, he did some tests and – and – " Now Tracy was crying, and Will took over again.

"He says the defect has gotten worse and Isaac is going to need surgery. It's a fairly common surgery, I guess, but it's still risky. Sometimes – sometimes the baby – dies."

"Not this baby!" Gracie said loudly. "He's not gonna die!" Tears were running down her cheeks and dripping onto the blue bunny receiving blanket, but her grip was sure and her voice commanding.

"God won't do that to Isaac."

"Hush, child," Pearl said, and Gracie subsided at once. "We are going to pray for Isaac and ask the Lord to heal him and keep him safe. He is always in God's hands."

"Yes, ma'am," Gracie whispered, sitting on the floor at Tracy's feet.

"Allison," John said, "you know a lot about sick babies. Is this a routine thing?"

"Yes and no," she said. "No surgery is without risks. But Dr. Gable has a great reputation. And I've seen cases a lot worse than Isaac's. I think he'll be fine."

"I'd trust that more if you didn't look like you've been crying your eyes out," Tracy said, frowning at Allison.

"Honey..." Will began, but Allison cut him off.

"I don't blame you for thinking that way," she told Tracy. "I have been crying. But not because I think Isaac's going to die. I'm just so sad that you and Will have to go through all this. It's hard, and I wish you didn't have to."

"Thank you," Will said.

"I think the best use of our time at this point is prayer," John suggested, and everyone nodded agreement. "Pastor Miles?"

"I'll get us started," Miles said, "and then anyone who wants to can just jump in. When we're all finished, I'll close." He bowed his head. "Father in Heaven – "

"Hey, Mr. Ryersen!"

Will turned to see Eddie, from his infamous study hall of last year, bearing down on him across the feed-store parking lot, where Will had his father's truck backed up to the loading dock to fill it with dog food and salt blocks and feed for the cattle. Will stripped off his worn leather gloves and waved.

"Hi, Eddie."

The youth stopped in front of Will and hesitated for a moment. His acne-marked cheeks became redder than their sunburn, but he drew breath and forged ahead:

"I heard about your baby," Eddie said. "We're praying for him at our church, and I just wanted to say – well, I'm sorry he's sick and I hope he gets better. See ya!" He took off in the opposite direction even faster than he had come.

Huh. That was nice of Eddie. Sure is the sign of a small town, though, that churches I don't even know are aware of our business.

"All set?" Matthew asked, coming out the back door onto the dock and seeing Will leaning on the closed tailgate.

"Yes."

"I appreciate your helping with the loading and unloading. I like to spare Ed from the heavy stuff whenever I can."

"No problem," Will said, getting into the passenger seat and buckling his seat belt as Matthew did the same on the driver's side. "You worried about Ed?"

"Naw. Just trying to be thoughtful. I need him for the mechanical stuff."

"For sure. I can't help with that, even if I wanted to."

Matthew drove smoothly out of town and onto the country road toward the farm. "You start school next week, right?"

"Yes. Next Tuesday is orientation day for teachers, then classes begin Thursday." Will laughed. "I think they give everyone a two-day opening week to break us in gently, not that it really does."

"So when do you and Tracy see the surgeon?"

Will's heart slammed against his ribs. He hadn't been thinking about that! "Uh – I think Wednesday. It was the soonest they could get us in. At least I can go with her without having to take time off school."

"We're praying for you, Son," Matthew said, reaching over to pat Will's knee without taking his eyes off the road.

Will unaccountably felt his eyes filling with tears again. "I know, Dad. Thanks."

"John and I were talking," Matthew said slowly, still keeping his eyes on the road.

"And..."

"And we wonder whether you would have the elders pray over Isaac."

"What does that involve?"

"Well, they all gather around him and lay hands on him and anoint him with oil and pray one at a time... It's biblical, you know."

Yeah? It sounds like a B movie to me. What's the big deal about the elders – they're just a bunch of men who wear suits to church and lead groups. I don't like people I don't know touching Isaac. Or me. Or Tracy.

"I don't know, Dad. It sounds kind of – odd – to me. People are already praying. Just before you came out, a kid from school saw me and said his church is praying for Isaac. We're covered."

"Of course you are. But the elders are – well, they're anointed by God to be like shepherds over the congregation. They're special, like Pastor Miles. You don't mind when Miles prays for you."

"That's different. He's – he's almost like family. Look, I don't know how to explain, but I don't want this to be a big show. I don't want everybody knowing everything about our business. We can handle this without everybody and his brother being in the middle of it."

"Oh. I guess I figured the more, the better. Sorry. Didn't mean to interfere."

Oh, nuts. "No, you're not interfering, Dad. I just don't want to – it's private."

They said no more as they pulled into the barn area and unloaded the truck. Will took his chore list and continued to do odd jobs until the sun began to set.

"You missed supper," Gracie said as she came up to Will, who was tightening the wires on some fencing. "Cassie saved you a plate. Daddy told me not to call you. I think that was stupid." Her little face turned crimson in the rays of the setting sun. "I don't mean Daddy is stupid!" she gasped. "I just mean you should have come in to eat with us."

"I get it, Gracie. Don't worry. I have to go home now, anyway. Tracy and Isaac should be home from her mom's house by now. She'll feed me something."

"Won't be as good as Cassie's meatloaf," Gracie warned.

"No, probably not. But that's okay." Will put away his tools and tucked his gloves into the pocket of his jeans. He fished his car keys out of the opposite pocket and walked with Gracie to the Toyota. "I'll see you Sunday, kiddo."

"I love you, Will," she said, giving him an unexpected hug. "It's going to be all right."

"Of course it is," he agreed automatically, hugging her briefly and then getting into his car. "'Bye, Johanna Grace. Be good."

All the way home, Will argued with God about the way the universe should be run. *I need for* You *to take care of Isaac,* he insisted, *not a bunch of elders or well-meaning relatives. You. The God Who Heals.*

You can do it, so You need to do it now. Before some stranger puts a knife to my son's heart. Now.

"THERE WAS A MESSAGE FROM DR. GABLE'S OFFICE," TRACY SAID ALmost before Will had come through the door.

He walked over to her and put his arms around her, forgetting that he was sweaty and smelly and anointed with various bovine substances. "What did it say?"

Tracy burrowed in, not shy of farmers and their working conditions. "It said the surgery will be Monday, September tenth. Dr. Gable and a Dr. Austin will do it. We have to take Isaac in for blood work and tests on the fourth."

He felt her shaking – at least he thought it was she. "So we're down to it. Wow."

"Oh, Will, what if something terrible happens? What if he dies?"

"It won't," Will insisted. "I won't let it. He isn't going to die!"

"But how do you know?" Tracy cried, pulling back to look into her husband's eyes. "You aren't God, Will!"

He drew her back against him so she couldn't see his face. "No, I'm not God, but I'm not going to let anything happen to Isaac." *Do You hear me? You can't let anything happen to our son. He's ours now – You gave him to us, and You can't have him back!*

Chapter 34

WILL TRIED TO GIVE HIS CLASSES HIS BEST. THE STUDENTS were a nice enough group of kids, and the material was easy for him, and the other teachers were verbal in their compassion and support for what the Ryersens were going through. But he resented every moment he spent there, away from Isaac and Tracy, and his mind wandered away so easily he wondered whether he had early dementia instead of worry.

"Is there anything Anita and I can do?" Wayne asked over lunch. He and Will were sitting alone at the small table in the back corner of the teachers' lounge, safe from cafeteria duty and the overabundance of gossipy female teachers, sharing a sub sandwich so overstuffed its fragrant contents kept spilling out on the way from napkin to mouth. Some of the juices were decorating Wayne's pale blue shirt and yellow tie in colorful patterns.

Will swallowed hard to make his small mouthful go down. "Thank you, but there isn't anything anyone can do except pray – and I know you're doing that. He had the tests yesterday, and unless they tell us otherwise, the surgery will be next Monday."

"How's Tracy doing?"

"Fine. She's scared, but she's strong in her faith."

"And you?" Wayne wiped his mouth on a paper napkin and took another bite.

"I'm fine." Will put the sandwich down on its napkin. No point trying to force it down; he knew what would come of that.

"Well, let us know, okay? We care about you guys and we want to be there for you. Anita would love to cook you some meals, and we can come be with you at the hospital if you want us to."

Will sternly commanded his tear ducts to shut down immediately as he stood and pitched the sandwich into the overflowing trash can by the coffee machine. "Thank you, Wayne," he managed. "We'll let you know."

WHEN HE PULLED UP TO THE APARTMENT PARKING AREA, WILL SPOTTED his father-in-law's new Lexus parked in his spot. *Perfect. I get to park in the boonies and enjoy my in-laws' company for the evening. I know they invited themselves for dinner. Tracy wouldn't do that without warning me. Wonder why she didn't call?*

He hefted his backpack and computer case over one shoulder and trudged back across the lot to the building. Living on the second floor wasn't bad, especially after trekking six stories up to his loft in Iowa, but Will felt every one of these twenty-two steps as if he weighed six hundred pounds. Even from outside the front door to their apartment he could hear Anita Showalter's refined, piercing voice lecturing her daughter.

"I'm home," he announced, bulling his way inside hard and fast. "Hello, folks."

"Oh. Will," Anita said. "Hello."

Tracy flew at him, throwing her arms around him as if she didn't mean to let go, forcing a grin to his grim features.

"Hey, honey, let me put down the load here and make this hug worthwhile."

"I'm glad you're here, Will," Eric said, ignoring the display of affection between his daughter and her husband. "There are some things we need to discuss with you."

"Where's Isaac?" Will asked, bypassing everything else to get to the most important part.

"He's sleeping," Tracy said, still holding on.

"All right, I'll just go in and check on him, and then we can talk. Want to come with me?" he asked Tracy, tugging on her hand.

"I guess so," she laughed, following.

In the bedroom Will went directly to the cradle and gazed down at his sleeping son, so perfect and still in his pale green pajamas. "Is he all right?"

"He's fine," Tracy whispered. "Will, I'm sorry about Mom and Dad. I didn't know they were coming; they just turned up about fifteen minutes before you did. Mom has been at me ever since. I'm so glad you're home!"

"What's it all about this time?"

"Isaac. They think – well, I know they're going to tell you all about it."

"Then we might as well face the music – unless you want me to throw them out."

"No, of course not! That would be so rude!"

Will took a deep breath, in through the nose, out through the lips. "If you say so."

As they returned to the living room, Will observed how carefully Anita and Eric arranged themselves to dominate the room. *I wonder whether they even know they do it.*

"Have a seat," Eric said, gesturing to the two low chairs separated from each other by the sofa, where he and Anita were enthroned.

Will understood that he and Tracy were to be separated this way, but he wasn't going to play the game. He kept hold of Tracy's hand and drew her down onto his lap, hiding a smile at the looks of distaste Eric and Anita both had to disguise.

"The reason we're here," Anita began, "in addition to seeing our daughter and our grandson, is to talk with you about Isaac's ... condition. We have consulted with our family physician, and with several experts he recommended, and we want you to cancel Isaac's surgery and take him to either the Mayo Clinic or the Denton Heart Center in Texas. We will pay for it all, of course, since we know you can't afford it, Will. We want our grandson to have the very best."

Will noted in a corner of his mind that Tracy's fingernails were biting into his wrist hard enough to draw blood.

"That's kind of you," he said slowly. "And we appreciate your concern. I know you want what's best for Isaac. We do, too."

"Of course you do," Eric agreed. "So I have here the names and numbers for you to call." He thrust a piece of heavy, monogramed stationary at Will, expecting Will to rise and fetch it.

Will stayed seated, leaving Eric's arm extended in empty space until the older man finally put the paper on the coffee table.

"Now, when you let us know which hospital you prefer, I will make all your plane and hotel reservations and arrange a rental car," Anita said, "first for the consultation trip and then for the surgery stay. You don't need to worry about a thing."

"How long do you think it will take to get a consultation with these bigwigs?" Will asked.

"Oh, don't be silly!" his mother-in-law rejoined. "I've already set up those consultation appointments for this Friday – at both hospitals. When you let me know which one you choose, I'll cancel the other one. It wasn't too difficult to preempt an appointment; we have friends..."

"Of course you do." Will pried Tracy's fingernails out of his flesh and looked at the deep red crescents she had made. No blood, surprisingly. "Thank you both for your interest in the matter. Tracy and I will discuss it and let you know." He stood and walked to the front door, clearly indicating that the interview was over, routing the unwanted guests while maintaining a bland smile.

"I can't believe the way you handled that!" Tracy said, half-laughing. "I expected you to hit my father or something – at least to cuss – and you were so cool – "

"Sometimes God gives grace, I guess," Will said, scrubbing his hand through his hair with the very same gesture Matthew always used. "So how do you feel about it?"

Tracy sat down again, hugging herself, looking up at him. "I don't know. I mean, I know they mean well, they always do, and usually I just let it go at that if we don't want to do what they want. But this time – I mean, it's Isaac's life, Will."

"I know. That's why I didn't throw them out on their ears, honey. Because maybe this time it is about what money can buy."

"So what do we do? Besides pray, I mean."

Lord, this would be a good time for a loud, clear Voice or a text message or something. You can't jerk us around about Isaac's life!

"I don't know," Will said, shaking his head. "I don't have the faintest idea."

From the bedroom came the first faint whimpers of Isaac waking up hungry. "I need to nurse him," Tracy said, hurrying toward the door.

"You do that," Will said, "and I'm – I'm going to drive around for a while and think."

"What about dinner?" she asked.

"Not hungry. Big lunch. I'll catch something later."

"Okay," she said, but she was already gone.

ALTHOUGH THE FIRST WEEK OF SEPTEMBER IN NORTHWEST OHIO TENDED to brutal heat and humidity, this was a perfect day, warm and sunny, with a light breeze hinting at showers later in the evening. Will drove the Toyota at speed limit over straight and curving county roads, admiring in spite of himself corn and soybeans in the fields, the very occasional black-and-white herd of cattle, the farm which raised Belgian horses, with its spiffy red-and-white barns and stables and lush pastures. The sun was not even considering setting yet, and the heavy, dark green leaves in the woodlots gleamed like emeralds. If he had not been listening to an Iron Maiden CD he would have heard sleepy late-day chatter from larks and wood thrushes and other small birds in the woods.

But over it all was the image of Isaac, his little mouth turning blue as he nursed, his arms and legs skinny where other babies had rolls of fat and dimples.

"What should we do? Is Texas really that much better than Toledo? If I tell Tracy to stick with what we have, am I putting Isaac at more risk?"

You fool! No matter what you do, nothing is going to save that mewling infant.

"I am not hearing that," Will snarled between gritted teeth. "No. Not hearing it." He drove on until the light was waning, the gas gauge suggested filling up in the near future and his head was pounding. And there was the driveway to the Abbott farm.

"Good job, God," Will muttered, turning in.

Gracie must have spotted the car from the window, because she was waiting for him on the porch.

"Will! Hi!" she called, running down the steps to hug him as he climbed out of the car.

"Hi, Gracie! How's it going?"

"Great! What are you doing here without Tracy and the baby?"

"Ah, Grace, you wound me to the heart," Will declaimed, clasping one hand to his shirtfront. "I thought you loved me for myself, and it's really only for my wife and child."

"Don't be so silly," she scoffed. "Where are they?"

"Truth is, I hit them over the head and buried them in the back yard, whaddaya think?"

"I think you invented silly," Grace laughed. "So they're home, but you're here. Did you come to see Daddy?"

"I guess I did. Is he around?"

"He's reading the paper in the living room. Come on in."

Will loped up the porch steps and into the house, a trip he had made hundreds of times over the years, noticing it felt as close to coming home as anything ever had. He found John sitting in his chair in the living room.

"Will!" John said, laying aside the paper to stand up and greet him. "What brings you this way? Did I forget something?"

"No," Will laughed, "your memory is intact. I was driving around, trying to sort some things out – and here I am. May I sit down?"

"Of course! Want coffee?"

"No, thank you." Will sat on the couch opposite John's chair.

"Gracie, Will and I are in need of some serious conversation, here, so will you please go upstairs to do your homework or watch TV?"

"Hmpf!" Gracie snorted. "I know when I'm not wanted. See you later, Will." She ran lightly up the stairs to her room, no evidence of anger in her stride.

"She's a great kid," Will said, smiling after her.

"Yes, she is. A lot like her mother, but with a streak of Pearl thrown in there – God knows how; they aren't related... But that's not why you're here." John sat down again and settled back.

"No."

"Things all right with Tracy?"

Will was startled that John's mind had gone in that direction. "Yes, fine. Really. This is – something else. About Isaac."

John went immediately on alert. "Is he worse?"

"Oh, no. Nothing like that. It's just – " He explained the meeting with the Showalters, shaking his head. "I hate it when they interfere, when they think their money is necessary to make Tracy happy. But this is different. They might be right, and what kind of father would I be to deny the best to Isaac?"

"You recognize that they care, too, and you don't resent their trying to help."

"Right. I'd do it in a minute! But I don't know whether it's the right thing to do."

"Have you and Tracy prayed about it?"

Will hung his head. "Not yet. I've been driving around for a couple of hours, thinking – maybe praying a little."

"I gather you haven't gained any big insights, because if you had, you would have gone home."

"You're right." Will shifted uncomfortably on the cushions. "When I tried to pray, I heard that other voice – the bad one – "

"Can you recite Romans 8:1?" John asked.

Will considered. "Oh. Sure. 'There is now, therefore, no condemnation for him who is in Christ Jesus.'"

"So that other voice is the enemy who wants to destroy you, telling you lies. You know that, right?"

"I do." Will felt the Ryersen flush creeping over him. This time it seemed to be starting at his toes.

"When you hear that voice, you need to tell it, 'Shut up and be gone in Jesus' Name.' Can you do that?"

Will met John's clear blue eyes directly for the first time. "Yes, I can. I have. At least, I will. But that doesn't help with the problem, John. What's the best thing for Isaac? I have to keep him safe and get him well!"

John broke eye contact first, sighing and rubbing his chin, where Will could hear the rasp of the day's whiskers. "I remember standing at David's bedside, years ago, with the machines clicking and the i.v. bags hanging and the nurses coming in and out. I remember telling God to heal my son and give him back to me." He looked up again, and Will was horrified to see tears in his eyes. "And he died," John said, the sound of the tears in his voice. "And it was the worst thing that ever happened to me – until Carolyn died. I was so angry with God and everyone." He took out a handkerchief and wiped his eyes.

"I wasn't around then," Will said. "What did you do?"

"I did what every grieving person does, I guess," John answered. "I went through all those stages – you know, denial and bargaining and anger – and anger – until the Lord broke through to me and started the healing. It nearly finished our marriage, but we survived that and it was better than before. I finally understood I'm not in control of anything but my attitude and my behavior; but God really is good, Will, and He knows what He's doing. He just doesn't always explain it to us."

"That's for sure! If He really loves Isaac, why doesn't He just heal the little guy?"

"Ah, the 'why' question. I don't know the answer to that one, and nobody else does, either." John shook his head ruefully. "I wish I could tell you."

"Well, I wish you could, too!" Will got up and started pacing around the room. "Can you at least tell me what to do about changing the surgery?"

"No, I can't. I can pray with you for God to make it clear, though. Would you sit down and pray with me?"

"Sure, why not?" Will threw himself back down on the couch and leaned forward over his knees, hands clasped. "It can't hurt."

Whether it would help remained to be seen. Will didn't really hear what John was praying, and his own prayer continued to be a series of non-negotiable demands.

Finally John stopped and said, "I think I'll go up and see how Gracie's doing. Stay here as long as you want, Will." He stood up and gestured to his chair. "Sit here and think a while, like your dad used to do. It always seemed to help him. Oh, and one other thing – " John walked a couple of steps to the bookcase and picked up the carved bust of Jesus, handing it to Will. "Take a good look at your dad's handiwork and see if it doesn't say something to you."

Will took the bust reflexively and looked at it with distaste. "I've never liked this thing."

"I know. It's ugly, and it's painful to consider. Just sit in my chair and do it anyway, as a favor to me, okay?"

Will nodded and dropped down into John's chair as the farmer left the room and went upstairs. The living room was suddenly very quiet as Will turned the wood carving over and over in his hands, feeling the ridges and valleys his father's hands had made to create the face before him. Will remembered how those knives felt in the hand; he had stolen one from his father and tried to kill himself with it. That had taken some nerve, but no skill. This work must have taken many, many hours up close and personal with the man whose likeness

Will now studied.

You know what it means to suffer, don't You? You must have been afraid, and You didn't have to do it – so why would You? And if He loved You, why would God let you do it? I wouldn't ever let something like this happen to Isaac if I could stop it!

As his father had, many years before, Will looked deep into the eyes of the carving and saw there the same compassion and love Matthew had seen. This was the God Will had met in the woods, Whom he had trusted enough to say he gave himself to Him, with Whom he seemed to have been wrestling ever since. The agonized eyes wept and offered everything Jesus had to anyone willing to see it there.

Crocodile tears, the bad voice said. *All fake. You plan to trust your son to a liar?*

"Shut up and go away, in Jesus' Name," Will said aloud, feeling foolish.

"Persistent, isn't he?" John said, coming back into the room.

Will leaped up to vacate John's chair, moving to Carolyn's instead. "Yes, it is, sometimes. I don't hear it so much anymore, at least not until recently."

"The enemy comes at us when we're most vulnerable," John said. "Tired, sick, scared, lonely, worried... You know." He settled into his chair again. "Gracie's finished her homework; now I have her watching TV Probably not the most responsible parenting choice, but I wanted time to finish our conversation. Any insights from looking at the face of Jesus while I was gone?"

"No." Will popped up again to return the bust to its place on the bookshelf. "I'm telling you, that thing is creepy and I don't like it." He stood there, shifting from foot to foot. "Maybe I should go home. I've been gone a long time."

John nodded. "If you want. And if you want to stay, I don't have anything more important to do than be with you and try to sort things out."

"You used to do this for my dad a lot, didn't you?"

"I did. Or tried to, anyway. And a time or two he sorted me instead. I never would have made it through David's death without Matthew and Ed and Pearl and all the other people who were praying and hanging onto me so I couldn't slip any deeper into the pit than

I did. The Lord has blessed us with so many loving family members, Will."

Will sat down again in Carolyn's chair. "It's hard for me to trust people, you know that," he said, "but you and Ed and Grandma – and mostly Dad and Allison now, I guess – and Tracy – that's a lot more than I ever would have imagined. And Trey. I trust Trey. I miss him."

"Have you talked with him recently?" John asked.

"No. I should have. I haven't even talked to him but once since he accepted Jesus. I've been so wrapped up in Isaac... Man, that's rude!"

John laughed. "I imagine he'll forgive you if you call him."

"He would. He's that kind of friend. I'll call him tonight."

"So you have a number of people you can trust. What about trusting God?"

"What do you mean?" Will snapped. "Of course I trust God."

"Really? Oh, I know you trust Him with the weather and things like that, maybe with your job – but have you really turned everything in your life over to Him?"

"Isn't that what becoming a Christian means?"

"It's supposed to," John said easily, "but sometimes we hold back parts of ourselves."

"That's crazy!" Will replied, frowning at John. "I don't know what you're talking about!"

"Well, let's just pretend for a minute. Say you have a behavior you're really fond of, a habit, you know, like smoking or drinking or looking at Internet porn. You know those things get a bad rap in church, but you don't think your habit is so bad. It doesn't really mess up your life in any way. So you accept Jesus as your Lord and Savior, whatever that means, and start going to church and learning the lingo and the way we do things. You get a good study Bible and study it, take classes, volunteer for things – if anyone would ask you, you'd say you're a good Christian. You don't count that habit, because you don't see it as being in the way of your relationship with Jesus.

"Then maybe you hear your pastor say one Sunday, 'Be careful when you sing this song, because you need to be sure you really mean it, or else you're lying to God as well as to yourself.' And the song is 'I Surrender All.' And you never thought about the words before, just sang along with everybody else. But the words say, '...All to thee, my precious Jesus/I surrender all.'

"And that day, when the words come up on the screen and you read them, you can't quite make them come out of your mouth, because you're thinking, 'Huh. I surrender some... I surrender most... but all...?' And then you think of that habit, and you know you don't surrender that!"

"John, I don't have any secret vices I'm covering up and holding onto. None of that stuff you mentioned. You're being insulting."

"I don't mean to be," John countered. "You know that. But there are things in your life you haven't surrendered to Jesus, things you don't trust Him to handle without your help."

Will stood up, glowering. "I suppose you're going to say Isaac is one of those things, aren't you?"

"Do you think he is?"

"If I wanted a shrink, I'd go to Toledo and hire one!" Will snarled. "God needs to follow through on His promises. If that's lack of trust and failure to surrender, so be it!"

"TRACY, ARE YOU AWAKE?" WILL WHISPERED AS HE CRAWLED INTO BED in the dark room.

She rolled over and put her arms around him. "Mostly. Where have you been? I was getting worried."

"I ended up at John's place," Will said, sliding his arm under her neck and drawing her close to him. "We talked – prayed – stuff like that."

"'Stuff,' Professor?"

"Seriously, Trace, he gave me a lot to think about – maybe – "

"God spoke to you!" Tracy sat up and turned on the light, excitement driving any traces of sleep from her face.

"No."

"Oh."

"Did you hear anything?"

Now it was Tracy's turn to shake her head. "All I really heard was, 'Trust Me.' I can do that, Will; can you?"

"I hope so," he answered, turning out the light again and spooning her to him for sleep. *I hope so...*

Chapter 35

On Thursday, Will came home from school to find a strange car in his parking place again. It was a Lexus, but not his father-in-law's, and it had an Ohio license plate.

"Who – ?" he grumbled to himself as he once again parked at the far side of the lot and trekked to his building in the brassy afternoon sun.

The owner of the Lexus stood in the middle of Will's living room, beer in hand, grinning like a fool. "Surprise!" Trey said, laughing.

It was Will's turn to grin like a fool as he gave his best friend a ferocious bear-hug and stepped back to look at him. "Man, it's good to see you!" He paused dramatically. "You don't look any different..."

"Well, you do," Trey said. "Older, but not wiser. How are you?"

Will turned away, pretending to put his laptop on the coffee table. "Fine."

"Buddy," Trey said, "don't pull that stuff with me. I came all the way back to Ohio because I knew you were in trouble, and I'm here to help. Don't shut me off, okay?"

Will spun back to look at Trey. "What do you mean, you knew I was in trouble? Did somebody call you?"

Trey took a swig of his beer. "Uh – well – things don't happen the way they used to, you know? I was praying for you guys and I felt like the Lord just picked me up by the scruff of the neck and pointed me at Lewiston. And I told myself, 'You're nuts. Just forget it.' And then the very next day I got this call from Gracie – that kid's a menace with a cell phone! And, anyway, I thought maybe you could use a friend, so here I am."

"Wait here," Will said. "I need one of those." He gestured toward the beer. As he went to the kitchen, he asked, "By the way, where's Tracy?"

"Her mother came and carried her off, along with the Young Prince. I think there was a lecture in the making, but I could be wrong."

"I wish." Will plopped down on the couch and gestured for Trey to sit, also. "Her parents are so hot for taking Isaac to one of the big hospitals and specialists – they went ahead and scheduled appointments for us."

"What you going to do?"

"Darned if I know," Will said, running his free hand through his hair. "Tracy says we're supposed to 'trust God.' Whatever that means in this case."

Trey frowned a little and leaned forward from the armchair to look more closely at Will. "Well, isn't that what we're supposed to do, trust God?"

Will startled visibly and shook his head. "I forgot. You came to Jesus while I wasn't looking. I should have said 'congratulations' the minute I saw you."

"You should have called me the minute Gracie told you," Trey laughed. "But I get it that you're pretty preoccupied with Isaac. It's taking some getting used to, I have to admit, and my parents are totally bewildered. But Claire has been super, and I found a Bible study for men on Thursday mornings like you told me to. Now there's devotion! We meet at five-forty-five a.m.! Anyway, I hear a lot about trusting God and giving everything over to Him. The guys in my group are serious prayer people. They're praying for Isaac, by the way."

Will didn't try to stop the tears that welled up this time. "Thank you," he said, his voice breaking a little. "That means a lot to me. It means a lot that you're here. I can't believe you came all this way..."

"Even before we were brothers in Christ, we were brothers," Trey said. "Where else would I be when my brother's hurting like this?" He walked over to the couch, sat by Will and put his arm around him.

Will wept, and his brother hung on. And in a moment Will knew in his very bones that Trey was praying for him. He could feel it, bringing the first peace he'd had in weeks.

"Here," Trey said, shoving a handful of tissues at him, "blow your snotty nose. You're messing up my shirt, you big sissy."

"Thank you," Will responded, covering a multitude of things, mopping himself up and moving away, embarrassed as much as he was relieved.

"Don't be a dork," Trey said, going back to his chair and his beer.

TRACY CAME HOME AT SUPPERTIME, BEARING PIZZA AND PROFUSE APOLO-gies. "I know this is no way to treat a guest," she fussed, blushing as she avoided eye-contact with Trey. "I'm so sorry!"

"No problem," Trey said easily. "Pizza goes with the beer we've been drinking, and I like it just fine. Except for anchovies. Tell me you didn't get anchovies."

"Of course not," she said, relaxing a little. "Will would gag on an-chovies."

"Ah, maligned again," Will sighed to Isaac, who was watching his father intently.

As they ate pizza from paper plates around the coffee table, Will finally asked, "So what did your mother have to say?"

"Same old, same old," Tracy said. "I told her we haven't made a decision. But, Will, we have to decide, like now. Those appointments are scheduled tomorrow!"

"Want me to take a walk or a nap or something?" Trey asked.

"Of course not!" Tracy said. "You can pray with us."

"I'd like to finish my pizza," Will lied, folding the slice in half so it would look like he had eaten more than one bite.

A little while later, when the remains of the meal were reposing in the trash, the three of them came back into the living room and sat on the floor in a circle. Trey took Tracy's hand on one side and Will's on the other, and Will had no choice but to hold on to them. He watched, eyes open, as Trey and Tracy bowed their heads. It was so weird, Trey at prayer.

"Dear Jesus," Trey began, "thank You for my brother Will and my sister Tracy, and for little Isaac, such a gift from You. Thank You for being the one, true God, in Whom we can put all our trust and hope and faith. Lord, we come to You tonight to ask what You want Will and Tracy to do – to cancel Isaac's surgery here and go to the big specialists, or to stay here and follow the original plan. We can see 'reasons' for doing either one, but we want to do Your will. So we ask, in faith believing You will always answer us when we seek Your will. Jesus, what do You want them to do?"

Will had nothing to say, so he just sat there and tried to listen. He could see that Tracy was crying a little, but her face was calm under the sheen of tears. *All right, Lord. We're here. We're listening. Can You just give us a hint?*

More time passed. Will could feel again the peace that came from Trey – and the peace that began coming from Tracy on his other side. He heard himself give a huge sigh and began to feel his muscles relaxing. He waited some more, but now it was in silence, inside as well as out.

He didn't know how long they had been sitting there holding hands, but suddenly the silence was broken by a cry from Isaac.

"I'll go," Will said, standing quickly.

"Hey, baby," he murmured to the squalling infant, picking him up to calm him. "It's all right, little guy, Daddy's got you. It's all right."

Isaac quieted immediately, although he began to chew on his fist, a warning that feeding time was at hand.

"Let me change your diaper first," Will said softly, "then we'll get Mommy." He laid Isaac on the changing table and began the routine with the surety of practice. Isaac looked up from his fist and grinned, a full-gums grin that showed Ryersen dimples in both cheeks. Will felt his heart breaking as he smiled back through a rainbow of tears.

"I can't live without you, baby. I just can't. You have to get better. God, You have to heal him!"

"Aw, Will," Trey said from the doorway, "it's gonna be all right. Hey, can I hold him?"

"Sure." Will handed the blanket-packaged baby to Trey without hesitation, only after the transfer thinking to ask, "Have you ever held a baby before?"

"Uh – probably. I mean, I must have sometime. It's kinda like holding a football, isn't it?" He balanced the infant expertly in the crook of his arm and headed for the living room and Tracy. Will followed helplessly.

"Thank you," Tracy said, taking the handoff. "Good job, Uncle

Trey!"

"I like the sound of that!" Trey said. "Seriously. Maybe someday I'll be handing my kid to Uncle Will and Aunt Tracy. Claire really is going to marry me, y'know."

"I'm going to go into the bedroom and nurse Isaac," Tracy said, smiling at Trey. "You feel free to tell Will what we heard."

"You heard something?" Will asked.

"Well, yeah, Tracy and I both did, and it was the same thing, pretty much. How about you?"

"Nada." Even the word was bitter on his tongue. *Not me. I'm only his father.*

"Let's sit down," Trey said, suiting actions to words by sprawling on one end of the couch. As Will took the other end, Trey continued, "We both think God is telling you guys to stay with the original plan, here. Tracy seems to have real peace about it. She said if it's okay with you, she'll call in the morning and cancel those out-of-town appointments."

"Fine."

"Will?"

"No, it's fine."

"You seem kind of torqued, man."

"Oh, really? And why do you suppose that would be?"

"Uh – I don't know."

Will stood up and began pacing around the living room, a short trip with many sharp about-faces. "Do you think it could be because I've prayed and prayed and haven't heard a thing, prayed for healing and He hasn't done it, and you and Tracy just waltz right in and pray one little prayer and He answers you? What's the matter with me that God won't pay any attention to me? Reminds me of my dad when I was young."

Will turned back the other way so he wouldn't have to see the pity in Trey's eyes. "I mean – Isaac's my kid, my responsibility, not yours!"

"I'm sorry, Will," Trey said softly, "but, really, what difference does it make who God gives the message to, as long as you get it?"

"You don't understand! It's the story of my life – never good enough. Never wanted. Never – ah, s – " Will threw open the front door and took off down the steps. He found the car keys in his hand and ran across the parking lot to his car.

"Will!" Trey yelled from the open doorway, but Will didn't answer. He drove away without a backward glance.

It didn't take long to get to Matthew and Allison's house after he figured out where he was going. In the long twilight, he could see lights on in several different rooms and was grateful his father was still up, although he had no idea what he was going to say to Matthew – or what he wanted from him.

Will stepped out of the car and braced himself for Tucker's welcome, which included paws on shoulders and a brisk face-washing with the dog's huge tongue.

"Get down, you big dummy," Will said, attempting to extricate himself from the fragrant canine embrace. "Yeah, yeah, I love you, too. Just get down."

"Tucker!" came Allison's voice from the porch and the dog dropped down to grovel in the driveway.

"Don't worry," Will told him. "She isn't mad at you."

"Come on up!" Allison called, and Will met her by the door, Tucker close behind.

"No, Tucker, you lie down out here," Allison said, and the huge dog dropped to the porch floor with a loud sigh. "Come on in, Will. What brings you our way? I thought you would be with Trey."

"I was," he answered as they went into the living room, "but I just needed to get out for a while. I thought maybe, if Dad's still up – "

"I am," Matthew said, coming in from the kitchen with a glass of milk and a cookie. "Want some dessert?"

"No, thanks. Dad, I – if you have time – "

"I think I'll take a bath," Allison said. "A long bath, with bubbles." She winked at Matthew so blatantly Will couldn't miss it, which seemed to be her intent. "You and your dad have a nice talk, Will." She kissed his cheek and left the room.

"Subtle, she isn't," Matthew remarked, sitting in his chair and taking a small bite of the cookie. Oatmeal-raisin-chocolate chip, Will noticed, Carolyn's recipe, Matthew's favorite. "Gracie makes them for us now," Matthew said, catching Will's glance.

"That's nice."

"How's Trey?"

"How does everyone know he's here? I didn't know he was coming."

"Don't be miffed, Son. Word just got around, but it was kind of a spur of the moment thing, I gathered."

"Oh. Well, he's fine. Better than fine, really. He's got himself a Bible study group and seems to be taking to Christianity like the proverbial duck to water. He's a praying fool!"

"This is where Pastor Miles would say, 'Um-hm' or 'I see.' I hate it when he does that, so I'm not going to do it to you. You do seem kinda put out about Trey, though."

Will sat down on the couch and ran his hand over his face. "I'm sorry. It's really childish and stupid, but I think maybe I'm jealous. He seems so – so comfortable and secure in his relationship with the Lord. I've been at it a lot longer than he has, but I don't ever feel the way he looks. Well, hardly ever."

"I get that," Matthew said, washing down the last of the cookie with the last of the milk. He held the glass in his hand and swirled the last few drops around and around, making a thin film on the glass. "John would say only a fool compares his insides to somebody else's outsides. John would also say some of us are more hard-headed than others and can't seem to learn the easy way. That'd be me."

"And me." Will laughed, a bitter-edged sound. "Like father, like son, right?"

"In this case, I'm afraid so. I'm sorry, Will. I'd like to be a better example for you. But in the meantime, how can I help?"

Will's hand scraped across his face again. "Dad, we've been trying to decide what to do about Isaac – you know that – and tonight Trey suggested we pray together about it. We all sat in a circle, and Trey prayed, and then we just – sat – like a Quaker meeting, I think. Then Isaac woke up and I went in to change him, and when I came back, Tracy and Trey had all the answers. They said God wants us to stay here and go with the original surgery."

"I'm glad you know what to do now," Matthew said. "Not knowing is so hard. Are you okay with it, Son?"

"No! I mean, yes, I'm okay with staying here, but I'm not okay with God talking to everyone but me. I'm responsible for Isaac. I have to take care of him. God should be telling me what He wants, not Trey! How can I keep Isaac safe if I don't know what I'm supposed to do?"

Matthew sighed and shook his head. "Do you really think you can keep him safe, Son?"

"What kind of question is that! Of course I can; it's my job!"

"I wanted to keep you safe," Matthew said quietly, "but I couldn't do it. You almost died because I couldn't save you. I'm not the one who delivered you, if you'll remember; it was God. I had to trust Him to take care of you when you went away, and for all those years you didn't come back – and He did."

"That's different," Will insisted. "Isaac is just a baby."

"So were you, once," Matthew said, "although I wasn't around to see it. God took care of you in all kinds of tough situations over your lifetime, even though you didn't know Him or even want to know Him. He took care of me, too. Your grandfather could have killed me instead of just messing up my knee."

"He messed up a lot more than your knee," Will replied, "and God let all kinds of bad things happen to me."

"It took me a long time to trust Him," Matthew nodded. "It's always a leap of faith. Been reading your Bible much lately?"

"No."

"Figured. That's how it was with me when things got bad – turn the other way. Just remember some key verses, like, 'I will never leave you or forsake you' and 'I know the plans I have for you – plans to prosper you and not to harm you; plans to give you hope and a future.' That's true for you, and it's true for Isaac. You can trust God with Isaac. He isn't going to drop that baby, Son, he really isn't."

Will felt himself close to tears yet again. "I want to trust Him, Dad – but I just can't."

"I think trust is maybe a choice," Matthew said slowly, "like forgiveness and love are choices. So you can say, 'Lord, I choose to trust you with my mind and will, even though my feelings don't match.'"

"Thanks, Dad, for listening and not judging. I'd better go home to Tracy. I appreciate your being here and letting me say what I feel."

"I love you, Will," Matthew said, hugging his son as they walked to the door. "And I'm here any time you want to talk, or to pray. I'm going to take Tucker for a walk, and we'll pray you home, how's that?"

"WHAT ARE YOU DOING?" TRACY ASKED OUT OF THE DARKNESS, HER voice furry with sleep.

"Uh – nothing," Will replied softly.

"Well, come back to bed and do it here," she said. "It's three o'clock in the morning, and you need your sleep."

"In a minute," he whispered, but he continued to stand there looking down into the cradle, where just enough light from the parking lot seeped in through the adjacent window to let him see Isaac's sleeping form. The baby slept with abandon, arms flung out to his sides, little brow slightly furrowed, as if sleeping were hard work. But Will knew better. It was breathing that was hard work. So he stayed where he was, as he had the night Isaac was born, willing his son to take and release each breath.

When Will struggled out of the shower and into the kitchen for breakfast, he found Trey and Tracy waiting for him – or, really, going on without him, as they tucked into Tracy's delectable gruyere and tomato omelets.

"Have a seat!" Trey said, unaware the cheeriness of his voice put him in mortal peril. "Your wife's a great cook!"

"Thank you, sir," she smiled, refilling his coffee cup. "Would you like eggs, Will?"

"How could he not?" Trey asked.

"Oh, he eats like his father a lot of the time," Tracy sighed. "No matter what I cook, I never know."

"Come on," Will groaned, sitting down and picking up his juice glass. "I love your cooking. I'm just tired."

"I guess that means no eggs," Tracy said, nodding to herself. "Toast?"

"Juice is fine," Will insisted, taking an exploratory swallow. "Or not." He set the glass down again. "So how'd you sleep, brother? You look pretty wide-awake and spiffy."

"Slept like a log," Trey agreed. "And spiffed up to join you for church this morning." He preened the front of his blazingly white Armani shirt and the YSL tie with its abstract swirl of blues, soft greens and – violet? – that on any lesser man would have suggested gender identity issues.

Will felt positively grubby in his khakis and navy polo shirt, especially as he realized Tracy had dressed up more than usual, *Probably so she'll look good with Trey.* He sighed and stood up again. "I'll change."

"You don't have to do that!" Tracy protested. "You look fine – as always."

"Yes, he does," Trey contradicted. "He'll feel better if he dresses up to your level." He grinned at Will and took another bite of his omelet.

Reconfigured in his own white shirt (JC Penney) and blue-striped tie (Target), Will carried Isaac into the church, followed by Tracy, with the diaper bag, and Trey, who was looking around like a kid at the zoo. They were stopped a number of times crossing the lobby by people who wanted to coo at Isaac, give hugs to Tracy and Will, accompanied by words of comfort, or meet the handsome stranger. Trey handled it with the grace he brought to every social situation, the country club finesse Will had always envied but never begrudged.

"We used to sit up front," Will said as they approached the door to the sanctuary, "but since we've had a baby, we sit in the cheap seats in the back so we can get up and go out if he gets fussy."

"No problem," Trey said easily. "I figure the Holy Spirit fills the room, right?"

"Suck-up," Will muttered, softening his comment with a grin.

"Boys, boys," Tracy murmured, taking a bulletin from the usher at the door and lightly shoving Will into the sanctuary.

The Abbott pew had simply moved from third from the front to third from the back on the right side. They were all there – Ed, Pearl, John and Gracie, Allison and Matthew – holding the rest of the pew with Bibles and purses.

"They wouldn't have to do that," Will muttered to Trey. "Everybody knows the whole family sits together here." He stepped back to let Tracy slide in next to Matthew. He sat next to her, the diaper bag between their feet, leaving the aisle for Trey. "In case you feel like making a break for it."

"I suspect you're the one who always has to have the aisle seat," Trey returned.

"Me and my dad. It's cool to see him sitting in the middle these days."

The canned music was cut off abruptly, and Pastor Miles walked out onto the platform to welcome everyone. His tall, lanky frame seemed more awkward than usual this morning, and he was accompanied by his wife, Penny, who seemed equally stork-like and ill at ease.

Where's the worship team? Will wondered. *What's up?*

"Good morning," Pastor Miles said, and the congregation responded, "Good morning!"

"We're doing things a little differently this morning," Miles said, still not smiling, "and I want you to know I'm not any more comfortable with it than you are. I had a sermon all prepared, as you can see by the sermon notes page in your bulletins, and the worship team was prepared to lead a number of songs. But we won't be doing that."

He hesitated, and an audible buzz went through the large room. Tracy put her hand on Will's arm for reassurance. None of them was comfortable with unannounced change, obviously.

"Does he do this stuff often?" Trey whispered.

"Never," Will whispered back.

"This morning when I woke up," Pastor Miles said, "I felt – unsettled, I guess is the right word – like something just wasn't right. So I did what I always tell you to do and took it to the Lord in prayer, which led me to the passage about the rich young ruler, the man who came to Jesus asking what he must do to achieve eternal life.

"This is a really important passage, so much so that it occurs in Matthew nineteen, Mark ten and Luke eighteen. And we all know how it ends. Jesus tells the rich young man to sell all he has and give it to the poor and lay up treasures in heaven. But the young ruler goes away sorrowing and misses his chance because he just can't give up this one thing."

Pastor Miles stopped for a moment and took a sip of water from a glass sitting on the lectern. He held out his hand to Penny and she clung to it. Not a sound came from the congregation; even the babies were silent.

"One of the songs we had planned for this morning is that good old standard, 'I Surrender All,'" Miles continued, "and I started singing it – well, inside my head," he laughed, joined by the congregation, who were aware in which direction their pastor's talents did not lie. "And I remembered being told when I was young, and telling you from time to time, 'Be careful when you sing that you really mean the words coming out of your mouth. Can you – no, can I – really sing, 'I surrender all' and mean it? Maybe I can sing, 'I surrender some,' or even 'I surrender most.' But is that what my Lord is asking of me? No, it isn't."

He took another sip of water.

"I felt pretty sure by the end of that prayer time that I was supposed to scrap today's message and just bring this to you. I believe God is asking us to lay it down and leave it at the altar – whatever 'it' is. Whatever the idol in your life is, if you want eternal life, you need to leave it here.

"I know that isn't appealing. I know it isn't easy. I'm reminded, though, also, of Abraham taking his only son, Isaac, into the wilderness, up the mountain, to sacrifice him to the Lord. Isaac, whom he had waited for all those years; Isaac, who was to be the future of his father's people; Isaac, whom Abraham loved more than anything in this world – his only son.

"But Abraham trusted God and obeyed, even though he couldn't imagine the outcome. And when Isaac said, 'Father, I see the wood, but where is the lamb for the sacrifice?' his father responded immediately, 'My son, God will provide the lamb,' knowing full well the lamb being provided was Isaac. So he took his son and bound him to the altar and lifted his knife over the boy's heart, ready to strike the blow that would kill his own heart, too."

Will looked down at his own son, sleeping so trustingly in his father's arms, warm and limp in his little white terrycloth sleeper. A horrible suspicion began growing in Will's mind.

"We don't know for sure," Miles said, "but maybe even during the downstroke of that knife, God said to Abraham, 'Stop!' And He spared the life of Isaac because Abraham had been willing to lay it down.

"Penny and I have been struggling for some time now with an Isaac of our own. You know our oldest girl married a missionary and is serving on the mission field in Peru. Six or eight months ago they wrote to us and asked us to consider joining them there. Penny – " His voice broke and she moved in to hug him as he cleared his throat and continued, "Penny took a little while to get used to the idea, but in a few months she was ready to go. Not me." He looked out over the congregation. "I've been here such a long time, and I love my job. No, really, I love you. I love being your pastor and sharing in your lives and being present at the miracles God does among us. I don't want to be anywhere but here, ever.

"But this morning I realized our church, our church life here, is my idol, the thing I don't want to lay down and surrender to the Lord. I don't want to go to Peru, or anyplace else, either. And I've had all kinds of good reasons, you know: I don't speak Spanish, although Penny does. We own a home, and what if we can't sell it? How can I take my wife into a place where there may be political unrest and danger? What if we have a medical emergency beyond what Band-Aids and Kaopectate can handle?

"And God says, 'Trust me. Trust me, Miles, and lay it down. Lay your Isaac down on the altar and see what I will do.'

"So here I am this morning, laying it down before the Lord, and before you." He bowed his head and closed his eyes. "Father, you say, 'Trust me.' And today I say, yes, I choose to trust you. If Peru is where you want us, we will follow."

Audible sounds of weeping began to spring up around the sanctuary, whether from grief over the loss of their pastor or conviction about their own lives, Will couldn't tell. He looked around, wild-eyed, the notion pressing against his breastbone from inside, to see Trey nodding calmly and Tracy, eyes closed, obviously praying. He also saw his father looking at him, and John.

"I have a challenge for you this morning," Pastor Miles finally said, looking at them again. "Don't be like I was, don't be like the rich young ruler. Whatever your Isaac is – right now, this morning, trust God and lay it down. If you want to, use the sermon notes part of the bulletin to write it down, then bring it up here and put it at the foot of the cross on the platform. If you don't want to write it down, come forward anyway as a sign to yourself and others and tell Him what you're laying at His feet.

"The worship team is going to sing now, while we are surrendering, and if you want someone to pray with you, the elders are available up front or in the back." Pastor Miles gave a signal and the team came onto the platform to begin singing, using only the piano and a couple of acoustic guitars. They began with "I Surrender All" as Pastor Miles pulled a piece of paper out of his pocket and laid it on the floor.

No, Will begged. *Please, no! How can I?*

At first maybe only half a dozen people tentatively left their pews and moved toward the front. Two of them held the pages torn from their bulletins; the others were empty-handed. But behind them came more and more people, some with bulletin pages, some with other objects in their hands.

I can't. I can't.

The worship team began singing, "I trust in Jesus, my strong deliverer..."

"It's a choice," Matthew's voice said inside his head.

Only a fool would trust a god who kills babies.

Will found himself on his feet, Isaac in his arms, stepping over Trey while Tracy said out loud, "What are you *doing*!"

By now the aisles were crowded with people, but Will didn't care. He began to push against the people ahead of him. Suddenly he found Trey on one side of him and Matthew on the other and the rest of the family following behind as the crowd parted for them and a clear path ran from where they stood all the way to the altar.

He couldn't see very well, because the tears were flowing, and he felt as wobbly as a new calf, but his brother and his father braced him and went with him every step of the way. When they came to the edge of the platform, Will looked down at Isaac, still sleeping, secure in his father's arms.

"I love you so much," he told his son, unaware at this point that he could be heard in the sudden silence. "Jesus, I choose to trust You. I lay my Isaac down."

He laid the baby on the floor of the platform and took a step back.

Epilogue

"GRANDPA, READ US THE ONE ABOUT ABRAHAM AND Isaac," Isaac demanded, squirming closer under Matthew's encircling arm and giving him his most winsome smile.

From across the room, where he was working on his laptop, Will had to smile to himself at the sight of those two Ryersens face to face. *Like father, like son, like grandson,* Will thought. *We look like we were stamped out with a cookie cutter – and we act so much alike it's scary. I hope Isaac never hates that idea the way I used to.*

"No!" John Matthew said from Matthew's other side. "I want you to read us Daddy's book!"

From the superior wisdom of his six full years, Isaac explained to his four-year-old brother, "Mommy says we're too young to read Daddy's book yet. We have to be teenagers." He sighed. "That's a long time. Besides, Joy wants to hear Abraham and Isaac."

"She does not!" John Matthew said, poking the chubby baby with wispy black curls who reclined on Matthew's lap sucking her thumb. "She's too little to understand anything anyway. You just want that story because it's about you."

"Boys," Will said without looking up from the laptop, "please don't be rude to one another."

"Yes, sir," they chorused, bringing an exchange of grins between Will and Matthew.

Isaac, however, was prone to having the last word. "And Joy can, too, understand. I was littler than her when I did."

"When you did what?" Matthew asked.

"When I understood grown-up stuff going on."

"Tell me about that," Matthew said, shifting Joy into the crook of his arm and looking straight at Isaac, who returned his slatey gaze openly.

"It was when I was sick and we were in church and Daddy lied me on the floor and Jesus came."

Will's head snapped up again and he stared at Isaac. "Isaac, you couldn't have – you were so tiny – babies can't – "

"Oh, Daddy, sure they can. Jesus talks to them all the time. It's grown-ups who can't hear Him. He said I would get well and you would figure out who loves you. And He was right – wasn't He."

Will put the laptop aside and sat down beside Isaac. He did his best to gather all three children and his father into one embrace, because Isaac was right. That was exactly what the Lord had told him, and it was true.

END

Mary Mueller loves her God, her family and friends, her life and her books. A graduate of the University of Dayton, she has been writing since she was nine, and has published poems, short stories and devotions, as well as her four novels, *Stargazer* and The Ryersen Trilogy (*The Redemption of Matthew Ryersen, Mirror Images, and Burnt Offering*).When not working on her next novel, she keeps out of trouble by volunteering, directing (and sometimes writing and acting in) skits and dramatic musical productions for her church. Mary welcomes (no, she loves) feedback and opportunities to interact with people, so she is available for speaking engagements, radio interviews and e-mail conversations. (She maintains she is too old to text and tweet, but that could change...)

Contact Mary: mmad4him@gmail.com or via White Feather Press, whitefeatherpress.com.